Beyond McCarron's Corner:

Sassy's Story

Sharon K. Middleton

BLACK ROSE
writing™

The final approval for this literary material is granted by the author.

First printing

This is a work of fiction. Names, characters, businesses, places, events and incidents are either the products of the author's imagination or used in a fictitious manner. Any resemblance to actual persons, living or dead, or actual events is purely coincidental.

ISBN: 978-1-61296-991-6
PUBLISHED BY BLACK ROSE WRITING
www.blackrosewriting.com

Printed in the United States of America
Suggested Retail Price (SRP) $19.95

Beyond McCarron's Corner: Sassy's Story is printed in Adobe Caslon Pro

Special thanks to my husband, Gary, who puts up with me writing and neglecting the house when my head is full of stories. And for inspiring my sex scenes!

Special thanks to my dear friends, Judi Steckman Broussard, and Dawn Anderson, who have helped me with proof reading and listening to countless hours of story plotting.

Special thanks to my son, Scott Middleton, for introducing me to the beauty of Northern Georgia, which is the site for McCarron's Corner.

Beyond McCarron's Corner:

Sassy's Story

Prologue

It is said that grief never ends, but it changes. It is a passage, not a place to stay. Grief is not a sign of weakness, nor a lack of faith. It is the price of love.

My name is Sarah Alinora Winslow. My family has called me Sassy as long as I can remember. They called me Sarah Alinora if I was in serious trouble. I am 34 years old. My husband died a few months ago. He just turned 50. We were married 14 years. We both worked hard, and we saved a lot during our marriage, so that we could buy a lake house near my brother and his family, who live in Kennesaw, Georgia, just outside of Atlanta. We were so excited to buy that house at Lake Allatoona, 20 minutes away from Jim and his family. Owen bought his boat he had talked about for years, and was thrilled that we had found the house we wanted, for when we retired in a few more years. Our son, Rick, would be living there while he attends Med School at Emory. We had been moving the first load into the house, when my damned husband had a heart attack, and just had to up and die.

Isn't that just like a man?

I was so ready for this desolate time in my life to change. To move on to the passage to the next stage in the grief process, for movement to the next phase in recovering. Because when all is said and done, grief sucks. It hurts like hell.

Maybe I was better. Maybe I was progressing. I knew I was going through the passage. Some days, I felt like it was the slow boat to hell. But then, change is not always pleasant, especially secondary to the death of someone loved as much as I loved Owen. I just knew I was ready to stop hurting.

My Owen was dead, and I was struggling to go on. Breathing was hard. I hurt. I know that grief is said to be love's unwillingness to let go. He was missing from me. Right now, thinking about life without him was almost unbearable.

Prologue

Chapter One

I graduated high school a year early when I was 17, and started at Trinity that fall. In the spring, I took a class in Early American History taught by the renowned Dr. Owen Winslow, who had the reputation of being one of the foremost authorities on Colonial American History in the country.

I hated the illustrious Dr. Winslow from the very first day.

I typically run a program on my computer to record my classes. That way, I can listen but not have to take notes. I have an accurate recollection of every word the professor says. It's easier to explain than the fact that I have a photographic memory.

We got off to a bang up start that first day, when he called roll for Sarah Searcy.

"I'm here, sir, and I would prefer to be called Ms. Searcy."

His head whipped up at that. Lips thinned, and he took his glasses off, tilted his head, and stared at me, frowning, before he put them back on. I was unsure whether I was going to pee myself or laugh. I must have made the wrong choice because I laughed, and it caused his lips to narrow more. He glanced at me again, and said, "Ah, yes, the Saucy Miss Searcy." I tried not to chuckle as he pronounced Searcy like 'Sussy,' which I assumed was due to his New England accent. "I will make a point of NOT calling you Sarah."

I smiled, fascinated by his accent. "Thank you, Dr. Winslow."

About 45 minutes into the lecture, he realized I was not taking notes. In fact, in typical Saucy Sassy Searcy Style (as it came to be known), I was sewing while he lectured. "Could our Saucy Miss Searcy manage to pull herself away from her important task in her hands to pay attention to this lecture?"

I smiled, and kept sewing. "I am listening to you, sir. I am quite capable of multitasking."

The hall was silent except for a shuffling of seats. Eyes grew wide around me as students seemed to move away from me, in fear of the explosion to come.

He took his glasses off again, his grey eyes cold as ice, as he gave me that thin-lipped smile. I learned right then that when Dr. Winslow smiled, it was not necessarily a good thing. "Fine, Little Miss Multitasker." I bit back a grin as he dropped the 'er' on the end of Multitasker, so it sounded like 'Multitaskah.' "What did I say before I asked you to stop your handwork, or whatever it is that is so very important that you are doing?"

Okay, A-hole, I thought. *Bring it on. You may have one sexy accent, but you are just plain rude, every bit as rude as Gramma always says Yankees are.* I smiled, as I glanced at my computer screen over the transcription from his words of his lesson. "At what point in the lecture, sir?"

His cheeks were turning bright red. "I beg your pardon?"

I kept sewing. "Well, you've been talking for 45 minutes. At what point would you like me to recount what you said?"

He smiled again. "How about 5 minutes ago. No. Make that 7 ½ minutes ago." The Cheshire cat looked like he had swallowed the mouse whole.

I shut my eyes, visualizing what he had said then. "In 1765, King George III and Parliament agreed that the colonists would pay taxes on all printed material to help pay for the French and Indian War. Colonists were angry. Since they had a self-government, they thought Parliament had no right to tax them. At that point, the colonists determined that without representation, they were little more than slaves. Hence, the famous words 'no taxation without representation.' The cornerstones of the prospective Revolution were laid at that very moment."

The shit eating grin was off his face. He blinked and then he blinked again. I thought his jaw was going to hit the floor. It was word for word what he had lectured. After about a minute, he snapped his jaw shut, and shuffled his papers. "Very good. Continue... whatever," he waved his hand in the air as if to make light of me.

I smiled and continued to stitch. "Thank you, Dr. Winslow."

As class ended, I started picking up my things to leave when he said, "Just a minute, Miss Searcy. I need to speak with you."

My heart sank. *Great, Miss Sassy Mouth,* I thought. *I pissed this dude off, and he's gonna kick me out of the class. Damn, I really wanted to take this class.*

He took his time in gathering his own papers up to put them in his briefcase. At last, he asked the question he had apparently made me wait to hear. "Can you always do that?"

I gulped. He was making me late for my next class. Worried, I glanced at my watch. "Uh, sir..."

"Answer me, girl! Can you?" He glared at me, his grey eyes blazing.

I sighed as the bell for the next class rang. "Okay, I'm late now anyway. Yes, sir. I have been able to do that all my life. Why does it matter to you?"

He stared at me. "And you can just sit there and sew or whatever, and know every word that was said?"

I nodded.

He grabbed me by the arm. "Come on!"

I dug my heels in. "Hey! What's going on? I have classes! I am already late for the next one now!"

He stopped and looked back at me. "Because, my dear Saucy Miss Sarah Searcy, I have need of you at a meeting. I'll talk to your professor, but you need to come with me. Now."

"Sassy," I said through gritted teeth.

He stopped and stared at me. "Saucy. Sassy. What's the difference?"

I shrugged. "People call me Sassy. Sarah Alinora Suarez Searcy. The initials spell SASS. Add the 'y' on the end from Searcy, and it spells Sassy. My family has called me Sassy since I was an infant. If you are forcing me to do something for you this afternoon, at least get my name right, sir."

He started laughing. "Saucy Sassy Searcy! I love it! That name fits you to a 'T'! Come on, girl, time's a'wastin'!"

And that was how I got conscripted into the job working in his office to record meetings unobtrusively. Don't ask me why he couldn't use a tape recorder. I always wondered if he had one going, too. I would sit in the corner, with the lap top, sewing, or apparently reading, while my photographic memory would record every freaking word for Himself.

As the semester progressed, we had to do a major research project. My paper was on the history of the quilt in the Colonies. I included a sample square for each significant quilting pattern that evolved during the Colonial

Period. It must have impressed him. He gave me the only A that semester, and surprised me when he asked me to be his Research Assistant on an article he was writing on Early American Textiles. I didn't know then that the article he had in mind would became a series of articles, which began with him writing about the importance of cotton to the economy of the colonies, why they wanted to produce their own textiles, and the financial impact it had on the colonies. Or that I would write articles about how they carded and wove the cotton into fabric, how they dyed the fabric, how they made print designs, especially chintzes which were so expensive to import from India, and were so highly in favor during the Colonial and Revolutionary War eras. We wrote about clothing styles affected by using cotton and linen instead of silks, and of course, I wrote in particular about quilting, applique, and embroidery. The articles evolved into a well-received book. I still smile at the memory of that very happy time in my life.

As time passed, the business relationship into which I was conscripted became a friendship. I started working as Owen's Research Assistant that summer, even though I didn't take classes then. Gramma insisted I take a break from studies in the summer. I now know that working as Owen Winslow's RA full-time was harder than classes would have been. In fact, he cut a deal with the Dean that I received college credits for my work that summer. Seems if you write articles in your area which are published, you get college credits, if your professor is ethical enough to give you credit for writing the articles!

The fall semester started, and I continued with my research for Dr. Winslow, dying pot after stinking pot of fabrics, from all sorts of natural dyes known to the Colonials. By spring, I began making patterned fabric, using the lost wax techniques still used in India to this day, that they used in Colonial Williamsburg. I became accustomed to him calling me Saucy Sassy. In private, I even started calling him Doc, or on rare occasions, Owen. Even so, we were still very much in a professional relationship, just a lot more cordial and friendlier than the year before. We both joked and teased a bit, although more times than not, I had to jerk my head up and look at him to see if he was teasing or serious. The sparkle in those grey eyes would always give it away even before that twitch of a grin hinting on his lips. Damn, he had a good poker face, but I was learning his 'tells'.

Owen shocked me when he asked me to go with him to Williamsburg that summer. I told him he had to ask my Gramma and get her permission. My maternal grandmother raised my brother, Jim, and me after our parents died. She was very 'old world' Spanish, descended from *los Canarios* who were the first settlers to San Antonio in the 1700's. He went with me to the house, and bowed to kiss her hand when I introduced them. "*Mucho gusto en conocerle, Sra. Suarez*," he said in remarkably good Spanish.

"I didn't know you speak Spanish," I blurted.

He flashed a grin at me. "*Si, como no*?"

Gramma blushed, and said, "Oh, please, Dr. Winslow. Call me Alinora."

My eyebrows just about popped off my head. My aristocratic, elegant, very proper *abuelita* never asked anyone to call her by her first name that fast.

"*Solamente si usted me llama* Owen. Only if *you* call me Owen." He smiled, "M*uchisimas gracias, Alinora. Con su permiso*." With a slight bow, he bent to kiss her hand as my Gramma blushed again. He stayed for dinner, explaining why he wanted me to go to Williamsburg. They talked about the project, and what I would be doing. He told her how much he admired my work and admired me as a human being, in fact, that I was an exemplary human being. That one totally surprised me, I remember.

"Really?" I interjected.

He reached over to squeeze my hand. "*De veras*. Really, Sassy."

Gramma adored Owen from almost the first moment she met him. He flirted with her, and I swear he could have charmed the panties right off that sweet old lady. This was a different Dr. Winslow than I knew at school. This Dr. Winslow rather fascinated and terrified me. By the end of the evening, Owen had Gramma eating out of his hand. Literally. He was feeding her candied fruit. She told him I could go with him to Williamsburg, since I would be living in a boarding house with the other female students working there for the summer. She stressed that no men were to be allowed in the boarding house where I stayed. Owen assured her that I would be well guarded, before he left me some patterns. Gramma and I sewed up my clothing for Williamsburg.

"That man is falling in love with you, Sassy," Gramma said one evening after Owen left.

My head jerked up at her words. "Oh, Gramma, *yo no creo*. I don't think so..."

She nodded her head, as she watched him walking to his car. "No, *m'hija*, this old woman can tell you a few things about love. *De veras*, *m'hija*. Believe me, Owen Winslow loves you."

My throat felt dry at her words.

"You be careful this summer, Sassy. *Con cuidado*. Don't let him take liberties with you."

Silent, I nodded. I swallowed, hard, more than once. "Don't worry. You raised me better than that, Gramma."

She smiled. "Yes, I know, *m'hija*, but passion is a funny thing. It can make a strong woman weak. Just... be careful. And remember: don't make permanent decisions based on temporary feelings."

Williamsburg was quite an experience, to say the least. I worked my ass off at the dye vats every day from dawn till dusk. Owen enjoyed telling people I was his little Mexican indentured servant. Believe me, he got a real dirty look the first time he said that. I all but chewed his head off and spat out the pieces when he laughed and told another man dressed as a planter that I was a real little hot tamale. In fact, I was so angry that I stomped right out of the dye vats and went back to my room.

Working in the vats was hot, smelly, exhausting work, but by summer's end, I was able to produce museum quality dyed cottons which were produced as yardage and which they began selling in the shops. I was so proud of my work. Owen took photos of the fabrics, and I took some yardage back with us to Texas to use in quilting pieces for the book our articles were evolving into. I was most pleased because the prints I made duplicated original Colonial prints popular during the Revolution. I was especially pleased with the results of my Jefferson chintz, the same pattern as the curtains in the parlor at Monticello. Owen said if it had been made when Martha Jefferson lived, that you could not have told my copy from the original. That was pretty high praise coming from Owen.

I also realized the very proper Dr. Winslow had a wicked sense of humor, and could be rather charming and flirtatious at times. I guess I should have perceived that with the 'hot tamale' comment. I tried my best to ignore the flirtatious behaviors as nothing more than the Good Professor was away from school enjoying himself role-playing in Williamsburg. Still, there was a swat or two on my butt that got him some really dirty looks, and once I even raised my hand as if to slap him, to which the men watching had howled in laughter. "*No, me tocas esta vez.* Don't touch me like that. Sometimes, you get way too much into this role of planter with the little indentured Mexican girl, Owen," I muttered through gritted teeth. The men howled again as he gave me a wolfish grin as he arched an eyebrow at me.

The following semester, a couple of things happened. Back at Trinity, he was Dr. Winslow again, replete with tweed suits, bow ties, and crisp New England accent. I had enough hours to be a senior, even though it was just my third year. That's what happens when you get credit for working your tail off in the summers in Williamsburg. Dr. Winslow had definitely become Owen to me, at least out of the classroom. He'd best not try to pop me on the butt again, but we were definitely friends.

I could tell if he had his way, we would be more.

And then one afternoon in late October, Owen surprised me when he told me that he had filed for divorce that morning.

"*Que dices*?" My head jerked up in shocked surprise when he told me, even though I knew his marriage had been rocky for the past couple of years. "I'm sorry. Um... why are you telling me this?"

He stared at me a long time, with this rather sad smile on his face. He reached out, as if to touch me, and after a second, he smoothed my hair back from my face. I was unsure whether to feel relieved or disappointed that the touch was so insignificant, so ... not a caress. "Oh, my sweet Saucy Sassy. You are the one person I wanted to tell. I trust you, Sass. Perhaps more than you will ever know."

When he left his wife, he took their son, Rick, who was 9 years old. I often worked at the office on Saturday, to conduct dye experiments with fabric, to sew, and to write. Owen would bring Rick with him on Saturdays. He would even leave Rick with me, if he had to run errands or go to the library to do research.

Rick and I bonded in no time at all. He enjoyed my quirky sense of humor, and I just plain liked the kid. He taught me how to play Pokemon. I taught him how to play poker while pots of dye processed. Rick learned how to help me with the dyes, and developed a critically discerning eye where it came to them. Periodically, Owen would walk through, and smile when he saw us laughing at cards or analyzing and grading dye lots. Rick was also learning Spanish, and enjoyed knowing words his dad didn't know.

Rick was just about the same age Jim and I were when our parents died in the crash. We related to each other. He began telling me things he wasn't telling anyone else. Like his dad, Rick needed a friend, and he chose me to be the friend he trusted.

In November, there was a hearing on temporary orders. The Saturday before the hearing, Kathryn wanted to meet with Owen to 'talk'. He was pretty nervous about it and admitted he told her he was unwilling to meet.

"Why not?" I asked. "Afraid she might try to get you in the sack?"

Owen looked horrified. "Oh, that's <u>not</u> going to happen! Not even with a 100-foot pole and Dean Sander's dick!"

Owen asked a couple of students and teachers to come to the hearing as witnesses. I was one. I told the judge I worked for Dr. Winslow, and sometimes I babysat, if that was the correct term, for Rick. I told the judge Rick talked to me about concerns about his mom and his desires.

"What does the boy say he wants, Miss Searcy?" The Judge surprised me when he asked the question. I understood the lawyers couldn't ask me that. Something about hearsay, I think Owen's lawyer said.

I looked at Owen's attorney, and the judge before I answered. "Judge Hinojosa, he says he loves his mother, but he doesn't want to live like that again."

The judge studied me before asking it. "Like what?"

Her lawyer objected, and the judge waved a hand in the air. "I asked the question. I want an answer. Of course, I can always appoint an amicus attorney, but that will cost your client more money and I am not sure she can afford it. And if push comes to shove, I won't make Dr. Winslow pay for her fees to an amicus attorney, who winds up appointed due to your arrogance."

I dreaded answering these questions, but I knew Rick needed a friend to stand up for him. "He says he was living in constant fear."

"Why? Why was he in constant fear, Miss Searcy?" the judge asked.

"He says that his mother is addicted to heroin, your honor."

All hell broke out with that. Kathryn Winslow was screaming I was a lying Mexican whore, whereupon Judge Hinojosa held her in contempt. As I heard her attorney say to Kathryn: don't call the witness a Mexican whore in front of the Hispanic judge. Not your coolest move. Anyway, the Bailiff then handcuffed her as the Judge ordered she submit *instanter* to drug tests. She tested positive for heroin, just like Rick said she would.

At the completion of the hearing, Owen had custody of Rick.

I had an enemy named Kathryn Winslow.

After the hearing, people started looking at me differently. Sometimes they would stop talking when I came into a room. Sometimes, they would move away from me. One day, I came into a classroom when everyone stopped talking when I came in. I remember I frowned, and asked, "Okay, what gives? Do I have body odor? Bad breath? Lice? What's up?"

Most of the students tittered, a few looking away. One of the jocks sauntered over to me, and leered down at me. "Nothing, Saucy Sassy. Why?"

"Leave her alone, Brice. She's okay," interjected Tim Brown, the computer geek who was one of my study partners.

Brice Waters gave Tim a dirty look, and made a move towards him. "Shut up, twerp. She's his whore. Everyone here knows she is his whore." He turned his head back to me, leering at me again. "Aren't you, Saucy Sassy?"

I felt the color fade from my face. Without thinking, my hand whipped out and slapped him hard, one, two, three times. When I realized what I had done, I threw my hands over my mouth. My hand print stood out on his face as if I had painted it there.

He touched it gingerly. "Saucy." His eyes narrowed as he reached for me again, but I stepped back, and jerked my arm out of his reach. "One for the whore. But watch out. I'll score next time."

Heart racing, I moved to the front of the class before I sat down. I think it was the one class in college I could never remember a word from later on.

Kathryn showed up late that Friday night at about 6:15, with a big show of love and affection before they left. Rick looked back over his shoulder at me, mouthing, 'save me'. It broke my heart, but there was nothing I could do. *Look kid*, I wanted to say, *I can't save you. You're on your own here.* I waited till I saw them leave the building through the window before I turned off the lights and locked up the office to head home.

Gramma's house was two blocks off campus, three blocks from the Chandler Building in which the department office was located. Most days, I walked back and forth unless it was raining or dark when I left. That evening, it was drizzling, and would soon become dark. I'd hoped Owen would get back from his staff meeting in time to give me a lift home, but when he wasn't back, I figured I could handle walking a couple of blocks in light drizzle. After all, South Texas isn't very cold in November.

I was about halfway down the block heading off campus when I heard steps behind me. I glanced back, half expecting to see Owen, shocked to see Brice Waters leering at me. I hurried up to get away from the brute, but he grabbed my arm and swung me around. I felt a jolt of pain shoot through my jaw as he slugged me. I fell backwards, and saw stars when my head hit the concrete curb. He fell on top of me, laughing like a maniac as he began rip at my clothing.

I began screaming, as I pummeled him ineffectively with my fists. He ripped my blouse open, and was ripping my skirt apart. Hell, he just about stripped me right there on the edge of campus, less than three blocks from the safety of my home. As I lay there in the cold, damp grass, my head throbbing with pain, all I could think was this monster is going to rape me because of something Kathryn Winslow is spreading around about me. I sobbed, begging him to stop, in Spanish. "*No, me tocas, por favor, no me tocas*!" I tend to revert to Spanish when I am very stressed, scared or angry.

Then, Owen was there, pulling Brice off me. He hit Brice again and again, until the Dean ran up and pulled Owen off Brice. My friend, Lucy, followed along behind them, and rushed to my side, Lucy gathered me in her arms as I cried, struggling to pull something over me. She slipped her sweater off to cover my bruised breasts. Campus security showed up, and escorted Brice away in handcuffs, his nose still bleeding from the pummeling Owen gave him.

"Went a little overboard there, Owen," the Dean said. "There's gonna be repercussions from that."

"I don't give a fuck, Jack. You saw what that bastard was doing."

Dean Sanders nodded. "Yep. But we're gonna have a load of shit from his parents."

"That bastard was about to rape her, Jack. We all saw it. Let them bring it on. I don't care. That boy has to learn he can't rape women." Owen glanced at him in scorn, as he knelt down beside me and scooped me up into his arms. "I am so damned sick of entitled students who think they own the campus. He shouldn't get away with that, not here, not anywhere. Let's get you into the car, sweetheart. Lucy, can you come with us?"

Eyes wide, Lucy nodded, silent, as she hurried to help Owen get me into the car.

The security guard standing there shot into motion. "Dr. Winslow, we need to debrief her."

"Talk to her tomorrow. If you dumb asses had been doing your job, she would not have just about been raped right here tonight." He stood up, with me still crying, my arms tight around his neck, as he carried me to the car. "On the fucking campus. This is outrageous."

My grandmother swooned when she opened the door. "Sassy! Owen! What happened?"

It was hours later that I realized he called me sweetheart. Or realized he kissed me when he raised me up. Or that I kissed him back as I clung to him.

Brice was arrested, but his family bonded him out the next day. Kathryn came in smirking two weeks later, but the smirk wiped off her face pretty quick when she realized an armed security officer was waiting for her there with me. As she started to leave with Rick, she nodded at me, and said, "Round one for the whore."

I knew what she meant but I wasn't going to give her the satisfaction of acknowledging that. "You haven't won anything, Kathryn. And please, don't belittle yourself like that in front of your child."

Angry, she slammed the door so hard the glass in it shattered.

Soon, it was the next spring, and I would graduate in May. The students still looked at me strangely, but was more in awe because I survived the Waters attack, lived to tell about it, and Brice had been expelled. I kept waiting at the office for Kathryn on her Fridays, often in the company of Lucy, my Gramma, my brother, and security. Security was always there when Owen was not in the office with me. Rick thought it was fun to have our Friday afternoon parties. We all knew we were protecting my reputation.

In early March, Owen came looking for me in a Home Economics class one afternoon. He looked shaken. "Miss Searcy," he always called me Miss Searcy in class, "I need to speak with you in the hall, please."

My heart plummeted. Something was wrong, terribly wrong, if Owen came to another professor's class to find me. I rushed out of the class to his side. "What's wrong? What's happened?"

"Your grandmother is in the hospital. Jim called and asked me to bring you right away."

"*Ai, dios mio*!" I rushed back in the class, told my professor where I was going, and rushed right back out. We were at the hospital minutes later.

Gramma had a mild stroke after Owen brought me home the night Brice attacked me. Her health had been delicate ever since. Now, at 72, she'd suffered a major stroke. It devastated me. Jim and my Gramma were my whole family, after Mom and Dad died 10 years before.

"Gramma? It's Sassy. *Estoy aqui.* I'm here. I love you. *Yo te amo, mi abuelita.*"

My Gramma's beautiful green eyes opened, and she reached for me. I took her hand, and began to pat the delicate skin on her hand, shocked to see how infirm she looked. I knew she'd been failing, but I'd been unable to admit to myself how frail she had become. I held her hand up to my face, and she stroked my hair, as she had done all my life. She motioned for Jim, who came over beside us. I was surprised she motioned for Owen, who joined us at her bedside, also.

"When I'm gone..." she began, her voice weak and tremulous.

"Don't talk like that," I said, as I began crying. "You aren't going anywhere."

She tried to smile, and gently squeezed my hand. "Shush, *m'hija*. When I'm gone, you men look after my girl..."

"Gramma, please, please don't say that..." I sobbed. "Please, Gram, please. *Por favor, mi abuelita. No te vayas!* Please don't go! Please."

Owen placed his hand over mine. Jim's slid beneath Gram's and mine. They looked at each other.

"We'll take care of her, Alinora," Owen promised.

"Always," Jim said.

She passed that night.

The next week, Kathryn Winslow tried to get custody of Rick back. She hit hard, accusing Owen and me of adultery. I must have looked totally shocked. The Judge interrupted her, and called me up to the bench.

"Miss Searcy, are you having an affair with Dr. Winslow?" he asked, his voice stern.

I objected with unexpected violence. "No, sir, I promise. I'll take a lie detector test, Judge. Right now, if you want. I think a lot of Dr. Winslow. He's a good man. But I'm not having an affair with him. My grandmother didn't raise me like that." I choked up at the reference of my grandmother. "I'm sorry, Judge Hinojosa. My grandmother just died last week..." I struggled hold back my unbidden tears.

Owen's attorney asked if how many visits Kathryn had missed with Rick. "Eight."

The judge's eyes popped up. "How do you know that, Miss Searcy?"

I'd regained my composure by then, so I squared my shoulders and looked at the judge. Kathryn was shooting me daggers. I knew I'd start shaking again if I looked at her right then. "I work in the office on Friday afternoons. Dr. Winslow attends a staff meeting at 6..."

"Ha! He's out drinking," Kathryn interjected.

Judge Hinojosa frowned. "Counsel, control your client. Mrs. Winslow, I will hold you in contempt again if you do not comport yourself appropriately. This is a court of law. You know I mean it. I've done it before. Don't make me do it again. Proceed, Miss Searcy. What happens then?"

"I stay at the office with Rick for his mom to come pick him up."

"Do you know the dates when she has picked him up?"

I nodded. "Yes, sir, I mark it on Dr. Winslow's calendar."

The judge's eyebrows popped up again. "Did you bring the calendar?"

I smiled. "Yes, sir, I did." I pulled it out of my bag. "I marked the times she came in blue, along with the time she showed up. I marked the times she didn't show up in red."

"How late would you wait for her?"

"Until at least 6:30." I responded. "We stayed til 6:45 once when she called and said she had been stuck in traffic."

"Please hand me the calendar." Judge Hinojosa reached for the book, which I handed to him.

Kathryn picked Rick up 4 times since the hearing in November. She did not pick him up for Thanksgiving and just took him for one day at Christmas. She could have had him for a week. She didn't pick him up again until the weekend before the hearing, when she showed up at 6:35, just before we were all about to leave.

"What was this date with the big circle around it?"

I paled. "That was the date of her first visit, sir, after the last hearing. After I turned Rick over to his mom, I started out to walk home."

"What time?" the Judge asked.

"She picked him up at 6:15. It was a little later when I left. I always lock up the office before I leave."

The Judge frowned. "Why is it circled?"

I could feel myself shaking, and I began rubbing my hands together. They were cold as ice. I took a ragged breath. "I was assaulted on the way home that night."

The Judge stared at me before he spoke. "You may sit down, Miss Searcy. Dr. Winslow, please take the stand."

Owen stood up, straightened his tie, and took the witness seat. "Yes, your Honor?"

"Are you having an affair with this girl?" he asked.

Owen turned to look the judge right in the face. "No, sir. I have great admiration and respect for Sarah Winslow, but I am not having an affair with her."

The judge tilted his head at him. "Oh, really? Little Freudian slip there?"

Owen realized what he had said, and laughed as his face reddened. "You may just be right, Judge. But I am not having an affair with Ms. Searcy. I have far too much respect for her as well as for the University where I work to do that. And like she says, her Grandmother did not raise her like that. She's a fine young woman, with a keen sense of morality."

The judge studied his face again. He nodded and said, "What happened on the night of November 24th?"

"A male student followed Ms. Searcy and attempted to rape her, sir. The Dean and I were walking back to my offices and heard her screams for help. We interceded and were able to stop it."

The judge looked back at me, but my head was down. I was shaking horribly as I tried not to cry. Kathryn sat there like a cat who had been given a saucer of milk. The judge looked back at Owen.

"Was it ever determined why he attacked her?" he asked.

Owen nodded. "Yes, sir. The boy admitted in criminal court last week that he attacked Ms. Searcy because my wife spread the rumor I was sleeping with Sassy."

The Judge gave a pointed look to Kathryn. "Did you do that?" he demanded.

She shrugged. "Well, if the shoe fits..."

She looked completely lost when the judge told her he was not changing custody.

A week later, Kathryn Winslow overdosed on heroin.

No one was at the secretary's desk that Friday afternoon when I came into the History Office. The phone was ringing, so I slung down my backpack, and grabbed it.

"Sassy? This is Dean Sanders. Is Owen okay?"

The question surprised me. "I guess so, sir. I just came in. Would you like to talk to him?"

"Yes, please. See if he is okay, and let me know if I need to come over. Right now, Sassy. I'll hang on."

I didn't know what was going on. "Yes, sir."

I put the phone on hold, and knocked on Owen's door. He did not answer, so I pushed the door open. He stood at the window, staring out across the beautiful campus, deep in thought. I walked up, and laid a hand on his shoulder.

"Owen?" When he didn't answer, I rubbed his shoulder, to get his attention, and asked, "Owen? Are you okay?"

Wordless, he reached to my hand. "Oh, Sassy, I didn't hear you come in. Um... no... no, not really."

I had never seen him quite so white faced before. I pulled him around to face me. "Owen, what's the matter?"

He pulled me to him and laid his head on my shoulder. I realized there were tears running down his face. "She ... killed herself, Sassy. Kathryn killed herself."

"Oh, my God." I swear, I went numb. I swear I felt like I had killed her with my testimony. I knew that wasn't true; chances were heroin killed her. Mouth dry, I got the words out. "Umm... Dean wants to know if he needs to come over."

Owen shook his head. "No."

I started to pull away, to go back to tell the Dean what Owen said and how he was. Owen didn't release my hand. Instead, he pulled me closer. "Owen, I have to..."

He dipped his head to kiss me. "I have wanted to do that for so long," he whispered, his voice hoarse. He lowered his head towards me again. I could feel months if not years of yearning in that kiss, my own yearning as much as his. He had never so much as pecked me on the cheek before except for the kiss the night he took me home to my Gramma after the attack.

I wanted so badly to kiss back. To reach my arms up around his shoulders, to run my fingers through his tawny blond hair. And before I thought, I was kissing him back. But with a start, I realized I couldn't do this, not now. We both deserved so much more. I felt the blood drain from my face. I pulled back, my hands shaking like a leaf. Stammering, I pulled away from his arms, and rushed to the other room, but I made sure I locked Owen's door before I left his office. I didn't want to be tempted to go back in there. Not right then.

"Dean? He says Kathryn ... yes, exactly. He is pretty shaken up. He said you shouldn't come, but I think you should. I locked him in there. I didn't want anyone else walking in."

I hung up the phone, and turned, to see Owen standing in the doorway his hands extended to me, beseeching me to stay. "Please, Sassy. Don't go."

"I can't do this. I can't. Not now." I whispered the words as I backed away from him. "Please, Owen, don't... Not now. She just died, for God's sake, Owen. Not now. Please."

Just then, my friend, Alice, walked in. I grabbed my backpack, and with tears streaming down my face, I hurried towards her. "Come on, Alice, we need to go pick up Jim."

Alice kinda had the hots for Jim and would do just about anything for him back then. I remember she looked from Owen, to me, and back again, before she nodded. "I'll drive," she said.

That was good, since I didn't have a car.

I would be lying if I said I hadn't realized Owen was falling for me or that I was falling in love with him. He was always very proper at Trinity. You know, that New England bow tie and tweed suit, puffing on a pipe kind of guy. That kiss was the first real kiss we ever shared, other than that kiss when he took me home after the attack. For well over a year, he did little more than pat my back or pat my hand, except for those few occasions at Williamsburg which I tended to blame on play acting and a bit too much bourbon. But in the weeks after the attack, he became more solicitous of me. Much more solicitous. His pats on my hand would linger a little longer than necessary. Sometimes, it seemed as though his pats to my back were becoming caresses. At first, I thought it was just my imagination, but I hadn't stopped it. I knew, just like my Gramma had known, that Owen loved me. I knew, just as my Gramma had known, that I loved my crotchety curmudgeon. When my Gramma put his hand on mine, I knew she was telling us both that she approved. Despite the age difference. Despite the fact that he was not yet divorced, which was quite shocking from my very Catholic Gramma. She gave us her blessing.

I just wasn't sure that afternoon what I felt about Owen Winslow. It was complicated. Some days, I knew I loved him with all my heart and soul and wanted to spend my life with him. Other days, I hated him to the very essence of my being. I often told him that he could be a real ass. He had a temper and rarely apologized after he blew. He hurt my feelings any number of times, and sometimes, he made me cry. But in all our years together, I never let him see me cry when he hurt my feelings.

But, as the days became weeks, and weeks months, and months became years, I knew, deep down in my soul that my feelings for Dr. Owen Winslow had changed. He was more than my professor or my mentor. He was more than a friend. Dammit. My professor had become my first love. I refused to be a cliché, a Research Assistant sleeping with her boss. I saw too much of that in other departments, and I was determined to stay above that. I saw too many girls ridiculed and even run out of school over that. I didn't intend to ever be called *puta* again. So, I said over and over to myself, don't make permanent decisions based on temporary feelings. In other words, Sassy girl, don't go jump into that fine kettle of fish. I'd heard Owen say, 'fine kettle of fish' a jillion times. Okay, maybe not a jillion, but a lot.

I had trouble sleeping that Friday night. I tossed and turned. I remembered Gramma used to say, a year from now, *m'hija,* everything you are stressing about won't even be important. Keep moving, girl! Just keep moving! So, I determined to move into sleep mode. I went hog wild and drank a whole glass of Gramma's vintage fine Spanish wine. Dotted some of her lavender on my temples, my wrists, and sprinkled some on my pillow like she used to do when I couldn't sleep. With the wine and the lavender, I finally drifted off to sleep. When I awoke the next morning, more of Gramma's words rang in my head. Love isn't what you say, Sassy. Love is what you do.

Then the damned phone began to ring, over and over again from Owen. I sighed, and picked it up. "Yes, sir?" I hoped if I kept it all business, he might, too. Maybe. But in my heart, I knew we moved past that yesterday, both with Kathryn's death and with those kisses.

He wanted me to go with Rick and him, to run some errands. After significant wheedling on his part, I relented and agreed. He arrived an hour later grinning like a school boy, with Rick in tow.

"Have you told him?" I whispered.

He sobered a bit. "No. I ... I don't know what to say."

I was dismayed. "Owen! I will do a lot of shit for you, but this is not, I repeat, not, in my job description. Nowhere does my job description say I am to be the bearer of bad news to your child." Owen just stared at me, despair clouding his grey eyes to hazel. "Oh, hell, Owen. Come on." I felt disgusted with myself for giving into those damned puppy dog eyes.

We went to lunch, and took Rick shopping for some new clothes. Around 4, we got to the San Antonio Art Institute, one of Rick's favorite places. I planned to wander off, leave the two guys alone, and Owen would at last man up and tell Rick about Kathryn's death. No such luck.

As I started to wander away, Owen grabbed my arm. He looked frantic and sounded almost desperate as he said, "Sassy, please stay here with us."

My lips thinned in anger. "Owen, you need to talk to your son." He gave me his damned 'I'm helpless – help me – I'm all alone here' look again. I didn't know whether to hug him or slug him. So, I sighed, and sat down. "Dammit. Rick, we all need to talk."

Rick turned around from studying the painting before him, and grinned. "What's the matter? Dad get you knocked up?"

I gasped. "Richard! Of course not!"

Owen looked shocked. "Richard, you need to apologize to Sassy. Right now."

Rick chuckled. "I'm sorry, Sassy. Mom spouts off like that all the time.

I'm just teasing. Honest, I know better. For the record, I can't think of any one I would rather have for a Mom than you."

I turned very pale. Owen stared in shocked silence.

Rick spoke first, his voice far too serious for a boy his age. "Okay, what is it?"

Owen swallowed, hard, and then turned to me. "I can't do it," he whispered, his voice cracking with emotion.

I hate you, I mouthed to Owen. *I love you*, he signed back, with just the faintest hint of a smile.

I shut my eyes tight for a minute, as I struggled for words. *This is so unfair*, I thought, as I opened my eyes and cut daggers at him. Finally, I turned to Rick, and placed my hand on the boy's arm. "Rick, your mother died yesterday."

He stared at me a long moment before he answered, and when he did, Rick's eyes shown with unshed tears. "I told her she would kill herself with that shit."

"Don't talk like that, Rick," Owen said automatically.

I frowned at him. *"Ai, dios mio*! For the love of God, Owen. Don't do that to him. He's your son, for God's sake. Have a little sympathy. *Es su hijo*! I just told him his mother is dead. Show a little compassion."

His eyes flashed in anger at me. "I want him to grow up to have some manners."

"Then don't act like an ass," I snapped back.

Rick began to laugh through his tears. "See? She's strong enough to deal with you, Dad. I loved Mom, but she was weak. Sassy, well, Sassy ..."

"Is not your mother," I finished for him.

His smile was bittersweet. "I still wish you were."

I hugged him to me.

Rick turned 10 the day of his mother's funeral.

Owen asked me to marry him the afternoon I graduated. I knew the proposal was coming, and I accepted. We were married six weeks later in the Trinity Chapel. With us were Jim, Rick, the Dean, and my friend, Alice. Owen gave notice to Trinity, and accepted a job at Harvard as head of their American History Department. They'd been trying to steal him away for a couple of years, but he liked the temperate weather in San Antonio. He wouldn't have left if we had not fallen in love. We found a cute apartment near campus for the three of us, and managed to move in just before the fall semester started. Suddenly, I was living in Boston, the wife of a Harvard professor, the step-mother of a pre-teen, while I went to graduate school at Harvard.

For Christmas, Owen brought home a little ball of wriggly fur that he told me was a Skye terrier. Rick was thrilled. He'd never had a dog before. Of course, I wound up the one who loved the dog, and the one who cared for him.

That was fourteen years ago. I finished my master's degree in American History at Harvard and then I adopted Rick when he was 12. A year later, I finished my doctorate. By then, I had lost all traces of the Hispanic accent I still had when we went to Boston, although if I was raging mad, I lapsed into Spanish as I yelled at Owen. I began teaching at another local college. Four years later, we moved to Williamsburg. Owen became the Dean at William and Mary and I became a history professor. Owen hated the cold in Boston, and we both saw this move as the chance of a life time for us both. We continued to write about the Revolutionary War.

We were both still at W&M when we bought the lake house. The plan was Rick would live there while attending Med School at Emory, in Atlanta, and we could stay there when we visited Rick as well as Jim and his family. Jim had a thriving legal practice in Marietta, just outside Atlanta. Owen and I would live at the lake house when we retired.

And then my damned husband had to up and die.

A Harvard friend told me once, "No wonder he loves you," to which I bit back the angry retort on my lips. Owen loved me for so much more than the fact that I was a good Research Assistant, even if he bragged I was the best damned RA he ever had. My friend didn't understand at all why Owen loved me. Even now, it's hard for me to verbalize it. I loved Owen, don't misunderstand. But sometimes, I think maybe I married Owen because I loved Rick so damned much. But don't ever doubt I loved my Owen, body, heart and soul, long before he died.

Now, the man I loved is gone. I understand grief is love's unwillingness to let go. I wasn't ready for Owen to leave. I sure wasn't ready to say goodbye. He's missing from me. I realize that I am no longer who I was. My loss is reshaping me.

Like I said, love is complicated.

Chapter Two

I arrived in Acworth about dusk on the first of July. I had tendered my resignation to W&M, and the sale of our row house in Williamsburg closed a few days before that. I would start teaching at Emory that fall. I had no place to go but ahead, as Owen would have said. My brother, Jim, and his family were out of the country visiting his wife's family in a long-planned family reunion and vacation. I did not want to be a bucket of cold water on them, and elected to stay home, to organize my new house. Europe was always fun, but Moldova was just not where I needed to be that summer.

Rick would continue to live with me while he finished med school at Emory in Atlanta. Rick is the first to admit that he was a difficult child for this stepmother at times. He said he couldn't imagine wanting anyone else to be his mom but once the reality of his new life set in, I was to blame for all his problems in his mind, at least until he decided his dad was the cause of all his problems. I adopted him when Rick decided again that he loved me and wanted me to be his mother. Since Owen and I never had other children, Rick, Jim, Jim's family and I were basically all the family we had now. Owen's mother had little to do with us, often calling me 'Owen's little wetback' despite the fact that my 'back is not wet', as we say in South Texas. I am a legal U.S. citizen, just like Nell Winslow is. She is such a nice Progressive lady. You know the type. God bless Owen, he wouldn't tolerate her treatment of me, and he finally cut her off when she kept throwing slurs as well as punches at me.

Rick announced he was 'not available' on the 4th of July. I took that to mean he had a better offer than hot dogs, fishing, and fireworks with Mom at Historic Acworth for the 4th. I couldn't blame him for taking that pretty blonde over me. She was a knockout and smart as a whip.

So, all alone by my sweet little self, I decided to do something crazy and drive up past the Cohutta Wilderness to look at a piece of property I might buy. In this day and age, who doesn't need a bug out camp? Armed with a map from the realtor, who was unavailable for a property showing on the 4th of July weekend, and with my two Skye terriers in tow, I headed north, until I turned between the towns of Ellijay and Blue Ridge. I followed the road on through the Cohutta, past the Wilderness, almost to the state line between Georgia and Tennessee.

I planned to then go off road just past Little Frog Holler, in search of the legendary McCarron's Corner. I say legendary because McCarron's Corner was known historically to have been a settlement all the way back to colonial days. However, in the past twenty years, a famous romance writer immortalized McCarron's Corner with a series of books which dealt largely with life during the Colonial Period and the Revolutionary War. With a hunky hero and a smart and brassy heroine, the books were big hits and made the author quite rich.

Owen and I loved hiking, and we had hiked various trails in the Cohutta Wilderness as well as around Lake Allatoona, but I had not struck out on my own since Owen died. Somehow, I thought having the dogs would help to keep me safe 'just in case', so, I brought the two hooligans with me 'for protection'. I was not at all sure who would protect me from my hooligans. I brought along more practical items as well, a canteen of water, a couple of peanut butter and bacon sandwiches, a compass, lighter, a fire starter, and my old, ever-faithful Swiss army knife. I also brought water purification tablets, flash light, a little fold-up fishing pole and gear, a rain parka, a little sewing kit, and even a little package of the fix all, duct tape. I even carried a solar powered phone charger, just to be safe. I also threw in a couple of extra pairs of socks, since I would be crossing both the Jacks River, Little Frog Creek and McCarron's Creek several times while heading to McCarron's Corner. It wasn't a long hike, but it was known to be a pain in the southbound end of a northbound mule. All just basic survival gear which I keep in my day pack. I threw in the dogs' collapsible food bowls replete with a two day supply of kibble. As an afterthought, I also threw in a super nutritious pack of chocolate chip cookies, and a large Diet Coke for good measure, so I was ready to make the day. I had more than I needed, but I was venturing into new territory and I would rather be safe with a little bit too much gear than sorry. Being a good ol' redneck girl from Texas, now residing in Georgia, I knew it was better to be prepared 'just in case' for my foray into anything approaching Wilderness. Little Frog Holler and McCarron's Corner were definitely located in The Wilderness.

The turn from the main road north of Ellijay was a few miles out of town, easy enough to follow. I went as far up the road as possible, past the hiking trails in the Cohutta Wilderness, just shifting into four-wheel drive after I passed Cohutta Creek. When the road finally became virtually unpassable, as I had been warned, about 25 miles past Little Frog Holler, I pulled over and parked Owen's four-wheel drive SUV off the road behind a dilapidated barn. The dogs were excited to get out and start our hike. It should be a few miles further, but it would be rough going, with water crossings 2 to 3 feet deep, that could be running pretty fast.

"It's not a bad hike," my realtor said. "Well... I take it back. It *is* bad. I hate it. But you're an experienced hiker. You can handle it far berter than I can. Just remember: don't wander off from the trail."

"Why?" I said, startled, as I glanced at her from the map in my hands. "Is Big Foot gonna get me?"

She laughed, worry marring her face. "Um... might. People disappear up there. Just stay on the trail, and everything should be fine."

"So I'm going to get kidnaped in Deliverance Country? Are you telling me to listen for the banjoes playing? Or will I disappear through some portal to another world? Will I hear the music from Twilight Zone, or from Deliverance?" I teased.

She laughed, nervous, and I noticed her hands began to shake. "No, nothing like that. Just be careful. And don't wander off the trail."

I rolled my eyes. Non-hikers can be such sissies over the least little inconvenience. Still, I had a fleeting question of how many people had ever disappeared. In fact, the fact that people had disappeared was why I took my brave and stalwart long haired albeit short legged companions with me. I left a note for Rick telling him where I was headed, and not to worry if I were late, but that I should be back by the 6th at the latest. After all, he was 24 years old, in med school, and quite capable of being alone by himself for a few days. He could manage a day or two without Mom.

The terrain was beautiful but quite rugged. The hike was easy at first. As

I descended into a lush, green waterfall-filled river valley, I was awed by the views. This was the kind of remote beauty I was hoping to find, a pocket isolated from the modern world we could access in a couple of hours for weekends away from the hustle and bustle of Atlanta. I envisioned a little cabin nestled beneath the towering pines, beside a babbling brook, where Rick could study and I could sew.

An hour later, as I struggled over a nasty rocky outcrop, I decided the area didn't look half as pretty as I first thought. Old hemlocks shaded younger deciduous trees, creating a living canopy of myriad shades of greens. The forest floor was rich with ferns and wild flowers. Vividly colored mushrooms thrived in abundance. Nonetheless, I was now cursing those same sparkling, splashing waters that enchanted me an hour earlier. By the third time I crossed that damned creek, slipping off the rocks into three-foot-deep cold water, I was aggravated, frustrated, and approaching exhaustion. The dogs, on the other hand, thought it was great fun. Thank God, they could swim!

It was the middle of the summer and hotter than hell. It looked like rain might finally be coming to North Georgia after a lengthy drought. All I needed was to get stuck up here in a flash flood. Rain clouds hovered above, causing the heat and humidity level to rise from merely 'hot and humid' to 'walking in a miasma of hot steam.' It was hideous, to say the least. At least our periodic falls into the creeks cooled us off. The brush was so high and the trail so bad it was almost impossible to know if you were on the old, worn path or not. In places, the mosquitoes swarmed in hordes of tiny, evil little demons, their pitchforks striking anywhere and everywhere. I was sick and tired of the little beasts! Sweat poured off my body, stinging all the places the mosquitoes had bitten. I knew this trail was rated hard, but this was insane. With visions of being captured for nefarious reasons out here in Deliverance Country, I continued, with my two energetic Skye terriers through the creeks as well as thickets. I cringed every time the dogs caught their coats, lush and show ready just that morning, as we stumbled along through brush and brambles. I definitely should have left them at home. It would take a good year to get those coats back into condition. They already looked like ragged little street urchins. I dreaded to think what combing them out would be like!

As the dogs and I crossed what I thought was Jackson Creek, the 'trail' (and I use that phrase very loosely) leveled out for a bit, passing one of the lovely waterfalls in the area. The dogs and I took that opportunity to rest, and I broke out one of my sandwiches and my Diet Coke. The spot looked much more enchanting after I rested and ate. I checked my map again, and realized with relief that the cut to McCarron's Creek was just past my current location. Once we switched to the McCarron's Creek trail, we would go 4.3 miles further to a hilltop spring and waterfall beside the old abandoned settlement of McCarron's Corner, the property I was considering buying. One thing for sure, in this remote location, it would make a fabulous bug out cabin. I called the dogs, wrapped up my trash, tucked it into my backpack, and we started hiking back uphill again (oh, joy), following along the ridge to the outcrop where I should be able to see our destination. In fact, everything would have been fine, *if* Hawk had not dragged me off the trail into a meadow after a damned rabbit. Of course, as soon as he took off in high pursuit, Mimi followed behind. I took off after the troublesome two, wincing as tree branches slapped against my face. That was when, as the old saying goes, the fertilizer hit the ventilator. All of a sudden, we were enveloped by a hideous, high pitched, shrill sound which put the dogs into a frenzy of barking.

And I would have sworn we were falling.

Chapter Three

The dogs woke me up licking my face. I figured I hit my head because it sure was hurting something awful, and that I must have fainted, even though I had never fainted before in my life. Disoriented and sick to my stomach, a wave of vertigo hit me as I tried to raise up. It felt like I was falling again, even though I was on solid ground. I slowly raised myself up, and looked around.

This was undoubtedly the hardest freaking couple of miles I ever attempted to hike. I startled, at gun fire in the distance. *Must be hunters,* I mused. *Odd they are hunting way out of hunting season in July though.* "Come on, guys, let's find that trail and get to blasted McCarron's Corner."

I was not quitting at this point. Still, I was much less interested in buying the property than four hours before when I left the SUV. Not one to give up without a fight, however nervous I might be, the dogs and I continued in the direction of the shooting. I began to sing, my voice off-key but loud, with the dogs barking in syncopated disharmony as we approached the intermittent booms of the gun fire. Owen always said I sang like a tone deaf drunk. I didn't want a hunter shooting us, and I felt growing unease that anyone was hunting out of season here. After all, if some good ol' boy in the backwoods would break the law and be hunting up here in broad daylight, they might not be people I wanted to encounter all by myself. With no trail visible in the heavy undergrowth, I focused more on finding people and avoiding stepping on a Western rattlesnake who might be sunning on this hot Georgia summer day than in perusing real estate out here in what I was now calling this 'God Forsaken Corner of Hell'.

Three hours later, and a half a dozen more circles wandering around, I had still found a big fat nothing. I grew increasing nervous after hiking for seven hours, fretting I might not make my destination before the light began to dim. Hell, I wasn't nervous, I was scared. Shitless. I wanted to be home. I wanted my Mommy. I wanted anything but McCarron's Freaking Corner. As we stumbled back into the meadow we had landed in over and over, I sank onto a rock that should now have my name written on it. The dogs, also tired, sank down beside me. I sighed, and thinking we might just camp here overnight, I dug out their bowls and kibble. The little hooligans ate like they were starving, totally oblivious to my growing fears.

I tried my cell phone jillions of times. Each time, it had no reception. *Wouldn't it just figure? The one time in my lifetime that I go hiking alone, and I get lost. I even have a full charge, and a solar powered charger with me! And I have no freaking phone reception. Wouldn't it just figure?*

With another sigh, I pulled out the other half of the sandwich I had eaten earlier, and began to nibble at it. I was far too nervous to be hungry, but I knew I needed the energy from the peanut butter and bacon. After I finished, I pulled out the 35-mm. pin hair brush from my pack. Owen used to laugh at me for using a dog brush for my hair. I always told him, but it is a very nice dog brush that cost a lot of money! I unbraided my long hair, and shook it out to allow me to rinse the sweat soaked strands in the creek. After I soaked my hair, I flung my hair back, gasping as the icy chill ran down my back. It felt so good to be rid of the sweat and to have a cool head again! I worked out the snarls from the long strands, and then re-braided it. I called Hawk to my side, and began brushing the mats from his now ravaged, once beautiful show coat. "Dammit, I can't believe I brought you guys out here. Your coat is shattered."

"White woman talks to dog?"

I jumped up, heart pounding, and whirled around to see a tall man dressed in what appeared to be Native American attire, replete with buckskins, bead work, and tall moccasins. His long, black braids glistened in the fading light, with long turkey feathers rakishly sticking up from behind his head. He carried both a long rifle and a bow and arrows. A skinning knife was sheathed at his waist. He slung the dead deer he'd been carrying across his shoulders down beside him.

"*Ai, dios mio*!" *It must have been him shooting*, I mused, my mouth dry. "Where did you come from?"

He nodded. "You talk to dogs and worry about where I come from?"

I nodded. "Yes, I ... I guess that seems silly to you."

He looked confused, as if trying to understand the meaning of my words. "White women often seem silly to me." And then he grinned.

I continued to study his clothing, and realized his attire looked very much like that worn by Cherokees in North Carolina. "Are you Cherokee?"

He stared at me again before answering. After an uncomfortable pause, he said, "Yes, I am one of the People of a Different Speech, the AniYunwiya. Is this white woman lost?" I nodded. He grunted. He squatted down, to pick up one of my chocolate chip cookies.

A look of surprise passed his face as he tasted the cookie. His eyebrows arched, and he nodded.

"Food good."

"Thank you. Yes, I am lost."

"Mmph," he said, as he swallowed a bite of the cookie. "Hmm. Then, maybe I call you Lost Woman. You wear good clothes. Most white women do not wear leggings." He pointed to my jeans.

I laughed. "Well, I am glad I wore these in this brush today."

He nodded as he grunted his approval. "Yes, that was wise."

I was also glad I wore a loose cotton top, which helped wick perspiration away from my body. I loved that top because I bought it before years in the Mercado in San Antonio with Owen. Handwoven in Mexico, bright red, it was my favorite top. I was glad I had on my comfortable, well-worn hiking boots.

He continued to chew the cookie. Finally, he swallowed it, he looked from the two dogs and me. "Where you come from?"

I frowned. "From Acworth, down by Lake Allatoona. Why?"

He frowned, as if he did not know where Lake Allatoona was. It occurred to me he might not know where I meant.

I was sorely tempted to say, 'Way Down Yonder by the Pawpaw Patch,' but I had a pretty good hunch that would get me another blank look. Instead, I said, "Allatoona Pass. In the southern part of Cherokee County."

His eyes narrowed and he grunted. "Long walk to Allatoona Pass. That would take four days to walk here from there. Maybe longer." His eyes narrowed as he looked me over again. He nodded abruptly. "You come from Beyond?"

I shrugged, not at all sure of his meaning. "Yes, I came from beyond the Pass. Why?"

His bronzed skin paled at my words. He dropped his eyes from my gaze. "Yes, Lost Woman is the right name. Now I understand. It was fated that I come by here today. Where you go now?"

"Um... I was headed to McCarron's Corner."

He nodded. "Not far. You have come far, but do not have far to go now. Come. I will show you."

I blinked as he hoisted the deer back up across his shoulders, whirled around and started away. He stopped after a few steps, and looked back at me. "Lost Woman, come. I take you to McCarron."

I hesitated, as I wondered just how wise it would be to follow some unknown man wearing Cherokee garb, carrying a skinning knife, bow and arrows, and carrying a muzzle loader musket, replete with powder horn, not to mention a dead deer slung across his shoulders. I've seen hunters all my life, but I I'd never seen anyone carrying a muzzle loader before, except at re-enactments. They are pretty common at Williamsburg, and a gunsmith there recreates them, for a hefty price. Owen had one hanging on his study wall. Anyway, I thought about my options. It did not seem I had any option other than stay here and just continue to go in circles. I raised myself up, and grabbed my backpack.

"Thank you." I whistled. "Come on, dogs! *Vamonos*! Let's go!"

I almost had to run to keep up with his long strides. He knew where he was headed. In less than thirty minutes, we stood beneath the tall hemlocks and pines near an opening to a cleared meadow, where I saw plowed farmland and six cottages. One cabin appeared to have burned at some time in the past, and a man was repairing it. In the distance, I saw a larger house as well. The Cherokee nodded towards the houses. He slung the dead deer down to me. I sagged under the weight of the deer, but I could manage it. "McCarron lives there. You go now. Take the deer with you."

He wheeled about as if to leave. I grabbed his sleeve. "Thank you so much! What is your name?"

He looked startled at the question, and then his eyes narrowed. "Why?"

"I would like to say who helped me, and who sent the deer. And to mention you in my prayers of thanksgiving to, um, the Great Father."

He studied me again, as if he could peer right into my soul. After another of his long pauses, he nodded. "Tell McCarron his brother, Shadow Wolf, brought this Lost Woman to him."

I nodded. "I will."

"Tell him I leave the deer as a gift to my friend. For caring for another one from Beyond."

Mute, I nodded.

"Be sure to tell McCarron you came from Beyond to come to this place."

I nodded again. This seemed very important to Shadow Wolf. I figured I better tell whoever McCarron was what he said. "Lost Woman will tell McCarron you helped me, Shadow Wolf. And that I came from beyond to find him. I am sure he would thank you for the deer. Thank you again. You're a life saver."

I hadn't known anyone named McCarron still lived around here. I still had no idea where 'beyond' was, or just where this adventure had brought me, or where it would take me. Most of all, little did I know how true those words I uttered to Shadow Wolf were.

He had been a life saver.

Chapter Four

Dusk was fast approaching, but people were still working in the fields and around the cottages. All sounds of hustle and bustle around the farms ceased as I walked out of the forest into the meadow. A dog barked, and mine barked in response. People working in the fields stopped and stared. One woman pointed towards me, dropped her scythe, grabbed up a toddler, and ran for her cabin.

Odd, I thought. I thought this was an old, abandoned village, but looked straight out of the 18th century. I've worked Williamsburg enough to know what one looked like. But, that would be impossible. Stranger still, the people were dressed in colonial styled clothes. The women wore long sleeved shifts, sleeves pushed up, with long aprons tucked up at the waist to form pockets, big sun bonnets or broad brimmed straw hats. The men wore pants and homespun shirts, opened at the neck. Many of the men had their sleeves rolled up, with handkerchiefs round their necks. Most of the men wore broad brimmed hats. All were sweating and dirty from working in the fields all day. Nah… They just couldn't be from the 18th century. After all, it wasn't like I fell through a hole in time, and wound up somewhere in the distant past!

Was this how Alice felt when she fell down the rabbit hole? I wondered, trepidation filling my heart. I decided I must have discovered a group of people recreating a community like what could have been here during the Revolution. Yes, that must be it. That made the most sense. I was damned tired, or I would never thought for a second something as silly as 'hole in time' or time travel. I just needed to stop reading those silly romance novels. They were starting to affect my mind! Hole in time, my Aunt Soledad! Ha!

I smiled, and waved to the people I was approaching. "Hello! I am so glad to find people!"

One tall, slender woman with masses of curly, red hair with a white streak at her widow's peak, stood arguing with several men pointing towards me. She lifted her apron, wiped her hands, and strode towards me. "Hello! I am Lily McCarron! How come you to these parts?"

The woman's soft, Southern accent lilted rhythmically as she spoke. Just like Liliana McCarron's voice was described in the books, I thought. Pure Southern to the soul, Lily grew up in Georgia, and had the beautiful accent of a native Georgian. My heart began to beat about 90 to nothing. Actually, I guess that would have been about 190 to nothing. *Madre de dios! Holy Mother of us all! Maybe I did slide down that rabbit hole. Was this how Alice felt when she met the Mad Hatter?* I blinked again as I wiped the perspiration from my face where it was sliding into my eyes. That 'hole in time' joke I made to the realtor didn't seem as farfetched as when I made it, or even a few minutes before. Had I somehow managed to come through a portal to another world, another time? My mouth quite parched, I wasn't sure I wouldn't pass out. In fact, I wasn't sure I already had passed out, that I was hallucinating this entire thing. "Um... my name is Sassy Winslow..."

A look of pure pleasure crossed Liliana McCarron's face. "Cousin Sassy! We thought you would never arrive! Marcus, look who is here! It is my cousin, Sassy! She finally arrived! Sassy, I haven't seen you since we were children!"

I sidled up beside her. I spoke, my voice low and warning. "Uh, Mrs. McCarron, I don't think I am your cousin."

A look of irritation crossed her face. I was startled to see her cognac colored eyes, just like the books described, and that the striking color turned even more yellow with irritation. Her voice low enough that just I could hear, she replied, "Of course you aren't, you ninny, but don't tell these people that. Let them think you are my cousin. Jeans and that shirt? I can bet where you came from. Or rather, when. Quick, now. Where are you from?"

"Acworth. Just came here from outside Williamsburg. Boston before that. Oh, I guess that could cause problems… Um… I grew up in San Antonio, if that helps."

"Yes, there's at least one here who knows both Williamsburg and Boston. San Antonio works. Remember it's Mexico, a Spanish colony, not yet Texas. Now, come along. We can talk later. Marc, look, my cousin Sassy finally arrived! Our prayers have been answered! Sassy, this is my husband, Marcus

McCarron. Sassy came from Beyond the Allatoona Pass to find us."

A startled look of immediate recognition crossed the clear, dark green eyes of tall, blonde-haired Marcus McCarron. He looked like an Irish warrior of old, bronzed golden skin, erect posture, broad shoulders, and hard, taut muscles. Marc reached out and clasped a large hand on my shoulder, and then pulled me to him. My stomach literally turned to jelly at his touch. *My God, he looks just like I always envisioned him when I read those books about McCarron's Corner!*

"Ah, lass, we were a'feared you would never arrive! Our prayers are indeed answered! Tis high time ye made yer way here!" He said, his lilting Irish accent thrilling to my ears, as he wrapped me into a bear hug extraordinaire. He then stepped back, still holding me in his grasp. "Let me have a look at ye, lass. Well, Lee, ye always said she was a wee bonnie lass."

Everyone laughed at his words. Except for one man, not quite as tall as Marc, dark, brooding, not at all buying the story we were selling. His ice-cold eyes appeared untrusting, narrowed and suspicious.

"How convenient. Wolf comes up and drops off your long-lost cousin, Lily. Doesn't this smack you as a little off?"

Brooding. Angry. Frowning. I decided right then and there that he would henceforth be known to me as Big Angry. I didn't have to take this, even if I'm not Lily McCarron's long-lost cousin. Bristling, I stepped towards him. "Chill, Dude. What did I do to you? What's got your panties in a wad?"

Okay, I admit it was a crazy thing to ask the man. Do not ask me to explain why on earth I chose to say that to an 18th century man! I was pretty tired, maybe a little slap happy. Heck, maybe a lot.

Marcus McCarron had to turn away, as he guffawed. Lily dropped her head, to cover a smile.

Tall, lean and angry just continued to glower at me. "I don't recall addressing my comments to you, madam. And my name is not 'Dude'."

The man had a lovely, old South, Virginian accent, but nonetheless, I shrugged in an obvious lack of concern about who he was. In my best attempt at a Virginian accent, I replied, "Well, prithee, do tell?"

That set Marc off into new paroxysms of laughter. Now tall, lean and angry's mouth narrowed into a thin, hard line, as his steely blue eyes perused me from head to foot. "Marc, you don't have any questions at all why Shadow Wolf, of all people, brought this ... this ... besom here? Of course, you have questions, plenty o' questions. You're not a naive man."

Hawk growled and bristled at the man's tone, sidling between the man and me. His growl became louder and louder, as the ruff around his neck stood up, but the angry man did not seem to notice. Even my little Mimi bristled and she began to growl as Big Angry came closer and closer. Mimi loves everyone and never fusses like that. I stood myself up to every bit of my 5'4", and finally answered. "Besom? That's the best you can do? Really, Dude? Tsk." and as the dogs' growling increased, I added, "Better watch out, Dude. My dogs are going to bite you."

He looked down, scorn written across his face. "Oh, yeah? And do what? Attack my ankles? Well, my boots are pretty stout. I think they can withstand any paltry nibbles from your little ol' puppy dogs. Nobody's gonna be afraid of those little ol' pups. And I have no idea who 'Dude' is, but he sure ain't me."

Marc laughed out loud. When Big Angry cut Marc one of his patently furious looks, Marc held up a hand, in an effort to stop laughing. "Sorry, Will. Sorry." He wiped the tears from his eyes from laughing so hard.

Lily gave Marc a sharp glance, and then answered the angry man. "Well, I recognized her immediately. We used to see each other in the summers. I do know my own cousin, Will. Don't be an ass."

Big Angry sneered at me. So, I did the one thing I thought of. I kicked the big lout. Hard, right in the shin. Now, bear in mind I never kicked another living human in my life, unless maybe it was my brother when we were kids. Come to think of it, I did kick Jim once when he broke my doll. Still, I couldn't believe what I was doing. Hell, I suspected I had totally lost my mind!

A look of shock crossed the big guy's face that turned to rage. "What the bloody hell..."

"I can attack you all by myself, you big bully. Never underestimate the abilities of an angry Skye terrier, much less an angry woman, no matter how small she is." And with that, I flounced around the Big Angry man to traipse up the path to the McCarron Big House after Lily McCarron, my brand new, 'long lost cousin.'

The 'Big House,' as they called the largest house at McCarron's Corner, was the one in which the McCarron's resided. It always made me laugh to hear it called that, because in the future, 'Big House' is a colloquial term used for 'prison'. The house was a two storied, log cabin set up on the bluff above the creek about a mile from the other cabins and cottages, much like it had been described in the books. Downstairs, there was a large parlor, which opened to a kitchen and dining room. Across the hall were Marc's study and a large room used for Lily's infirmary. If memory served me right, there was a bedroom upstairs, for Marc and Lily, and a second room where their fifteen-year-old son, Michael, slept. There was also a guest bedroom. It was almost twice the size of the smaller cabin we passed with the roof damaged from a recent fire. She crossed to the fire, silent, to light a faggot to ignite the lantern. It was clear she was trying to collect herself from laughing all the way back to the house. "Now, tell me how you came to be here." Her odd-colored eyes sparkled like warm topaz in the lantern's light, as a whimsical smile teased her lips.

I looked about the room in the subdued light, taking in the reality and comparing it to my idea of these rooms from the books I'd loved for so long. It was a comfortable room, one where I knew I would always feel safe and welcome. There was the settee that had been brought from England and hauled up here, with considerable effort, from Savannah. It took about three weeks, as I remembered from the books. Even a short trip to Savannah was 6 or 7 days of hard riding. A quilt was thrown over it, obscuring the fabric beneath. It should be a green and pink colored floral print that came from France in 1777, smuggled into Georgia past the British embargo line. Two French styled rococo lamps sat on tables, one on each side of the settee. Lily's Irish harp sat across from the settee, with a stool and a music stand. Next to the harp was a large easy chair, which I knew was Marc's, covered in sturdy, old fashioned green fabric popular in the first half of the century. It was unexpectedly elegant, refreshing in this backwater village at the edge of what was to one day become the northwest corner of the State of Georgia. I fingered a worn place where the applique of the Whig's rose had come loose.

"It was the 4th of July, 2018. I decided to hike up here to see the site of the McCarron's Creek novels. I love Judith Barker's characters and descriptions of 18th century America, during the Seven Year War and the

Revolutionary War." I realized the light had faded from her eyes. In fact, she looked downright stunned. "Um, Lily?"

She seemed to snap back, and nodded her head tersely. "Judith Barker writes about us?"

"Uh, yes." I nodded. "She published several now."

She narrowed her lips into a thin slash across her face. "Oh, my." She nodded. "Yes, I know her. She came 'from beyond' several times over the years. I thought she was a dear friend, someone, like myself, with a secret about where we are from and how we got here. Marc will be so upset. Damn!"

I felt rather stumped at that one. She was so upset that Barker had written about their lives in the future. I could understand her anger and frustration, but I sure as hell did not want her to become untrusting of me. I paused as seconds ticked by into minutes. Finally, I began again. "Um, I didn't dream I could come. I sure didn't know time travel was real. Looks like those Ancient Alien shows that say that there are portals to other worlds and other times are correct. People talk about time travel, but I never met anyone before who actually claimed to have fallen through a portal to another time. Wow, and now I guess that I am the nutball who will be claiming that! I guess time is fluid, like they say 'gender is fluid' back home. I sure didn't come to cause trouble or to upset you."

She reached over and patted my arm. "Of course, not, Sassy. I didn't mean to indicate I thought you came with ulterior motives. Believe me, you have a purpose here or you wouldn't have been able to come here. But whatever do you mean when you say, 'gender is fluid'?"

"Oh, girl, sometimes truth is stranger than fiction. Back home, they say gender is fluid. Men can use the women's rest room if they 'identify' with being a woman that given day. It's a crime in California now to use the wrong pronoun. You can go to jail for calling someone 'he' who thinks he is a 'she'. Well, let me tell you, I identify with being rich and beautiful, but that ain't happening. Anyway, it's clear from the books that Judith adores you. I'm pretty sure she put a lot of fiction into the books." Lily gave me a sharp look, but said nothing. I cleared my throat and began again. "No one knows the books were based on real people. I mean, who would dream that Marcus is the son of an Irish lord, or that he was captured by pirates? Or sold into slavery, to then be bought and freed by Lord, what's his name, Lord Ransom?"

"Ranscome. But that is what happened, Sassy." Lily looked distressed as the color drained from her face. "And that is a part of his life Marc does not like to talk about. He'll be horrified to know Judith put it in a popular book in the future."

I flinched. Note to self: do not discuss Marcus's past life unless he raises the issue. I sure wasn't going to mention that a popular television series was also based on the books. I looked around for a sewing box, determined to mend the loosened section of the beautiful quilt. "Anyway, I used Barker's maps, and found where I thought McCarron's Corner had been. Sure enough, there's a McCarron's Creek up here. The map looked like the spring up here was the source of the creek, which in turn, runs into the Little Frog Creek, and later into the Jacks River. I learned there was still a little remnant of a settlement established around 1760, which reportedly had not been inhabited since just before the Battle of Allatoona, during the latter part of the Civil War. And, low and behold, I found out the land was for sale..."

"For sale?" I whipped my head around at the sound of Marcus McCarron's sultry Irish burr. "Ye mean t' tell me that someone claimed my land was for sale?"

Fortunately, I realized Big Angry was right behind Marcus, still glowering like I had molested his dog or something. The idea made me chuckle. I noted in dismay the eyes of both Marc and Big Angry narrowed at my laughter.

I nodded. "Um, yes, I was told by a woman ... um ... down south near Allatoona Pass that the property was for sale. I told her I doubted my cousin's husband would sell his land. She said everything is for sale for the right price." I found Lily's sewing box, opened it, and threaded a needle before I sat down and began repairing the loosened stitches.

Marcus relaxed a bit and nodded abruptly. "Not no way no how I'm gonna sell this land. I worked too damned hard for it. Hell, I literally slaved for this land. As it is, I got 1000 acres from Lord Ranscome during the French and Indian War. I received an additional 50 acres for each male settler who came with me. Six more men joined me, so I was awarded another 300 acres for building the settlement. I received an additional 300 for fighting at Saratoga last year. I have 1600 acres of prime wilderness land. God willing, I'll obtain more in the future."

"That was what I told her. Anyway, I set out, and came on up on my own. It just got a little rough in the last 5 or 10 miles. The trail was really hard to follow."

"How long did it take you to walk here?" The Big Angry man's voice was deceptively soft.

I thought fast, with the needle stopped in mid-air. I sure couldn't plausibly explain how I sat out from Acworth that morning, drove 2 hours north in my car, and then wandered around lost for almost 7 hours before finally being led here by a Cherokee warrior named Shadow Wolf, who Big Angry apparently dislikes, for some untold reason. I mentally calculated how far I could have walked in one day. With a nod, I began stitching again. "From Mexico or from Little Froggy? Or from Allatoona Pass? I left Texas after my husband died in April. We planned to leave sooner, but his illness delayed my departure. I almost decided not to come at all. Took a ship from Tres Palacios to Biloxi, where I bought a wagon and mule. I got to Rome a week or so ago, and left there the next day. Hard trek from there as we came into the mountains. I left from Little Froggy this morning." It was close enough to truth. I drove through Augusta the week before, and it took me way too long to get here from Little Froggy today.

He grunted. "Long way for a woman alone with just two little puny ol' dogs along to protect her. What is it? Fifteen or twenty miles?"

Marcus stopped trying to light his pipe long enough to answer. "About that." He took a long draw on the pipe to get the tobacco to catch hold of the tiny flame.

"I thought the trail was about 10 miles. It took all day, and the trail was a lot harder than I expected. The danged mule went lame going into some little town the other side of Little Froggy. I left the mule there yesterday. Got 5 pounds for her. Not bad for a surly tempered, lame mule."

"Five pounds, huh?" Big Trouble looked pointedly at Marcus. "Just think, Marcus, a lame mule was worth 5 pounds. Kinda ironic, ain't it?"

"Shut up," Marcus McCarron cut his eyes at Big Angry. "That is not amusing, William."

"No, it isn't," Lily snapped. "Don't tease."

That nagged at some memory I should remember but couldn't quite place at the moment. "I figured I could make it by foot. I never dreamed how rough these mountains would be. When I left Little Froggy, I expected about ten miles at most. I knew it would be a pretty hard hike today, but I did not realize the terrain would be quite so challenging, or that it was almost twice as far as expected."

Marc nodded. "Ye sound like a woman who has experience trekking through the wilderness. You do nice work, lass. Lee, m'love, look what she's done while sitting here but a few minutes. I think she has almost finished repairing the quilt."

"Oh, this is simple. I love to do applique work." My head bobbed up and down as I remembered he tended to call Lily simply Lee. "Well, to tell the truth, any kind of handwork. And yes, we used to trek about a bit. Owen loved to explore."

Oh, great, I thought. *You can explain trekking through Appalachia and the Cumberland Trail. Just remember not to mention the Sangria Mountains, much less the Grand Canyon*!

Lily McCarron is every bit as sharp witted as Judith Barker portrayed her in the books. She turned around from cooking at the kitchen fire, and with a look of surprise, she said, "Oh, Sassy, you do beautiful work! Thank you so much! And that's right. Your husband just died, didn't he, dear?"

I nodded, surprised that the tears were stinging at my eyes. Dammit, it was past time to quit crying every time I thought of Owen. Throat tight, I could not squeeze out any words. "Yes. In April. That is why I was so late getting here. We hoped to arrive in the spring, but then Owen up and died and ... I ... I ..." My voice cracked as an unwanted tear slid down my cheek. "*Tu me manques*," I whispered.

"What?" Lily asked, with a frown furrowing her brow.

I tried to smile. "It's French. *Tu me manques*. It means..."

"You are missing from me." The big angry man looked stunned at my words.

I nodded, determined not to allow my tears to spill over. "Yes."

Lily put her arm around my shoulder. "You needn't talk about it right now, Sassy. We have plenty of time. Would you like to clean up and rest a bit before supper?"

I nodded. "That would be wonderful." I handed the quilt back to her before she led me into another room. She lit a lantern and showed me to the pitcher of water and a fresh towel. I could smell some interesting, pungent herbs, tansy, lavender, chamomile, and I figured this was her infirmary. I poured a bit of water into the ceramic bowl, and washed off my hands and face. "Thanks. I'll be okay..."

"Of course, you will dear. It's been a hard day for you. Believe me, I know just how hard it has been. The good news is that things get easier. And cheer up, sweet girl. You came from Beyond. You're going to love again someday, and it will be magnificent. Now, rest a bit. Dinner will be ready before you know it – and I'll keep Will Selk away from you."

"That was Will Selk? But I thought he was handsome, witty, urbane, quite the lady's man?" I cringed. "That nasty old beard looks like something from Duck Dynasty. Does it have mice nesting in it? And, well, to be frank, that man smells like he's been rolling in pig shit!"

"I assure you there are no mice. But, what in heaven's name is 'Duck Dynasty?" Lily asked, laughing.

I explained it is a popular television show in the future, and described the general premise of the show. Lily giggled at my description in light of my comparison to Big Angry.

"Well, he can clean up quite nice with proper motivation. He doesn't always look like the back woods mountain man. But sometimes he acts like he still owns Marcus, and Marcus does not appreciate it when Will gets all uppity like that. Will reminding Marc that Lord Ranscome bought Marc for 5£ was low, even for William when he is in one of his moods."

I nodded again, as I realized why Selk's 5£ comment was significant. Yikes! Wouldn't it just figure I had to say that? Lord Ranscome bought Marcus at a slave auction in San Juan, Puerto Rico, when Marc was about 12 years old, ragged, dirty, rebellious even though half beaten to death. The previous owner thought he made a good sale when he got 5 pounds for the obnoxious Irish boy. When Lord Ranscome realized Marcus was kidnaped son of an Irishman, more serious about his education than were the Selk boys, Lord Ranscome freed Marcus and raised and educated him with his own sons, Thomas and William.

So Big Angry is none other than William Selk. Wouldn't that just figure?

Hateful cretin, I thought to myself, as I sat on the bed's edge and bent over to remove my hiking boots and rubbed my aching feet. *And wouldn't it just figure he was the only one who understood what I said. Well, no way he could understand this unrelenting pain. Not that man.*

As I stretched out on the small bed, relief swept over my exhausted body. I sank down into the soft feather mattress on the rope bed, relief washing over me as my body sagged against the softness of the down. I was finally out of the heat, out of the sun, out of the mosquitoes and stinging gnats. My skin ached from the newly received sunburn covering my face, arms and hands. I was in a place that felt safe and inviting. It was hot and still, and my legs ached from the long walk. I pulled a quilt across my legs as Hawk jumped up on the bed, and curled around my feet. It never occurred to me that Lily might not want dogs on the bed. In just a few minutes, I heard Hawk snoring. Mimi jumped up, circled around me, and then snuggled against my butt. After a few minutes of graciously licking me, she also slipped into a quiet sleep.

Tu me manques, Owen. You're missing from me. Maybe I stumbled down the Drunkard's Path. Maybe I had found my way to the Brave New World. In any event, within minutes, I joined the dogs in my slumbers as well.

I should fill you in on a little back story about Marcus and Lily, in case you haven't read Judith Barker's books. Liliana Van der Houghton was raised just outside of Atlanta, Georgia. Her father died in Vietnam before she was born. She grew up with her mother and step-father and visiting her grandmother every summer. Her mom and step-dad divorced while she was in high school. At 17, she began classes at Kennesaw State, and two years later, she began pre-med classes at Emory. After she graduated, Lily stayed at Emory for med school. Her mother remarried and moved to Portugal the same year Lily began med school. After her internship, Lily went to Duke for her residency.

In the spring of 2001, Lily finished her residency at Duke. She struggled to decide whether to join the Marines as a surgeon or do another residency in Ob-Gyn. She knew a few years in the battlefield would hone the skills she learned at Duke doing her residency in Emergency Medicine. She was leaning towards the Marines; her father had been a Marine. But Lily knew it would be a tough basic training for her. At the same time, she was increasingly drawn towards Ob-Gyn. Lily enjoyed hiking, and she decided a hike into the Cohutta Wilderness would help give her the answer, and to clear her head. The Cohutta had been a big challenge to her for many years, since she was lost in it as a child while hiking with family. She felt confident that if she could manage the Cohutta Wilderness alone, she was ready for the Marines.

Instead, she fell through what she calls 'a wild card hole in time', and wound up at McCarron's Corner, where she did both emergency medicine and Ob-Gyn work, along with a myriad of other kinds of medicine. She was the sole medical provider for hundreds of miles around, the shaman for the local Cherokee village and the white healer for the people at the Corner.

Marcus Fitz Simmons was born in Ireland in 1730, the second son of Meara McCarron and Micah Fitz Simmons. His mother died when he was about 5. He had an older brother, Jay, and an older sister, Dara. When Marc was 10, the family moved to Sardinia, where Lord Fitz Simmons was the new Ambassador. One day, Marcus and Dara were on the beach, when they were overtaken by pirates and were taken prisoners. That is not something the attractive son of an Irish Earl, with strawberry blonde hair, intelligent eyes, and a ready smile wants to happen. Even worse for Marcus was the fact that his beautiful sister was also captured. To this day, Marcus still has recurring nightmares about Dara's fate.

Marcus never dreamed the pirates would sell them. He was sure they would be ransom them back to their father. But unfortunate for the children, on a swelteringly hot August day so long ago, both were sold in Tangiers.

Marc also never anticipated that he would wind up in the clutches of psychotic pedophiles. Marc fought his new owners every chance he had, but the young boy was still hurt in ways I will not describe. You cannot imagine the horrors that he endured. To add insult to injury, he was lashed for refusing his master's advances more than once. Since his master was also a pirate, Marcus found himself traveling through the Mediterranean and on to the New World. Marc tried to escape in the Canaries and again at San Juan, only to be recaptured both times with sound floggings. After the second attempted escape in San Juan, the pirate dragged Marcus off the ship to the slave auctions, where he told the auctioneer to sell the boy for anything he could get for the trouble making boy's worthless carcass.

That day, in the crowd was a tall, handsome, aristocratic man and his two sons from Virginia. The younger son, a gangly, dark haired lad about Marc's age, was horror stricken to see a white boy about to be sold as a slave. He knew whites as well as blacks were often sold into slavery, but Will had never witnessed a white person on the block before. From the looks of the slave boy, he'd been having a damned hard time. The ragged, blonde-haired boy had a black eye, numerous bruises across his shoulders and his hips, as well as scars crisscrossing his shoulders. His shoulder blades stuck out as did his ribs, from lack of nourishment and loss of weight. The aristocrat's younger son convinced his father to buy Marc.

Once purchased, Marc steadfastly refused to give Lord Ranscome his surname. Finally, he gave his mother's surname, claiming his name to be Marcus McCarron. Thus, Marcus Aurelius Fitz Simmons became the chattel of Lord Ranscome, Josiah Selk, father of Thomas and William Selk, for the impressive price of 5£.

After Marcus grew up, and was trained to be overseer of Lord Ranscome's numerous properties, Marc was sent out west to survey wilderness property. He loved seclusion of the Cohutta Wilderness, the wild, rugged terrain, and the calm he gained from listening to the falls by the spring he loved so much. Marcus realized he was no longer that lost and broken boy. He was a man who had found the place to be his own home.

Not long after that, Marc encouraged his friends among the Cherokee to move to the Cohutta Wilderness. The terms of the settlement of the French and Indian War required the Cherokee to move west of currently inhabited colonies into what would be called Indian Territory. Three years later, Marc's friend, Shadow Wolf, and he were hunting for Wolf's errant son one afternoon, when they heard the child crying for help. The child had fallen into the springs beneath the falls. As both men rushed to the springs, they watched a young woman dive into the waters, rescue the boy, and work to make the boy start to breathe again. Wolf called it magic. She called it CPR.

Wolf realized that Lily came from what the Cherokees called 'Beyond'. Wolf told Marcus when a woman came from Beyond, she was the Lost Woman of the one who found her. Wolf was married to the love of his life. Marc was without a woman. Marc needed a woman. Thus, the Lost Woman, Lily, must be meant to be Marc's Found Woman.

Marc thought the whole story was hogwash, but he had to admit the woman tugged at his heart from the first. Lily said that her heart found its home when her hand was placed in Marc's hand. Marcus often said that Lily was more precious to him than any sum of diamonds or gold. Will often teased that she was Marc's Diamond Lil.

In remembering the story, something else from their stories hit home. Five pounds. Jeez Louise, no wonder my story of selling the mule for 5 pounds struck home. When I remembered the back story, I understood a little better why Will Selk was so protective of Marc, even though Will could be 'uppity', or what I would have called snarky, when it suited Will. Marc was like a brother to Will Selk. After all, Will was the son of the aristocrat who convinced his father to buy the bruised and battered Irish boy in 1743, some 35 years ago in San Juan.

But why on earth was Will Selk here in the backwoods of the Indian Territory at McCarron's Corner?

—

"Then, we will put it to a vote! The Colony of Georgia accepted the Articles of Confederation, and wishes to be determined to be one of these United States of America. All in favor of accepting the Georgia into the United States, please raise your hands." Every hand raised. Men began to cheer and pat each other on the backs. Old Button Gwinnet beamed from ear to ear. His hard work was coming to fruition. He was the second to sign the Declaration of Independence, and it was high time that Georgia became a State of the Union.

"Let it be noted that on this date, the Continental Congress voted to approve allowing Georgia to become the 11th state in the Union. Hip, hip, hooray!"

Chapter Five

Jim frowned and lowered the telephone receiver to the hotel lobby phone. "Odd. Sassy doesn't answer her phone. She always answers if she has reception. Where is she?"

His wife looked up from the baby she was feeding. "What's wrong?"

"I still can't get Sassy on the phone. I've called her five or six times now, and can't get her. It's just not like her. I'm sure something is wrong. Very wrong."

Sue smiled at her worried husband. One of the things she loved the most about Jim was his devotion to family. When she would be away from home, he always made sure to call and check that she was okay. And he had an uncanny connection with Sassy. He said twins were that way, even if they were as different as Sassy and he were. Since Sassy's husband died a few months before, Jim had been attentive to his sister's needs, and often called to check on her just like he did Sue. She patted him on the arm. "She'll be fine. I bet she went out on the lake with friends. You know the phone reception can be horrible on the Lake. You'll hear from her tomorrow, you'll see."

Jim nodded. "Maybe. It just doesn't feel right. Not at all."

"Did you talk to Rick? Maybe he knows where she is." Sue glanced up from the cooing baby to her husband.

"Rick says he hasn't heard from her either since she went to the Cohutta Wilderness the other day to go hiking. She planned to go for the day, and told him she wouldn't be gone more than one or two days at most. She even took the dogs with her. He's worried, too."

Sue shrugged, trying not to show her husband the worry that was now nagging at her belly, also. "We fly home in two days. We'll be home soon. I'm sure that she will turn up before then. She is very resourceful. She just went off somewhere and forgot to let anyone know. Rick said she went hiking. You know she loves to go tramping around out in the woods."

Jim looked unpersuaded. "I hope so. But, this is so unlike her to just disappear without a word. It's not at all like her."

His sassy little sister always let someone know where she was going. Jim just flat knew something was wrong. He could always feel Sassy. Wherever they both were, they had both said before, each always could feel the other. They could never explain it to other people. Now, he couldn't feel her. It wasn't that she was dead.

She was just gone. She was missing from him.

...

Rick Winslow trekked up the long path past the waterfall, hoping against hope he would find some sign of his mom. *Still nothing, dammit. Mom, where have you gone????*

....

News Bulletin: There was rioting today in Atlanta as people rebelled against the new laws ordering that all monuments erected to fallen Confederate heroes be torn down. Three were killed at Stone Mountain in the riots as the government pulled down the historic Civil War monument to Confederate heroes.

—

And A Brief History Lesson from Widow Winslow: A Southern Prospective

Georgians made two attempts to take Florida from the British in 1776 and 1777. Their third attempt to take Florida from the British failed in the summer of 1778. At that time, Gov. John Houstoun (yep, that is the correct spelling) commanded the Georgia Militia, Gen. Robert Howe commanded the Continental Army, and Gen. Andrew Williamson commanded the Carolinas militia. Lack of communication as well as lack of coordination of efforts resulted in the same dismal failure to secure the southern borderlands as had occurred twice before.

The Patriots had two small victories that fall. Howe's regulars managed to drive Lt. Col. Thomas Brown and his East Florida Rangers from Ft. Tony on the St. Mary's River, and the Georgia militia skirmished with the Rangers and a company of Royal Americans on Alligator Creek. With that limited success, the invaders returned to Georgia. As more than one brave Patriot said, 'any victory is better than no victory at all'. You know, kinda like Gramma told me the Aggies would do when they will even kiss when their opponents make a touchdown in bad years. Seems kind of silly, but hey, a kiss is a kiss, and if your team can't make a touchdown, then you kiss when the other team makes one.

General Augustin Prevost conducted a cattle raid into the lower Georgia counties that failed, also. As a diversion, Lt. Col. Lewis Fuser demonstrated against Ft. Morris at Sunbury. When Morris demanded the surrender of the fort, its commander, Lt. Col. John McIntosh, said, "Come and take it!" Fuser withdrew. Georgia hailed McIntosh as a hero, and the phrase became a battle cry of Americans throughout the Revolutionary War as well as subsequent wars. It was later the cry at Goliad during the Texas War for Independence. The flag with the drawing of the cannon from Goliad is often used to show American courage in the face of terrible odds. Owen talked to me about the importance of the battle cry more than once. A small copy of the flag flew in Owen's office in every home we ever lived in. He thought it ranked right up with the Don't Tread On Me flag.

Around that same time, a group of Southern governors assured Lord George Germain, the American Secretary in Britain, that hundreds of Loyalists in the southern colonial backwoods bided their time, awaiting the King's troops. They assured Lord Germain the southern Loyalists would support a southern British attack.

As a result, Lt. Col. Archibald Campbell was ordered to bring 3000 troops to invade Georgia, and restore British rule in Georgia. Gen. Sir Henry Clinton intended to set an example for the other colonies.

Chapter Six

As days stretched into weeks and weeks into months, I settled into the rhythm of the little village called McCarron's Corner. Lily told me I fell through a wild card hole in time, apparently the same one that she fell through in 1763, some 25 years before. She called it a wild card because the actual location of the portal would be in the meadow, but changed with the seasons and weather. It wasn't a standing stone or circle of stones, that were always in one place. It also would not work for everyone to pass. You had to be meant to pass through it to travel through to another time. While the portal could bring a person back in time, it rarely took people to the future. The Cherokee claimed other women had come through the same portal over many years. To return to the time from which you came, she heard there were other portals, a stone circle on Lewis in Scotland and similar stone circles in Ireland and Scotland. Some stories said you had to be soaked in alcohol to be able to go forward in time. We laughed about that, thinking it sounded like a waste of good corn whisky, and figuring the poor person who went forward in time would probably be arrested for drunk and disorderly in public. Lily decided years ago to stay here with Marcus and their son. Right now, for me, Scotland and Ireland were both a very long way away, so it looked like I was staying, too.

So, with no other realistic choice, I settled in. I worked on weeding and harvesting crops. The corn and okra would soon be ready to harvest. My tomatoes, corn, potatoes, peppers, and herbs were all producing like mad. Believe me, I had a stellar crop of jalapenos that fall. I fed livestock, and learned how to butcher a hog and how to dress a deer. I learned how to make sausage and to render fat. I often helped Lily in her clinic, enjoying the work of helping others who were more in need than me. I pieced quilts for the coming winter, my heart always at peace as I sewed. Sewing had always been my redemption, my safe place, and that was true at McCarron's Corner as it had been elsewhere throughout my life. I worked mash along with the other women, finding the sweet, intoxicating scent, comforting in some odd way. I fished in the creek, and even managed to catch a swim now and then.

My least favorite job other than making lye soap was washing clothes in an iron pot over a fire. It was hot and tedious work, altogether a job unfit for humans. I hate the burning, acrid smell of the lye soap almost as much as I hated what it did to my skin! And yet, in a way, the acrid stench was comforting, reminding me of those happy days at Williamsburg stirring fabric into pot after pot of dye, with Owen watching me as he leaned against that white picket fence, puffing away at his pipe.

Some days, I didn't think of my Owen much at all. Other days, all I knew was *tu me manques, mon amour. You are missing from me, my love*. Funny a Hispanic girl always thought that in French, hmm?

I made friends with locals. I was most comfortable with Marcus, Lily, and Mike, of course. They knew where I came from, and were old hands at keeping such information private. I was fond of an older couple, Emmett and Jeannette Sullivan, who were a tad slow, almost appearing to be 'teched in the haid', as Marc would say. Both were of low average intelligence, and both appeared to have numerous other issues, but both were good as gold, people you could depend on in a pinch. There wasn't a person at McCarron's Corner I would want to pray for me more than old Emmett! His tiny, grey-haired wife of 50-plus years was so hard of hearing that it was hilarious at times as he screamed at her so she could understand him. Then again, perhaps that was all an act, so she didn't have to pay close attention to Emmett's long winded narratives about whatever oddity occurred that day. And while Jeannette was slow, she was one fine cook, and often helped Lily with meals.

I knew how to dress in the 18th century. Owen and I spent long hours at Williamsburg reenacting living history. Dress was more casual on the frontier than at Williamsburg, albeit hotter. I often wore a short shift, jumps, and petticoat with a fichu and an apron in the summer, where at Williamsburg I would have worn a camisole, short shift, two petticoats, stays, and an apron. I had a couple of serviceable petticoats, as they called skirts, and a set of leather jumps. I had a dressier 'Sunday go to meeting' gown, which I wore with stays. For an average work day, I could get away with the shift and apron. I understood the reasons to wear a cap over my hair for modesty and as a kind of 18th century female dew rag. The cotton cap soaked up sweat and tended to keep your head cooled with the layer of soaked cotton. It might look crappy, but it had a function I used. I was enchanted with bergere hats that looked so feminine when tied with colorful ribbons. One hat could coordinate with all my outfits. That way, my hair looked presentable for dressier occasions or just when working in the sun. After all, a lady had to preserve her complexion, Lily kept telling me, and with my Spanish blood, I tan pretty dark, even with my dishwater blonde hair. Castilian blood, you know.

It felt strange lacking that connection to Jim and Rick that I had felt for so many years. Especially Jim. My twin and I had always been able to 'feel' each other. I had to keep reminding myself it wasn't that they were dead; they just weren't born yet.

The sole thorn in my butt was Big Angry Will Selk, who came around regular as a bad penny every month or so. He was always frowning, always cranky, always snarky, at least with me. He seemed pleasant enough with the other settlers. I saw him laugh and joke, his blue eyes sparkling with mischief or merriment, with Marcus and the men. I now included myself as one of the settlers at McCarron's Corner. Thank heaven, with Marc's help, I was learning how to irritate Will without being irritated by him. And I suspected he might just be a lot of fun to know if I could ever break through his 'tude with me.

That morning, Michael and I were re-roofing the cabin that burned before I arrived. Michael hammered as I handed him the next shingles and nails.

Michael was clad in buckskin breeches, and his boots. His shirt came off a few hours before, as the handsome teen began sweating profusely in the heat. I wore an unbleached muslin shift, jumps, and my brown Linsey Woolsey work skirt, hiked up to my knees. I wore once-white stockings, now mostly brown with dirt stains, on beneath the skirt, and an apron over the skirt. My cap fell off earlier, and I was sweating like crazy with my long braid hanging down my back, recalcitrant tendrils sneaking out of my braid. Roofing was hard, hot work, especially when dressed in Linsey Woolsey in the heat.

I was giving serious thought to removing the damned skirt when I heard the dogs barking down below. Nothing unusual in that. However, I didn't expect to have my butt struck with a rock. As my head jerked around to see what moron hit me in the rear with a rock, I lost my balance. I shrieked as I fell through the air, landing with a thump in the arms of no less than Big Angry Will Selk. He was back a good two weeks before expected, based on his visits since my 'untimely arrival' on July 4th.

I looked up at his startling blue eyes, and laughed. "Well, hello, Mr. Selk! Mighty nice of you to catch me!"

He looked unsure of what to do with me now that he had caught me, or just how to dislodge me from his arms. Since he was almost a foot taller than me, I hoped he wouldn't drop me; the fall would have been a couple feet to the ground. Finally, he just cracked the teeniest bit of a smile and asked, "Were you missin' me, girl?"

Before I could reply to his odd question, Lily ran over. "Are you okay?" She sounded worried.

I nodded, and slipped an arm around Mr. Selk's neck. "Oh, yes, I'm fine. It was very thoughtful of Mr. Selk to catch me." And I'll never know what ever possessed me, but with that, I leaned over, and kissed him right on his scratchy, old whiskery cheek! His face went dark red with embarrassment. I remember thinking, hot damn! Look at those beautiful baby blues next to his beet red face!

His eyes began to glow silver glints as he slowly slid me down the length of his body, toward the ground. I was a bit shocked to feel his 'manly parts' standing at attention as I slid past. As I dangled about a foot off the ground, he bent towards my face, and said, "Darlin', that's not the way to thank a man for catching you. This is how you thank a man..."

And damned if that big lug didn't bend me over ass backwards and kissed me, you know, like you see on the front of romance novels. Believe me, the man could kiss, and with an unexpected, brooding passion I sure didn't expect. Damn, that kiss curled my toes! Literally! It was all I could do to refrain myself from climbing him like a monkey climbs the banana tree for an extra succulent treat. I now had an inkling of why Judith described him as 'charming, urbane, often called irresistible to women.' I somehow managed not to totally humiliate myself and refrained from my scandalous tree climbing monkey imitation. I was breathless as he lowered me to the ground, while still holding me in his arms. I staggered a little as my feet found the floor and I realized I was no longer in his arms.

You should appreciate the moment of a first kiss, because it might be the last time you own your heart. I was reluctant to think this man could in any way bring peace and calm to my chaotic heart. That applied to my Owen. It was with his first kiss that I totally lost my heart 15 years before, at least the part he didn't already have. But that hot afternoon in what would someday be North Georgia, with Will's kiss, I realized I no longer owned a heart to lose. With a jolt, I understood what 'heart of my heart' meant.

And then the damned man smiled. When he smiled, his whole face changed. His eyes glowed with deep turquoise glints. I read that some kisses are given with the eyes. Will's eyes were still kissing me. My throat went tight with longing for more. And the damned man had dimples! I hadn't noticed them before because of his whiskers, but up close and personal, you would have to be blind to miss dimples like those when he smiled, even with his Duck Dynasty style whiskers. All at once, I realized he didn't look Big Angry now.

He looked like Big Sexy.

I blinked. Damn, this was not good! I didn't need to get involved with anyone like Will Selk, not in this or any other century. He was too controlling, too argumentative, too... too much an 18th century male! Owen played that part all too well, and he wasn't even from this era.

I smacked his arm with my hand. "La! Mr. Selk, behave yourself!" I stepped out of reach of his long arms, and began to straighten my shift, making sure the fichu was tucked back into my shift. How did that thing come loose anyway??? I tucked my hair behind my ears, and tossed my long braid back behind me, before I turned to walk away.

It would just figure that I would stumble. Double damn. And then I heard him chuckle. "*Oui, cherie, tu me manques,*" he said, his voice low and husky, so I alone could hear him.

"*Jamais!*" I replied as he continued to laugh. Dratted man! It would just figure he kissed me so well I couldn't even walk straight.

I told myself over and over I did not need to get involved with this man.

He would be nothing but trouble. I didn't care how strong he was, or how he caught and held me with no effort at all. I didn't care how damned good the man kissed. Did I mention he's a super good kisser? I was afraid that he kissed me so hard that I'd never be able to get the taste of him out of my mouth, and to my surprise, l liked the taste of Will Selk.

I missed my Owen. I would not, could not miss Will Selk. I would not, could not fall in love with Will Selk. No way, *mi tia* Soledad.

After all these years, he still did not know from where Lily originated. If Lily and Marc wouldn't tell him, despite how close he was to Marc, there had to be a reason. No, I could not get involved with Big Angry/Sexy Will Selk. Maybe he was missing me, but I was not about to miss him. Period. Case closed.

So why did I feel like I might have already lost that battle before I ever knew it was being fought???

—

"Whatever did you think you were doing to her?" Lily McCarron sounded irritated.

Will shrugged and scratched his whiskers before he answered. "I just caught her when she fell."

Lily frowned, shaking her head. "Oh, bull, don't play that game with me. I saw you pitch that pebble up and hit her square on the arse. Whatever possessed you?"

Well stretched out his long legs and grinned. "Well, Lil, I just decided it was high time I ..."

"Quit being an arse with the lass?" Marc surmised, succinct as ever.

Will chuckled, a bit embarrassed at his friend's unexpected crudity. "Yeah, I guess so. First off, she's still here. She's like a little tornado. She's worked damned hard to fit in. She made a serious effort to fit in. I have to admit, I like her spunk."

Lily blinked. "You..."

"I like her spunk. She's a tough little thing. Feisty. She's a survivor."

Lily began to laugh, with Marc chiming in. Soon, they were hanging on to each other as they both laughed uproariously. "Spunk!" Marcus sputtered.

"Lee, he likes her spunk."

"Yep, even if she is a damned hardheaded little vixen. She's the kind of woman we need in this country. She's a woman well worth the effort to get to know."

Lily held her hand to her stomach as she tried to catch her breath. "Oh, if you just knew just how spunky she is, William. If you just knew!"

"And she is right pretty, too, you big lug!" Marc slugged Will's arm.

Will blushed again, but nodded. "Yep, sure enough. Right pretty. I like all that golden brown hair curling around her face, and those big green eyes. Lord, I do love that woman's pretty hair."

"Not to mention that figure?" Marc quizzed.

Will blushed again. "Well, now that you mention it..."

Marc's eyes narrowed. "So, why did you come back so soon? Tis sure I am 'twas not just to see a pretty woman."

Will's features sobered. "Yep. That's part of it, but it ain't all. I thought you'd want to know Georgia became the eleventh colony to sign the Articles of Confederation. It's official now. It's part of the United States of America, and they are drafting a Constitution."

Marcus jumped up and pounded on Will's back in excitement. "That's wonderful news, Will! But Georgia's already part of the U.S. Remember ol' Button Gwinnett was head of Georgia's Continental battalion? He voted for independence and was even one of the signers of the Declaration of Independence."

"When did this happen?"

"Sometime in July, around the time I passed through here." It hit him with a start. That was around the time Sassy showed up here. *Well, by damn*, he thought to himself, *I'm definitely goin' to have to get to know that little gal a whole lot better.*

Will Selk realized he was a complex person few people understood. Raised between a tobacco plantation in Virginia, and a sugar plantation in Puerto Rico, he was accustomed to travel. As the second son, it was easy for him to take his expected life at sea after he finished his education at William and Mary. Now he was the captain of the Ranscome shipping fleet, that hauled goods produced at his family's plantations and goods he secured both near each plantation as well as further away, out past Fort Heard and even past Augusta all the way here in Indian Territory. Like Marc, he was sure someday this would-be part of Georgia. He made it a point to come to the Corner often.

No one expected his sister to die in childbirth at age 23, or his mother to die a little over a year later. No one expected his father to die just a few years after that, a heartbroken, lonely man, unable to overcome his grief over the loss of the love of his life. Josiah Selk loved his Belle from the time he laid eyes on her when she was just 16 in 1716 until she died in 1766. As his daddy used to say, fifty years was a long time to love a woman, but it wasn't near enough. He never recovered from her death. Will was sure they were together again in the Hereafter, but he still missed them both. And, Will never expected his brother to die two years ago at the Battle of Saratoga. Damn, Tom just had a scratch! Who would have ever dreamed that piddly little ol' flesh wound would go septic, as Lily put it, much less that it would kill Tom in a matter of days? And what the hell was 'septic' anyway?

Tom was loyal and faithful to family as well as to his country. He worked long and hard to make the plantations successful. He was a damned good soldier and a crack shot who was sorely missed after his death. Stephen Heard, Elijah Clarke, and even General Washington himself commented what a loss it was to the Cause when Tom Selk died.

Tom was sorely missed by Will, too.

In fact, the sole thing Tom Selk failed to do was to produce an heir. His wife, Charlotte, died of typhus years before, and their son died but three days later. Tom was devastated. He loved Charlotte and never remarried. No other woman ever filled his heart like she had.

Will never married such that was accepted in Virginia. Years ago, he met Hortense, and fell head over heels in love with the beautiful young woman, but it was complicated. She was what they called 'a free woman of color'. While they could never marry in Virginia, he made it clear to one and all he loved Hortense with his whole heart, as well as the daughters she gave him. They moved to Puerto Rico, where they legally married. It just about killed him when she died in childbirth in '64 much like his sister died earlier the same year. He managed to raise the three girls well. He'd arranged good marriages for Natalie and Marie Therese, and hopefully, in another few years, Genevieve would find a happy marriage as well, assuming he could find a decent man to put up with his beautiful, headstrong, spoiled daughter – and assuming he ever found a man good enough for the daughter that looked so much like his sister, Ginny Lee. For now, Genevieve was tucked away at a convent school in San Juan. Hopefully, the nuns would keep her safe and could teach her how to be a lady.

Will was the last male Selk left. His girls could not inherit in Virginia. He had the shipping line and Irish properties to manage in addition to the plantations. He was the first to admit he enjoyed the shipping more than managing plantations. He tried more than a few times to get Marcus to come back to help him oversee the plantations.

Daddy educated Marcus to become the overseer for the plantations. That did not go as planned, when Marc fell in love with this wild corner of land which became Indian Territory under the terms of the settlement of the French and Indian War, and then with the wild haired woman he met out here. They went back to Belle Rose for a while, but wouldn't stay. Marc and Tom didn't get along, with Tom often saying rude things to Marc designed to 'keep that boy in his place'. After a nasty fight between the two men, Marc and Lily returned to this wild corner of the country, determined to spend their lives out here. Thus far, Marc refused Will's generous offers to come back to oversee even one of the two plantations. Will couldn't even shame Marc back when he wrote Marc that Fancy had been attacked by the no-good overseer. Marc was pretty upset but just kept telling Will to bring Fancy here instead. He might just have to do that.

Will was the first to admit he enjoyed this part of his job, going out and securing other things to trade, tramping around from place to place, ever so much more than even the high seas. It allowed him to see old friends and old haunts. He knew what Sassy meant when she said that not all who wander are lost. He enjoyed the wandering, the searching, the endless quest. He realized Sassy and he were of the same mind, maybe cut from the same cloth.

Traveling also enabled him to secure information about the War to pass along to the General, while passing bad information to the Tories. It allowed him to see people he loved, like Marc and Lil. Good people. They always raised his spirits, although he always left saddened that Marc wasn't going with him on another adventure. Sometimes, he wished Marc wasn't so danged important to him, but they'd been like brothers since that hot summer day long ago when Will made Daddy buy the boy off the slave auction block. These were people he needed to see.

Shadow Wolf was another. Will didn't enjoy seeing Wolf, and it sure as hell did not make him feel better to see him. He had never forgiven Wolf for bringing Ginny out here. Now, her children were being raised way out here by that Godless heathen. But, Will felt he owed it to Ginny to check on her children and her husband every now and then, no matter how sour the taste it left in his mouth.

Now there was this little Sassy gal. He wasn't sure how she made him feel yet, but by damn, he intended to figure it out. And soon. As he trekked through the mountains in the past weeks, collecting and trading goods and information from farmers and hunters, he did a lot of thinking about Lily McCarron's cousin. Something about that little bit o' Texas Sass just irritated the heck out of him. He didn't know why, he couldn't put his finger on it. But she also intrigued him. Hell, he was almost afraid to say it, but the smart mouthed wench enchanted him. She was a tough little gal with an incredible amount of intestinal fortitude.

He realized when he was gone, she was missing from him. Her spunk, her courage, her love of life. He needed those things in his life again. And after that kiss, well, hot damn, he wanted more. It had been a long time since he felt that way about a woman. Maybe he could drown all his demons in her kisses. Who knew, maybe she could save him from those demons. But he definitely wanted more. Like Marc was quick to point out, Sassy Winslow was mighty damned easy on the eyes, too, with all that gorgeous hair, and those flashing green eyes. He reckoned she could prettify mighty nice. He knew most men didn't like freckles or suntanned skin on a woman. Will always kinda liked it when a woman looked like she could handle in the sun, with her skin golden, and with a smattering of freckles across her nose and cheeks. Hortense used to get freckles, he mused. Not that Sassy Winslow was in any way like Tennie, who was sweet, loving, amiable and lived to please him. Sassy was very different. Biting, acerbic, tart, like homemade raspberry pie. Always had to get the last word in. Yep, Sassy was the perfect nickname for Sarah Alinora Winslow. She was the most fascinating woman he had met in a long time. In about fourteen years, to be exact.

Tom was dead. It was up to Will to produce an heir. He was finally contemplating finding him a wife and doing just that. Will had not quite figured that out yet, but he was working on it.

—

I tried to keep my distance from Mr. Selk that evening. He grinned each time I passed by, and swatted me on the rump once. As I wheeled around at him, a bit shocked by his forwardness, he grinned then chuckled. "What's the matter, Little Bit?"

"You keep your hands to yourself, Will Selk. *No me tocas esta vez*. And don't call me that."

"Yep, you ain't nothin' but a little bit o' Texas Sass." Will leaned back in his chair, and just laughed. "But it's okay for you to call me Dude? Who is this Dude fella anyway?"

"No one you would know," I muttered, with a fleeting thought about The Big Lebowski, as Will laughed again.

Something was different about him. He was more relaxed. More pleasant. Less like he had a sharp stick up his butt sideways. In fact, he was almost attractive after he had a bath, in his clean buckskins with a smile. He'd trimmed that beard, so he almost looked presentable. Well, almost. Owen never wore facial hair and it always seemed a bit 'off' to me. I can't tell you how many times Owen said a gentleman in the 18th century did not sport facial hair. Even all cleaned up, Will Selk still had 'wild mountain man' written all over him. And Will was the real deal, not just a wannabe. Since he trimmed his beard, that damned smile made those dimples so plain to see. Damn, it galled me he was so handsome all cleaned up like that. He reminded me of someone, but for the life of me, I couldn't figure out who.

I noticed Lily and Marcus glanced at each other, and Marc turned away to laugh. He tried to cover his laugh with a cough, but I knew he was laughing at me. "You cut that out, Marcus McCarron. Do not encourage that man!"

Will grinned again. "See, I told you. Spunky. And she sure does prettify right nice!"

Lily turned away as well, struggling not to laugh.

I finally got enough of their laughing, and got up to head for the cabin we reroofed that afternoon. "I'm going to my cabin."

Selk's eyebrows shot up. "Her cabin??"

Marc nodded. 'Aye, we thought she could use a bit of space to herself. They finished the roof and she is all moved in. The cabin has the extra room which will be good for her sewing."

He looked surprised that I could do anything as domesticated as sew. "You sew?"

I nodded. "Of course. Don't all women?"

Lily chimed in, "She sews like a dream. She has a true gift for piece work. Her quilts are works of art. She's getting a lot of orders for custom quilts. She gets good money for them, too. People as far as Blue Ridge and Rome come over to order quilts from her."

Lily and Marc knew that in my prior life 'beyond', I taught American History, but my avocation and love were sewing and quilting. I taught classes in quilting at Williamsburg, in addition to my classes in fabric dying. I could make clothing, but my real forte was dying cloth, hand piecing, applique, embroidery, and quilting.

'Back home' I had always been saving quilt patterns on my phone. I had over 1000 patterns downloaded on it. While I couldn't phone home from here, I had a solar battery charger, and I could refer to all those patterns I saved over the past years. I had a couple hundred blocks to piece and to applique sketched out for reference. That enabled me to make quilts from patterns that other women here didn't have yet. Better yet, I knew shortcut methods to all the old tried and true patterns, which meant I could make quilts faster than most women, even stitching by hand. I was glad I learned applique and hand quilting skills from Gramma many years ago. She would never have guessed just how handy they would come in when I went back in time to 1778.

Will's eyes narrowed. "How much do you get paid for a quilt?"

I shrugged. "Depends if they want me to make it from their fabric, and it is just for warmth, just basic piecework, I charge less than I charge for a quilt that I am making with new material, selected for a project, with embroidery and applique work. For basic, everyday quilts, from 5£ to 15£. For custom quilts, 15£ and up, depending on detail. The one I am working on now is highly customized, a very detailed pattern with exquisite applique work, if I do say so, on both in the center medallion as well as on the borders. I quoted them a fee of 35£. They paid half up front."

Will's eyebrows shot up. "They did? Well, I'll be danged! I think I'll just mosey along with Little Bit here, and make sure she gets back to her cabin all right. That way, I can see her sewing."

"That is not necessary," I snapped as I glowered at the smirking man.

He grinned again. "Might not be necessary, darlin', but I'm comin'. It would please me to take a gander at your work. I could sell things for you, up north in the big cities, if you're interested. Come on, dogs, let's go!"

My traitorous dogs jumped up, tails wagging, to follow the big man now flashing that lazy, easy smile. Damned dimples must have charmed them, too.

Oh, I was in so much trouble.

Chapter Seven

"Did you find any sign of her?" the worry evident in Jim's voice, as it had been for the past months since Sassy disappeared. "Anything at all?"

"No. I don't know what else to do. It's been three months. I go up there every weekend, but nothing. The first time I went up, I saw some faint tracks, but those are long gone now." Rick sighed.

"Same here. I go up on my days off, but … nothing. I feel nothing. She is missing from me. I don't know what to think. It is just like she fell off the face of the earth. Fell in a hole and disappeared."

"I agree, Uncle Jim. With all the craziness in the world right now, who knows? They busted a white slavery ring up in Chattanooga not far from where Mom was headed. Who would dream they had white slavery in Chattanooga of all places? It scares me witless that one of those groups got their hands on my Mom. Damn, she's still a fine looking woman. Would you go one more time with me this weekend? I'd sure appreciate the help." Rick sounded tired and defeated, and he wasn't one to admit defeat.

Jim sighed. "Yeah, let's hit it one more time. Maybe we'll turn something up with two pair of eyes searching. We should go talk to the Sheriff again. They just aren't taking this seriously at all. But Rick, if we don't find her, you have to focus on school. Sassy would hate to be the cause of you flunking out your last year in med school."

Rick sighed. "I know. I won't let that happen. But you know as well as I do that Mom would not just disappear."

Jim frowned. "No, Sassy would not just take a powder."

Jim worried something very bad had happened to his sister. Like his nephew, he worried she might have been taken by one of the white slavery groups popping up across the country. Who would ever have dreamed things like this would happen in the United States of America? But ever since the news had come out about Hollywood, more and more white slavery rings were becoming known across this beautiful land.

They located Sassy's SUV tucked back behind an old abandoned building a few miles past Little Froggy the first time they both went up there in July, right after Jim and his family returned from Europe. Apparently, the road got too rough for her to try to drive further. They were both so excited over finding the car and hoped was a good sign. In hindsight, it didn't appear to have been the portent of good luck they had hoped.

Jim was afraid to tell Rick they might not ever find Sassy. The kid had been through too much in the past year, with his Dad's death, and now Sassy's disappearance. But as Jim had thought at least a thousand times since Sassy disappeared, she was missing from him.

Please, dear God in Heaven, Jim prayed. *Let us find her alive and well. Please. Por favor, Dios mio.*

He wasn't sure how his nephew would hold up if they learned that Sassy was dead. To be honest, Jim was not at all sure how he would hold up himself. But she didn't feel dead. She just didn't... feel. He could not feel her at all. For the first time in his life. Nothing. No Sass. Just ... nothing. She was simply missing from him in a way that never had happened to the twins before. It was almost as if she had never been born.

Sassy, where the hell are you????

—

About the end of September, Lily sent for me. I'd been struggling to stretch a double bed sized quilt onto my quilting frame unassisted, never a pretty job at best. Delighted to take a break from the onerous job, I tidied my hair and clothes before I headed towards Lily's house.

When I arrived, I found Lily chatting in the parlor with an attractive young woman. Her wavy, ginger hair was tied back under her tignon, the way I had seen some free women of color wear their hair in this time, although it was not required for women of mixed blood yet as it would be later. In fact, it was the tignon more than anything that gave away her mixed heritage to me. Without it, I would not have suspected she was mixed.

"Sassy, this is Fancy. She's looking for work. She sews beautifully and loves to quilt. I thought you might be interested in talking to her about being your assistant."

My mouth fell open. "Lily, I need help, but I'm not sure I could afford to hire a lady..."

"Oh, no, ma'am, I ain't no lady. I'm jus' a servant." The girl blushed to her roots.

"I don't think she would expect much salary, Sassy. But she needs a safe place to stay." Lily paused. "For herself as well as her baby."

I blinked. Oh, great, now they expect me to take on a young woman and her child? After thinking about how I might tactfully extricate myself from this awkward situation, and finding none, I sighed. "Okay. Fancy, would you like to come with me down to the cabin where we can talk?"

The young woman nodded her head with vigor. "Oh, yes, ma'am, I sure would. Thank you, ma'am."

"I'll watch the baby while you two talk," said Lily, as she dandled a lovely little girl with dark curls and bright blue eyes on her knee.

Wordless, I nodded again, and headed for the door, with Fancy right behind me. We walked silent to the cabin. When we entered it, Fancy smiled.

"Oh, Miss Sassy, this is nice! You fixed it up right pretty."

I smiled. "Thank you. Why don't you have a seat while I fix some tea for us?"

Fancy jumped up, heading to the back to my kitchen. "Oh, no, ma'am, let me!" The girl ran to fill the kettle and hung it from the hook over my fire.

I sighed again. It seemed more and more like there was a foregone conclusion that I would hire Fancy. "Let's go look in my sewing room while the water heats." With a flourish, I motioned for her to come with me into the second room, where I sewed.

Fancy gasped when we walked in. "Oh, Miss Sassy! I ain't never seen so much pretty fabric before!" She walked over and stroked some pretty rose and green fabric. "Where on earth did you ever find this?"

I could feel tension start to leave my body. "I made it."

She gasped. "No!"

"Well, let me explain. I dyed the fabric that light grass green, and then I painted the roses on it. I set it with vinegar. If cared for, the colors will hold true for a long time."

"You painted it? How?" as she stroked the fabric almost reverentially.

We talked for about two hours. She wanted to see my fabrics, my sketches, and all my projects under way at the time. She helped me stretch that quilt onto the frame, and to start basting it. I noticed she had a fine hand, her stitches even and smooth. We were pouncing the powder on the first section to quilt, when I finally asked the essential question. "Why have you come to live here?"

She paled a bit, swallowed, and looked towards the floor, as if afraid to look at me. "Uh…"

I patted her shoulder. "It's okay, Fancy. But, why here? We are a long way from just about anywhere."

"Well, Miss Sassy, that's part of the reason why here. I was livin' at a big plantation in Virginia, and the owner died. The overseer ... the overseer ..." She stifled a sob. "Well, Mr. Selk said the McCarron's would help take care of Bella and me so nothing like that would happen to us in the future. And he said you sew, and you might could use someone to help you."

I was stunned. "Do you mean to tell me that Will Selk told you to come here but didn't bother to bring you? My God, he is such an ass sometimes."

"Oh, no, Miss Sassy! It warn't like that! He done brought me as far as he could befo' he had to gwine on to Rome. We didn't have very far to come a'foot, just a few miles. Even with wild Injuns and bears and rattlesnakes and wildcats and... and who knows what else is out there in them thar woods, I wasn't near as skeered as I was back home..." She stifled a sob. "At least Simon Le Grande ain't here. I just couldn't stay there any longer."

I sighed. "I can give you room and board..."

Her eyes lit up. "Oh, thank you, Miss Sassy!"

I frowned. "I'll pay you for your work. I am not sure what I can afford right now, but I propose to pay you a commission on work produced. Would that work for you?"

"Oh, Miss Sassy, I never dreamed you might pay me!"

I closed my eyes in frustration. "You're not my slave. I won't own a slave. It is not right for one human being to own another."

"No, ma'am. I ain't never been a slave." She held her head up, proud.

I smiled. "If you can live with that, you have a job. Come on, I'll show you the rest of my house, and then we can go get Bella. But Lily feeds us tonight."

Thus, I became a woman of means, who now had help of her own. And I guess kind of an abolitionist at that, since I had been making it clear that I did not 'cotton' to slavery. God save me! My wild, outlandish ideas might get me into all kinds of trouble yet back here in 1778!

By the end of October, I'd lived at McCarron's Corner for almost four months. The leaves had turned, and there was a welcome autumn crispness in the air. We were harvesting crops, in addition to gathering in stores for the forthcoming winter. We had already put up jars of tomato sauce, and made all kinds of pickles and jams from local fruits and vegetables. Potatoes, onions, wheat, beans, corn, peas, beans and garlic were stored for winter. If I had to put up any more pickled okra or sauerkraut that I would puke. God, I hate pickled okra, not to mention sauerkraut! The thought of having to eat that crap all winter long was not cheering me along. Oh, well, I'd lose weight this winter. By spring I ought to be pretty trim.

Fancy was a good match for me. We worked long hours, but they flew by with her at my side. The young woman was intelligent, quick, and very willing to please. She was quite adept at clothing construction. With her skills, we soon made additional clothing for the three of us. Soon, Fancy was taking orders for custom made clothing I wouldn't have attempted to make. She could work with silk and fancy materials far better that I ever would. I am basically a quilter. I love to work with cotton. I work some with silk and velvet, but cotton and linen are my 'thing'.

Fancy's stitches were all tiny, uniform, and exquisitely made. She could stitch 10 even spaced stitches per inch when quilting. I can stitch 12 per inch, but not many can. She learned my piecing techniques, and sometimes showed me new ways to piece which I had not considered before. And she was just plain fun to have working across from me when we were quilting. That job that can be tedious if done alone, in a day and age with no television or radio to help break the silent monotony. Yes, Fancy was becoming more and more like a sister to me, and little Bella was just about the age of my brother's daughter. They brought a lot of joy to my otherwise tedious and always challenging life.

There was a barn raising the last weekend of the month. People from as far as Little Froggy to the south and Big Froggy to the north came to help, and for the party once the barn raising was completed. I never saw a barn raising before. It was exciting to see the men building the sections of the barn, and to hoist them up. The barn was raised before dinner was ready. The men would roof it later.

Before we served the food, many of the women changed into fresh garments. Lily changed into a pretty plaid overdress, and insisted I change as well. Since I had but three outfits other than a couple of shifts I wore in the fields other than my jeans and red blouse, it was not a hard decision on what to wear. There was my usual work outfit, that I wore the day Will Selk showed up when I was roofing my cabin with Mike. Pretty plain Jane. There was my outfit I wore when sewing. It was a little nicer, cleaner, but still nothing to write home and brag about, a dark green homespun petticoat I had dyed, an unbleached muslin chemise, leather jumps, and a gingham apron. Both were serviceable and practical, but not at all exciting.

And then there was my 'Sunday go to meeting' outfit, which Lily and Fancy insisted I wear that night. I had to put on real stays, a true 18th century corset, with boning, and OMG! I hated that corset, even if it did make my waist look minuscule, and pushed my itty bitty titties up almost to my neck. I always wore real stays at Williamsburg; Owen insisted. But, my stays back home were made for me and fitted better. Still, I looked pretty in the indigo quilted petticoat with yellow jonquils embroidered around the hem, the creamy linen shift, and the indigo blue stays, making a fresh, pretty outfit. I donned my beloved straw hat, tied with a bright blue ribbon, and tied a matching piece of ribbon around my neck. It was time for me wear half mourning attire, but I was glad not to be in black or the drab shade of brown, grey or lavender that widows were generally allowed to wear after six months. Lily and Fancy said that it was fine, that we were on the frontier, and no one would care. No one here knew Owen. Although they knew I was a widow, they didn't know how long he'd been dead. Apparently, they were correct, because all I'd heard about the outfit were that it was pretty and well made. I felt quite fetching, 'all prettified', if I did say so that sunny autumn evening. I was bound and determined to have a good time, with or without Mr. Selk in attendance.

A number of the Cherokee from Shadow Wolf's tribe came over to help that day as well. Marcus always welcomed them, although some of the locals were not as welcoming. Of course, Marc was here since before the treaty was signed in 1760 and was very comfortable with the Cherokees. At times, he seemed more comfortable with the Cherokees than with the settlers.

The Cherokee village was a couple of miles away. They sat up in the large pasture, where crops had already been brought in, and they began roasting venison, corn and potatoes for the feast that night. The smells were inviting and my mouth watered in anticipation.

As the men finished hoisting the last side of the barn up, and nailed it into place, we loaded food onto boards set out for serving the meal. The Indian women came to the boards with the venison and roasted corn and potatoes they'd prepared. We put all the food out on the boards along with fish, barbecued pork, beans, sauerkraut, fried okra, as well as a variety of fresh fruits. Jugs of cold milk and water were available at each table. The men had the hard cider and moonshine under the table, to be monitored so the children would not get into those, at least not too badly. I helped serve the food as the hungry men crowded around the table, ready for the feast after the long day of barn building.

I had hoped Will Selk to be there, even though it hadn't been very long since his last trip. I watched for him throughout the day, and felt disappointed he hadn't showed up. We'd worked out an agreement for Will to market and sell pieces for me on his journeys. I had a number of items ready for him to take with him, assuming he came. I sighed. Oh well. *Sea lo que sea.* I knew I shouldn't get involved with Will Selk or any man. I was here now, but I couldn't stay forever. At some point in time, I had to figure out how to go back home to my family, to my 'real' life.

Yet with each passing day, this was becoming my real life. Life in the future was becoming harder and harder to remember, to remember why I needed to go back, why I even wanted to go back. Don't get me wrong: I love my family. I also love electricity, running water, indoor plumbing, and flushing toilets. Believe me, I so missed flushing toilets. But I was learning to love life in 1778. It was exciting to be living in the history that Owen and I researched for years. I wished Owen could have lived this, also. He would have so loved it!

We cleared away the dinner plates, and moved the boards back to make room for dancing. By then, the musicians were tuning their fiddles, and one man was beginning to strum rhythmically on his bodhran. As one began to play a merry jig on his tin whistle, the fiddles began to chime in, with Lily on her harp, and the bodhran keeping the beat. My foot began to tap in time with the music, and I began to clap with the music, as did many who were not yet dancing. This tune was a variant of American Colonial Dance, which was a variant of English Country Dance. In another 50 years or so, this style dancing would become good old American Square Dancing. People on the frontier loved to dance as a relief from the hard work and tedium of the life. A barn raising was a great opportunity for a party and dancing. I was so glad I had learned all sorts of unnecessary trivia including how to dance this while married to a history professor for 15 years.

I smelled the man before I saw him. Not in a bad way; he had bathed. I could feel the warmth of his body rolling off him and enveloping me in that musky scent I had begun to associate with Will. Some gentleman's scent he'd picked up somewhere in his travels, the smell of ambergris and spice mingled with his ever present buckskins, Lily said. Not a bad smell at all. The smell of Will.

"You look mighty pretty tonight, Miss Sassy," he murmured into my ear, and my heart leapt. Who would have dreamed it would mean so much for this man to tell me I looked pretty? "*Tu me manques, cherie*."

And before I could think, he bent to kiss my nape. Who would ever imagine the power of such a kiss? No one should ever underestimate the awesome power of a kiss gently placed on the back of a woman's neck. I trembled as unexpected electricity rushed through me from the touch of his lips to my bare skin.

"You clean up pretty nice yourself, Will Selk," I reached up without thinking and stroked his hand, realizing what I was doing as he chuckled.

"Want to dance, Little Bit?" He reached over and eased an errant tendril from my face.

I nodded and smiled up at him. I liked this softer and gentler Will that had been showing himself on recent trips. Less suspicious and glowering. Almost romantic, like he was courting me. Of course, that was just foolish conjecture, even if he did tell me he had to come back each time because I was missing from him. *Mais tu me manques,* he said, with that lopsided grin.

You were missing from me. What could I do but just shake my head and laugh? But he sure could clean up nice, after a bath, with his hair combed and his whiskers trimmed. I thought fleetingly again that he reminded me of someone, but I could not remember who it was. Maybe someday he'd shave off that silly beard and I could figure it out.

Will took my hand and led me out to where the others were dancing. He bowed, I curtseyed, and we began the intricate steps, as the rhythm began leading us weaving in and out among the other dancers. We finished that tune, and danced two more sets before I finally begged to sit down and catch my breath. As Will went to fetch some cider, Lily sidled over to me, with a sly grin on her face.

"Glad we made you change?" she asked. "I do believe he's quite taken with you."

That surprised me. I thought he was just a flirt, just enjoying a brief interlude with a passably attractive woman in the backwoods of what would someday be Western Georgia. "That man? The one who hates me? Are you serious? That man just likes to flirt, and I am the sole person around here of flirtable age for him. Well, other than maybe Fancy, but she's a little young for him."

She nodded. "Oh, he doesn't hate you. You know better than that. Yes, that big, tall, handsome man, with the dark hair and those amazing blue eyes. I have known him for 14 years and I have never seen him express interest in a woman before. Other than Hortense, of course. I never met her, but he used to talk about her a lot. Her death just about killed him. It took him a long time to show interest in another woman. It's high time."

That startled me. I knew his wife died years before in childbirth, but I imagined that typical of most men of that era, he had, ahem, 'dated' other women since then. You know, down at the local bordello if nowhere else. I was rattled to hear he had not. I didn't know if I wanted anything like a permanent relationship with a man in 1778. A fling might be nice, but I still had to get back to the future at some point in time. I just knew that my son, my brother, and his family were all missing me, and I needed to go home.

Well, someday, I guessed.

And then I looked up into the bottomless pools of azure in the face of that damned big sexy man again. I remembered his words again, and I sighed. Will Selk flashed me a lazy, sexilicious smile while he led me out onto the dance floor again. It had been Will in my thoughts more and more, and Owen less and less with each passing day. Oh, well, damn the torpedoes, and full speed ahead. I still had to earn enough money for my passage to Scotland to ever be able to go home. And that was a long ways off.

We danced until way after midnight. Finally, the musicians packed it in for the night. I helped Lily and the other ladies put everything up. As I started to lift a basket to take home, Bright Star came over to me.

Star is one of the young Cherokee women from Shadow Wolf's tribe. She's been very friendly with me since I arrived. All this land should be Cherokee land. The Cherokee get along with Marc, and tolerate settlers being here, but under the Proclamation Line of 1763, settlers were not supposed to come this far west. Some who were already were here when the Proclamation Line came into effect, like Marcus and Lily and their little settlement, were allowed to stay. Some others came later, and were generally welcomed by the Cherokee, in clear difference to the manner in which the Creeks dealt with settlers further south.

People told me that Star was a 'breed', meaning half Cherokee and half white. Her mother was a white woman who married into the tribe. I was startled when Will straightened up, frowning, at the young woman. He said something to her in the Cherokee language, and she blushed beet red. She answered him, and then pushed past Will, and thrust a bundle into my hands.

"Lost Woman, my father asked me to give you this." She cut her eyes in defiance at Will, and then said something else to him in her own language, before she turned abruptly to leave.

"Thank you, Bright Star!" I called out to her, as she retreated. She nodded and waved back at me without another word.

Will tried to take the bundle from my arms. "What the blazes did that red savage send to you?"

"Oh, for God's sake!" I made an impatient sound, as I held tight to my package. "My guess is venison. She brings me meat twice a month." I slapped at Will's hands. "Cut it out, William! I am quite capable of carrying this!"

I realized that everyone around me had become quiet. Will appeared livid. "Wolf sends you venison a couple of times a month?" A tiny muscle twitched by his jaw.

I nodded. "I guess so. Bright Star brings it, and I appreciate the gift. I couldn't say if it is from the tribe, or from Star, or from her dad. But, hey, it ensures that Fancy, Bella and I have enough to eat. Now, quit that! It is mine and you're not taking it!"

"Hell, Sassy! Don't you understand what he is asking when he sends you that venison?"

I shrugged my shoulders. "He's not asking me anything, Will. It is a gift. No ulterior motive. It's just a simple gift from a friend."

He snatched the bundle of venison from my hands. "No, you silly little ninny. Men and women can't be friends. It ain't natural. Wolf's asking you to marry him."

I was aware that all the eyes were focused on me. Several women tittered, and a couple of the men snickered.

"Oh, bull hockey!" I lifted my chin in stubborn defiance of the Gospel According to Will Selk. "That is the most ridiculous thing I ever heard."

He shut his eyes, frustrated. "Woman, you can be so dadblamed naive at times that it's downright painful. Lil, explain what it signifies when a Cherokee brave sends a woman venison."

Lily cleared her voice, and stepped over to me. "He's right, Sassy. It means the tribal elders have approved his petition to court you." I swear my jaw hit my feet when she said that. "Courting commences when he then brings her venison."

I felt like the ground was beginning to spin around me. I was quite sure the color had drained from my face. "To... court... me? Me??"

She nodded.

Wouldn't it just figure that I am not an expert on indigenous Americans??? "But why wouldn't he tell me? I mean, how would I know?" I felt color rising in my cheeks.

"It's common knowledge among people who live near the Cherokee. Marcus has been here almost 20 years now. Sassy, what did you do with the venison he sent to you?" Lily looked quite worried.

Everyone appeared to be waiting for my answer with proverbial 'baited breath'.

"I cooked it. We ate it. What would you think I would do with it? Roll naked in it??" I had to throw a little sass in my answer.

Several of the ladies tittered with embarrassed laughter. Lily rolled her eyes, as Marc turned aside in laughter. "You are so incredibly inappropriate sometimes," she muttered.

You could almost see the steam rising from around Will's collar. "Did you send any back to Wolf?"

I smiled. "Why?"

"Sarah Alinora, I'm asking you one more time: Did… you… send… any… back... to... Wolf?" He snapped the words out like they tasted bad in his mouth.

I looked around at the people still there, and realized this was serious.

"No. And do not call me Sarah Alinora. You are not my Daddy. You don't have the right to call me that. Besides, why does it matter?"

The tension seemed to go out of Will. He turned away, and rubbed his face. "Good."

"William!" I grabbed his sleeve. "Okay, I'll ask it again. Why does it matter whether I sent any of the venison back to him?" I snapped.

Lily came up and slipped her arm around me. "By accepting the venison in the first place, you agreed to allow him to court you. If you cook his meat and send it back, you accept his proposal of marriage."

"Well, f..." I felt my spine stiffen. "Why that low down, sneaking hound dog..." I picked up the bundle of venison and started across the pasture towards the tents.

"Where the hell are you going?" Will snarled, as he caught up with me and grabbed my arm.

I shook his arm off mine. "I'm taking this meat right back to him and telling him what I think of him."

Lily ran up to me as well. "No, no, you can't do that. It would dishonor him in front of his people. Just don't accept it in the future. And do NOT send him cooked venison back."

"Fine. Who wants this meat?" I dropped it to the ground, and then struck out for my cabin.

Will picked it up, and started after me. "Little Bit, there is no reason to throw away good meat at this point."

I swung around at him, my eyes blazing. "Oh, will you please quit telling me what to do? You are worse than the Democrats back home, always telling a person what they can and cannot do, what they can and cannot say, even what they can and cannot think. First, you tell me I can't take it. Now you tell me to take it. Well, let me tell you this: you are not the boss of me, William Ranscome Selk, and don't you forget it! You... are... not... the... boss... of... me!!!!"

I jerked my arm away from him and marched to my cabin. *I will not cry. I will not cry I will not cry I will not cry. That damned man will not see me cry!* Once inside, I slammed the door shut, leaned against it, and burst into tears. Dratted man. This evening was not going the way I had hoped. Not at all. *Dammit. I wanted those kisses to lead to some nice, unbridled sex, not the fight of the century. Sweaty, down and dirty sex. Dammit, dammit, dammit, dammit. Damned man. Dammit!*

Fancy came running to my side. "Miss Sassy, are you all right? Whoever upset you, girl?"

I'd learned her mama was one-fourth black, her father some white planter. With her light complexion, turquoise eyes, and pretty hair, not to mention her beautiful figure, she would have brought a high price in New Orleans at its annual Quadroon Ball, to be set up as a rich man's fancy woman. I suspected that had been her father's intention, given her odd name. He probably thought that would be the best possible life for her. Since she was at a plantation somewhere along the coast, Fancy would have been perceived as a threat by many white women and had not had an easy time in life. She was definitely not accustomed to many white women who treated her as anything little more than a slave. Even though she was not a slave, and never had been one, many people treated her as inferior based on the sole basis that she was part black. Add to it the fact that she had a baby out of wedlock from the last place where she had worked, when her employer raped her, and then apparently threw her out, and you understood this woman had a life far harder and more difficult than any woman had to live in the USA the future where I had lived. I'd heard women in the future whine and fuss about discrimination and their hard lives. I remember when Whoopi Goldberg complained that she 'only' earned $1,000,000 a year and she felt like a slave! Goldberg didn't have a clue it felt like to be a slave. This girl had a hard life that few could even imagine, in this world or the one I came from.

I realized Fancy had excellent sewing skills and could tailor just about any item of clothing. I wasn't thrilled Will Selk sent her to me but she made my life one heck of a lot easier than it was before she showed up. I knew I couldn't manage without her. She had also become my dear friend.

"Did you know that by accepting the venison from Shadow Wolf, I apparently gave him permission to court me?" I asked.

Her eyes widened and she began to shake her head back and forth. "No, ma'am, Miss Sassy, I ain't never heard nothing like that before. I don't know nothing about them Cherokees. There weren't none where I lived befo'. I would 'a told you if I'd 'a known that."

"Well, I'm sorry, but we can't accept the meat from him in the future. It has caused quite a scandal that I accepted meat from him. We'll manage somehow."

She patted me on the arm. "It's all right, Miss Sassy, everything will be jus' fine. Now, let's get you ready fo' bed."

I let her lead me up the narrow stairs to my little bedroom, where I slipped out of my Sunday Go To Meeting Clothes, and into my night gown, which was nothing more than an old shift that Lily gave me. As I sat curled up on my bed, brushing my waist length hair, I heard the door swung open and footsteps clunk up the stairs towards my room.

"William Selk, you ain't got no reason to be comin' into this cabin this late at night," Fancy began fussing.

He waved her off. "Get out of here, Fancy. Go take care of your child. This is between Miss Sassy and me."

Fancy looked uncertain, as she glanced from Will to me. Finally, she nodded. "I'll be in my room, Miss Sassy, if you need me."

I didn't respond to what she said, but stopped brushing my hair long enough to give him what I hoped was an imperious look down my nose. When he didn't respond, I finally said, "We have nothing to discuss. It's late. You're not wanted here. Goodnight."

The time when you were wanted here was before you made the big scene, you big dope. Earlier, I wanted a back rub, a few shots of whisky, and some really great sex. Now just go away, I thought glumly. *You pretty well ruined your chances of getting lucky tonight, bucko.*

I resumed brushing my hair, having dismissed him. It threw me when he did not turn tail and leave. I lowered the brush again, and curtly asked, "Why are you still here?"

"I reckon you don't know why I dislike him."

It was true: I couldn't guess why he had such animus towards Shadow Wolf. "True. I cannot fathom what Wolf did to alienate you, but to be blunt, it doesn't matter, William. I don't care. Not my duck. Now, go away."

"Not your duck?" He tilted his head as he studied me, trying to interpret the saying.

I nodded. "Not my duck. I have no horse in the race. No dog in the show. It is none of my business, Will Selk. It does not involve me."

He turned the chair back towards me, and straddled it. I sighed. The damned man was not going away. So much for my twenty-first century analogies. He sighed as he raked his hands through his hair. He looked downwards to the floor, and then up at me, two, three, four times, before he finally responded. "Bright Star's mother was my sister."

I literally thought my eyes were going to pop out of my head. "What??? Oh, bull hockey. Your sister was a white woman. At a plantation on the coast. How? I don't understand."

"Back then, Wolf's tribe lived near there. He was a good friend. He used to come around, and we boys all went hunting and fishing all the time. Tom, Marc, Wolf, and me. George went with us some of the time, too, but he was more Tom's friend than mine. Ginny tagged along as she got older. Ginny was about 14 when Wolf first started noticing my little sister. Pretty soon, he was sending venison over."

The brush and my hand fell to my lap. "Then what happened?"

"Mama and Ginny cooked up that venison into one fine stew. Mama told Ginny it would be the polite thing to do to take some back to Wolf to thank him for the meat. We didn't know what the meat meant. No idea at all. So, my sweet little baby sister took a kettle full of venison stew to the Cherokee settlement and presented it to Wolf."

My throat was tight. I was almost afraid to ask, but I did anyway. "And...?"

"Wolf told her he was delighted she had agreed to be his wife. Ginny Lee was stunned but thrilled. Here was this handsome brave, the chief's son, in line to be the next chief, telling her they were engaged. My foolish baby sister found it all rather romantic. She didn't know what her life would be like. So..."

"What?" I prodded him to continue.

"They were married in the Indian way." Will said. "I will admit it was a right pretty ceremony."

"How long did she live with them?" I was surprised my voice seemed calm considering the shock I felt.

"About 5, almost 6 years. She had two sons, Grey Wolf and Running Bear, and then Star." His voice broke.

"What happened to Ginny?" I asked, as my hand rubbed his hand.

"They married in '58. In '60, Wolf's tribe moved out here. Four years later, Ginny died in childbirth. That was 14 years ago. My sister was 23 years old when she died. Don't you see, Sassy? It's a hard life on the frontier for a white woman. It killed my sister. Mama died of a broken heart after Ginny died. It dang near killed her when Ginny went to live with Wolf in the first place."

It occurred to me with a start that his sister would have been about my age.

"But, it wasn't Wolf's fault she died in childbirth. Many women do, even with excellent medical care. In fact, one in two women dies in childbirth. And to be frank, what does all this have to do with me?"

He nodded, just half listening to me, as he progressed with his story. "But she didn't have the option of having any kind of real medical care, Sassy. Wolf and his tribe moved out here, to this God forsaken wilderness, after the war. It's a lot harder place here than it was back home. I want a better life for you. Better than to be married to a red savage and live in a hut made out of sticks and mud." His voice cracked, and I reached out for him, but he was already standing up. "Don't marry him, Sassy. Just... don't... marry him."

And then he turned and left. Well, I thought, I hadn't expected that, but I still was not sure what his purpose was in telling me the story about his sister and Wolf. Finally, half to myself, I murmured, "I thought he loved the wilderness."

"Him? Oh, no, ma'am. He loves big, fancy houses. Nice clothes. Beautiful horses. Beautiful women. Fine wines. But you know what I think he loves the most?" Fancy as she peeked around the door into my room. "You. Will Selk loves you. He's got it real bad for you, Miss Sassy."

My head jerked towards her. "Oh, I don't think so..."

"No ma'am, I knows I ain't supposed to argue wif' no white woman, but I tell you, I have known that man long enough that I can say he is plum dab crazy fo' you. You wait and see, Miss Sassy. You jus' wait and see. Oh, and by the way. You got some mighty strong feelings for him, too. But you gonna have to figure that out for your own self."

The next morning, I was up earlier than usual. I pulled on my everyday clothes, and headed over to where the Indians were still tented from the night before. As I approached Wolf's tent, Bright Star came flying out to greet me.

"My friend! We are always so pleased for you to come visit us!" She pecked me on both cheeks, as I did her.

I studied my friend, and saw signs I should have recognized months ago. Azure eyes under aristocratic, high brows. That elegant, long, straight nose. And those same damned dimples, sans whiskers. How could I have failed to recognize that this beautiful girl was related to Will with those dimples? I kissed her back, and squeezed her hand. "I must talk to your father, my friend."

Her eyes lit up, and she started to dart back to his tent.

"Alone, Star! I must speak to him privately. This is serious."

She stopped in her tracks, and turned to me observing no smile on my face. She studied my face with apparent sadness. Her shoulders sagged with disappointment as the excited light faded from her eyes. "Are you sure, Sassy?"

I nodded. She turned back and entered his tent. Moments later, Wolf came out, uncertainty written across his face.

"We need to talk."

I turned towards the tall hemlock trees at the edge of the clearing. He followed after me. When I reached the trees, I wheeled back towards him. "Why, Wolf? Why didn't you tell me what the venison meant when you brought it over?"

He appeared surprised by my question. "I thought all knew the meaning of the venison when provided by a Cherokee brave to an eligible woman. I did not know that..."

"Oh, come now, Wolf. You know how long I have been here. You know where I came from. You actually thought I would know the meaning of the gift?" I snapped the words at him.

He blinked. "Yes. I thought you would know..."

"Bull hockey. You know damned well I didn't know what it meant. Did you hope to trick me into marriage like you did Ginny Selk?"

His eyes flashed with anger as they narrowed. "I did not trick my Ginny Blue Eyes. I loved her. She loved me. She was my whole world. She knew what the venison meant when I sent it. She told me to send it when I told her I wanted to marry her. She knew what it meant if she cooked it and sent it back to me. She was destined to be my wife. I miss her every day..."

I blinked as his voice cracked with emotion.

"But you never mentioned her to me, did you? That you were married to another white woman in the past? That you had children? Much less that she was Will Selk's sister? Or that Will never forgave you when she died in childbirth."

He stared at me before answering. "We do not talk about our Dead among our people. Besides, you are from Beyond. You are special, sent from the Great Spirit. I thought you were sent for me. I never considered you might not know our customs. You came from the Great Spirit. He sent you. He had to send you with the knowledge you needed to live here."

"Oh, stuff and bother! That is nonsense, and you know it!"

"No, Sassy. It is not bother stuff. You have told me how you and your husband studied this time, wrote about these years, taught about it. Why would I think you would not know our ways?" He stared at me again, like he could look straight to my soul. "You love someone else."

My jaw hit the ground in shock. "Are you kidding me?? My husband just died a little while ago. I loved him very much. I'm still getting over that. Heck, I'm still getting over winding up here instead of still being there. How on earth could you think the Great Spirit sent me for you?"

He shrugged. "When a Cherokee dies, it is appropriate for his widow to marry again. To have a provider. And when a woman comes from Beyond, she is meant for someone here. I found you when you were lost. I believed that you became <u>my</u> Lost Woman then. I thought you knew. For me, it was obvious. Just as it was obvious to me years ago that Lily was a Lost Woman, intended for Marcus."

"Huh. That idea must have gone over well." I snorted in disbelief.

He smiled. "It met with some initial resistance from both until they realized it was meant to be."

"Humph. Well, let me be clear: I am not your Lost Woman. I am not your anything. I thought we could be friends. You have been kind to me, very kind, and I thought you were a friend. I didn't know you were ... lusting after me!"

A smile tugged at Shadow Wolf's lips. "You are a beautiful woman, Sassy Winslow. It is normal for a man to lust after a woman as beautiful as you. Men and women can never be friends. They can love and respect each other. I thought the Great Spirit was being most kind to me after all these long, empty years."

"Jesus Christ, Will Selk said the same thing." I rubbed my forehead, which was beginning to ache horribly. "I can't marry you. I can't marry anyone at this time..."

"And in the future?" He interjected, his eyes sparkling again.

I stopped mid-sentence. "No, Wolf. Not in the future. I don't know where the future will take me, but I can't ever marry you. I'm not Ginny. I'm not that courageous."

I couldn't tell him I was unwilling to be the mother of Cherokee children who might someday die on the Trail of Tears, that horrible forced march to Oklahoma in which so many would die along the way. I was not that brave.

Besides, I didn't love him.

His shoulders slumped. He looked at the ground as he shuffled his feet in the dirt and leaves. He finally nodded. "I understand."

"Good." After a pause, I frowned. "Wait. What do you understand? Tell me what you think I am saying."

He looked at my face again. "I understand that you love Will Selk. You are his Lost Woman. When you both face that, you will be found again."

I am pretty sure my jaw hit the ground at that. "Wha ... what????? Where the blazes do you get these crazy ideas??? First, of all, not all who wander are lost!"

He nodded. "Ah, but you must be lost to be found, Sassy. I have seen it coming. I hoped I was wrong, that you were meant for me. But I could see the attraction between you two. And Selk ... does not like me..."

I stared before I asked the question. "You say that, having been married to Will's baby sister? After Ginny died out here, in child birth, hundreds of miles away from the nearest doctor? Do you blame him? After all, you married his little sister, you brought her here, and she died having your baby. Can you <u>not</u> understand how he feels at all? Is Star her child?"

He nodded. "I understand. It was my loss as well. My greatest loss. I loved my Ginny very much. She was beautiful through and through. Her soul shone with the beauty of the heavens. She was the other half of my heart. When she died, half of my heart died as well. The day she died, my world went dark. And yes, my beautiful Bright Star is Ginny's child. Ginny died giving me Star. But she was not hundreds of miles from a doctor. Lily was here, and Lily could not save her. Even Selk says Lily is the best doctor in the Colonies."

His words touched me more than I wanted him to know. To have a love like that... Wow. To say Ginny's heart shone with the beauty of the heavens, that she was the other half of his heart. That the world went dark for him the day she died. I could not imagine such words ever even occurring to Owen Winslow, much less him ever uttering them. Smirking if he heard someone say that, perhaps, but never say it about me. For a man so capable of writing, he had a hard time verbalizing his feelings. He could be very passionate, and could show me his feelings with his touch, but he rarely stated his love for me. When he did, I could tell it was almost painful for Owen to utter the words. I figured it was his uptight New England upbringing.

I blinked, determined not to cry over Wolf's great love for Ginny. I took a breath, and started another tact. "And you have sons, also? Red Bull and Squatting Duck?"

He laughed, and patted my back. "You tease me, Sassy Winslow. Grey Wolf and Running Bear. Red Bull would be a good name, but I would never name a child Squatting Duck."

I smiled, pleased I had lightened the mood a little bit with the joke. After a few moments, I asked, "Why do you say I love Will Selk?"

His smile was bittersweet. "Ah, sweet Sassy, you must figure that out for yourself. You alone know what is in your heart, just as Will alone knows what is in heart."

He bent to kiss my brow, and then after a long pause, turned and walked away into the forest. I stood there watching him go, as I pondered his words. *I understand you love Will Selk.*

How could he understand that? It surprised the living day lights out of me when he uttered those words. Just as it surprised the living day lights out of me when Fancy said virtually the same thing the night before. Deep in thought, I did not hear the footsteps approaching.

"Well, don't that just beat all. I come up here to make sure you're all right, and I find that man kissing you??? After all I told you last night???"

I wheeled around, startled not just by the sound of another person but the sound of this particular person. *I understand you love Will Selk.* How in hell's bells could I even begin to explain that entire conversation to Will at this point in time? It was one of those moments when Owen would have said that life is like a dick and sometimes it's hard for no reason. I blinked as the reputed recipient of my undeserved love strode up, anger boiling to the point of rage in every word, every step, every inch of his overly taut muscles.

Oh, hell. Big Angry had returned.

"Oh..." I caught my breath. "Shut up. Will, do not jump to conclusions. As they say back home, you know nothing, Jon Snow."

His lips narrowed even thinner in anger at my words. "Well, who the hell is this Jon Snow fellow? Another man you been kissin'? Have you been going around kissin' everybody? I bared my soul to you last night, and this morning, you're down here, kissing that damned Injun. What the blazes are you thinking?"

"Oh, good grief. You are the most obnoxious, self-absorbed, unmitigated ass in the shape of a man I ever met, and I thought Owen Winslow had that title all wrapped up and tied with a bow. Dude, I came to tell him I'm not the woman for him..."

"Damned right." I tried to calm and center myself, but he continued with his rant. "I told you before my name is not Dude. Don't you walk away from me like this, you sassy little piece of baggage. Woman, don't you dare walk away from me like this!"

"I have no reason to stay." I was shaking. I wanted so desperately to tell him not to ever use that tone of voice with me again, not to ever demand anything from me in such a rage of anger. I heard that tone too many times in the past – future?? – from a man I loved, and I did not ever intend to fall victim to loving a man who would talk to me like that again. I long ago realized the dumbest thing you can ever do is love each other but you can't be together. 'Not be together' does not necessarily mean you are apart, distance-wise. It means you are apart, in your thinking. It meant *tu me manques* in the truest sense of the words. Instead of trying to explain any more, shaking with my own anger and frustration, at my own rage, at my own self-perceived weakness, I raised up my right hand, and made a dismissive motion known to all men in the world I came from, as I kept walking, and said, "What… ever."

Owen, Rick and Jim knew that meant This Is All Done, Do Not Push Me Any More. Stick Me With a Fork, Because I. Am. All. Done. Apparently, Selk didn't know that, and came right after me, ranting and fussing all the way. With nothing else said, by me at least, I marched right straight to my cabin, where I literally slammed the door in his face. I turned around to Fancy, who was wide eyed with mouth agape.

"Do <u>not</u> let that damned man in."

I started up to the loft, as the door slammed open behind me.

"Sassy! Sarah Alinora Winslow..."

I wheeled around, ready to kick ass and take names. "Who the hell do you think you are coming into this house like this? And why the hell do you think you have the right to use that tone of voice with me anyway? This is <u>my</u> house. This is <u>my</u> life. Do <u>not</u> call me that! You are not my Mama or my Daddy! Get the hell out and stay the hell out, William Selk!" I shook as I finished, tears stinging at my eyes. Damned tears better not fall. I would not look like some mewling, weak kneed woman right now. I… would… not.

He didn't move. He stared, shocked, for about thirty seconds before he responded. Lips again thinned to a narrow, angry line, azure eyes sparking with silvered outrage, he started up the stairs, three at a time, until he caught my arm. I tried to shake him off as he pulled me close.

"Let me go, Will! I swear, I'll scream!"

"You <u>have</u> been screaming. Everyone between here and Augusta, hell, maybe all the way to Savannah, heard you." With one fell swoop, he threw me up over his shoulder and strode on up the steps to the landing while I ineffectively pummeled his back, causing nothing more than to make his anger grow.

"Will! Stop this right now! You have to stop this right now!" Dammit, the blasted tears started despite my earnest determination not to allow them to occur. I realized we were falling. I didn't know anyone could dump a person onto a bed while falling onto it themselves. Somehow, Will did both.

"Shut up, Sassy! Don't you know how much I love you yet?"

Shocked, I quit fighting, although the tears were still flowing. "Wh... what did you say?"

Will looked me, his eyes serious. "I love you, dammit, woman. I didn't mean to. I swore I'd never love another woman, but I love you, Sassy." He waited for my response. Breathing hard, but waiting.

"Oh. I ... I didn't know. You really love me?" I squeaked out.

Wordless, he nodded.

I thought of all the things I wanted to say, that I needed to say. That Wolf had been telling me that Will loved me, telling me that I loved Will, that I was intended to be Will's woman, like Lily was Marc's. I knew how Owen used to feel: I could not utter the words. Not yet, anyway. I was at that moment when you have to take that deep breath before speaking because you are just so damned close to crying. Again. I swiped my hand across my tear dampened cheek, and pushed back hard against his chest. "Well, this is a piss poor way to show it. You <u>cannot</u> just go around telling me you love me while trying to rape me. This… is… not… acceptable."

He stopped, panting, and leaned back on one elbow. "What? Damn it, woman!!! I'm not trying to... to... rape you! All right, maybe seduce you a little bit, but..."

"Well, slow down, William. You say you love me. Slow down. Woo me. Talk nice to me. Be nice to me. Smile at me now and then. Tell me I look pretty sometimes. You were doing pretty good last night until you got mad. But don't ever think you can bully your way into my bed, bucko. It won't happen."

He laughed, eyes sparking with those turquoise glints. "Why not, Lil Bit?"

He leaned towards me again, his lips dropping towards mine. *Kiss me,* I thought, *kiss me now. Kiss me hard. Kiss the hell out of me.*

Chapter Eight

"Ahem." We both paused as we heard the feminine sound of a throat being cleared. I struggled to hold back laughter as Will pulled back to see who was interrupting us. I expected anger as he saw Fancy. Instead, he began to stammer.

"Uh... uh... Lil, uh, uh, it's not how it looks..."

"Oh, bull crap, Captain Selk. Now, get out of the lady's bedroom, and I do mean lady, and march your horny self right down those stairs. Sassy is not some sailor's doxy, this is not that sort of establishment, and you are damned sure not going to treat my cousin like she belongs in one. You are not going to rape my cousin, in this house or anywhere. Now, get out!"

I never saw a man jump so fast in all my life as he did in response to Lily's words. Will was still pulling his shirt back on (which I had never seen come off) as he ran down the stairs like a frightened school boy. I was not going to giggle. As we heard the door slam as he rushed out, I pushed my hair back and grinned. "Thank you. But I think I had it under control."

"Yeah. Sure." Lily tried to look stern as she stood there, hands on her hips, shaking her head at me. Finally, she answered, struggling not to laugh. "Fancy said you needed me. Urgently."

"I did. But, I was handling it okay. I'm still glad you showed up when you did."

She came over and stared into my face. "You were handling it? That's what you call it? Give me a freaking break. Will was all over you. How did he get up here? Come on, let's fix your clothing. My God in heaven, woman! You're falling out of your things. You must figure out what you feel for him. No conjugal visits until the two of you decide where this is headed. This is the 18th century, for heaven's sake. It's simple: no wedding, no bedding. Agreed?"

"Agreed. And he wasn't going to rape me, well, maybe seduce me, he said, but not rape me. That's what I was trying to tell him. But, he was having a hard time taking 'no' for an answer."

I began straightening my hair and then noticed my jumps, which had somehow come untied. I slipped one errant breast back into my shift, and then dropped my hands to the laces, and began to tighten them back up to tie the jumps again. "How did I ever get like this?" I murmured.

"The same way his shirt came off, you dimwitted ninny." Lily looked frustrated. "Lust does things to a person's brain. Not always good things. A man on fire with lust can do all sorts of things you would never dream possible. This is different than where you came from, Sassy. Men are not in the least enlightened about women's needs and wants. And this man all but had you undressed, slick as a peeled onion. Do you understand?" Fancy, who had been hovering behind Lily, came over with the hair brush to begin working the tangled snarls from my hair. Lily clucked like a mother hen over her chick again, and then said she was leaving. As she headed down the stairs, Fancy began smoothing my tresses into place, before she began to braid it again. I have a real love hate relationship with my hair, and this innate ability it has to tangle.

"I'm sorry, Miss Sassy. He skeered me, and you was screaming fo' help, so's I went fo' Miss Lily..."

"And by the time you two got back, it was under control. Well, more or less. It's okay, Fancy."

She looked very uncomfortable. "I almos' tried to make him go my own self, but I ain't never talked back to no white man like that since Mista' Simon..."

Her hands were still shaking. I realized Fancy was willing to risk her own life for me. I was stunned with the realization. I hugged her. "Oh, Fancy, that is the kindest thing anyone ever did for me. God bless you, dear. You are a true friend."

"I just warn't gonna let him rape you. That ain't' nothing no woman should ever have to endure." Fancy was blushing almost as bad as I was just minutes before. "Oh, Miss Sassy, you treat me different than any white person ever did befo' exceptin' fo' my Daddy. He taught me to not never, not never ever, to say 'no' to a white man. Cause if I did, the man would beat me." Shaking, head bowed, her voice broke off. "And I don' ever want to get beaten again."

I stiffened at her words, my mouth too dry to even think of spitting. "Your father beat you?"

She looked up, shocked by my words. "Oh, my land, no, Miss Sassy! He done switched me a time or two, but he never beat me. But he knew the ways o' the world, and he warned me not to ever sass no white man or tell one no."

"Fancy, who beat you?"

"Mr. Simon. He said everybody knew a woman with even one drop of colored blood was nothin' but a whore, that she would spread her legs for anyone. So he beat me."

"For refusing him?"

She nodded. I slipped my arm around her, and pulled her close. I was filled with anger that anyone ever beat this lovely young woman for any reason. If there was one thing I could not tolerate, it was domestic violence. Whoever Simon was, he had no right to beat Fancy just because she rebuffed his advances. "No one will ever beat you again, Sassy. Not even for saying no to them. I promise. You're a free woman of color. No man, white or black, is your Master. And I'm just Sassy. You don't need to call me Miss Sassy."

Her eyes flew open in alarm. "But, Miss Sassy, I ain't never called no white lady just by her given name in a long time. There was a real nice lady who was kinda like a mama to me. Besides her, I'm supposed to always say Miss in front of a white woman's given name. That's what my daddy said."

"Did you call your daddy Mista' Daddy?"

"Oh, my land, Miss Sassy! He was my Daddy Jo! Around other folks, I just said yes, suh, or no, suh."

I sat back on my haunches, and scratched my head. "Okay, did you ever call Mista' Tom just Tom?"

I suspected Mista' Tom was her half-brother.

She looked horrified. "Oh, Miss Sassy, he didn't like that. He was the young Mista'! Oh, you just don' understand!!!"

I shook my head. Apparently, it was permissible in the crazy world Fancy grew up in to call your Daddy, who was the Mista', just Daddy, but not to call your white half-brother by his given name. Go figure. I grew up believing no living person, white or black, is responsible for what other white or black people did generations ago. Now that I was living 'then', it hit me with a shock at what I was witnessing first hand to be done to other people on the basis of their skin color or in Fancy's case, that there was even one drop of black blood in a person.

There were times that living in the eighteenth century sucked.

"Okay, let's try this. You call me Sassy when we are alone and Miss Sassy when someone is around who would object to you just calling me by my given name. I won't fuss if you call me Miss Sassy. You won't fuss if I remind you to just call me Sassy." I held out my hand to her. "Shake?"

She stared me long and hard before responding. Finally, she swallowed hard, and then she spat into her palm, and extended it to me. "Shake, Sassy. You got a deal."

We'd been sewing a couple of hours on a custom order before Fancy raised her big fear. Fancy shook her head, and then gave me a little half smile. "I know you'll watch after me, Miss Sassy, I mean, Sassy, but..."

"But what, Fancy?"

"What happens when you leave?"

That stumped me. "Uh... why do you think I'm going to leave?"

She shrugged. "Good folks always leave. Mama did. Daddy did. Even Mistah Tom did."

That stumped me, yet I could understand her position. I knew someday, I might leave – if I could ever go home. And I sure couldn't stop bad things from happening to her or Bella if I was not here. I thought for what seemed like a long time then before I answered. "If I leave, I'll take Bella and you with me, if you want to go with me. Agreed? I promise not to leave you at the mercy of some stupid assed man ever again."

I contemplated the differences in her world and the one I left behind. I frowned as I remembered something unsavory from the hours of history lessons I taught over the years about the South. "You are a free woman, Sassy. So is your daughter. Just remember, the laws changed in 1775 and it is not as safe now as it was for you before."

She laughed drily. "Believe me, I know. Simon beat me and had his way with me back in '77 after he took the job as overseer. He said no one would ever believe a nigga over a white man. Well, they always said, don' let no one know you can read or write, Fancy." Tears burned bright in her eyes.

I felt a shock of raging anger rush down my spine at her cavalier use of the 'n' word, as we say in the Beyond. I took her by the shoulders and gave her a little shake. "Do not talk about yourself like that. That 'n' word is so derogatory to anyone of color. Please, don't refer to yourself like that around me." She blushed and looked downward. With a start, I realized the other part of what she had said. "Can you read and write?"

She nodded. "Yes 'm. I can cipher, too."

"Which tells me that you can speak better than you do most of the time, right?" She blushed and nodded as I reached over pat her hand. "You don't have to 'dumb down' for me. It'll be all right, you'll see. If go anywhere, I will take Bella and you with me. If I have to send you someplace for me, I will send you with permission to go so no slave catcher can claim you."

I sure would hate to have to hunt down and kill some damned slave catcher or anyone who tried to beat or otherwise hurt this beautiful young woman ever again. I would if need be. No one was going to hurt Fancy or Bella while on my watch.

It was late when Marcus came by. Nervous, he finally handed me the letter. "Will asked me to give you this."

I stared at him, numbed by his words and the letter he was holding out to me. "Why didn't he bring it himself?" I asked, almost afraid to hear the answer.

Marcus scowled. "He left, Sassy."

Hands shaking, I took the letter, stunned by his words. I felt like my throat was closing. "He

... left? He just up and left? Without a damned word? Today?"

Marcus nodded again. "Aye. And I have to say, I never thought Will Selk would act the coward. I'm sorry."

I realized with a shock that nothing in life ever prepares us to lose someone we love. And I realized with an even bigger shock I had just admitted to myself that I loved Will. And yet, in the blink of an eye, the damned man was gone, without one word.

Damn it. He was right.

Tu me manques.

—

Rick and Jim sat in silent disbelief in the Sheriff's Office. Finally, Jim responded. "You mean to tell me women have disappeared up here for years and you haven't shut this trail down? And not one damned person is willing to keep searching for my sister, let alone the other women?" And before the Sheriff could respond, Jim continued. "Well, that just sucks toads. I cannot believe that you people aren't trying to figure out what the hell is happening to these women. Your 'oh, well' attitude is unbelievable." Jim stood up. "Come on, Rick. They may give up, but I haven't, and I know you haven't, either. We're going to hunt until we learn what the hell happened to Sassy."

Rick felt bereft. "The Sheriff all but said Mom is dead. I can't believe that. I won't believe that. Surely, we'd feel something, we'd know something, if she were dead, Uncle Jim. And ... and ..."

Jim put his arm around Rick's shoulders. "We'll find her, Rick. Your mom's not dead. I would know it if she were. She's my twin. I've known all our lives if something was wrong with her. I swear we'll find Sassy and we'll learn the secret of that damned trail. Right now, we are going to the press. We are breaking this bad boy wide open."

"Mom says grief never ends, but it changes. It's a passage, not a place to stay. Grief is not a sign of weakness, nor a lack of faith. It's the price of love."

Jim nodded. He heard his sister say that for years.

"Well, I'm grieving. I lost my Dad this year. Looks like I lost my Mom, too. But damn it, Jim, does grieving have to hurt so freaking bad? It hurts so bad, every day, this missing people who were here for me, and now are gone."

Jim didn't answer. He knew there were no words he could offer that would help ease Rick's pain. He couldn't begin to explain how he knew his sister wasn't dead, but Jim flat knew that she wasn't dead. With every fiber of his being, he knew it. She was missing from him. He just had no idea where she was.

—

News Release: The President today issued an Executive Order, abolishing Freedom of Speech, warning that people must maintain political correctness and any perceived slights to others, no matter how unintended, would not be tolerated.

—

News Release: The President today issued an Executive Order, abolishing Freedom of Religion. Henceforth, such antiquated ideas will be considered of the same ilk as the Jim Crow laws of the last century. It will not be considered to be politically correct for people to talk about their religion as if it were true to non-believers.

—

"Well, hell, Uncle Jim, it looks like we violated the New World Order by criticizing that Sheriff." Rick scratched his head in disbelief.

Jim snatched the newspaper from Rick's hands. "My God. I would never have believed I would live to see the day that our Government abolished rights delineated in the Constitution and Bill of Rights."

Rick nodded. "They say they are 'progressively modernizing it.' Antifa says their goal is the abolishment of our Constitution and Bill of Rights. Dad must be turning over in his grave." He looked at Jim.

They both started to laugh.

"I can just hear your dad ranting and raving about this now. 'How dare they attempt to circumvent the Constitution and Bill of Rights by Executive Order???'"

Rick nodded his head. "Dad would be having fits." He grew more serious. "Thank God he didn't live to see the mess this country is in."

Jim nodded, too. "Or to see your Mom went missing and we couldn't get the damned authorities to help us search for her."

Both men grew quiet. Finally, Rick spoke. "My Dad would be damned pissed about that."

Chapter Nine

It was still hot in East Florida in November, but it was always hot in this God forsaken hellhole, thought Sir Henry Clayton. He sipped his tea as he surveyed his officers with a jaundiced eye. The tea was strong and brewed the way he liked it, and his men were attentive and ready to do his bidding. He smiled, his lips thinned into a conniving faux smile.

"Lt. Col. Campbell shall soon sail from New York to Savannah with Fraser's Highlanders and the other forces under his command. They will meet with the local Tory Specials and other troops at Tybee Island. Even allowing for bad weather at this time of the year, the troops should all be in place and ready to attack Savannah by Christmas Day. Not even those crazy Georgian Whigs would expect us to stage an attack at Christmas!"

His officers laughed in agreement, eager for this much needed invasive win. Clayton smiled again, chuckling to himself. The foolish and presumptuous Continentals attempted to invade East Florida during the summer with dismal results after having the audacity to sign the so-called Articles of Incorporation. Now, it was time for His Majesty's troops to pay back those bumpkins for the defeats the British suffered of late at the hands of this Continental riffraff. He straightened his shoulders as he took another sip of tea. The lovely capitol of Georgia would be his at Christmas, come hell or high water, and Savannah was a much more pleasant and civilized locale for him to be located in than Eastern Florida, he thought, as he swatted at yet another blasted mosquito.

He never noticed the tall, handsome figure slip out of the conference room. Within minutes, the silent officer swung up onto his sleek, black stallion and headed north, towards Savannah.

—

After I 'came' to McCarron's Corner in July, or as Wolf would say, found my way here, I often came up to the Ridge, where I could sit in the shade, and look at the lovely springs below. At times, I swam in the spring, an easy if cold way to bathe. The drop from the ridge to the water was about 20 feet, and the spring itself varied from just over 20 to 40 feet deep. I dropped in enough to figure out it was safe to dive. It was a tremendous rush to stand up on the Ridge, and to dive into the crystal clear waters below.

About six weeks after Will slunked off without saying anything, I was up at the Ridge. It was mid-December, unusually warm and sunny. I figured I'd enjoy the weather while it was still nice. I went to the Ridge, where I 'shucked down' to swim in the springs. I often swam to clear my head as well as to bathe. I poised in my dive before I sprung, making a smooth, clean descent into the clean, cold waters below.

I was more than a little shocked when I kicked my way to the surface and found Will staring at me, worry written across his face. I swam to the side of the spring, where I shook the water out of my eyes, and slung my hair back from my face. "Imagine finding you here."

Worried, he chewed at his lip. "You okay? You scared the piss out of me when you dove in the water like that."

I laughed. "I'm fine. I've been swimming since I was a kid. What brings you back?"

"It was a very impressive dive." He held my towel and my well-worn shift out to me. "We need to talk."

"About damned time," I muttered as I snatched the towel and the shift from his hand. I toweled off before I pulled the worn shift over my head, and slipped into my petticoat and jumps. I then braided my hair, before we walked in uncomfortable silence back to Lily and Marc's house.

I was startled when Will held the door open for me when we got to the house. "Thanks."

I wasn't surprised to see Marc and Lily waiting for us in the house. I just had no idea what was going on. It was early afternoon, but Marc already stood by the fireplace, sipping what I suspected was some of his best blended malt whisky.

I entered the parlor and sat down beside Lily. "Okay, I'm game. What's up?"

Will took the glass of golden fire that Marc extended to him, and took a sip, closing his eyes as he savored the golden heat of Marc's home brew. "The Governor of Georgia asked me to invite you fine people to his annual Christmas regalia."

Lily cut her eyes at me, silent and worried. Finally, she spoke first. "Where will it be held?"

Will took a sip of the whisky. "Savannah. Of course. Where else?"

Lily and I looked at each other again before I answered. "I have no desire to go to Savannah for Christmas."

"Me either," Lily chimed in. "No desire. At all."

Will stared at us both before he responded. "I came here thinking I would have a hard time convincing you ladies not to go. Now, I find myself wondering why neither of you want to go?"

Lily and I glanced at each other again. Will's eyed narrowed; he appeared to be catching our nonverbal communications with bells on. "What do you two know about Christmas in Savannah?"

I cleared my voice, but Lily answered before me, cool and glib as always. "It must be a week's travel from here to Savannah, and then a week back again. We could have a sudden severe drop in temperature. I wouldn't want to be traveling and have a snow storm hit. Augusta would be a long enough trip; Savannah sounds insane."

Man, that southern drawl of hers was laying it on thick.

"But Sassy was just out swimming in the spring." Neither Lily nor I said anything in response. Will shook his head in disgust, and then raked his hands through his hair before he turned abruptly to Marc. "Do they know? Dammit, Marcus, did you tell them?"

Marc was succinct. "No."

Lily tensed, fire flashing in her eyes, and she snapped, "Tell us what, Will? Marc hasn't said anything to either of us. Just what the hell are you suggesting Marc told us? Marc?"

Marc looked first at his wife and then at Will. "I haven't said a damned thing to them, William. You know me well enough to know that. But, now you opened up this creel of worms. You tell them what's going on."

I stood up. I knew what would happen at Savannah after Christmas, but I didn't want to explain to Mr. Selk how I knew what was coming. In fact, a letter came from the Governor a week before, asking us to the Christmas festivities in Savannah. Lily, Marc and I discussed it and we all agreed we'd stay far away from Savannah anywhere near Christmas. "I'll go back to my house. This sounds like a personal family issue..."

"You just hold your horses, Little Bit, and sit right back down on that settee. You aren't going anywhere just yet." Will sounded furious. I thought I'd heard him angry before, but this had potential to get worse than the day he stomped off in November.

Why on earth was I falling for another man with a blasted Irish temper? God knew when Will Selk blew, all the Black Irish in his genes came boiling out. *Why me, God? Why two men in one lifetime with blasted Irish tempers? What did I ever do to deserve this*? I shrugged, trying not to show the trepidation I felt at his harsh tone, determined not to let him see my hands shaking or the pulse of the blood thrumming frantic through the vein in my neck. I sat back down. "Fine. Whatever."

He cut his eyes back at me but did not utter a word. *Well, that's a start,* I thought.

Will frowned again, and his shoulders sagged. He sighed, and then sat down abruptly next to me on the settee. It was clear he was wrestling with telling us something important. Finally, he turned towards me and whispered, as if worried someone outside of the room might hear his words. "I believe the British may attack the Colonists at Savannah around Christmas."

This was our turn to look at him in shocked surprise. Mouths agape, we looked from one to the other, unsure what to say in response. Finally, I said, with wit and aplomb, "Say what???"

His eyes narrowed again, as his lips thinned. "Sassy, you know something. Talk."

I tried my hardest to give him my best 'who, moi?' look. "Will, I don't know what you mean."

He just glared at me, impatient.

Lily cleared her throat. "All this love talk is quite endearing, but I want to know what the hell you think my husband told us. Just what have you two men been up to??"

Will looked from Lily, to me, to Marc, and back around to each of us again. "Aw, shit." He sighed, and nodded in acquiescence. "I, uh, sometimes am able to secure information that is helpful for General Washington and the war effort."

It hit me like a load of bricks and slipped out before I even thought. "You're one of the Culpers!!!"

Marcus and Lily stared at me in stunned silence while Will turned beet red. "I knew it! You are a spy!"

And then the words just spilled out like oil in the Gulf after a tanker collision. "Oh, bull hockey, Will Selk! You're the spy. You're one of Washington's spies!" And then it was just like the dam broke as I couldn't control the flood of words that came out. "I'm just a woman who fell through a hole in time and wound up here. Owen and I wrote about the Culpers. Uh... OMG! Oh no!!!" Trembling, I slapped my hand over my mouth as it hit me that I had literally spilled the proverbial beans.

Will's jaw hit the floor as my face turned as red as his had been minutes before.

Fine kettle of fish, Sassy. Ayup. And, now the jig is up.

We all talked long into the night, with Lily and Marcus confirming my story of coming from Beyond, as well as Lily's story of coming from Beyond years before. Once Will got past his initial reluctance to believe the 'crazy, ridiculous, not to mention outlandish fairy tale', interspersed with numerous interjections of the ever-popular 'bull hockey!', he gradually came around with fascinated excitement about our knowledge of events to come. Like Marc years before, Will wanted to change the future. Lily and I tried to explain we couldn't change the future, unless you counted the people Lily healed over the years who might otherwise have died. Will stubbornly clung to the idea that perhaps we could influence the future, even assist the Culpers and Washington with our knowledge.

"So, what are you saying, Will? You believe us?" I grinned as he nodded his head.

"Yes, but I must admit that it would all be a lot simpler if you were a British spy." He grinned, his gorgeous eyes sparkling. "But not nearly as much fun as this."

I chuckled. His response sounded much like what I remembered Marc reportedly said when he learned where Lily was from years before. "Bottom line: I damned sure don't want to be in Savannah at Christmas. The Redcoats are going to whup the snot out of us."

"What?" Will whipped his head back around at me in dismay. "How?"

I shrugged. "The commander doesn't have a lick of common sense and doesn't strike when he should. He virtually lets the English take the town. Damned fool even gets word the Redcoats are at Tybee Island waiting to attack, and he still fails to act timely. He's a four star moron."

Will nodded his head as he sat silent, chewing his lip as he considered the information. "That's pretty much my opinion of him, too."

"And, bucko, if you think you want any kind of relationship with me in the future, then you best not be in the middle of the fighting, you understand? Virtually all our soldiers are killed or taken captive at Savannah on December 28, 1778. Dammit, Selk, I lost one husband in the past year. I'm not about to get involved with you now and have you get killed in 2 freaking weeks. Not gonna happen, Dude!"

"Don't call me Dude," he muttered as if by rote. His head jerked up and he grinned. "Hey, did you say we're in a relationship, Sassy?"

"Play your cards right, big boy, and we could be. But you better never take off without telling me goodbye again. Understand? I may never get over that, you big dope."

He literally leapt up, rushed over to me, and gathered me into his arms. Before I could react, he swept me into my new most passionate kiss of my life. Heavens! I felt it all the way to my toes!

He walked me back to my cabin, holding hands like two school kids, stopping and kissing every few steps. Kisses extended to loving caresses. Soon, we were 'making out', as we used to say 'in the day', all but making love standing up outside in broad moon light.

"I do love your hair," he murmured as his hands stroked it.

I giggled. "My mouse brown hair? Are you serious?"

He took a tendril into his hand to examine it. "Not mouse brown at all. Golden brown, the color of good corn whisky when firelight shines through the bottle."

I laughed out loud. "My hair is the color of whisky?"

He blushed. "Don't make fun, Sass. I'm tryin' to be romantical."

—

Lily stared after Will and Sassy as they headed back to her cabin. "Should we tell her?" she finally asked.

Marc frowned. Tell 'who'? And what, pray tell, are we goin' to tell?"

Lily turned towards her husband. Tell Sassy about Fancy."

He walked to the window, and stared out after the kissing couple. "No. Not before I tell Fancy. I'm not even sure Will knows."

Lily frowned. "I bet he knows."

"I doubt it." How would Marc manage to tell the lass the greatest secret of his adult life? He'd kept his promise to Jo all these years and never spilled his soul to the beautiful girl. How could he tell her now, after all she'd been through? Her life could have been so different, if he had just spoken up sooner... He sighed. Why was life so damned hard sometimes?

—

After the previous time, Will wasn't about to enter my cabin without an invitation. I grinned as I motioned for him to come in, and with a big grin, he swung me up in this arms, and carried me into my sewing room, where he settled me onto the small couch, more or less sprawling beside me, more off than on it. We began kissing again, and the fire was definitely growing within us by leaps and bounds. As I helped Will unlace my jumps, we both heard the ominous sound of a hammer being set on a flintlock.

"William Ranscome Selk, I don' care if you are my brother, you get off Sassy right now. Miss Lily already done told you there will be no rape in this house. Now, move!" Fancy was shaking so badly I feared she might pull the trigger by accident.

Will jumped back, hands in the air. "Fancy, this isn't anything like that!"

Fancy's words hit me hard, almost like I had walked into the broad side of a brick shit house. "Your brother???" I shouted, shock reverberating in my two simple words.

Fancy nodded while keeping the musket aimed at Will.

Wordless, Will also nodded.

I exploded. "Why the hell didn't someone bother to tell me you two are related???"

Will shrugged. "I thought everybody knew."

"Dude, you know damned good and well that I didn't know. Jeez Louise, who do you think I am? The Great Houdini? You think I am a mind reader or something? Hell, you just lied to me. Again."

"You're talking about stuff you don't understand, Sassy," Will warned, cutting his eyes at Fancy. "And I'd be mighty careful about calling people liars right about now, girl."

Fancy looked stunned by my words. "But, you knew Will sent me to you because he said you would protect me."

"Yes, but you sure as hell never told me he's your brother!"

"Well, there is that," she muttered.

"Put the freaking gun down, Fancy! You don't even know how to shoot it! I cannot believe, you," I pointed to Will, "sent your sister to me for protection and never bothered to mention she is your sister. And you didn't even have the common decency to bring her all the way here! Do Marcus and Lily know she's your sister?"

He nodded his head. "Marc knows who she is."

I put my head in my hands. "You two never cease to amaze me. So, did you kill Simon when you learned what the sorry POS did to Fancy?"

He looked puzzled. "What is a POS?"

"Piece of shit. POS."

He tried not to laugh, shaking his head. "No, I horsewhipped the son of a bitch, tarred and feathered him, then took him to Maryland where I pitched him out, buck assed naked."

"Well, why the Sam Hill didn't you kill the mother hunchin' bastard?"

He looked shocked at the idea. "Sassy, he's a white man. You don't kill a white man for raping a ..."

"Do not say that word, William. And do not refer to your sister like that never again. Am I clear?"

He nodded. I swear he looked afraid to say another word.

"Well, now, Sassy, technically I'm his…" Fancy began.

"Oh, shut up." I pushed my hair, newly defined as the color of corn whisky, back and gave them both what I hoped was my 'evil glare'. Both squirmed but did not look like they were intimidated. "I'm getting a God Awful headache. I cannot believe all this. Go back up to Marc's tonight, William. We can talk about this in the morning. No, let me correct that: we shall talk. Don't you dare leave before we talk, do you understand? Because if you walk off without a word again, we are done. D.O.N.E. Stick me with a fork, 'cause I will be All Done."

"Yes, ma'am," he mumbled. "But you remember you got secrets of your own, Little Bit. I'm not the sole individual in this room that failed to give the other some pretty important information. And, who is Sam Hill?"

"Just shut up, William. STFU. You're not helping matters in the least," I responded as I glanced at Fancy, who looked at me curiosity all over her face. "Tomorrow, we talk. All of us. No more secrets."

Will turned back at the door, glaring at us both. "In my whole damned life, I never thought my own damned sister would pull a gun on me. I swear, I do not know what is getting into modern women these days." With that, he turned and walked out the door into the darkness of the night.

Morning came early even if we did turn in late the night before. I groaned as light seeped through the window, and pulled the pillow over my head. "I… do… not... want… to… get… up."

Fancy strode in and threw the covers off me. "Too bad. It's way past time to rise and shine. Will's downstairs, drinking coffee, raising Cain that I need to get you up."

"Did you tell him it's not in your job description?" I groaned again. "Can't he come back later?"

She shook her head. "No, ma'am. It is past 8, and he says he's here to clear the air. Time to face the music, Sass. Get up." She thrust a steaming hot cup of coffee into my hands.

I peeled one eyelid open. "Jesus. I've had three hours of sleep. Maybe. Cream?"

Fancy nodded.

"Sugar?"

She nodded again, chuckling. "Two lumps."

I moaned as I shoved my hair back over my shoulder. "Fine, I'll be right down."

A few minutes later, I straggled down the stairs. I cheated and put on my nicest outfit since Will was waiting for me. I brushed the tangles out my hair and pulled it into a chignon, with a little lace cap, to look as presentable as possible with a paltry three hours of sleep. After all, a girl wants to look pretty for her beau.

Will grinned when I walked into the kitchen, to pour myself another cup of coffee. After I gulped down that second cup of the dark, rich brew, I sighed. "Okay. I think I may live now. So, William, hit me with your best shot. What do you want to know?"

Will looked at me before answering. "Are we going to talk in front of Fancy?"

I shrugged as I took another long sip of coffee. "I don't know why not. She's family. She's your sister. She's my friend and lives here with me. She's like a sister to me already. She should know these things."

He nodded. "To a certain degree. If it won't endanger her."

I nodded. "Agreed."

Fancy looked from Will to me and back again. "What are you two talking about?"

I chuckled. "Who starts, Will? You or me?"

"Me. My story is easier." He walked across to the window. "Fancy, sometimes I go on these trips to..."

"Gather information for the General," she interjected. "I knew that for a long time now."

Will looked surprised. "How did you figure this out?"

She grinned. "Tom told me way befo' he went to Saratoga. He told me to be patient with you, because sometimes you might have things on your mind that would distractify you around the plantation." She grinned again. "So, what's next?"

Will's jaw had just about hit the floor. He looked speechless. Finally, he stammered, "Tom told you? My brother, Tom?"

She nodded. "Our brother, Tom. Yes."

"Well, damn. And you never said a word to me about it?"

"Not my place to discuss it with you. Unless you brought it up."

"I wish all women felt that way," Will muttered.

"Well, I have a question." I said.

Will tilted his head at me. "Of course, you do. You always have questions. What is it this time?"

I smiled. "What do we say if British soldiers come here looking for you?"

He blinked. "Damn. I hadn't thought of that. We're so far west, I can't see them comin' to Indian Territory. Why might they come out here, Sass? You know something we should know?"

I grinned, shaking my head. "No, but I know a number of the Southern Governors have loyalist leanings. I wouldn't be surprised if they led the Brits to believe there's a lot of loyalists in the backwaters who would fight for King and Country. So, what if they show up?"

He pondered the question before he brightened, and said, "I've got it! Wouldn't they ask for Lord Ranscome?"

Fancy and grinned at each other. "I never met any Lord Ranscome here. Much less looked like a lord! But what if they ask for William Selk?"

"Then you aren't sure how long it's been since you saw the sorry ol' reprobate. Selk's not someone who sticks in your mind."

I snorted. "Yeah, sure."

Will grinned at me. "Do I stick in your mind, girl?"

I just rolled my eyes. "Not gonna give you the pleasure of the answer to that one, you old reprobate. What if you're here?"

That appeared to stump him. "Well, now, that could be a problem. What do you think?"

We puzzled over that as we sipped our coffee. Finally, Fancy slapped her hands together. "I know!"

"What, Fancy?" Will asked.

"Sassy's husband was named Owen. If they are here when you show up, or if you're already here when they show up, we just tell them that you're Owen Winslow, Sassy's husband." She sat back, a self-satisfied smile playing on her lips. "The name is the code that the Redcoats are here."

Will tilted his head at me. "What do you think, Sassy?"

"I think your baby sister is pretty smart. Maybe she should be the spy and you should just play the role of my husband. There isn't another Owen Winslow here about that I know of. It would warn us all if they showed up looking for Lord Ranscome or Will Selk. Likewise, it would be a clear warning to the others if you introduced yourself as Owen, or one of us called you Owen, that the Redcoats were here. Yes, I think it would work!"

We spent the morning fine tuning the details of our safety net if we ever needed it. After lunch, Will and I went to explain the plan to Marcus and Lily. Lily acted surprised to learn Fancy was Will's half-sister. Marc kept quiet, with a smile playing on his lips.

Finally, I spoke up. "You knew who she was, didn't you?"

He nodded. "I remember a beautiful little girl named Fancy at Belle Rose."

"Why didn't you tell?"

He stopped puffing on his pipe long enough to answer. "Wasn't my place to tell. It's not like she's my relative. If Will wanted you to know, he would tell you."

I frowned. "Don't you think that's kind of weird?"

Marcus grinned at me. "Girl, I've lived through weird, and this is not the weird stuff. Believe me. I figured if William didn't say who Fancy was, he had his reasons."

I just stood there gaping at him. Will came over, tapped my chin, and whispered, "Shut your mouth, Little Bit. Don't let the flies in."

I snapped my mouth shut. "Don't call me that."

"Then don't call me Dude."

I rolled my eyes. "You are such a pain in the ass, William Selk. I don't know why – oh, never mind..."

He grinned. "Don't know why 'what', Sass?"

I sighed. "You never cut me a break, you know it?"

He grinned, those damned dimples showing through that hideous beard. "Neither one of us ever cuts the other one a break, Little Bit. What don't you know?"

I sighed again, and plopped down into a chair as I took the proffered cup of Marc's brew. "Oh, dammit, Will. I do not for the life of me know why I had to go and fall in love with a man like you. Especially with that hideous old scratchy beard!"

Will grinned at Marc. "I told you she would admit it."

Marcus looked woeful at his last unopened bottle of 12 year old whisky.

"Aye, and a promise is a promise. Here it is. Take the damned stuff."

Lily and I looked back and forth, confused by their words. Finally, I answered. "You bet the man I would tell you I love you?"

Will nodded. "Before Christmas. Marcus thought it would take until February."

As his words sank in, I realized what he was saying. "You jerk! I cannot believe you two bet not just whether I would fall in love with you, but how soon! You sorry ..."

"Calm down, Sassy," Lily said. "You do love this jerk. I love my jerk. All men are jerks. We can't live with them and we can't live without them."

I realized she was right. I loved Will. He loved me. But it was complicated. It would always be complicated. Lord knew we were from different worlds. I knew it was both a blessing and a curse to feel everything as I felt right now, as I figured I would feel as long as this man was in my life, and beyond.

Will leaned close to me. "I love you, Little Bit. I told you that in November. I hoped you'd realize you loved me soon. I glad you did. I'm sorry I upset you." He kissed my cheek. "Will you forgive me?"

I tried to look fierce with little success. "Fine."

"Will you? Forgive me?" He delivered little butterfly kisses down the side of my face to my neck.

"Kiss me again proper and I'll think about it."

That was when I realized that crow tastes a lot like McCarron's 12 year old whisky. Not so bad, with a good kiss. As I pulled back from Will's lingering caresses, I grinned. "Want to know what Wolf told me that day? When he kissed me by the camp?"

Will bristled at the memory, and then nodded abruptly. "Yeah. What did that heathen devil say?"

"He said he thought this Lost Woman, who came from Beyond, was meant to be his Found Woman, but he was wrong. I was a Lost Woman when I came, but you were the one meant to find me and love me. I was meant to love you, and when I realized that, I would be a Lost Woman no more, but I would be your Found Woman. Because you have to be lost to be found."

Will's eyes widened in surprise. "Wolf said that? For real?"

Wordless, I nodded.

Will looked shamefaced. "What was it you called me that day?"

"Dim-witted knucklehead comes to mind."

He tried to hide the grin that shimmered across his face as he turned and walked towards the fence, where he stood staring in the direction of the Cherokee village. "Looks like I owe him an apology."

I nodded, as I slipped under his arm to snuggle close. "I think it might be very timely."

Will pulled me tight to him and bent down for another deep, long kiss. When it ended, he smiled. I thought, yep. Tastes a lot like McCarron's 12 year old blended whisky. And that's pretty danged good.

He began to fumble as he unbuttoned his pocket, and finally pulled something out. "Sassy, I meant to ask this before when I came, when I acted like a dim-witted knucklehead."

I laughed. He abruptly dropped to one knee. As I realized what he was doing, my heart dropped to my toes.

"Sarah Alinora Winslow, will you do me the honor of marryin' me?"

Words would not come. I batted at the tears flooding my eyes, and nodded, wordless. Finally, I whispered, "Yes."

I didn't even fuss at him for calling me Sarah Alinora.

He bent over my hands and kissed them. Sweetest thing a man had ever done, I swear. And then, he slid the object he had pulled from his pocket onto my ring finger. It was an elegant ring with a central emerald-cut pink stone surrounded by rose cut diamonds. A delicate gold rope trim surrounded the gold setting. Made in the Georgian style, it had gold across the back of the foiled stones. With tears in my eyes, I whispered, "It's beautiful, Will. I love it."

I was surprised to see his eyes mist over, too. He stood up again, and he leaned his head down against mine. "It was my mama's engagement ring. The big stone's not a diamond; my daddy said it's a pink tourmaline, but it has rose cut diamonds all around it. I hope you don't mind."

My heart lurched. It was very special he gave me the ring his father gave his mother in 1718, sixty years before. Jewelry often followed in families from generation to generation. "I don't mind at all. I'm honored you gave it to me. It's exquisite, a beautiful ring. I will treasure it, William. But..."

He frowned. "But what, darlin'?"

I gulped. "Your mama's dead, right? I didn't dream that?"

"Yes, but, why?" he nodded, with a puzzled look.

"Oh, no reason. Just checking." I would not tell him how mean Owen's mother was to me, calling me everything from a wetback to a trashy little Mexican whore. It didn't matter that my mother's family was Spanish, that we could trace our family back to Spain, and that I had a Ph.D. in history. All that mattered was that I somehow stole Nell's son. Shit, he was married to Kathryn 10 years before he married me! Of course, who knew what kind of poison Kathryn fed her. I would never again marry a man whose mother lived. Not after the way she treated me. When she learned Owen and I reconciled and she socked me in the face and broke my nose. Of course, she always said she had a demon on her back. I believed her. If anyone was demon possessed, it was Nell. I didn't even tell her when Owen died until after the services and he was buried. And I was the one who forced him to go see his mother every time he saw her after she attacked me until he died. Mean old woman just couldn't die while Owen lived.

Will bent down to kiss me again, and I reached around his neck to pull him closer to me.

I felt more special, more loved, more cherished than I felt in a long, long time. Maybe my whole life. Our kisses continued, right there in front of God and everyone, until finally Will swept me into his arms. I held on tight as he walked back to my little house, and began climbing the stairs to my room. As he passed Fancy, he gave her a look that precluded any discussion. I tucked my head to his chest after I saw her scurry towards Bella, grab her up, and run out the door.

"She's gone for the night," I murmured.

"Good."

Different from the last time he carried me up the stairs in November, he was gentle as he laid me onto the bed, before laying down beside me. I trembled as the length of his body pressed against me and the rope mattress swayed beneath the weight of our bodies. I began to unlace my jumps until impatient, Will could wait no longer and finished the job for me as I giggled.

He spread my jumps apart, and eased my breasts out of my shift. He lowered his head to my brush his face across one and then the other. I quivered at the seductive rasp of his whiskers against my bare skin. Such an unexpected delight! I pressed my breasts against his face, exulting in the pure sensuality of the sensation of skin on skin.

It had been a long time. Far too long.

I sighed and leaned up on one crooked arm, enjoying the sight as he eased his shirt off, and began to unlace his breeches. As he undressed, I loosened my chignon and shook my hair loose with my fingers. When he realized I was watching him, he stopped, and raised an eyebrow. "Everything okay?"

I nodded, a smile on my lips, as I shook my hair over my shoulders. "Very okay. Please, don't let me disturb you. Continue."

He grinned at my blatant invitation, and he shucked out of his breeches and small clothes. In the blink of an eye, he was back on the bed beside me, and he untied my petticoat and slid it down over my hips and from me with a flourish as it slipped away from my feet. He then eased my shoes off. It was a bit shocking to realize I was lying there darned near stark assed naked except for my stockings! He paused for a moment at my stockings, and then with a wicked grin I knew I should know from someplace in the future, he trailed kisses from my foot up the stocking until he came to the garters. He untied the garters with his teeth, and then tugged the stockings off with another row of seductive kisses.

I panted as he finished his homage to my worn and tattered stockings.

"What's this?" Will leaned over, tracing the words etched on my foot. I realized he probably had never seen a woman with a tattoo before. He grinned. "Not all who wander are lost."

"As in, some of us just like to travel. Or maybe, some of us are looking for home."

"Well, you naughty little thing, you found home." He blew out the candle. "They say 'home is where the heart is,' and I danged sure hope your heart is with me. What's that word you use, sexy? Well, girl, that little tattoo on your foot might just be the sexiest thing I ever discovered hidden on a woman."

With a sigh of relief, I pulled him back to me. I was his Found Woman now, no longer lost. "Not all who wander are lost, but you must be lost to be found. I am your Found Woman, Will."

It was approaching 7 the next morning before I arose. I stretched, luxuriating in that glow you have after a night of really fabulous sex. You know, extraordinary sex. Mind blowing sex. I mean, Owen was good, but oh my God, Becky! This was Best Sex in Your Life Sex. With a smug smile playing on my lips, I came downstairs, and poured myself a cup of my morning brew. As I took a sip, I looked around, my JBF hair still all around my shoulders and down my back, and asked, "Where's Will?"

Fancy looked at me in dismay. "Sassy, don't you tell me you don't know where that man is. He went for his horse. He's headed out."

"He left? Without telling me?" I choked on my coffee, spitting it everywhere.

She nodded, and pointed towards the stables. "Not more 'n five minutes ago. You better run if you plan to catch him, girl."

"He left? Are you serious? I'll freaking kill him if he takes off again without a word!" I exclaimed, as I slammed down the cup and rushed to peer out the window. Before Fancy could answer, I grabbed a shawl to throw around my shoulders over my shift, and scurried out of the cabin barefooted. Long hair trailing wild behind me, I ran towards the lone figure on the big black stallion headed out of McCarron's Corner.

"William Selk, don't you dare leave like this!" I exclaimed as I raced towards him.

I had a catch in my side by the time I caught up with him. Will wheeled the horse around, and looked shocked to see I was following him. He spurred the big black to gallop back to me. As he approached, unconsciously, I must have reached up towards him, because he reached down to swing me into his arms.

My heart sang as he pulled me close to his chest. I reached up, and pulled his head to me, where I met his lips with mine with eager abandon. And right then, I wanted to show him with that kiss was that he had never been loved like this before. I wanted him to feel with one kiss that I could make love to his soul for all eternity.

I realized with a start that was what 'soul mate' meant.

"Don't ever do that again, Selk," I warned, my voice tremulous. "You can't just ride off into the sunset."

Will laughed. "Sun's just come up, Little Bit. I wasn't gonna leave before

I came back to tell you goodbye for now, darlin'. I'm headed to talk to Wolf."

He bent his head down to touch his lips to mine in the barest angel kiss, before he grinned, and then plunged back to plunder my mouth with his own. I moaned into his mouth, as I arched closer to him, sure I had died and gone to heaven. He finally pulled back, as he chuckled, and said, "I'll be back, darlin', don't you fret. Come spring time, I will be back for you." He kissed me again.

As I pulled back, I struggled to smile. My voice trembling, I said, "You better. And don't you dare go to Savannah."

He grinned, and nodded before he eased me off the horse. He trailed his fingers down the side of my face to my throat before he answered. "I won't. I promise. Don't much like to get my ass whupped. I'm going to talk to Wolf before I leave. I owe him that apology. Now, can I have a lock of your pretty hair to take with me?"

I nodded, as he pulled out his knife and sliced off a tendril, before he bent over from his horse to kiss me again. "I love you."

I stood on the ridge overlooking the trail to the north as he rode off. *Please, dear God, please take care of this man. Please bring him back to me, safe and sound. Por favor.*

As he disappeared into the horizon, I realized there was a nip in the air. I smiled wryly. Finally. Winter Is Coming. I shivered, praying it would not be a Westeros - Game of Thrones kind of hard winter.

Chapter Ten

It was cold. Damned cold. Lily said it was the coldest winter she could remember, including the winter she spent with the Cherokees in '63-64. Winter in Westeros could not be any worse, although I doubted there were any White Walkers out and about. By Christmas, we couldn't have gone to Savannah if we tried. Snow drifts were already well over two feet deep, with winter just begun. The stock was brought into the barns, and ropes stretched from the houses to the barns, so we could feed the animals every day. Other ropes reached to the necessaries, for obvious reasons.

I shivered, as I pulled the rough wool shawl up tighter around my shoulders, wishing I could turn up the central heating. But, central heat had not been invented because humans had no idea yet what electricity could do. I lifted the heavy, frozen logs to carry them back into the house. The fire was burning low, and we needed more firewood. No central air and heat. No gas stoves. Hell, no wood stoves for that matter. Just fireplaces out here in the backwoods wilderness. And we couldn't let the fire die down or we would die. It was just that simple. If the fire went out, we would freeze to death. I didn't plan to let that happen.

I'd hoped it wouldn't be so bad, not having Will there for Christmas. But it was cold, bleak, dreary. And I was lonely. Even surrounded with friends, I was damned lonely. After all, it was the first Christmas in my entire life I was not with family. Friends, yes, but not my family, even if friends can become your chosen family. It was the first Christmas I would not be with the man I had finally accepted that I loved. The man I had finally accepted as my soul mate. The man the Good Lord brought me here to meet. The man who was missing from me even before he even left town.

Jim and I are twins, even though we were born in different years. He was born just before midnight on December 31, and I was born minutes later on

January 1st. It was part of the reason he always loved bragging that he was my older brother. Anyway, I missed Jim and home more than usual that New Year's Eve and New Year's Day. It was the first birthday my brother had not been with me to celebrate. He was also missing from me. And in fact, he hadn't even been born yet. I wondered if that somehow meant I was the older one now, since I was living more than 200 years before Jim (or I) were born in the Beyond.

Love is a funny thing. It can make you happy. It can make you sad. Sometimes, it can just about kill you with longing. I missed Will so damned bad that it hurt physically as well as mentally. I missed his voice, his smile, his smell, his touch, his hugs and kisses. His jokes, however lame they could be at times. Even his temper. I missed my man and how my man made me feel. I missed everything about my Will.

Tu me manques.

I realized I was no longer the woman I was the year before. Losing Owen changed me. Loving Will changed me more. Life, death and a new love had reshaped me. Loving someone who was not with me was hard. It hurts when you love someone who has captured your heart but you can't have them in your arms. But he was in my soul, part of me now, and I hoped it all was making me stronger, more resilient. After all, as Tolkien said, not all who wander are lost. I had realized you have to be lost to be found. And as I had told Will, I was his Found Woman, lost no more.

Still, that Christmas, and New Year's, away from the ones I loved, I was lonely. Empty. Bleak. I knew I'd stop missing Will when I was with him again. Patience is a good thing to have, when you love a man who is gone, when you love a man who is missing from you. But distance can't stop what is meant to be, and I was meant to be here, in 1779, head over heels in love with Will Selk.

It was ironic. Thinking about Will kept me awake at night, while dreaming about him could keep me asleep, even when I needed to get up and fetch more logs to keep the fire burning.

Shivering, I remembered the words of the old Christmas carol, not yet written:

In the bleak midwinter, frosty wind made moan,

Earth stood hard as iron, water like a stone;

Snow had fallen, snow on snow, snow on snow,

In the bleak midwinter, long, long ago.

I smiled wryly. I always loved that song. I sure never thought I would literally live that first verse. I knew the song dealt with Jesus coming to save us, hence the reference to the bleakness before He came. But the words sang true, so true, that God awful frozen morning. In the warmth of my centrally heated homes, I had never understood the truth of the phrase, 'bleak midwinter'. Frosty winds did make the house moan, sometimes so loud you thought the timbers were cracking and that they might fall. The earth was indeed frozen hard as iron. We had two die that winter, and they were literally stacked like cord wood in the ice house until the spring thaw. The ground was hard as iron, far too hard to dig holes in which to bury them. Water was frozen hard as a stone. It was hard to thaw it even pouring hot water on top of the frozen. And snow. So much snow! I'd never seen so much snow, not even when Owen and I lived in Boston for those years while at Harvard. *Pahk the cah in Hahvahd yahd,* I mused, in my sad attempt at a 'Hahvahd' accent, as I watched the snow falling relentless, without end. And to think I had looked forward to the snow in Northern Georgia when we moved!

Snow was falling, snow on snow, snow on snow.

I sighed. The battle at Savannah occurred as I foretold on December 28th. Campbell's army landed unopposed on a bluff below Savannah as the weather took an unexpected turn for the worse. The seasoned British soldiers located an unguarded sheep path and crept with great stealth around General Howe's defenders, effectively cutting them off from the city. The battle was soon over. Campbell lost virtually no soldiers. In contrast, most all of the brave but grossly unprepared and unorganized patriots of Georgia either died or were captured as a rare snow began falling along the Georgia coast.

It was reported to have been a sad day for the new Republic, and a glorious day to be British.

In the weeks that followed, it seemed the Redcoats could not be stopped. Campbell waited for the arrival of Prevost's Royal Americans and Brown's Rangers from Florida. On January 24th, in a heavy snow, they began their march to Augusta through the back country. They said later that except for a minor skirmish at the Burke County Courthouse, Campbell's men were unopposed, and by January 31, 1779, they took Augusta. It seemed the British Southern Strategy had worked. Fourteen hundred Loyalists enlisted in the royal militia.

But I knew the Battle of Kettle Creek was soon to come. And I knew the tides of war would change with that important battle.

The true bleakness for me in the winter of 1778 - 1779 was the fact that Will – my Will – was not with me. I didn't know if he had listened to me and stayed away from Savannah. I didn't know if he was warm. If he missed me. If he was safe. Or if he was injured somewhere, with no one to help him.

Or worse, if he were dead.

I stifled a sob, and blinked the tears already freezing on my lashes, and started back towards the cabin. You can't think that way, Sassy, I thought. But relentless as the winds and the snow itself, the words of the old song circled through my brain again and again. Snow had fallen, snow on snow, snow on snow, In the bleak midwinter, long, long ago.

—

The winter of 2018 was bleak, Jim thought. Grey, cold and bleak.

A gentle hand tugged at his sleeve. "Come on, darling. We need to turn back. It is too rough to go on up there today."

Jim stared at the frozen waters ahead of them as he pondered whether he could make it across the ice if he pushed himself hard enough. He knew it could get cold in Georgia, but he'd never seen so much ice or snow since moving here five years before. Of course, this was a lot further north than Kennesaw, and definitely not just outside Atlanta. His shoulders sagged, and with a sigh, he nodded to his wife. "Okay. Let's go back."

She nodded. "You have to let this all go, Jim. It's time. You have to face it, and let it go. You're not going to find her."

Jim didn't say it, as one word rang through his mind.

Never.

—

Backwater Georgia has always been known for its stubbornness. Just because

Campbell took Augusta did not mean he won the war. Just because 1400 Loyalists enlisted did not mean he would win the war.

In early January, Marcus received the muster call he had been expecting to go to Kettle Creek. He talked to the men in the village, and almost to a man they agreed to go fight for the Cause, even though we were in Indian Territory, not Georgia. They were unwilling to resume taxation without representation, even out here in our remote little unknown corner of the world.

On February 3, 1779, Marcus and Lily left with 30 ragtag but hale and hardy men from McCarron's Corner to rally to the call. They left old Emmett as the man in charge in their absence, and left me as virtual dictator to run the little village in their absence.

I knew we would win at Kettle Creek. I also knew we would have losses. I was pretty sure Will would meet them there, and I was scared pissless. So as the snow fell, as the wind raged, as the wood stack got smaller, and as the food supplies dwindled, I reigned over my little band of women and children, with one valiant old man to help me.

Please, God, let my Will come back. Please. And as I prayed, I remembered an old tune, which I thought came from the Civil War.

When Johnny comes marching home again, hoorah, hoorah!

We'll give a hearty welcome again, hoorah, hoorah!

The men will cheer and the boys will shout,

The ladies they will all turn out.

And we'll all be glad when Johnny comes marching home.

I chuckled. For a tone deaf woman, I love music. My love's name wasn't Johnny. But I would be glad, so glad, when my William came marching home.

When you are married to a man for 14 years, who specialized in the Revolutionary War period, and when you become a history professor under his tutelage, you learn a lot of trivia about the war years. For instance, I knew that the winter of 1777 - 1778 was a horribly harsh winter, when 2500 men died at Valley Forge, due to the harsh weather and lack of food. And I knew that the winter of 1778-'79 was harsh in the South, in fact, had long been considered to have been the harshest winter in the South for at least 100 years, before or after. Even harsher than the winter of 1779 - 1780, the Hard

Winter, in which far less people died than had that fateful winter at Valley Forge. But knowing it, is different than living through anything like that.

Snow had fallen, I mused, snow on snow. Snow on freaking snow. Snow fell almost every day for 2 months now. As the end of February approached, spring should have been approaching with it. Yet, a new blizzard blew in. I guesstimated the temperature had dropped to about 400 degrees below zero. And that seemed generous. I never in my life have known such God awful, excruciating, bone chilling cold, such insufferable unending snow. Chilblains are a terrible thing to suffer.

Such bleakness. I decided hell was not a pit of fire; it was endless, unrelenting, bitter cold. The kind of cold we had that winter.

On the morning of February 26th, the winds and snows had blown for fourteen days without break. The men and Lily had been gone for a little over 3 weeks. I coaxed everyone to move into my house. We were using far too much fire wood trying to keep the cabins heated when we could all huddle together in one large room and share heat to try to survive the endless soul searing, gut wrenching cold. I hoped with us all together, we might better conserve our foodstuffs, too, because we were running low on just about everything right now, except, cringe, you guessed it, pickled okra and sauerkraut. I have to admit, more than once, I wished we were still getting that venison from the Cherokee every week.

I have to admit, more than once, I wished we were still getting venison from Shadow Wolf every week. Fancy even offered to trek over to find a brave who would bring her meat, but I told her it was too dangerous.

"Death's too dangerous, Sass. We need food," she retorted. But the snow was too deep and she couldn't find the trail.

Everyone brought extra clothing and bedding. I even broke out fabric yardage to serve as extra bedding. Frozen people surrounded with piles of unused fabric would be just plain stupid. I could wash the fabric later for use, once the water thawed out, but right now, we had to stay warm enough to survive. So, everyone had a thrown together quilt of sorts, in addition to anything else they brought over for warmth.

Fancy and I made a big pot of stew that afternoon, with the last of the potatoes, carrots, and a bit of leftover meat. It was more gravy than anything else, but people ate like they were starving, sopping it up with the biscuits we made from some of the last of the flour.

That helped, but the food was not going to last much longer at all, and we had children and old people to feed. I was relatively young and healthy. I could wait a few more days for much of anything to eat. I knew a person could go a month without food. I hadn't gone near that long yet. I lost some poundage, and I wasn't about to complain about that.

If Lily and Marcus would just get back. I knew they would bring supplies we needed with the utmost urgency. And if my Will would somehow get back. I felt everything would be fine if Will got back. I needed to feel those strong arms wrap around me again. I even longed for the scratch of that scraggly old beard across my skin. Now, that was desperate, I thought!

I forced myself to eat a couple of pieces of pickled okra, my thoughts bleak. Oh, well, my throat ached and I didn't have much of an appetite anyway. I wanted chicken soup, and I was not going to kill a laying hen just to make myself a pot of soup.

By dark, the wind was howling like a crazed coyote. We could hear the shutters on one of the other houses rattling in the wind. People shifted nervously, worried if the roof would hold up to the weight of the unrelenting snow, growing heavier by the minute.

I coughed again as I realized the horses and cows had to be fed. I began bundling up to go out for the evening run to feed the critters. I pulled my rough, homespun woolen cloak around my shoulders, flipped the hood up, and tied the hood under my chin, coughing a few more times as I thought about venturing out in the bitter winds. As I finished pulling on my fur lined mittens, and reached for the door, it swung open.

My mouth fell open in shock, soon replaced with delight. Heart beating hard and fast, I rushed to the lone figure standing in the doorway, throwing my arms around him in a bear hug he had not expected.

My Will had come back to me.

"Oh, thank God," I murmured, as I swooned.

He pushed back the hood on my cloak, and stroked my hair. "Why, Little Bit? I told you I'd be back."

I grinned up at him. "I had been praying you would come sooner than spring, but I didn't expect to see you for another month with all this snow. And yet here you are, thank God! Oh, Will, we needed you here so badly. I

... I needed you here so badly," I choked out the words, overcome with emotion.

He bent back down to me, and kissed first one eyelid and then another. "Silly woman," he murmured, "I couldn't let anything happen to you, now, could I? Or to Fancy or little Bella. Or the rest of these good people. You have anything to eat?"

My heart sank. I gulped. "Not much. Would you like a biscuit and some stew?"

He laughed as he picked me up and spun me around. "No, you silly goose, I brought you food! Lily warned me that stores would be running low up here. Now, who wants some fine Virginia ham? I toted this thing all the way from Belle Rose for you people!"

Everyone came running at once.

Fancy had that ham sliced and on the table with sweet potatoes, rice, biscuits and gravy when Will and I got back from feeding the animals. A pot of coffee was boiling over the fire. The house felt warmer and cozier than I had dreamed possible, and I felt warmer than I had felt in weeks. Not a balanced meal, I thought, but one that would stick to our ribs and give us some much needed energy. Fancy and I emptied the two pails of fresh milk into glasses, and people soon had a warm meal filling their bellies. I leaned against Will, marveling again that he had somehow managed against great odds to come right when we needed him desperately. As babies began to fall asleep in their mama's arms, content with full tummies, I began to nod off myself snuggled against Will's strong shoulder. I remember he chuckled as I burrowed my head close against the place where his arm met his shoulder, and he pulled me closer to him.

His body warmth was wonderful.

"Damn, you're thin. And you have fever," he murmured. "I don't like that cough."

"I never run fever," I protested. "And the cough is nothing. I'll be fine. It's just a little cold. Besides, I wanted to lose weight."

He didn't answer as I began coughing again. My throat burned raw, and I ached all over. I could tell he was still worried, despite my earnest protestations. I burrowed closer against him. "Tell me again," I commanded.

He laughed. "You are the bossiest little bit of sass I ever met, skinny girl.

Okay. Where do I start this time?"

"At the beginning. Tell me everything that happened since you left in December."

Will explained that he had made his way to Charleston after he left in December, following my advice not to return to Savannah. From there, he sailed north to Virginia, where he was lucky enough to catch the Commander-in-Chief and talk plans for the coming year before Will began to wend his way back south towards Kettle Creek.

"Why?" I asked, my curiosity ripe.

"I damned sure wasn't going to miss the chance to be at Kettle Creek. Not when I knew it would be the battle that will change the tide of the war in the south," he grinned. "Kettle Creek flows into the Little River near the Tyrone Community in Wilkes County, Georgia." He took a sip of his hot coffee. "Fancy, that coffee sure tastes mighty fine this evening." She flashed a bright smile at him, and patted him on the back as she refilled his cup. "Anyway, the story was Boyd arrived at Wrightsborough on January 24th. I hear tell he was searching for guides to the frontier in the Carolinas. He established a camp over in South Carolina, and then with somethin' like 350 recruits, he set out for Augusta on February 5th. Along the way, he was joined by 250 additional Carolinians under the command of John Moore." He took another long sip of coffee before he continued. "I have to admit, it did not look good for our boys at first. Our men were ineffective in their pursuit of the Loyalists, heck fire, you could say they were three bricks shy of a load." Everyone laughed. "Boyd captured Ft. Independence and Broad Mouth Creek, in South Carolina. For some odd reason, he decided against attacking the garrison of McGowan's Blockhouse, located on the Cherokee Ford of the Savannah River. Instead, he decided to cross the river further north at Vann's Creek on February 11. The Cherokee Ford Garrison attacked Boyd's men at the crossing, but they were repulsed. Boyd must have felt pretty dadblamed confident as he sat camped with his men at Kettle Creek on February 14th, and he dispatched prisoners to Augusta. After all, so far, he was batting one thousand, ain't that what you say, Sass?"

I grinned at his reference to a baseball term I was prone to use, determined not to attempt to explain that one to the crowd right now. "Something like that, yes."

"Ol' Boyd didn't know the British troops he expected to rendezvous with him began their withdrawal that morning towards Savannah. In other words, the Loyalists were left high and dry by the British troops that the Loyalists were there to support. Boyd didn't get the help he was dependin' on."

"Serves the bastards right," shouted Emmett Sullivan. Jeannette smiled as she continued knitting.

Will grinned. I decided that history is definitely better when experienced firsthand, or at the retelling by a truly fabulous story teller like my man. "About the same time, 340 South Carolina and Georgia militiamen, under the direction of Col. Andrew Pickens of South Carolina, and Col. John Dooly and Lt. Col. Elijah Clark of Georgia were preparing to attack Boyd's camp at Kettle Creek. These brave Patriots had been bedeviling Loyalists at Robert Carr's Fort on Beaver Dam Creek. They abandoned their prey at Beaver Dam to intercept Boyd's party. Pickens led his 200 in a direct assault on Kettle Creek, while Dooley and Clarke attacked the camp across the creek from both the left and the right."

Everyone was cheering with excitement, but Will was not finished. "It got a little dicey there. You see, Pickens' advance guard disobeyed orders and fired on the Loyalist sentries, and that was a sure enough damned shame, because it announced the attack to the Loyalists. Boyd then led his troops in ambushing Pickens' troops while Dooly's and Clarke's men were struggling through the frozen swamp. Things were looking bad, even if Boyd's back up troops didn't show up."

The crowd murmured, as they shifted uneasily back and forth. Old Emmett asked the question everyone was thinking. "Well, then how the Sam Hill did we win the battle?"

I chuckled that he had picked up one of my expressions from the future.

"Well, you see, Emmett, the Good Lord was on our side. He sent us an unexpected bit of luck. That damned Irishman caught a shot and fell from a mortal wound. His men panicked with their leader down, and couldn't hold their ranks. They turned tail and ran."

"Like the cowards they are," Emmett muttered, with numerous heads nodding in agreement.

Will dissented. "Nope, they were fighting pretty damned good till Boyd fell. That just rattled them. They just had one leader and no back up plan in case of something like this, and they didn't know what to do. At final count, Boyd and 19 of his men were killed. Another 22 were taken prisoner right then. On our side, Pickens and Dooly lost 7 men, with 15 wounded. Another 150 of Boyd's men were taken prisoner later. I don't know what happened after that. Lily was patching up soldiers as fast as she could sew. I got my supplies together and headed here. They should be back in a few days."

I knew 7 of Boyd's men would hang for treason. Another 270 escaped and reached the British army.

Most important, my Will survived.

We all sat around talking for another hour or two. I fell asleep against Will's shoulder, and woke up when he shook me. "Wake up, Little Bit. It's late. Let's get you up to bed." I nodded groggily, and reached up to put my arms around his neck. He lifted me up, and carried me up to bed.

"Take your hat off and stay a spell," I coaxed.

He grinned. "Don't have time to take my hat off. God almighty, girl, I missed you somethin' awful."

I pulled him down to me, and threw the disreputable looking, battered old hat across the room. "I missed you, too. Come make love to me. Show me how much you missed me." I pulled his face to mine, and met his kiss mid-air as he bent to me.

It was hours before we fell asleep in each other's arms, and when we did, I was too tired to be aware of anything except my Will was back. I slept well that night in his arms.

The next morning, we arose early to make our way down from McCarron's Corner to Little Froggy. Will assured me it would just take a couple of hours. He tried to talk me out of going, but I wanted to spend all the time I could with him, and a silly little cold was not going to keep me at the Corner while he went for more supplies. I bundled up warm as possible, with long johns under my jeans, shift, a wool sweater over my shift, two quilted petticoats, and a quilted overskirt under my large, woolen overcoat. The overcoat was originally made for a man, but I had commandeered it as my own several weeks before when I became the person primarily responsible for feeding the animals. My feet were covered with two pairs of stockings and my hiking socks and hiking boots. Wool gloves beneath my fur lined mittens protected my hands. A wool scarf was tied around my head and a wool shawl was over my head and shoulders. I covered it all up with my long blue wool cloak. I was pretty sure I was dressed warm enough to tackle Antarctica, or at least I thought so until we had ridden a few miles.

We rode along in silence for some time, except for my coughing which was worse, with occasional sneezing bouts. I couldn't believe how deep the snow was in places. There were snowdrifts some places deeper than I am tall. The river was frozen over for the most part, hard enough that the horses could cross it with care without breaking through to the frigid waters below. I shivered as the north wind cut through my layers of woolens that seemed so warm a few miles ago. We made good time; the path was much easier on horseback, even in the heavy snow, than the path I took last summer with the dogs. I focused on Will's back as it became harder and harder to keep sitting in my saddle. My hands numb, my back and arms ached from the effort to stay on the horse. I could have sworn my butt froze through and through. I hoped Will know would not realize I was having a harder and harder time staying astride my horse. Mesmerized by the rhythmical movement of the horses, I began to doze off. Suddenly, I was falling.

"Sassy! What's wrong?" Will wheeled his horse around towards me as I apparently let out a shriek as I began slipping from the horse's back. Will pulled me out of the snow bank, as I set off into another bout of coughing. "Dammit, girl, I knew you were sick. I shouldn't have brought you with me."

"I'm not sick. It's just a little cold," I murmured as I started coughing yet again.

"Yeah, sure. Little liar. Stubborn as a danged mule. So, why'd you fall off the horse?"

I shrugged, embarrassed to admit I had fallen asleep. He pulled me up onto his horse, against his broad, warm chest, and wrapped his arms around me. "There, that should keep you safe. Not much further now anyway." He kissed my brow, and then frowned. "You feel awfully warm."

"I don't run fever," I answered automatically.

"Yeah, sure," he muttered again, through clinched teeth. "My stubborn little liar."

I learned a couple of things that morning. First, don't go out in the cold when you're already sick. Secondly, it takes a lot less time to traverse between McCarron's Corner to Little Froggy when you're on horseback. Third, it is colder than Hell if you fall into a snow bank. Fourth, Will is warm.

Within the hour, we arrived at Froggy. I had fallen asleep again, warm and safe snuggled up against my man's chest. The wool of his jacket scruffed against my cheek in a most comforting manner, I remember thinking as we rode.

When we arrived, Will shook me. "We're here, Sass. Wake up, darlin'."

I forced myself to rouse up. Eyes heavy with sleep can be hard to open, I realized. I nodded, as I realized I was thirsty.

"Und vat you haff here, Vilhelm?" fussed a feminine Germanic accent. I looked around to see a tall, slender woman with greying brown hair waddling towards the horses through the snow.

Will chuckled. "Hillie, I have my fiancée, Sassy Winslow. Sassy, this is Hildegard O'Brian. She's married to Angus O'Brian. They own the store here at Froggy. Everyone calls her Hillie. Hillie is from Bavaria originally."

"Nice to meet you," I murmured, and then I began to cough again.

Hillie frowned. "Vilhelm, she ist sick. Vhy you bring a sick voman out in dis veather, you schnook? Shame, boy, shame! Bring her in, und let her get varmed up by de fire!"

Hillie sounded like she was Eastern European. My guess was Russian based on her use of the word 'schnook'. Right then, all I cared about was getting off the horse into a warm bed. I was so cold I hurt.

Will helped me down from the horse, and I leaned against him as we went inside the small cabin. It was warm and cozy inside as I approached the fire. I sighed as I rubbed my hands up and down my arms, as the warmth began to seep into my body. For the first time in hours, I felt like I might thaw out.

Hillie came over, fussing again as she began to take my scarf and shawl off. "You need to get out of dese tings, girl. You are vet. Let me help you."

Like a statue, I stood there complacently as she unwound the scarf and shawl. Will frowned, and came over to help me out of my overcoat.

"Are you okay?" He fussed, worry written all over his face.

I nodded, my teeth still chattering. "Yes, I'll be fine. Just c... c... cold."

Hillie's hands stilled as one landed on my brow. "Child, you are burning up vit' fever!" she exclaimed, horror in her voice.

I pulled my mittens off. "No, I never run fever."

She shook her head right back. "Nein, nein! I have raised enough children to know vhen someone has a fever. Will, get her out of her clothes und into ze bed. Now!"

My eyes sprung open in shocked surprise. "But we have to go back today. They need supplies. Just let me rest a few minutes..."

Hillie looked grim. "Nein, nonsense. You are sick. You vill stay here. Vilhelm can take supplies back. Now, get into dat bed. I vill make you some nice bone broth. You need fluids."

I sank into the exquisite softness of the goose down mattress with a sigh. It felt so good, so warm, so comforting. I was dozing when she returned with the cup of broth.

"Here. Enjoy," Hillie said as she handed me the cup.

I drank it down without fuss as Hillie continued to fuss comfortingly at me, much like my Gramma used to fuss at me when I was a kid. With the last sip, I handed the mug back to her, and sank back down into the comforting bed. Within minutes, I was asleep.

Will hurried to gather additional supplies. Two more hams. A couple of rashers of bacon. Four dozen eggs. A 20 pound sack of taters. Another 20 pound sack of rice. Within a half hour, he had it loaded on the back of Sassy's mare, and was ready to head back to McCarron's Corner. "I'll be back later tonight, Hillie," he promised.

"*Nein, nein,* Vilhelm, is too much. You come back tomorrow. You need rest, also. I vill take care of her until you get back."

"What do you think it is?" Will asked in hushed tones.

"Pneumonia," was Hillie's curt response. "Und you better hope that Miss Lily gets back soon, because she is so much better at this than I am."

"What do we do?" Will asked, afraid of her answer.

Hillie thought before answering. "Pray. Now, take your supplies back to ze Corner. Do not come back until tomorrow. I do not need to have two patients. Pardon de French, but I vould need dat like I need a hole in my head. I vill take good care of your voman vhile you are gone. Now, get lost."

"But..."

"No buts. Pray, Vilhelm. Pray that Lily gets back. Pray that the Good Lord guides my hand und I help this girl the best I can. Pray she gets better. Pray that you have the sense to rest before you come back again. Now. Pray."

Will nodded, a lump in his throat. "Yes, ma'am."

He climbed up on his big, black stallion, and wheeled the horses back towards the Corner. "Dear Lord," he prayed, "help Hillie to keep her safe. And keep me safe on my journey. Because no matter what Hillie said, I will get back to my Sassy tonight."

It was late when Will returned. Hillie was shocked to hear him beating on the door but opened it when she realized it was Will. "Vhas you doing back here tonight? I told you come back tomorrow! I swear, you don't know from nothing! Vhas good are you to her if you drop dead from exhaustion?"

He tried to smile. "I couldn't have rested there without her. I had to be sure she was okay."

Hillie clucked like a mother hen. "Und you say she is stubborn like a mule. Tsk, tsk! She is still asleep. But her fever is down a little, I think."

Will felt Sassy's forehead. She felt a little cooler. A little. Maybe. "Should she still be asleep?"

Hillie shrugged. "I do not know. I am not a doctor. She is comfortable. She took a little more broth twice when I offered it to her. Her cough is not quite as bad. I am hoping she is a little better."

Will frowned again. "If Marc and Lily would just get here."

Hillie nodded. "Ja, Lily will know vhas to do for her."

They took turns sitting with Sassy through the night. As morning approached, Will dozed off in the chair by the bed where Sassy lay sleeping. Hillie began to shake his shoulder.

"Oh! I'm sorry, Hillie. I'm slacking at my job..." He murmured, his voice filled with exhaustion.

"Nein, you go climb in that bed vit' her und go to sleep, Vilhelm," she commanded. "You are about to drop vit' exhaustion. Und I do not need another patient! I should live so long!"

Will nodded, weary, and slipped off his boots before slipping into the bed beside Sassy.

Within minutes, he was asleep, with one arm slung protectively over the woman he loved.

I slept long and hard. Strange dreams tumbled one after another through my fevered mind, first with Owen laughing at me for being lost in time, sick and cold. But I knew Owen wouldn't laugh at me for my situation. If anything, he'd have been jealous of the opportunity, not to mention more than a little jealous of Will. I blinked, and the dream changed, to Gramma singing to me as a child, old Spanish *canciones* of a time long ago when *Los Canarios* came to Texas in the 1740's. Gramma telling me stories of Old San Antone, as natives call it, of the development along the River Walk, of parades along city streets and along the river. Gramma being Miss San Antonio when she was a teen. The history of the missions encircling the city, and of the Battle of the Alamo. The dreams of the songs would meld into dreams of Gramma dressed in a fancy ball gown on a river float, doing the royal wave to the admiring crowds, as Crockett and Travis guarded her back and Fess Parker sang "King of the Wild Frontier!" I felt the warmth of a summer day in south Texas, clear and crisp and hot on my skin. The heat would turn to fire as I felt my skin burning and crackling with heat. I would cry out in pain and discomfort, and then begin shivering again, as I dreamed of falling into a drift of snow and ice in my winter of hell. I dreamed of the time when Rick was in the hospital when he was 14. Brain fever, I thought. He must have had brain fever. I must have brain fever now.

Long I slumbered, by sound sleep overtaken, with strange dreams running over and over again through my fevered mind. Owen's laughing face, would melt into Rick's tearful face. *Tu me manques,* Sassy. Jim stood in the background soberly telling me, "I told you not to fall in the snow, little sister'. *Tu me manques,* I said to Jim. Long I slumbered, by sound sleep overtaken, until at last my strange dreams bade me awaken. Finally, with a start, gasping, my eyes opened. It was day light. I felt weak as a baby, my throat raw, my chest on fire, but I was alive.

"It's about damned time you woke up," said a familiar voice drily.

Lily checked my pulse. "We got here two days ago, Sleeping Beauty. Will's a nervous wreck. He's scared witless he might have killed you bringing you on this little joy ride."

I tried to laugh, but the sound caught in my throat and set me off coughing again. "Is he okay?"

She nodded. "Yes, he's fine. Just crazed with worry." She sat me up, and leaned her stethoscope against my back. "Now, cough again. And once more."

I coughed as requested, and then looked at her. "What is it?"

She didn't speak at first. She was busy writing notes into her journal. "You were as close to dying from pneumonia as I ever saw. Fortunately, you're improving, but you're still pretty sick."

I blinked. "Pneumonia??? But it was just a little cold!"

She shook her head. "Maybe it was just little cold before some brilliant woman with a Ph.D. in American History decided to trek 15 miles through the snow on horseback on one of the coldest days of the year, but it was one bad case of pneumonia when I got here. And people say I am stubborn! Good lord, woman! Now, drink the willow bark tea and then let's get you back into the bed."

"If we've been gone several days, we need to get back!" I protested.

"Nonsense. You are quite ill. You could have died. You will remain here until I say that you can go back home. That's final." Lily's lips narrowed into a line I knew meant business.

I pouted and flounced back on the pillows. "Fine. Be that way. I bet that poor cow is about to bust an udder by now."

Marcus and Michael are tending to the animals and chopping wood. Fancy's cooking. And you are staying put for at least another week while you get better. Understood?"

Grudgingly, I agreed. "Fine. What about my sewing?"

"Will brought work back for you to so you can sit in bed and stitch. Do not overdo."

"Bitch."

"You betcha," she retorted. "And mighty damned proud of it, too."

Chapter Eleven

They were all wrong. It was two more weeks before I was strong enough to go back to McCarron's Corner. Even then, I felt weak as a dishrag as we rode back with me nestled safe and secure in Will's arms. Three hours later, tucked into my bed, I shook with exhaustion. I slept for 18 hours straight before I woke up. Day by day, my strength returned as I mastered getting in and out of bed, dressing, walking up and down the stairs, and gradually doing small tasks around the cabin. By the second week at home, I was almost back to my old self. Almost.

And it was way past time for Will to leave.

Fancy and I cooked a special supper for him that last night. Fried chicken, mashed potatoes, creamed gravy. Homemade biscuits. Green beans and fried okra. Pecan pie for dessert. We got ice from the ice house, to make iced tea the way I love it.

"Sassy, I consider you my wife now. In case anything happens, I want it known that you *are* my wife."

My mouth went dry at the thought of something bad happening to my Will. I nodded, unsure what to say.

"So, the Scots have this ceremony they call a hand fasting. They say you are married a year and a day after that. If you decide to stay together, you get married 'for real' at the kirk. Otherwise, you just kinda go your separate ways."

I nodded again, well aware of the ceremony.

"Would you agree to be hand fast until we can have a real wedding? Not that I intend leave you."

I smiled. "Yes, of course, Will."

Fancy's eyes got big. "No, wait! You need witnesses to make it legal! Wait!" She ran out of the house, towards the big house.

"What now?" I asked.

Will laughed. "We wait. But, do you have a length of cloth we could use in this ceremony?"

"Well, of course. Just a bit. What color?"

We went into my sewing room, and Will picked up three lengths of fabric, white, pink, and a third of green. He grinned, and said, "These will do just fine."

In a matter of minutes, Fancy returned with Michael, Marcus and Lily in tow. Lily's eyes were enormous as she realized what we were about to do. "Are you sure?"

I nodded. "Never more sure in my entire life."

Marcus stood in front of us, and looped the three pieces of fabric around our wrists, and then held the three pieces together. "Then, I, Marcus McCarron, as Laird of McCarron's Corner, say this: know now before you go further, since your lives have crossed in this life, you have formed eternal and sacred bonds. As ye seek to enter this state of matrimony, you should strive to make real the ideals that to you, give meaning to this ceremony and to the institution of marriage. With full awareness, know that within this circle of cloth you declare your intent to be hand fasted before your friends and family, and you speak that intent also to our Creator. The promises made today and the ties that are bound here greatly strengthen your union and will endure the years and lives of each soul's growth. Do ye, William Selk, still seek to enter this ceremony?"

Will nodded. "I do."

"And, Sarah Winslow, do ye pledge to be hand fast to this man?"

I nodded. "I do."

"Then I bid ye look into each other's eyes. I see that ye've chosen three colors for the cloth for this hand fasting. White, for new beginnings. Pink, for love. And green, for fertility. Will ye honor and respect one another and seek to never break that honor?"

We both answered, "We will."

Marcus look the length of white fabric, twisted it around our wrists, like an infinity knot, and tied it. "And so, the first binding is made. Will ye share each other's pain as well as seek to ease it?"

"We will."

Marcus draped the length of pink fabric around our wrists and tied it as he had done the first piece. "And so, the second binding is made. Will ye share yer burdens so yer spirits may grow in this union?"

"We will."

Marcus smiled as he looped and tied the third piece. "And the third binding is made. Lee, fetch a bit of red cloth as well, please, *mo leannan*."

Lily hurried into my sewing room, and came back with a length of red cloth, and Marcus continued. "Will ye share each other's laughter, and look for the brightness in life and the positive in each other?"

Will and I smiled at each other. "We will."

Marcus tied the fourth length of fabric around our wrists, and said, "And so the bindings are made. As yer hands are bound together now, so yer lives and spirits are joined in a union of love and trust. Above ye are the stars. Like the stars, yer love should be a constant source of light. Below ye is the earth. Like the earth, yer love should be a firm foundation on which to grow."

Marcus turned to the others. "Liliana McCarron, do you serve as a witness for this couple?"

She nodded. "I do."

"Fancy Selk, do you serve as a witness for your brother and Sassy?"

"I do."

"Michael McCarron, do you also agree to act as a witness to this ceremony?"

Michael stood up very straight and almost as tall as his father, and nodded. "Aye, Da, indeed I do."

"Then I declare that William Ranscome Selk and Sarah Alinora Winslow are now hand fast in marriage. This common law marriage will be duly noted as such in my magistrate's registry book of marriages, births and deaths. You may kiss your bride, William."

And kiss me he did. Long, hard, passionate. The kind of kiss a woman dreams of, longs for, craves. The kind of kiss that says I love you, and you are the most precious thing in my life. You are my reason for being. The kind of kiss that says you are my Beloved, and I am yours.

I almost wept when the kiss ended. "I'll send you some of Mama's dresses, if you like. You can remake them. The fabric is still in good condition, and they should make up into some nice gowns, Sassy."

I looked up in surprise. "Your mother's dresses? You wouldn't mind?"

He grinned. "Nah. She'd be thrilled to have them used. Better you than the moths, she would say. Some are pretty old fashioned, but I imagine Fancy can bring them up to snuff in no time."

I nodded, well aware of Fancy's ability to turn just about anything into a pretty garment. "When will you return?"

"Late May or early June. Plan on a July wedding in Virginia."

Two months. I hated to be without him that long, but I knew that was just the way it was. There was a war waging, and he was needed. I was lucky to see him when I did. I tried to smile, but I felt my face tremble with the effort. I didn't want him to go. Just knowing he was going to leave, made me miss him already. I knew with each passing minute after he would leave, I would miss him more until he returned.

Funny how a person could change so much in such a little amount of time, I thought. Two years ago, Owen and I were planning our move to Georgia. Now, Owen was dead, and I was planning to move to Virginia with Will.

And it hit me. Owen was dead almost a year. My eyes teared up at the thoughts rushing through my head. Dead almost a year and I was planning to marry another man. What guarantee did I have Will wouldn't die, too? Killed in a war that seemed so far away and yet so important to our country.

I pushed back from the table, and walked away, trying not to cry. Will frowned, pushed back his unfinished pie, and came over to hug me. "What's the matter, Little Bit?"

I couldn't put my words into any sort of coherent thoughts. I asked, "Didn't your mama had roses at Belle Rose?"

He laughed. "Well, yes, Mama loved roses. Why? You like roses?"

I nodded. "Yes, I do. But, if you don't mind, would you send me a rose bush or two when you send the things back?"

He sobered, and looked at me, his expression unfathomable. "Well, sure, Sassy, but why? I mean, you're coming to live at Belle Rose. Why do you want roses here?"

I plucked at an imaginary spot on the curtain before I answered, not at all sure he would understand. "Owen loved roses. He always had a little rose garden. I thought I would plant one or two here, kind of like a memorial for him. I know he isn't buried here, but... I don't want him to accompany us to Belle Rose. I want Owen's ghost to stay here when I leave."

Will stared at me before he nodded. "What color would he have liked, Sassy?"

"Red. For remembrance."

That night, I took Will to bed. He'd been helping me up and down the stairs every day, but that night, I grabbed his hand as he turned to leave. "Don't go."

He looked uncertain. "Are you sure?"

I nodded, and pulled his hand to my bosom, "Come to me, Will. I love you. I'm your wife now. Make me yours. Stay with me tonight."

I didn't have to ask twice. After just the slightest hesitation, my Big Sexy knelt down beside me, kissing my brow, then my eyes, nose, and my lips. I sighed, as my lips opened beneath his. His hand began to roam across my breasts, fondling, kneading, caressing, while he kissed me again and again. I pulled him beside me on the bed, and he rolled a leg over me. His eyes grew large as I pushed him back, and raised up, to ease my shift over my head, and toss it to the floor. With a gulp, he jerked his own shirt over his shoulders, and threw it down as well. I grappled with his laces to his trousers as we resumed kissing, until he broke apart from me, and hurried to strip off his clothing. Dressed in nothing except the finery God gave him, he lowered himself to me again.

I stopped him, and bent to look at his ankle. "What is this?" I asked, as my fingers traced the Mariner's Compass tattoo.

He blushed. "I had it done after I saw yours," he said, as he reached down, and caressed the arch of my foot.

I leaned toward Will to look closer at the tattoo and gasped. Encircled around the Mariner's Compass were the same words on my foot: Not all who wander are lost. He'd marked himself as my own.

Eyes shining bright, I laid back down. "Come to me, my love."

And he lowered himself to me. And lowered. And lowered.

I gasped as he clasped his hands to mine, and I realized where his tongue was traveling. As he reached my womanly center, as Owen would have called it, if he'd ever done such a thing, I arched my back in pure assed lust.

"Holy Mother of God..." I gasped.

Will raised his head long enough to grin at me. "I don't think she has anything to do with this, Little Bit."

I pulled his head back down. "Don't stop," I whispered hoarsely.

He grinned again, and then dipped his head back to me, laving and nibbling. I'd never experienced anything like this before. I arched over and over, moaning louder and louder as orgasms rolled over me like waves crashing against a coral reef. I worried Fancy would come to see if I were okay. Fortunately, she didn't appear in the doorway with the musket to try to warn her brother off. I fell deeper and deeper under the spell of William Selk, as it wended around me in paroxysm of lust-filled touch after lust-filled kiss.

Will pushed back, and raised up. I grabbed to stop him, but then I realized that he was just repositioning himself. I laid there panting as I waited for him to enter me.

And enter he did. Will's a big man, bigger than Owen was, and I never thought of Owen as small. "*Ai, Dios mio!*" I gasped as Will plunged deep within me. Riding wave after wave of pleasure, I threw back my head, exultant. Yep, Big Sexy was the right nick name. Hours later, I slept, better than I had dreamed possible, snug against the man I loved, with his fingers tangled through my hair.

He left the next morning after breakfast. He bent over from the saddle and pulled me up to kiss me goodbye. I refused to cry as he kissed me, and then lowered me back to the ground. "I'll be back," he promised.

"You better," I warned. "Or I'll hunt you down like a dog and drag you back to where you cannot escape me again."

He laughed, bent back down, kissed the top of my head, and brushed my hair from my face. "The end of May, Sass. And have a dress ready for our wedding, you understand? The General expects us to have a big, fancy 'do at Belle Rose, so make something nice."

I nodded, and snapped him a sharp salute. "Yes sir, Captain, I understand. Take care.

I love you."

He kissed his fingers and then held them up to me. "Always."

I 'caught' the kiss, and watched from the Ridge as long as I could see him and then some. My big man on his big black stallion riding back to war. Yes, I would love him.

Always.

Chapter Twelve

The girls in my class were coming along on their sewing. Four older girls were doing applique work on their quilt squares. Their future husbands would be proud of their stitching. The oldest girl, almost 15, was engaged and would marry that summer. She was making a whole piece quilt, already basted to the batting and the backing. She painstakingly stitched row after elegant row of flowers, cross-hatching, curves, circles, and waves, creating one of the prettiest quilts I had ever seen. Done all on dark blue velvet with pale pink stitching, I was more impressed every time I examined her handwork. It was a masterpiece worthy of a place at the Smithsonian someday, if it survived. I told her to put a label on the back of the quilt describing who made it, when, and of what fabric and thread type. She considered the idea amusing, but promised to do it. The youngest girls all mastered neat, even stitches, creating four- and nine-patch squares. I felt sure before I left, they would all have the basics for a quilt of which they could be proud to have made.

We'd stitched about an hour, when one of the boys ran into the cabin, shouting a rider was coming. The girls glanced up, but kept sewing. Fancy wandered over to the door, curious who the stranger might be. With a start, she let out a little cry, and rushed to the door.

"Uncle Tobias! I can't believe Will sent you! How are you?"

I put my own handwork aside, and walked over to the porch where Fancy was hugging an older gentleman who appeared to be of mixed heritage. "Fancy, introduce us."

She looked embarrassed as she pulled back. "Miss Sassy, this is my Gramma's half-brother, my Uncle Tobias. Mr. Will must have sent him down from Belle Rose."

Tobias nodded his white-haired head. He was tall and erect of carriage, slender of build, and with a light complexion and grey eyes. "Oh, yes, ma'am, Mr. Will sent me down. He asked me to bring some things to you ladies." His eyes sparkled with his words.

"Well, come on in here out of the sun, then, Mr. Tobias," I commanded. "Fancy, get your uncle something cold to drink. Girls, we're done for the day. I will see you all tomorrow at 9 a.m. sharp."

Most of the girls picked up their things, and put them into their baskets to take them back home. Two began to fuss that they didn't want to go home because their mama would make them do chores. Without a word, Fancy gave them the stink eye, and told them they could go milk my cow and feed my chickens if they didn't want to go home yet. With that, they both shut up, and shuffled reluctantly out of the cabin.

We walked out to the wagon that Tobias had brought from Belle Rose. There was a trunk, filled with pretty gowns from Will's mother's closet, as well as rich soil, roses, lavender, tansy, and other flowers. I squealed in excitement as I saw the lovely array of flowers. "I never dreamed he would send so much!"

He shrugged. "Mista' Will said it was impo'tant fo' you to have some niceties here in the back country. He thought them flowers would help make it more like home till he could come fetch you, Miss Sassy. I'm supposed to stay until he comes to take you home."

I knew the real reason he sent the flowers was to make a nice memorial to Owen, with the hope that I could, indeed, let go of Owen and leave his memory here when I went on to Belle Rose. I rushed inside and changed into my work clothes, and Tobias and I began to plant the flowers. Tobias was an unexpected treasure trove of information about flower gardening, and as the sun set, the little memorial garden was finished.

I didn't explain what the rose garden meant or why I wanted it. My feelings were too hard to put into words today. But I knew one thing. Owen was no longer missing from me. I had finally let him go since now I loved Will.

Owen had been dead a year today.

Goodbye, my love, I thought, as I tidied the soil around each plant one more time. You will not be forgotten. But you will not come with me in my new life.

I seemed to hear Owen laugh, and whisper, what, no more kettles, Sassy? Are you sure this is not just one more fine kettle of fish?

No more kettles of fish, I whispered back. I'll be fine, Owen. He's a good man. He loves me. He will protect me. And you will stay nice and dead in the future where you belong, while I make my new life here in the past we both loved so much. I raised up, and brushed the soil and the memories off my hands. "Done."

"Sure seems like a lot of work for a garden when you fixin' to leave here," Fancy said as we were setting the table for dinner.

I nodded. "Yes, I guess it seems pretty silly. But, we can enjoy it while we are here, and hopefully, the next family in this house will keep the garden nice."

After dinner, we opened the heavy trunk. We oohed and aahed as each lovely dress was pulled out, one after another. A short note was attached to each to tell me about the dress. A rich rose silk gown dripping with lace sleeves bore a note that his mother wore it once to a ball in Philadelphia. Another lovely green lustering gown was hand painted with exotic flowers and birds. The note said it was made in London on a trip once, and that Will always loved the way it made Belle's eyes look. Matching shoes were wrapped next to the dress. Since my eyes are reportedly close in color to hers, he selected the green dress to show off my eyes.

I gasped and then began to cry as I pulled out the last of the three gowns. It was so out of style, but the fabric was still beyond exquisite. Flowers, birds and harps were hand painted onto the cream colored silk fabric. The stomacher was beaded over the painted designs. The back was a' l'Anglais, with fitting that showed off the tight waist and cartridge pleated back. The elegant overskirt opened to reveal a delicate cream quilted silk petticoat, with more painted flowers and harps down low along the bottom, above the ruffle. My hands shook as I lifted it, and swung around while holding it up to me.

"Oh, Fancy! I love it! It's gorgeous!"

She waited until I quit dancing around with the dress before she told me. "It was Miss Belle's wedding dress, Sassy. Will sent you his mama's wedding dress."

I cried again.

I explained I saw this same dress in the Smithsonian years ago, how I marveled at the work, at the exquisite beauty of the hand painted fabric and the embroidery that echoed the portraitures of the birds, florals, and the harps. How Owen and Rick both laughed at me when I stood staring at the gown for well over a half hour until Owen insisted we move on.

How I told them it touched my soul.

They laughed even more when they saw it was worn by Sarah Winslow at the occasion of her marriage to William Selk, at Belle Rose Plantation on July 4, 1779. Owen teased me, asking if it belonged to me in a past life. I told him I didn't think so, but I did love the gown. I envied the woman who wore it long ago for her wedding. I'd forgotten that dress until that very moment. The memories flooded back with each touch of the exquisitely beautiful fabric. If I had any doubts about marrying Will, they disappeared with those long forgotten memories. I twirled around holding the beautiful gown up to me.

Fancy and I talked about how to best alter the court gown made in 1718, into a stylish gown of 1779. We drew sketches till late that night as we planned the dress, until we were both satisfied with the design. Full enough to still be quite elegant in 1779, while not being ridiculous. New furbelows down the front of the skirt, and additional embroidery and beading on the gown itself. A slight train in back for additional elegance. Still with the elegant a' l'Anglais cartridge pleated back I remembered from the Smithsonian. It wouldn't be a gown I wore every day, even in a day and age in which wedding gowns were used for more than just weddings. Fancy was eager to start on it the next day. she sketched how to alter the other two, as well, but they were simpler projects, not intended to be a wedding gown I knew would someday be exhibited in a position of honor at the Smithsonian.

Spring passed. As days lengthened and warmed, I felt summer approaching. I worked on a quilt I was making as a wedding gift for William, in greens and blues, reflective of the ocean he loved. With the Mariner's Compass in the middle, it would hold a special meaning for us both. Now pieced, I was embroidering the final touches of the words around the compass before sandwiching and quilting it. I tended to my little garden, and to my few animals. One of the sheep had twins. Mimi gave birth to a litter of 6 healthy, happy puppies, the first Skye terrier litter born in the Indian Territory. Hawk decided he liked Marcus better than the noisy puppies and took to spending a lot of time at the Big House. My girls came every morning, working on their quilts and other projects, as I continued working on the things I was commissioned to make in addition to the work on my dresses.

My wedding dress was shaping into a lovely gown, newly updated in the newer style that was so much more appropriate for colonial living than a court dress ever could have been. It had a slight train, just enough to give it a touch of elegance for the fancy plantation wedding I knew we would have in a few months. My girls pitched in, to help embroider the skirt much like the stomacher had been embroidered a half century before. Everything was going as expected, until that morning when the Redcoats arrived.

It was late April, a quiet morning, and I was out watering my roses before it got hot. I heard the horses coming up, but hadn't thought much about it; horses came up the trail now and then. My head jerked up in shock as an English accent asked for directions to Mistress Winslow's abode. Why the bloody hell were they looking for me? I quickly wiped the dirt off my hands, and turned to smile at the fresh-faced, young Lieutenant standing outside my garden. Rosy cheeked, with bright blue eyes peering at me underneath his regulation hat, the young man looked like the very picture of a British soldier in his distinctive scarlet jacket.

"Lovely roses, madam," he gallantly offered, as he doffed his hat and bowed for me. "I did not expect to find such an exquisite garden this morning."

I smiled and curtseyed, one of the few true curtseys I had done since I arrived almost a year before. "Why thank you, Captain," I purred, knowing full well this boy was no Captain. "You are so kind. Were you looking for me?"

He smiled, as he opened the small fence for me to walk through. "I am searching for a lady named Mistress Sarah Winslow, madam. But I am a mere Lieutenant. Might that be you?"

"Indeed, it is sir," I nodded, and motioned for him to follow me into the cabin. My heart was racing; why this man was looking for me? "And may I ask your name, Lieutenant, and inquire why you are searching for me here in the Indian Territory?"

"Oh, pardon my manners, madam! Lieutenant Rafael Gresham, at your service." He held the door for me as I swept past him.

Fancy's eyes opened wide in shock at the sight of his red coat. She snatched up Bella, and began to walk backwards towards the kitchen.

Hands shaking, I smiled. "Fancy, could you heat some water? I imagine the Lieutenant would enjoy a nice hot cup of tea this morning. I think we have a little bit left."

In reality, we had a lot of tea. Tobias brought a new supply with the dresses and plants two weeks earlier, but the officer did not need to know what we did and did not have.

Fancy curtseyed, the very picture of a docile domesticated servant. "Yes, ma'am, Miss Sassy, right away, ma'am. I'll fetch some biscuits fo' him, too."

I struggled not to laugh. "Very good."

I turned to the young lieutenant, and motioned for him to sit down. "Now, what can I do for you?"

He blushed a little. "I heard that you are an exemplary talent, madam. My mother is in England, and I would love to take her a little something home from the Colonies which would show her some of the quaint Colonial stitchery of which I have heard so much."

I tried to discern if this bozo actually wanted some little tidbit of craftiness for his mother, as a souvenir of his deployment to the Colonies, or whether he had some other hidden agenda. I smiled, and went to my desk, where I kept a notebook filled with drawings of items I could make. I opened it to a section that delineated pockets, scarves, and fichus, and made several suggestions to him before he agreed on a fichu with embroidered cream flowers on cream linen. I quoted him my price, and he paid the down payment quoted. With a smile, I told him that it would be ready to pick up in a week.

He then moved on to the true purpose of his visit to McCarron's Corner. "Have you seen a man named Lord Ranscome around about these parts, madam?"

I frowned. "What does he look like? The name does not ring a bell."

He smiled. "Tall, good looking rascal, I understand. Dark hair. Clean shaven. Rather striking blue eyes, I have been told.'" He coughed, and looked a bit uncomfortable. "They say that the ladies find him... um...quite appealing."

"Clean shaven? Good looking? Tall, dark, handsome? I can assure you no one fitting that description has been here since I arrived last summer," I said with an airy wave of my hand. "I'm certain I'd remember anyone who would even come close to fitting that description! And to tell the truth, I haven't seen any man I'd describe as 'quite appealing' since I came here, unless you count my cousin's husband, who is indeed quite handsome."

The young man laughed, self-conscious, his cheeks turning bright pink. "I'm supposed to inquire everywhere if anyone had seen the rogue. So, you just came here last summer, you say?"

I nodded. "Yes, my husband was reported killed. Indians, you know." I made a vague motion with my hand. "I moved here after I heard my dear Owen was murdered to be near my cousin, Mrs. McCarron."

He looked stricken. "Oh, I am so sorry, madam! I did not know."

You had every idea, I thought, grim. I bet you knew all about me before you showed up on my doorstep hunting for Will. "That is quite all right, young man. I've been widowed for over a year. I still miss Owen so much, but I'm accustomed to his absence. If one can ever become accustomed to such."

As unexpected tears stung at my eyes, I realized I was describing Will's absences, rather than Owen being gone due to death.

Fancy brought us our tea and biscuits, and I sent her up to Lily with Bella to fetch a cup of sugar. In reality, I sent her there to alert Marcus and Lily the Redcoats were here looking for Will. By the time Fancy returned with Lily in tow, the young man had left.

"What was that all about?" Lily looked worried.

I shrugged. "Said he wanted a souvenir of the New World to take home to his dear old mother when he returns to jolly old England. I'm making a fichu for her, with my lovely rustic stitchery. Reality was he's hunting for Will. Came up here snooping around for him. Odd thing was he knew my name."

Lily's eyes broadened in alarm. "Oh, my! Now what?"

"I suspect we just keep on keeping on, like the hippies will say one of these days. And hope Will doesn't run into them. But the good thing is they are looking for him all neat and clean shaven, not at all shaggy and scruffy. Heck, at this point, I'm not sure I would recognize him if he were clean shaven and looked like the man the Lieutenant just described!"

Lily laughed. "Oh, the change is remarkable. But you already love him, whiskers and all."

"No, I love him in spite of those awful whiskers. Although they do serve a purpose."

Found a purpose for that beard, did you?"

I nodded. "Oh, my, yes!"

Fancy arched an eyebrow at us and then shrugged, as Lily and I fell together laughing.

The week passed quickly. I planted crops, watered my flowers, made cheese. We sewed quilts, clothing, and the other things on order from clients. Every evening, Fancy worked on my wedding dress. We were both quite pleased at the way it was becoming a more modern dress. I kept working on the quilt for Will.

"I'll have this finished pretty soon," Fancy murmured one evening.

I looked up from the commissioned stomacher I was embroidering. "Wonderful. Then we can work on the others."

"Miss Belle was painted in this dress. I reckon she'd be mighty pleased you chose to wear it for your wedding. Will's gonna have to have you painted in it, too."

I smiled, pleased she thought I would look pretty in Will's mama's wedding dress.

"Strangest thing. Mr. Marc came by this morning again, like he had something to talk to me about. But then, he never says nothing." She frowned.

I shrugged. "Must not be important then."

Fancy frowned. "No, I get the impression it's important enough that words are failin' him. Miss Lily says he has a hard time talkin' sometimes. But you know, he wasn't always that way with me. They came to Belle Rose when I was little. I adored my Uncle Marc."

"Uncle Marc?"

She nodded. "By adoption. He was always sweet to me. I remember he brought me a pretty porcelain dolly from Ireland when I was about 5. She had red hair, like mine. It tickled him I named her Dara, cause his sister was named Dara. She had red hair, too."

We sat stitching for a while that morning, lost in thoughts about weddings and happy-ever-after endings, when I heard noises outside. With a frown, I arose, brushed off my skirt, and went to the window. My eyes grew wide as I realized Will had just ridden in. It wasn't even May, and my Will was back! I ran to the door, and flung it back, excited that my man was back earlier than expected. I was just about to call out to him, when I realized the Redcoats were there, also.

But, Will had been wounded. A dirty bandage was tied around his head, with blood still seeping through it. I grabbed a post on the front porch to steady myself, thinking how to best play this. "Owen! My darling husband! They said you were dead!" I began running to him, tears streaming down my face.

Will's head whipped up and around at me, his eyes narrowing as he looked around for the soldiers. Fancy ran out, and threw her hands over her mouth.

I ran to him, to help him off the grey gelding. "Are you okay?" I whispered to him.

He tried to grin. "I've been better, darlin'. You reckon you could send your girl to fetch Lily?"

I wheeled around to Fancy, and quickly snapped, "Go fetch Miss Lily right now, girl."

Fancy nodded and curtseyed to me. "Yes, ma'am, Miss Sassy, I sure 'nuff will!" she said in her broadest Southern accent. She took off running towards the big house before the words were out of her mouth.

I'd never seen Will look so scroungy. His clothes were incredibly filthy. His beard was tangled, his hair was matted to his scalp with blood. And the stench! I swear, I have never smelled such a stench in my entire life, before or since, as emanated from Will Selk that hot May morning! It was enough to puke a mule, as I have heard Will mutter at times. I wheeled around. "Tobias! Help me get my husband into the house!"

Tobias hustled over quickly to help Will down from the grey. "Let me help you into the house, Mistah Owen."

My heart lurched as Will grunted in pain, and leaned on Tobias as Tobias helped Will into the house. "What the hell happened?" I whispered.

"Tell you later, Little Bit," he whispered back. "Soon as Lily gets here. I need stitches. Quick."

About that time, Lt. Gresham dismounted from his own horse and came up quickly to help Tobias get 'Owen' into the house. "Mr. Winslow, I know your wife is delighted to see you're alive," he stated, quickly looking over my 'husband'.

Will nodded, and leaned onto poor Lt. Gresham. "Yessah, I sure hope so. I sure have missed my pretty little Sassy since them Redskins captured me. Still don't know how the hell I got away from one batch of 'em, just to be caught again yesterday by Creek."

I gasped. "Where?"

He shrugged. "About 25 miles southeast of here. That one brave tried his best to relieve me of my scalp, but I refused to let him have it."

I looked at Will's eyes. Yes, he appeared to be serious. "Let's get you inside, my love."

When we managed to soak the bandage off his head, we could tell he took a pretty good lick from the Creek warrior's skinning knife. I felt dizzy as I watched the blood begin to pour from the wound again as Lily cleaned it.

"Go sit down," she tersely snapped at me. "I don't need another patient right now."

I nodded, afraid I might either vomit or pass out. Or both. And Lily didn't need another invalid. My Will was hurt. Badly. He needed me. "Are you sure I can't get anything?"

"No. Fancy, get me more water. Hand your mistress some muslin. Sassy, tear that into bandages for me." She looked up and almost smiled as Marcus entered the cabin. "Oh, good, Marc! Owen showed up this morning, fresh from an Indian attack. Can you go get me some bear grease?"

"Jaysus, man!" Marcus paled as he took in the English soldiers standing by, as well as Will's condition. He nodded, and turned to hustle outside, where I heard him send Tobias to find bear grease.

"What is the bear grease for?" I asked faintly.

"Set the wound and helps it to start to heal once I get this mess cleaned and stitch it up," she said. "This is a nasty wound, sir. Were they trying to scalp you?"

Will flinched about then, from the prodding Lily was doing to the loosened skin on his skull. "Ouch! Yes, ma'am, I think he was. I managed to gut the man before he scalped me. I knew I was pretty close to here, so I pressed on, best I could. I thought I remembered Sassy said you knew a bit about healing. I sure was hopin' Sassy was right."

Jesus Christ, someone tried to scalp him! Tears filled my eyes at the thought I could have lost him, just like that. My hands were shaking, my stomach was rolling, my skin was clammy. I turned and ran for the back door, where I doubled over, as I vomited my breakfast into the herb garden. Fancy followed me outside, and held my hair away from my face as I vomited.

Chapter Thirteen

It had been a hard couple of months.

First, Sassy got pneumonia and she damn near died. Thank the Good Lord that Lil showed up in time to save her and his Lil Bit pulled through.

He'd never done anything as hard as leave her in March. They engaged in intimate relations as she healed. Marital relations, since they were now hand fasted. Will was thrilled she was as responsive to him as she was. He never expected to find a woman so open and free with her demonstration of love as Sassy showed him. It just about killed him to have to leave her, but he had a duty to the country he loved. He left to fulfill his duty and to help fulfill the destiny of the United States of America, the first Constitutional Republic.

Sassy made him prouder of this country than he had ever dreamed possible. She knew so much of the history of this great country. Not just things that already happened, not just things happening now. Things to come. And, she'd seen so much more of the country that was even known to exist yet, so many places he would more than she'd ever see. She had insights into this country that very wise, learned men could only dream of having. Insights he hoped they would be able to share with people who mattered in this country, who would write the Constitution and Bill of Rights, as Sassy called the documents to be crafted.

When he left in March, he went first to Savannah, to assess the situation there. It was still what Sassy called a hot mess. He then sailed north to the James River, stopping over night at Charleston on the way home. He knew from Sassy that Charleston, too, was going to fall soon, and he knew he needed to report as much as he could to the General. From there, he went on to the Potomac, and to home. It was good to be back at Belle Rose again. He hadn't been there since the short trip last fall when he fetched Fancy and

Bella and kicked that worthless overseer off the property. He figured if he got Fancy to McCarron's Corner, Sass would take her in, and he knew that Marcus would watch after them. It was bittersweet to go home without Tom. He went to ensure the servants understood a wife would be coming to live there with him soon, and they best get the house ready for her. It was sure enough a fair mess when he got there, with the furniture dusty, floors unpolished, even the silver tarnished. Mama would have died to see her house like that! It was never like that when Fancy was in charge. Of course, Mama and Daddy both would have died if they knew what happened to Fancy.

He gave firm instructions it was to be cleaned top to bottom for his wife before he got back, and that new bed clothes and window dressings were to be prepared for his Missus. It also gave him a chance to get some of Mama's pretty gowns together to send to Sassy, so Fancy could remake them into something pretty and modern for his soon-to-be lawfully wedded wife.

Lastly, he told Tobias to send herbs and roses to her. She might not remain long in Indian Territory, but she asked for the damned roses, and he would honor her request.

He managed to talk to George, Tom, Sam, and Jim. All good men devoted to the cause. All lived near Belle Rose, and they were able to meet before his ship sailed back to Charleston. It let him throw some ideas out at them that Sassy planted in his head, to see how they might react. And it allowed him to plan for the future.

Washington asked him – well, that meant ordered him – to head back south as soon as possible to continue his 'investigations'. So, within a matter of days, Will headed towards the Carolinas, wending his way from place to place, where Sassy had delineated future battle sites to him, to try to talk to Patriots and Loyalists alike to gather as much information as possible.

Will wasn't one of the Culpers in the truest sense. They were another ring of spies for the General, the original group. Tom helped George and Talmadge set up the network for the Culpers, and later, Tom set up the network for other spy rings as well. Will was assigned to keep an eye on the Southern front. He had a special ability to get up and down the coast, with his shipping line, since their daddy was an English lord. He could infiltrate the English with his looks, the well-educated English accent he could emulate with ease, and as his mama would have said, his uncanny debonair style and easy repartee.

He worried he'd been found out by Clayton last fall in Florida. He heard rumors the Brits were on his tail ever since. So far he hadn't run into any Redcoats hot on his trail, so *sea lo que sea,* as his daddy would have said. What would be, would be. He grinned, as he realized the expression was in Spanish, something his Little Bit o'Texas Sass would say, too.

He was dog assed tired by the time he headed back south towards the Cohutta Wilderness. He had expected not to get back till early June. It was looking like he might make it by early May. He was delighted his hard work paid off and he would be back to Little Bit early. He damned sure missed that little gal.

Later, Will reckoned his pondering of the future with his Beloved was why he didn't hear the warnings that the Indians were approaching. Lost in his thoughts, he was totally oblivious until the arrows began buzzing past his head. Will wheeled his black around, and found cover.

It wasn't good.

It was a small hunting party of Algonquins, further south than usual. Most of them lived further north, up into Virginia, Pennsylvania and along the Ohio River. He managed to shoot four before he realized the last one had slipped up behind him. The brave let out a yip of excitement as he grabbed Will's hair and yanked Will back from his gun. He flipped Will over to straddle him, skinning knife raised and ready.

It was a fight to the death. For a while, Will was pretty damned sure it was gonna be his death.

Will knew the brave was one hell of a fighter. Will managed to sucker punch the Algonquin brave, and to roll aside as the man grunted in pain. The man circled back to Will, wary and aware of his opponent. Finally, they lunged at each other, fighting hand to hand, as they rolled about in the dirt and debris. Will heard the horses neigh in protest as the men knocked into them, scattering as the men rolled about in their death struggle. Again and again Will slashed at the big warrior with his tomahawk in one hand and his skinning knife in the other, the brave slashing at Will, until both were covered with blood flowing free from their wounds. When the big brave rolled on top of Will, Will was sure his time was ending here on earth. He was exhausted, and unsure how much longer he could fight. When the brave raised his skinning knife again, Will knew he had but one chance left. He grit his teeth in agony as the bastard began to slice into his scalp. When the man was fair sure Will was dead, or at least incapacitated from pain, Will struck again. He slipped the long knife his daddy used to use to gut hogs out of his boot and twisted to slide it up towards the warrior's body. Will pushed the knife until he felt skin, and then pushed hard into the man's belly. The brave grunted, his eyes wide in surprise and pain as Will began to pull up as hard as he could into the man's ribs. The warrior quit slicing Will's scalp as he began to hit in desperation at Will, trying in vain to get Will to stop his assault. As Will forced the warrior's ribs to separate, he pushed harder, driving the knife higher and higher until the man shuddered, and fell against Will like the dead weight he was.

Shaken and bleeding, it took Will almost a half hour to manage to get the dead man off him. It took almost an hour more for Will to staunch his own bleeding, from his scalp and other injuries, and to get his horse to head out again. By then, covered with blood, dirt, the dead man's urine, and apparently some bear shit they'd managed to roll into, Will gathered up the warrior's weapons and headed back towards the trail. He grabbed the reins to the Algonquin warrior's grey horse, and turned away from the direction he'd been headed, towards Augusta, to head instead towards McCarron's Corner.

No time for dilly dallying now. He'd better high tail it to the Corner. He was about 40 miles from there, and he could make that in a hard day's ride. Lil was the best damned healer he'd ever known. And by damn, if he was gonna die, he'd be in the arms of his woman when it happened.

—

We got him on the kitchen table, which was just long enough to hold his body. I grabbed water, and began washing his face and head so that Lily could shave his head in preparation for surgery to come. "Jesus Christ, Dude, what did you roll in?"

"Some kind of shit, I think."

"Well, duh, I'd never have guessed that. Why does your head reek of piss?" It was so bad that I was gagging from the stench.

He tried to laugh. "I think the damned Injun peed on me at some point or other."

"No!"

He tried to laugh again. "Nah, I put horse piss on my head. Supposed to be good for cuts."

I gagged again. "Are you freaking serious?"

Lily nodded. "Old wives' tale. I didn't know you were a big enough dumb ass to believe that, Selk. Now, be still, we have to get this cleaned up."

We all grew quiet as Lily inspected the wound. The cut sliced from just above his left ear to almost the middle of the top of his head. "We can shave the rest of your head later, Will after we tend to this," Lily assured him. "Creek, huh? You sure about that?"

"No. Algonquins. North of here," he answered acerbically as he flinched. "Shit, Lil, take it easy! That hurts!"

"Where?" asked Marcus.

"East of Big Frog Wilderness. Shocked me they were so far south."

Marcus looked alarmed at the information. "That's odd. I haven't seen Algonquin anywhere near here in years."

"Sassy, go run get that thread cutter thing of yours, that looks like a little bitty scalpel."

I rushed to the other room for my embroidery scissors and my Tula Pink seam ripper. It really does look like a little scalpel, and Lily had often said it would make a great little surgical instrument. I rushed back, dropped both into a pan, and poured boiling water from the kettle over them. Lily nodded, pleased with my work. "Three minutes in the water, then bring them to me."

Three minutes later, I brought them to her. Will winced as the razor-sharp blade cut close to the severed flesh on his head. I held his hand tight, murmuring words of encouragement to him. "It'll be okay, darling. I promise."

He nodded, and shut his eyes again. He was not a person to complain about pain, and his wincing made me fear he was in serious pain. I stroked his hand as Lily began to prod the wound. She grunted a few times, as she spotted issues of concern, but I was doing okay until Lily got out the damned leeches.

"What are those for?" I snapped.

Lily never looked at me, but just began placing one small leech after another along the scalp line where Will had been cut. "They take down the blood," she stated. "That takes down the swelling. It's easier to stitch it up if it's not swollen."

"It's okay, Sass," Will whispered. "Lil knows what she is doing." He tried to smile, and winced again in pain.

I watched in horror as she allowed the leeches to suck their fill of the blood of the man I loved, until filled to satiation, they dropped from his scalp one by one. I felt sick but I was determined not to throw up again. I bit my lip and struggled not to watch the weird sight.

But when she got out the maggots, I gagged.

Lily glanced at me. "If you are going to vomit again, please leave. I have enough to deal with."

"Well, what the blazes are the maggots for?" I swallowed back bile.

"They remove the decay," she whispered, as she began easing dying flesh from his scalp.

After a few minutes, I realized I couldn't handle this. I pulled away, trying not to cry or puke on the man I loved. Fancy stepped back to move out of my way as I headed for the door. "That is undoubtedly the worst thing I ever saw in my life," I muttered.

Fancy didn't flinch. "You ain't seen much then, girl."

I puked again outside the kitchen door. I washed my face and hands, tears running down my cheeks, before I turned back towards Lily and Fancy, both working in silence on Will, spread out on my kitchen table. I began to shake as I realized just how bad the cut to his scalp was. At least 6 inches long, the knife must have slid under the scalp at least 3 inches, going right to the skull. I could see white bone glistening where Lily lifted skin to make sure all the dirt had been removed before stitching. "Will he recover?" I whispered.

Lily nodded as she kept working. "If you don't vomit on his head, yes, I think so. He is tough as nails. The maggots are eating the dying flesh out and should get the infection out, too..."

"Infection?" I yelped.

She nodded, face grim. "It's inevitable with this kind of injury. If I can get this cleaned up, and get it stitched, he should be okay. If we can control infection." She glared at me. "Don't you dare faint, Sassy. I don't have enough hands or time to deal with you fainting right now."

I nodded, silent.

"Get over there and boil some silk thread and needles. Same thing as before. At least three minutes to kill germs. And we are going to need them pretty damned quick now."

"You want my Neosporin Ointment?" I asked.

She frowned, frustration on her face. "Hell, yes, woman! Get it! That's a hell of a lot better than bear grease! Now!"

I kissed Will's cheek, and then hurried to the pantry for the tube of Neosporin which might save my Will's life, if we were lucky. While I was there, I grabbed the bottle of Marc's whiskey, too. Lily poured whiskey over the cut, as Will drew a breath in pain.

"Shit, Lil, I know you don't like me, but do you have to make it hurt worse?"

"If I didn't like you, I wouldn't help you, you big dumb ass," she retorted. "Now, shut the fuck up." Lily wiped the excess whiskey off his face, and began to apply the Neosporin to Will's scalp, gently shoving it in along the cut line, as far as she could get it under his scalp. He moaned again as she did this, his fingers clutching tight to my own. I saw it was God awful painful. "How could I not like you when you're Belle's child? You know I loved your Mama like she was my own. And without you, well, we would never have got Michael back when Jay kidnapped him. You big dumb ass. Thinking I don't like you." She pecked a kiss on his brow, much to his surprise. "Don't let that go to your head."

I rushed into the other room to gather up thread and needles. I brought the kettle back to a boil, and then dropped the needles and thread into the pan, where I poured boiling water over them. Three minutes later, I gingerly pulled them out with the tweezers I use for my sewing.

It took more than an hour to get the wound cleaned and stitched. As we stitched, we poured whiskey on the suture line, and then would go back over the line with Neosporin. We took turns, between Lily, Fancy and me, to stitch the tiniest stitches possible with my silk thread. Finally, Lily sat back, and smiled.

"That looks pretty good. Now, my dears, it is up to you two, and the

Good Lord up above."

We put on another good dose of the triple antibiotic ointment, and then bandaged his shaved head with clean muslin. Lily left me some elixir of poppies when she finished working on Will. "I wish we had more," Lily said.

"Me, too." I could not get over how scared my own voice sounded.

"Thank God you had the Neosporin. That may what saves him."

I was stunned by her words, my throat parched dry. "Why?"

She shrugged. "It's a hell of a nasty wound, Sassy. Thank God, he got to us when he did. I cannot imagine how he managed to ride here, half scalped like that."

I felt light headed again, as the darkness tried to push me into unconsciousness. I focused on Will's hand in mine, and refused to faint. "What now?" I whispered at last.

"Keep an eye on him. Give him the elixir of poppies for pain if he needs it. Not more than one spoonful in water every 4 to 6 hours. Remember, it's very addictive."

"I know."

"I wish I had some pain meds for him," she muttered. "I had laudanum, but I used it up last year when one of the Cherokee had a compound fracture that had to be amputated."

I snapped my head up at her words. "I have Aleve and Tramadol in my back pack," I said. "Do you want them?"

She frowned. "What are they?"

I realized both drugs had been developed after she had 'left' my world for this. "Aleve is a NSAID, made from Naproxen."

She looked surprised. "Hell yes, Naproxen would be great! Give him one when he awakens. And what is the other? Trazadone? Isn't that a sleep medication?"

"No, Tramadol. Pain medication. I take them now and then for arthritis."

"Well, I never in my life thought I would say thank God you have arthritis, but here I am saying it!" She grinned. "He's tough. My bet's on him. But he is gonna have a scar."

"Will his hair cover it up?" We both knew Will could be vain at times.

"It should grow back, although it won't grow right on that scar line. So, he should be able to cover it up with his hair, at least until he gets old and his hair line recedes," she laughed, her eyes beginning to sparkle again.

Fancy and I took turns that night sitting up with him. I tried to sleep a little while Fancy watched, but sleep was impossible. The following morning, Lily came back, and checked on him. He was sitting up, sipping a cup of tea and nibbling on a piece of toast when she arrived.

"Will, you look good. I think you might just live after all, despite your best efforts to get yourself killed."

He laughed. "Thank you, Lil."

"Get some real food into him, and then we all need to talk."

Will was happy to gobble down the ham, scrambled eggs and biscuits that Fancy brought him. As he wolfed down the last of it, Lily began to talk again.

"A woman is in labor at the Cherokee Village who needs me. I'm heading there next."

We looked at her in shock. "But what about Will?"

She looked at Will before answering. "How do you feel?" she asked him.

He grinned, sheepish. "My head hurts, but I think I might just make it. Why?"

She sighed. "That damned Lieutenant Gresham is still lurking about. I'd like to take you two with me to the Village. Marc thinks the Redcoats won't go there. Hell, they aren't even supposed to be here. They're prohibited from coming here by Treaty. From there, we can get you out of here, and head you back to Virginia."

I gasped. "But, Will almost died yesterday."

She nodded. "Yes, and he will die if they figure out who the hell he is. We have to get him out of here before someone slips up and lets them know who Owen Winslow is." She looked at Will. "Think you can ride?"

He nodded. "I could ride to get here. I can ride to get away. Just bring that medicine for my headache. It works like a charm."

I tried to laugh. He tried to grin, but didn't quite make it.

Lily stood up, and brushed her hands off. "Then grab yourselves a change of clothes and the medicine, and let's plan to head out to the Village in the next half hour."

I jumped up, unsure what to grab first. I ran to my back pack, and began to put the Aleve, Tramadol, Neosporin ointment, and of course, the elixir of poppies into it, along with a spoon to measure the elixir. Fancy took the bottle back out, and wrapped it in muslin, before reinserting it into my pack. I ran upstairs for my hair brush and some extra underwear and socks, and a pair of drawers Will left there in March. As I left the room, I wheeled back, and grabbed my jeans, my bra, a sleeveless top, a couple of well-worn shifts, the shawl Will had sent me from Virginia, my Bible, and my sewing kit. I could always do mending with the thread and needles in the sewing case if needed. Downstairs, I grabbed up my scissors, seam ripper, tweezers, cell phone and solar charger, compass, water purifier straw, and a few other items I rarely ever left home without, in this world or the next. I added some newly made venison jerky and fastened the backpack. I pulled on my divided skirt I'd made for riding, along with a cool shift and my jumps, and my hiking boots from last summer.

"I'm ready," I said breathlessly.

Fancy and Tobias had already gone to the barn to saddle up horses for Will and me. We'd washed Will's clothing the night before, so while still pretty ratty looking, it was clean and no longer smelled like piss, puke, and poop. They brought out the grey he rode in on the day before, as well as my mare. I knew that Tobias had Will's big black hidden at the barn behind Marcus and Lily's house. "Here you go, Mr. Owen," said Tobias, just as the English lieutenant rode up again. "Now, you take it easy and don't you go too far today."

I nodded to Tobias, relieved at his quick observation the British were back again. "What can we do for you, Lieutenant?" I asked, as I swung up onto the broad back of my pretty little sorrel.

The Lieutenant looked surprised to see us mounting up to ride out. "Why, Mr. Winslow, I'm surprised to see you up and about today."

Not as surprised as me, I thought.

Will smiled. "Well, seems we are needed at the Village. I have a headache, but I'll be just fine. No better healer in the Colonies than Mistress McCarron, you know."

He kicked the grey, and started down the trail. I wasn't sure why he chose to ride the grey rather than his big black, but right then I was glad he wasn't on the horse that might be identified as belonging to Will Selk. I followed close behind, heart pounding so hard in my chest that I was afraid Gresham would hear it. I watched in dismay as Lt. Gresham started after us.

Will turned slightly in his saddle, and then turned the horse towards the Englishman. "Any problem, sir?"

"Not at all. However, I am supposed to go to a Cherokee Village near here to speak to some Indian fellow called Chief Wolf Shadows. He apparently knows the man I am searching for," Gresham answered.

I gulped as Will cut his eyes at me. "Oh? Chief Wolf Shadows?" I sounded innocent and curious.

The young lieutenant nodded. "Yes, Mistress Winslow, apparently so. I'm supposed to find this Indian chap and see if he can give us any insight into the whereabouts of Lord Selk."

Will raised an eyebrow. "Lord Silk, you say? Ain't never heard of no one named that hereabouts."

The lieutenant laughed. "Well, I doubt he has been here, but we will see. Apparently, Mr. McCarron used to know him, and it was thought this Selk fellow might have stayed in touch with McCarron. McCarron swears he hasn't seen him this past year, but I am also supposed to talk to this Indian. We'll see what he says."

Por favor, Dios mio, I thought, please do not let Wolf give Will away.

Will was pale and swaying in the saddle by the time we rode to the Village. Tobias helped Will down, as Marcus rushed to find Wolf and explain the situation. I made sure Will was comfortable before I hurried to help Lily, trusting Marcus, Tobias, and Will to keep the story straight that Will was my long lost husband, Owen.

The girl was stoic but she in pain and tiring. Lily assessed the baby was breach. It took some doing, but with some serious massage like I'd never seen before, we managed to turn that baby. Before dark, a new, healthy brave was born to the clan. As we exited the birthing hut, I saw Marc and Will, posing as Owen, talking with Wolf near the perimeter of the Village, where the trees met the clearing. I could see Wolf look back at me from time to time. He nodded, and waved to me. Hopefully, that meant he was in agreement.

I noticed that many of the Cherokee who spoke English with us acting as if they could not understand our language. This enabled them to avoid having to talk to the English soldiers, who were not supposed to be there, and enabled them to report back to Wolf whatever they heard. Lily had already explained to the women in Cherokee that the English soldiers thought Will was my late husband, reportedly back from a long disappearance and believed to have been dead. Star in particular thought that was amusing, and did the best act of all the women, pretending not to understand a word of English while gathering important information from the fools as they ran their mouths about Lord William Selk, and the battles on the front to the East, as well as their low opinions of the Cherokee, who refused to assist the British against the Colonists. Once or twice, I saw her eyes flash with their derogatory comments, like when one referred to her as a 'damned blue eyed half breed c--t'. My own eyes widened with shock at his words, as Star turned to me, and said to me in Cherokee, "dumb son of a bitch, isn't he?"

I agreed, and added, "He undoubtedly has a very small manhood."

She nodded. "If he even has one." She left the hut.

I realized if the stupid corporal continued his rant against Bright Star, he might find himself minus said minuscule appendage before long. Shadow Wolf was no fool and was very protective of his family and his people. He would not tolerate any attempt by any man to act importunately with Star, or any other woman who was unwilling to accept a soldier's advances. Importunately, I thought with a slight smile. My lord, I was starting to even think in language like they speak here in 1779!

Shadow Wolf was grinning when we entered his lodge. "Owen Winslow, hmm? It is good to see you, my brother. I am glad to see that the Red Moon Woman was able to stitch you up. Now what?"

Will clasped Wolf's hand. "We head north to Belle Rose. Sure wish you could come, too. But whatever you do, don't head to Chickamauga. They are having some problems over there."

The men wandered off into another room, where I could hear them speaking in Cherokee. I sank down onto a chair, and shut my eyes, overwhelmed with fatigue. Lily came up, and put a hand on my shoulder. "You okay?"

I nodded, as I patted her hand. "I'll be fine. I'm just tired."

"Well, why don't you go lie down a bit?" she suggested.

"Time to sleep will come soon enough. There is too much to do right now." We helped Star to prepare dinner. After about a half hour, the men joined us.

I was surprised when Wolf spoke. "Star, please take Sassy and help her get ready."

Stunned, I looked up from my plate. "Ready? For what?"

Star giggled. "For your wedding, silly. Come."

Heart in my throat, I glanced at Will, who grinned. "But I have nothing to wear."

The men laughed. "I told you she would say that," Will said.

"It will be fine, Sassy," Star cajoled. "You can wear my dress."

Star had been working for months on her wedding dress, exquisitely crafted of white deerskin, with blue quill work, leather fringes, feathers, and beading. "But..."

"No 'but's," she said firmly. "You are my friend, and it will be a great honor for my Aunt to wear my dress."

With a start, I realized that when I married Will, I would indeed be Star's aunt. Warmed by the thought, I nodded, and rose, to go with her to get dressed for my wedding.

Star combed out my hair, and then braided blue beads and small blue feathers into it in small braids that overlaid the rest of my long hair hanging loose to my waist. She helped me put on the beautiful dress she'd made for her own wedding. I could not believe I was in her dress or that I was about to be married. As we came back downstairs, one of the women handed me a bouquet of blue bells and baby's breath.

Will took a sharp breath in. "Beautiful," he whispered in an awed tone.

Will had changed, also, into clean buckskins, also trimmed with blue quill work and beads. Shadow Wolf stood before us, and placed my left hand into Will's left hand before he started to speak.

"Great Spirit above, please protect the ones we love. This night, my brother, Iron Eagle, who is known among his people as William, marries his love, Sassy, who shall henceforth be known among our people as Pathfinder, for this Found Woman has found her path in this world."

Will began to speak. "Great Spirit, we honor all you have created as we pledge our hearts and lives together."

They looked at me expectantly. "What do I do?" I whispered.

"Repeat what I said," said Will.

"Um... Great Spirit, we honor all you have created, and we pledge our hearts to each other. We pledge our lives to each other." I glanced at Shadow Wolf. "Was that okay?"

He nodded. "Very okay."

Will smiled and continued. "We honor the Wind and ask that we sail through life safe and calm as if we were babes in our father's arms."

I nodded, and shivered at his words, as I also prayed for safe travels, a peaceful journey, and safe delivery in the months to come.

"We honor Fire and ask that our union be warm and glowing with love in our hearts," Will continued.

I was surprised he knew the words to this ceremony. Again, I nodded to indicate my agreement, and squeezed his hand as I repeated his words.

"We honor Water to clean and soothe this relationship, so that it may never thirst for love."

Tears welled in my eyes, at the simple beauty of the Cherokee ceremony. I nodded again, and whispered the words in echo to William's.

He smiled at me and squeezed my hand. "We honor Mother Earth and ask for our marriage to be abundant and grow stronger through the seasons."

Again, I nodded. I glanced at Star, standing next to me, and whispered, "Do I say anything?"

She nodded, and whispered the words into my ear for me to recite.

I smiled, took a breath, and said, "We pray for harmony and true happiness, always young together."

Will bent down and kissed me.

Wolf cleared his throat, and then began to speak again. "My brother, a man's highest calling is to protect his woman so she is free to walk the earth unharmed. Sassy came from Beyond to find you. It is your calling, your duty, given to you by the Great Spirit to protect this Found Woman and to keep her safe."

Will nodded. "I know. I accept the task."

Wolf turned to me. I noticed tears glistening in his eyes. "Sarah, who we call Sassy, a woman's highest calling is to lead a man to his soul and to unite him with the Source. It is why you came from Beyond, to be Will's soul mate. It is your calling, your duty, to do this for your man. It is why you are now called Pathfinder among the Cherokee."

Throat tight, I nodded. I figured I knew what to say. "I know. I accept the task."

Will said, "Gv-ge-yu-hi."

I had to figure out what he had said in Cherokee. I love you. "Gv-ge-yu-hi."

Wolf then wrapped a large, white blanket around us both, and then let out a yelp of excitement. "It is done! They are married!" He looked back down at me, and whispered, "I could not let him take you so far away without seeing that he married you, Sassy."

Wordless, I again nodded. If I spoke, I would cry.

About 10 p.m., one of the braves came in and whispered something to Star. After a brief conversation, she sidled over to me. "You need to go out back behind my asi."

I nodded, and after I changed out of Star's beautiful dress, I slipped out, to hurry out behind the asi. To my surprise, Tobias and Fancy were there with Will's big black stallion, my mare, and two pack mules, loaded with supplies. "We thought you might be needing these things, Miss Sassy,"

I hugged Fancy and then shook Tobias's hand. "Thank you so much! But aren't you two coming with us?"

"No, I don't think it would be best if I came with Bella. Uncle Tobias will get me to Savannah and then on up to Virginia on a ship. We'll most likely be there before you."

I was amazed at their sound logic, wishing that I could join them on the easier route to Virginia. I wasn't eager to travel 600 miles on horseback. In the summer. Through the roadless mountains of Appalachia. I would much prefer that quick trip to the coast and then up to the Potomac by ship instead of the way we were about to go.

I heard the whine when I turned to go back in. I looked down and saw my Hawk sitting at my feet, waiting for me to notice him. I dropped down to him, and hugged him tight. "Oh, Hawkie, my beautiful boy!" He began licking my face and wagging his tail as I cried. "He can't come with me, you know." It was about to break my heart to think of leaving my dogs in Indian Territory but I knew they would never survive a 600 mile trek through the wilderness.

Fancy smiled. "No, but I can take them in the wagon and they can come with me on the ship. I'll be bringing your dresses, the quilt, and some other things, too."

My jaw must have just about hit the ground by the expressions on their faces. "Oh, Fancy, you'll bring them to me?"

"Of course I will, you ninny. I am not about to leave Hawk, Mimi, and their babies here. We'll all be at Belle Rose when you get there next month."

It hit me with a start. Six hundred miles. That would take at least a month of hard riding. I swallowed, and glanced at Fancy, now anxious and worried.

"Did you tell him?" she asked in a soft voice.

"No. It's not the right time. I'm don't know for sure. And don't you dare tell either."

She gave me a hard look, shaking her head. I could tell she thought I was wrong. She eventually nodded. "Okay. I think you're making a mistake, but I'll keep quiet, at least for now. What will you do if you lose it?"

My throat tightened as tears burned at my eyes. "That's not going to happen."

She reached out to take hold of my hand. "Please come with us, Sassy. Don't try to do this. You're askin' too much of yourself. Will wouldn't want you to put your health in jeopardy, or that of a baby. Please."

I was adamant. "No, he needs me."

She looked crestfallen. "He needs you alive. Please think about this, Sassy. Please."

My throat tightened at the thought. Six hundred miles on horseback in the summer. Over mountains. With hostile Indians. And she wanted me to tell Will that maybe, just maybe, I was pregnant?

I squared my shoulders. Not gonna happen. My man needed me. I would stay with him.

Chapter Fourteen

The next morning, at 5 a.m., we headed north. It was just the 5th of May, but it was already hot and humid. Fortunately, mosquitoes were not too bad. Yet. Unfortunately, the gnats were another thing.

We pushed hard that first day, Will and Marc both determined to get well into Tennessee before sunset. They knew Redcoats would not follow us northward since they thought Will came from the South, towards Augusta, to get to McCarron's Corner. With two Cherokee braves as guides, we headed up the Appalachian Trail.

It was just a few miles until we were into Tennessee. From there, we had about fifteen miles to go to Big Frog Mountain, but the trail was hard going, with sixteen water crossings along the way, wild, raw timber country, uncut, untamed, true backwoods. Saying it was inaccessible by horses in places is an oversimplification. At times, we changed paths to find easier routes for our four-legged companions. The trail was just too steep.

By dusk that first night, I sighed in relief as I saw Big Frog Lake stretching before us. We were deep into Cherokee country, and the Cherokees were not renowned for their amiability towards the British. Thank God.

We started a fire, and the men threw some fishing lines out into the lake. In almost no time, they were catching bass. Lily and I grabbed those fish as quick as the men pulled them out of the water to clean and pitch them in the skillet. By dark, we had hot coffee, corn bread, and fried fish. Maybe not a balanced diet, but one that gave us lots of energy and sure filled our bellies. I managed to soak my swollen feet in the ice-cold water of the lake and to wash off my face and arms while Will fished. I would have liked a bath but realized that would have to wait at least until morning, perhaps longer. Sure enough, the next morning, the men had us up at 5 a.m. again, and on the road well before 6. I managed to jump into the lake for a quick, cold bath.

Marc said the faster we moved now, the further ahead we could get of the British before they realized where we went, the better it would be for us. It seemed easier the second day, perhaps because we were coming down off the mountain instead of climbing up it. But, I knew the trail would be going up and down for the whole way to Northeastern Virginia. Will estimated we made a good 35 miles that second day. We were all so exhausted, we just broke out leftover fish and jerky for dinner. I was asleep before the tea was even brewed.

I cried the third morning when Will woke me up at 5 a.m. "Come on, Little Bit, let's get a move on," he murmured into my ear.

I swatted at him. "No."

He laughed, thinking I was joking. "Come on, girl, we have a long way to go. We need to keep moving if we're ever going to get there."

It hit me that he was serious. It was morning. Or close to it, by a mountain man's internal clock. And damned if the tears didn't start. I swiped them away, unwilling for Will to see me wimping out. Grudgingly, I arose, and pulled on my divided skirt over the thin shift I slept in, and laced myself into my jumps. I shoved my hair back, brushed it and re-braided it. Within minutes, I walked to the camp fire, where Will handed me a cup of coffee.

"Thanks."

"There's some toast if you want it," he offered, eyeing me warily.

I picked up a piece of toast and began nibbling on it as I sipped my coffee. My stomach was rolling more than usual, and I was damned determined not to let Will know my suspicions until I knew. That meant I couldn't puke. Period. Once I finished, I helped pack up the items we unloaded the night before, and I mounted my mare. We were on the road by 5:30.

We rode hard again that day, Will estimating we traveled another 35 miles into the Carolinas. I had no clue where we were, other than somewhere further east and north than we had been that morning. If Will was right, we had come about 100 miles so far.

One sixth of the trip.

And so it went, day after tedious, hot, mosquito-ridden day. Up at 5. Ride till we couldn't see any more. Day stretched into unending, unrelenting day after day.

After 12 days, we made it into Virginia, and spent the night in a little hamlet called Fancy Gap. In the future, the trail we traveled would become much busier, and Fancy Gap would become a popular overnight stop. In 1779, it was little more than one two-story cabin, a mill, a single room store, a barn, and a couple of smaller cabins, where the Good Spur Road met the Flower Gap Trail. Will pulled up to the two-storied cabin, jumped off Zeus's broad black back, and hollered, "Letty! Leticia McEdwards! Are you here, woman?"

The door to the cabin flew open as a short, incredibly rotund woman flew out. Dressed in bright red plaid homespun, with a plain muslin apron, she looked about as plain as a mud hen. Ginger hair tidily pulled back into a bun, covered with a linen cap, with an abundance of freckles dancing across her cheeks and arms. Arms opened wide, she rushed to Will, and grabbed him, as he blushed deep red.

"My land, Will, I didn't expect to see you come back this way for another six months!" she gushed.

"Well, just remember if anyone comes looking for me that you haven't seen me in a coon's age, Letty."

She blinked her little eyes, which then narrowed in alarm as she sighted the bandage on his head. "What the hell happened to you, William?"

"Run in with Algonquins," Will explained. "One decided my scalp would look better on his belt than on my head."

She tilted her head, as she studied him. "Let's take that bandage off tonight and see how it's healing. Algonquins, hmm? Pretty far south for them."

Will nodded. "It was in Tennessee."

"Two weeks ago," I added. "Lily treated it, and we've been keeping it clean and dry."

She snorted. "I imagine that hasn't been an easy task with this boy. Well, come on, everyone! Get off those horses, and you gals get in here and set yourselves down! The men can take care of the animals and the gear."

The men were peering at Will's map when Letty announced supper was ready.

"See, we're just about half way there," Will pointed out to Marcus.

"Marcus nodded. "I thought the other route was quicker but this seems faster so far, Will. How did you find it?"

"Dan'l Boone showed it to me. He uses it often. I use it as a backup route. The English don't generally come this way."

The men understood the various tribes that lived out here 'on the frontier', and the dangers of each group. Will sure knew the dangers of the Algonquins first hand.

I have to admit I thought scalping was something that was intrinsic to the Plains tribes, but Will explained that all tribes would take scalps, as Europeans would, also. He wasn't sure if the Indians took the habit from the Europeans or vice versa. He added that Indians don't appreciate being called Red Skins, because in the course of curing scalps, the hide side is painted red, leading the scalp to be called a Red Skin. To apply it to Indians was a derogatory term, much akin to calling them 'loser'. I cringed at his words, once again realizing how close he came to be providing a Red Skin to the Algonquins.

We got the bandage off Will's head, and both Lily and Letty were pleased with the way it had healed. "I can take the stitches out, if you want, Will. It healed quite well."

He nodded. "I'd like that, Lily. They itch like the very blazes."

I held his hand as Lily snipped the stitches out. He winced once, and when she was finished, and had wiped it well with alcohol, he grinned and thanked her again.

She blushed. "It's nothing, Will."

He snorted. "You saved my life, woman. I think that counts for something."

"So do I," I interjected.

She shrugged. "It's what I do."

"I don't care, thank you anyway," I retorted. "I'm so grateful you were there when Will arrived..." I choked up at the thought of trying to fix that injury without Lily.

She reached over, and took my hand. "But I was there, and it's just fine now, Sassy. You'll see. Everything will be fine."

I beamed at her.

Letty went all out for 'her Will', as she insistently called my husband.

Virginia ham, mashed potatoes, creamed gravy, collard greens, and even apple pie for dessert. It was a meal fit for a king. We pushed back from the table. Lily and I helped Letty clean up, and then we all sat around the fire talking until I was falling asleep on Will's shoulder. With that, Lily suggested we turn in for the night.

Letty let Will and I have her bed. I protested, but she insisted. With a sly grin, she told me she could now tell people she at last got Will Selk into her bed. I tried maintain my composure, but it was impossible, as she stood there, all of about 4'10", almost as round as she was tall, grinning at me, as she lasciviously winked at my husband.

"You're terrible," I laughed.

"I keep telling him that, but he keeps telling me he has a woman who is so much worse than me that there is no point in my even trying," she said with another lascivious wink.

"It's true," I demurred. "No way you're even half as bad as me!"

It rained hard that night. I cannot tell you how good it felt to have a roof over our heads as that rain pelted down. I also cannot even begin to describe how good that lumpy homemade mattress felt. The finest Tempurpedic mattress ever made could not compare to the luxury of that mattress after 12 nights sleeping on the ground and another night in the Indian village on pallets. Warm and snug, with rain pattering down on the tin roof above, I had one of the best night's sleep in eons, but then, I was always partial to rain falling on a tin roof. Instant tranquilizer.

The next morning when I awoke, the sun was already up, the birds already singing. I pushed the covers back and jumped out of bed, grabbing on my clothing before I hustled downstairs.

"I am so sorry! I never dreamed it was so late! Why did you let me sleep?"

He grinned. "Marc and I decided we could all benefit from a bit of rest before we press on to Belle Rose. To be blunt, I'm not sure the horses or we can hold up to this pace. We'll stay here a couple of nights'. Letty's willing to have us. Then, we're going to work at going about 20 miles a day or so for the duration of the trip. That would get us there in about 15 days, at most. We may start running into Redcoats since we're gonna be closer to the coast and populated areas, so we may have to travel even slower than that. But we're half way there, and the roads are better from here on."

My jaw must have hit the floor. "We're that close? I knew we were in Virginia, but I hadn't realized we're half way there. That's wonderful!"

He leaned over and kissed the top of my head. "It'll be fine, Little Bit. I want you to rest today. You look plumb tuckered out. I can't have my girl getting sick on me."

I laughed, very self-conscious of my 'condition'. I was pretty sure I was pregnant by then. I'd missed two periods. I could read the writing on the wall even without a home pregnancy kit. "I'm not sick, Will. I'm healthy as a horse. But I am tired and I will enjoy the rest for a day or two."

It started raining again that afternoon. By midnight, it was a hard thunderstorm, what Will called a 'real gully whomper'.' The men all agreed it would be dangerous to try to go on until the weather improved. I was so glad we were someplace with a roof over our heads and not just out in the woods in the storm.

Three days later, the rains stopped. We were all pretty well rested by then, and in fact, getting a bit antsy to get on the move again. Will, Marc, and the Indians rode out to check if there was flooding towards the Clinch, up the Flower Gap Trail. Four hours later, they came back, with glum expressions. "The Clinch River is still way out of its banks," Will muttered in disgust.

I knew the Clinch ran northwards along the route we wanted to go, along with a series of other smaller rivers and creeks. We planned to head north through the Shenandoah Valley until we got to Front Royal, and then east to Belle Rose.

"We could cut east to Lynchville, and then north to Roanoke," Marcus suggested. "Then to Charlottesville, and on to Belle Rose. We're about what, 30 or 40 miles from there when we get to Charlottesville."

Will nodded. "Let's think about it today, and we can decide in the morning." He said something in Cherokee to the two scouts, who nodded soberly, and who then turned around, to mount their horses and head out in an easterly direction. "We'll see what they say when they get back."

Will surprised me a little later when he asked if I would like to go for a ride. I grinned, and nodded. We grabbed a picnic lunch to take with us. We rode a couple of miles out of town, up a steep slope, to what at first appeared to be a stone cairn. When we got closer, I could see an opening to a cave.

"What is this place, Will?" I asked, curious and excited.

He grinned. "They call it the Devil's Den. Don't ask me why. It's a cave, and it is pretty interesting. I thought it would make a nice place for a picnic, and as long as it's not flooded inside, it would be interesting for you to see."

We spread a blanket on the ground to eat our lunch, and after we ate, enjoyed laying on the blanket, under the cover of the trees as we kissed and fondled each other.

Will pushed back abruptly, and motioned for me to be silent. After a few seconds, he indicated I could get up and follow him. We grabbed the reins for the horses, the blanket, and the basket, and wordless, lead the horses into the cave. Finally, as Will held me close against a wall, I dared to whisper the question. "What's wrong?"

"Iroquois," he whispered. "Shush."

Soon, we could hear the men walking outside on the hill overlooking the cave. They noticed the traces of our visit, taking special note of the horse droppings. Excited, they argued in their language, of which I had not the slightest idea what they were saying. Will motioned again for me to remain quiet. Thank heaven, the horses remained still and silent as well.

After what seemed like an eternity, the men left. I sagged against Will in relief when they departed. Will indicated I should remain quiet inside the cave. He slipped out to see if it were safe for us to leave. After a few minutes, he came back, and waved for me to come out with the horses.

"I thought the Cherokee were part of the Iroquois?"

"No. The Iroquois have treaties with the English and are not generally friendly to us. They see us as usurping their lands here, pushing them further and further west from their traditional hunting grounds."

I nodded and mounted my mare. Indigenous Native Americans were not my strong suit. Will glanced back as we headed back down the mountain towards Fancy Gap. "They've become such a problem that Washington issued an edict to destroy the British-Iroquois alliance. This place is considered sacred to them. They might well have taken offense at us being here, even if they aren't aware of Washington's edict."

I gulped, to think how close we came to disaster just by Will showing me an interesting archeological site along our way. "How'd you find it?"

"Dan'l Boone showed it to me several years ago. I mentioned it to Wolf, and he told me the Iroquois consider it a portal to the Other World. He warned if I were found here, they might not take well to it. But it's spectacular inside and well worth seeing. I didn't know there were still any Iroquois around these parts."

"I think we just better high tail it back," I snapped.

He laughed. "I have to admit I would just as soon not be scalped again!"

I shuddered at his words. "Would they have scalped us?"

"I don't know, maybe, but I damned sure wasn't going to risk that or worse with you along, Little Bit," he muttered as I cringed.

We rode back to the McEdwards place, where Will and the other men began to peer at maps, talking in Cherokee about where to head next.

Lily came up and slipped an arm around my shoulders. "Don't you think it's time you tell him?"

I jerked my head around in surprise. "What?"

She grinned. "I'm a doctor. I know the symptoms. Don't you think it is time to tell him about this baby coming?"

I paled at her words. "Is it that obvious? I mean, I wasn't even positive when we left McCarron's Corner."

"Oh, for heaven's sake, Sassy, yes, it is that obvious! What are you, about five months along now?"

I stared at her in shock. "My God, no! I got pregnant in March, most likely the night of the hand fasting. Why would you think that?"

"Because you're bigger than that. Sassy, it's okay to tell me if you got pregnant in December."

"No, I swear, Lily, I had a period in December after Will left, as well as in January and February. I never missed a period until March. I thought I missed just because I'd been so sick, until I missed in April, too. I just now due for May, and we're already on the road. Oh, my God! I can't be five months along!"

She stared out the window for few minutes. "Let's go upstairs. I want to examine you."

I glanced at Will as we started upstairs. He'll be so upset with me, I thought. If I am wrong, he will just be livid.

Lily shut the door to the bedroom, and blocked it with a chair to keep anyone from coming in. She washed her hands in the basin, and performed a rather awkward gynecological exam on me while I blushed beet red, right down to my nether regions which she was examining. She looked at me, surprise written across her face, with her hand still on my cervix. "Is there a history of twins in your family?"

I could feel the red fading from my face, as I apparently turned white. "Uh... yes. Why?"

She paused, and then spoke again. "Okay, level with me. Who are the twins?"

"Jim and me. Mom and my Aunt Soledad. Gramma and her sister, my Tia Adelina. My great-gramma and her brother. That's as far back as I know."

Lily shut her eyes and shook her head. "Fuck."

"Why???"

"If you aren't four or five months along, then I bet you are carrying twins. It seems to be two fetuses, and they both seem to be the right size for 2- to 3-month fetuses, rather than one 5 month fetus."

That didn't shock me; I just told her they run in my family. "So... why the concern?"

She looked surprised by my response. "You idiot. Twins often come early. Haven't you ever been pregnant before?"

"No. Owen didn't want any other children after Richard was born. His first wife was a drug addict. He had a vasectomy... before we met."

Okay, so it wasn't the whole truth. He had that vasectomy just before we got married. But she didn't need to know about one of the major fights we had.

She arched her eyebrows at that. "Wow. Did you know that when you married him?"

I shrugged, but offered nothing else. Okay, so I lied. Again. It just wasn't her business. I learned he had the vasectomy a little before Christmas, after we got married. I started talking babies, and Owen finally told me. I just wasn't about to tell her I learned it 6 months after we got married.

She stood, silent, and then sighed. "And here you are trekking cross country 600 miles on a horse!" She pulled my skirts down, and stood up, to wash her hands in the sink again. "You must tell him. Today. It must be a factor considering how we get the rest of the way to Belle Rose. Now we have flooding in the direction we hoped to go, and may have hostile Indians in the other direction. Not to mention a much likelier possibility of running into Redcoats. Will and Marcus have to know this to make appropriate plans to get us to Belle Rose safe and sound. Understand?"

"But I didn't want to tell him till we get there."

"I don't care what you wanted to do. This is very serious. Do you understand?"

I nodded, numbed.

Shit.

I was pretty quiet that afternoon. We had a simple dinner of squirrel stew and biscuits, after which Will glanced at me several times, with questions in his eyes. I guess he never heard me ask for squirrel brains before, but I had a real craving for them boiled in vinegar in the skull, like Jeannette used to cook them at McCarron's Corner. You suck them out like you suck the heads on crawdads. Very tasty. Anyway, let's face it: he isn't used to a quiet Sassy, or one making unusual food requests. He's used to his Little Bit of Texas Sass, as he calls me, full of piss and vinegar.

After dinner with the much-desired boiled brains, the men played cards and smoked stogies while we womenfolk sewed. Sewing centers me, but that night, I kept making mistakes. Frowning, after I pricked my finger for the umpteenth time, I shoved my embroidery into my sewing case in disgust.

"Can't get it tonight?" Will asked from the poker table.

"Nope. I'm going to bed."

I headed upstairs, and slipped out of my clothes and into the old shift I generally slept in. I was brushing out my hair when he entered the room. He came up behind me, lifted my hair from my neck, and kissed me. I sighed, enchanted as always that he always knew just where to kiss me and when. I laid my brush down, and started to turn towards him.

My heart lurched as he laid his hand on my stomach. "Don't you think it's about time you tell me, darlin'?"

I gulped and started stammering. And he started laughing, which made me slap his hand. "Oh, stop it! Don't you dare laugh at me! I... I..."

And then damned if I didn't start crying.

He immediately quit laughing, and pulled me into his arms. I cried for several minutes, my face soaking his linen shirt. As my sobs and subsequent hiccups quelled, and as he stroked my unbound hair, he said, "It's okay, Sassy. I wasn't sure at first, but the squirrel brains pretty well convinced me for sure. I'm thrilled you're carrying my baby."

I started crying all over again.

"Darlin', I love you. Why are you crying? Everything will be fine. it must be those dadblamed squirrel brains. I knew you shouldn't eat them. But Sassy, you don't need to be scared. Women have babies every day."

I didn't remind him that one out of two women died in childbirth at this time in history, or that both his sister and the mother of his girls died in childbirth. I realized he was trying to console me, to comfort me, to calm me. Poor man was on a hard, long journey with an emotional, nervous wreck of a pregnant woman, and he didn't know the worst of it yet. So, of course, I blurted it out.

"Lily thinks I'm having twins," I sobbed.

His hand stopped stroking my hair, surprise written across his face. "She does? My mama had twin brothers. I never knew anyone else who had twins." He grinned. "I guess that goes to my virility."

My sobs changed to laughs mixed with hiccups, as I slapped at his hands. "No, you big goose, if I am having twins, it is from my side."

He arched his eyebrows in surprise. "Why? Anyone in your family a twin?"

I nodded, struggling not to start crying again. "Jim and I are twins."

"Well, I'll be danged. I never knew you could have a boy and a girl twin. I thought they were always one or t'other."

"No, there can be identical twins, which are the same sex and look alike, or they can be fraternal twins. Fraternal twins can be opposite sex, and even if the same sex, they don't necessarily look alike."

Will let out a low whistle. "Well, I'll be dadblamed. So, how soon are these babies gonna be born, Sassy? Can we make it to Belle Rose?"

I slapped his hands again. "Oh, don't be ridiculous, William. I'm just three months along, if that."

"Now, Sass, I have seen pregnant women before, and you sure look further along than that." He kissed my cheek. "Little liar."

I leaned against his face. "No, I swear. You didn't get me pregnant before March. But..."

"What then, darlin'?"

"Lily says twins come early a lot of the time."

He pondered that for a couple of minutes before answering, while he continued to stroke my hair. "Then, I reckon we better get home and get married right and proper, girl."

"Are you upset?" My voice quivered as I asked it.

He laughed. "No, Sassy, I'm delighted. I have to admit, I wish we were home first, but I'm thrilled we're going to be having a baby – babies – by year's end. What a great Christmas present you're giving me, woman!"

Chapter Fifteen

The four men headed out the next morning, heading up north to check the flooding situation. In two hours, they returned, Will morose and ill tempered, Marcus trying not to tease Will, and the Cherokees, as usual, laconic.

I could hold it no longer. "How bad did it look?"

Will cut me daggers with his eyes. Marcus stifled laughter, but responded, "It's pretty bad. We might go that way in a week, but no sooner. The river is well out of its banks, for at least a half mile headed there from this direction. We rode north a bit, but it didn't appear to be improving."

I peered over Will's shoulder at the map, as I rubbed his neck. It was tight as a rope, the muscles corded into knots. He sighed as I rubbed it, and I felt him start to relax a little. He reached up, and patted my hands. "Thank you, darlin', that feels mighty good."

I continued to study the map. The highways were not here, nor were many of the towns I knew from the future. But one name stood out: Roanoke. I basically knew the way to Roanoke and on. I kissed Will's head, now showing about a half inch of hair, and whispered, "What about north to Roanoke?"

He studied the map, too. After a pause as he pondered my question, he nodded. "It looks like it might be a better chance than going east at this point. I prefer not to head towards the coast yet. Too many Red Coats for too long a distance that way."

All the men murmured in agreement. I kept rubbing his neck.

"Why don't we ride out this afternoon and see if the creeks are low enough to cross?" Marcus suggested.

Will nodded abruptly and stood up. "Sounds like a plan. But I have a helluva headache I need to get under control before we head out in the sun again. Sass, you have any more of that headache medicine?"

"Yes, of course." I started to dash towards the stairs for it, and then paused, turned back to him, and frowned. "Which one do you want?"

"That little blue pill works mighty fine, if you have any more."

I turned to sprint up the stairs to fetch him an Aleve, which I brought back to him with a glass of water. He downed both, and sighed.

"Why don't you go rest a little bit before you guys ride out again?" I suggested, with another kiss to his neck.

He reached up and stroked my cheek. "I will if you come with me."

Giggling, I pulled him up from the chair, and up the stairs after me. As we reached the top of the stairs, he was no longer glowering, but was grinning in anticipation.

As we entered my room, I wheeled around to pull Will's shirt over his head. He grinned even broader as I dropped to my knees to unfasten his breeches. With a grin up at him, I ran my tongue over the head of his penis. His eyes grew wide in shock and surprise at the unexpected touch of my tongue on his organ as he shuddered in delight. He wrapped his hands around my hair, as I slid my mouth over him, and began to rhythmically slide up and down on his throbbing instrument. I was surprised it didn't take long, but in minutes, he shuddered, and spilled into my mouth.

At that point, Will and I both fell onto the bed. Will fell sound asleep within minutes, as I expected. An hour or so later, he awoke.

"You never cease to amaze me, Sassy."

I blushed, and snuggled closer to his shoulder.

"No, darlin', I just never expected... that... much less that you would be willing to..."

He was embarrassed at discussing this topic, so I just grinned up at him, and said, "Silly man, of course I swallowed. It's rude to spit."

I thought he'd choke laughing. He pulled me closer to him, and kissed me deep. "Girl, you may never fail to surprise me, but you're a true gem. I wonder if Owen knew how lucky he was."

I didn't say anything. In fourteen years, Owen never said anything like that to me. I knew Owen loved me, but he always wanted more, from both Rick and me. I smiled and snuggled closer to him. "I love you, Will."

"I love you, too, Little Bit." He started out of bed, where I knew he would head towards the door, and then turned around to grab me for another quick kiss. "I reckon you can call me Dude any time you want, Sassy."

Damn, that man has a killer smile! I kissed him one more time. "About time, Dude."

"Who was this Dude fella anyway?"

"It's a generic term, like 'man'. But there was a show called The Big Lebowski, and they call the hero Dude."

Will was quiet for a minute. "Was he good looking?"

I laughed. "Oh, very," I replied, although Dude Lebowski was not 'my type' at all.

He smiled. "Like I said, you can call me that any time, darlin'."

We laid back down again, snuggled up close, with Will running his fingers through my hair, until we dozed for perhaps another hour, before he climbed out of bed, pulled his clothes on, and strode downstairs with a new spring in his step. "Come on, guys! Let's get a move on! The day's half gone!"

Marcus looked confused. The Cherokees looked enigmatic. Lily just laughed and winked at me. "Did his headache go away?"

I smiled. "Oh, yes."

We both laughed.

Will, Marcus, Lone Wolf and Quiet Man all headed north, on the road to Roanoke an hour, crossing two streams, swollen but passable. Will breathed a sigh of relief. If they could cross those two streams, they could all get to Roanoke the next day.

"What now?" Marcus asked.

"Let's head back. Unless it rains again before morning, we'll be able to cross the river tomorrow towards Roanoke."

The others nodded in agreement, as they turned their horses back towards Fancy Gap.

Marcus looked about at the land. "This is right pretty land. Looks like crops would grow well."

Will nodded. "Yep. Worst thing about it is that it is in the mountains. Can't plant tobacco or cotton up here."

Marcus laughed. "Aye, but a man could have a prosperous farm. Raise some cattle, have a happy life."

"You gonna move?" Will sounded hopeful.

Marc laughed again. "Nah, I love the Cohutta, and it's far enough the war hasn't affected us too badly so far. Hopefully, my little village will remain safe."

—

It was hot and still in North Georgia in mid-June. Rick and Jim both wore short sleeved shirts, and both were still sweating, even with Sheriff Riley's window unit blowing cool air on them.

"So, you're basically telling us that she's dead?" Rick said, every word harshened with anger.

The sheriff sighed. "No, boy, you ain't listening to me. We can't find her. We can't find any trace of her. I have called off the search. It is just as if..."

"She disappeared into thin air," Jim said. "But we all know that couldn't have happened."

The sheriff nodded. "Yep, I don't see much chance she just up and disappeared. I already put enough man hours into scouring for her up there. We've been hunting for her a year now with no results. It's time to stop hunting, son."

Rick and Jim frowned, before they turned back to the sheriff. As if in one voice, they both said in unison, "Never."

The sheriff's eyebrows shot upwards. "What don't you guys understand?"

Jim stood up. "Oh, we understand. You're giving up on her. The case is beyond your capabilities to solve. Fine. Just understand this, Sheriff: Rick and I will NEVER give up looking for my sister. NEVER. Do you understand?"

The sheriff nodded. "Yep. Can't say I'd feel any different if it were my sister or my mother." He sighed, and lit his pipe. "But my hands are tied."

"Well, bollocks," shouted Rick. "Fucking ballocks. That is the biggest load of manure I ever fucking heard. You'd keep hunting for your mother, but not for mine? Fuck you, Sheriff, and the fucking horse you rode in on."

Jim reached over and touched Rick's arm. "Careful, son. Remember what your mom always said: don't make permanent decisions based on temporary feelings. Don't land yourself in jail disrespecting the sheriff."

"Oh, fuck the Executive Order of Her Majesty." Rick stood up, stiff with anger. "I will NEVER quit searching for my mother. NEVER. Understand?"

"Yep. And I didn't hear any disrespect for any law enforcement officer, young man. Nor for Herself."

Angry as he was, Jim refused to laugh. Apparently, the Sheriff shared the opinion of Herself as did most of the country.

Rick tried not to rage any more. He'd been protective of Sassy almost since he met her, first with his mother, and later with his dad and Grandmother Winslow. He didn't mention that to Jim. In fact, he wasn't sure Jim knew about that time when Mom almost divorced Dad. Or when Grandmother Winslow cold cocked her because Mom called off the divorce to Dad.

He never saw his grandmother since. He never would again either.

Of course, Rick still wasn't sure Mom made the right decision in taking Dad back.

—

We started towards Roanoke, early the next morning. We got about a third of the way there by nightfall. I let out a long sigh of exhaustion as I got off my mare, and stretched, trying to move muscles that sat too long in the saddle. "Is there any water around here, Will?"

"Yes, let me show you." He led Lily and me about 200 feet off the track to a little stream, rushing over the rocks. We both knelt down, and splashed water on our hands and faces. With but a moment's hesitation, I dunked my head into the cool water, shuddering with delight as the fresh chill washed over me.

"How did you get the scar on your neck?" Will kissed my nape.

My hand flew up to the old scar. I hadn't thought about that awful day in years. I sure hadn't thought about it since I met Will. I felt my heart racing as the memories began to flood my brain with endorphins and adrenaline again. "Uh... I had neck surgery."

He looked surprised. "Dang, I sure never knew anyone who had surgery on their neck before."

Lily walked over, and prodded the scar with the hands of a practiced surgeon, before she said, "I've wondered about that scar, too. Laminectomy?"

I nodded. "Yes, C 2-3 and C 3-4."

"Damn. Fusion, too, huh?" She let out a low whistle as Will and Marc just listened, obviously not sure what we were talking about. "When was that?"

I swallowed hard. Damn it, they were going to ask all sorts of questions now. My chest felt tight, and I could feel my breath quickening. "When we were Boston. I was twenty-seven."

She tilted her head at me. She's pretty good at reading me. "Wanna talk about it?"

I stood up abruptly as I dusted the dirt off my hands. "Nope."

Lily stared in stunned silence as I walked out. "Must be some story."

Will followed me after a few minutes. He pulled me close. I sighed as I smelled the ambergris and leather scent of my Will. "You know I love you?" he whispered to me.

I nodded. "I know."

He paused before saying it. "Sassy, if someone violated you..."

"No. I wasn't raped."

He stroked my hair, as he knew I love for him to do. He kissed my brow. "But what happened, darlin'?"

"I just tripped and fell down a flight of stairs. That's all. It was just a stupid mistake. I caught my heel and I just ... fell."

I felt Will stiffen at my words. "How? Why did you fall? Were you pushed?"

"No," I sighed, impatient, refusing to give all the details of that awful night yet again. My mouth was dry as stone. I shivered, more than from dread than from the cool of the night, and began to formulate the words to tell him of what happened in Boston years before. It was a simple enough story. I caught Owen with his RA doing the Monica Lewinsky. Oh, yeah, that should be easy to explain. Not. Anyway, I confronted them, with much yelling at him, right there in his Harvard office. I slapped him, and turned to run away. My foot caught on the ratty carpet, and the next thing I knew, I was plummeting down the stairs. The girl was screaming, I was screaming, even Owen was screaming.

When I woke up, I was in the hospital, where I learned I had managed to break my fool neck.

Owen kept saying he was sorry, that it would never happen again. He fired the RA. He thought I'd go back to work for him. He was wrong. I changed the locks, filed for divorce, and moved Rick and me to Williamsburg and a new job at William and Mary. He shocked me when he followed me a few months later. I shocked Rick six months after that when I took Owen back.

But then, I could never say no to Owen when he gave me those damned puppy dog eyes.

No, I would not tell them. At least, not now. Keep it simple, Sassy, I thought.

"Sassy? I lost you there. Are you okay?" Will sounded worried.

My head snapped around. "Yes, I was just remembering a lot of things." I swiped at a tear that was leaking out of the corner of my eye. I did not intend to tell him all of my memories. "Really, I caught my heel in frayed carpet, tripped and fell. That's all." It was all true. As far as it went.

I wondered if this was how Hillary Clinton felt when she tripped and fell, breaking her foot that time.

He still looked doubtful. "If you say so."

"I loved Owen, don't ever doubt that. He had a temper, but so do I. We would argue, but he never once hit me. Hell, he raised his voice, but he never once raised a hand to me."

But I could see it in his eyes. He didn't believe me. He thought my husband knocked me down the flight of stairs and broke my neck, which Owen most assuredly did not do. In fact, he never raised a hand to me, although he raised his voice at me in anger many times. I've seen him ball up his fists, but he never raised one to me. He got so mad at me that he hit the wall once and left a nasty hole in the plaster, but he never hit me. In contrast, that was just one of the times I struck Owen.

I loved Owen. I really did. But he was like the rest of us, perfectly imperfect.

I sure knew I was imperfect. I always wondered if Owen wasn't right, that I didn't really marry Owen because I loved Richard so damned much and the kid needed a mother, maybe almost as much as Owen needed a mother. His own mother sure wasn't much to write home and brag about.

Shit, I should have just told them I hurt my neck in a car wreck.

Chapter Sixteen

We headed north out of Roanoke towards Charlottesville. We arrived there ten days later. From Charlottesville, Will sent word to Belle Rose we would be there in 2 days. Just 70 miles to go! We'd been traveling for 7 weeks. Will was so excited to be approaching home.

I was tired to the bone, ready for a good, long, hot bubble bath, ready to rest, and most of all, ready to sleep for a month in a real bed. But, it would just be a week until our wedding when we would arrive at Belle Rose. No rest for the wicked, I thought, as I rubbed my aching back.

Three days later, as we were approaching Belle Rose, we were crossing Winter Haven Plantation. I pulled up my mare to stare at a small, dark skinned boy chained by the side of the road. The scrawny, half- starved, mud-spattered child wore a big, iron collar around his neck, and was shackled. Lash marks crisscrossed his shoulders. "Will, why on earth has this boy been treated like this? Why is this boy chained like this?"

"He's a runner, Sassy. Cutter can't keep him on the plantation."

I resisted the urge to ask if that was how his father would have treated a slave, but I decided maybe I needn't know. I felt sick. "The sign says the boy is for sale?"

Will looked surprised. "Yes, but he'll run, Sassy. Why would you buy him?"

I shrugged. "I guess for the same reason your father bought Marcus. Because this boy needs me." I looked around, and saw Mr. Cutter standing under a tree, talking to another planter. "Mr. Cutter? I'm Mrs. Selk. How much for the boy?" I motioned to the runner.

"Mrs. Selk?" He looked astonished. "Ma'am, you don't want that boy. He ain't nothin' but trouble."

"Fine, then you'll sell him cheap. How much?"

He looked at Will, who shrugged. "If she wants the boy, she can have him."

I bit my tongue as Will gave Cutter the money for the boy. But as Cutter loosened the boy's chains, and handed them to Will, I could hold my silence no longer. "Cut those damned chains off this child, Mr. Cutter. And take that awful collar off his neck."

He looked shocked. "You don' understand, Missus Selk. That boy will run."

"And he is mine now. That is <u>my</u> problem, not yours. Cut... This Child... Loose... NOW!" Even though my voice was like honed steel, I was shaking with rage as I finished shouting.

In shocked silence, Wilson Cutter cut the boy loose from his shackles and collar.

I reached down to the boy. "Can you swing up here, son?"

Untrusting eyes tried to comprehend what this crazy white lady was pulling. Finally, he nodded, and whispered, "Yes'm." He reached up to me, and I swung him up behind me.

Will cringed as the filthy child grabbed on to my skirt to hang on. "Sassy, he can ride behind me."

"No, he's my responsibility. Let's get home." I looked back at my tiny package. "What's your name, son?"

He looked surprised. "Ain't got no name, ma'am. I jus' Boy."

I ground my teeth in anger that any human being could be treated like this. "Your mama never called you by a name?"

He looked puzzzled. "Ain't got no mama."

I closed my eyes in frustration. "How old are you?"

"I don' rightly know, ma'am, but I thinks I's 7."

I cut my eyes at Will. He avoided my angry glare.

"Well, I'm Miss Sassy, and this is Mr. Will. From now on, your name is Gabriel Selk. How is that?"

The boy looked surprised. "Yes'm, that's right fine. Mighty fine, Miss Sassy."

I kicked my mare. "Then, let's get home, Gabriel. You could use a good bath."

He looked surprised again. "Ain't never had no bath before, Miss Sassy."

"Well, you're having one today. And you're getting some clean clothes and some good food in your tummy. Let's go."

Less than an hour later, I stopped to stare in stunned awe as we reached the long drive up to the Belle Rose Plantation. I knew in its heyday, this had been one of the most glorious old houses in the South. I never dreamed it looked anything like what I was seeing. We passed five miles of fields before we got to the drive to the house. The fields were neat and immaculately maintained. The industrious workers stopped and waved with huge smiles as we rode past. "It's Mistah Will! He done come home! Look! He done brung his Bride!"

Little Gabe's eyes bugged out as he saw the difference in this plantation and the one from which he had been liberated. I felt the tension ease out of his small body. I smiled as his little arms reached around me in a small show of gained trust. This little boy would never know how important that simple act was to me.

"Ooh, Miss Sassy, it's beautiful!"

"Yes, it is, Gabriel. Do you feel better now?"

He nodded. "Yes'm, cuz they all seem so happy. I ain't never seen no happy slaves before!"

I didn't tell him that over half of the servants he was seeing were not slaves, but were hired workers. There was time to tell him those things in the future.

The drive, as they called it, made a horseshoe up to the house, to let people out of carriages at the portico. On each side of the drive were tall trees, framing it much like Oak Alley would look some day in Louisiana. The trees created a shaded haven that broke the sun from bearing down on us for that last mile to the house.

And the house! Oh, in my wildest imagination, I had never fully understood what Belle Rose looked like in its heyday! I had visited the shell of a house, nothing like this. The house was covered with pale pink stucco and creamy trim. The impressive portico covered the carriages or riders as they disembarked to enter the house. The house stood there, three stories, of Georgian majesty. I could see at least 4 chimneys. The roof was red tile. Red roses framed the outside of the house, with a formal rose garden on each side.

"Oh, Will," I said breathlessly. "It's exquisite!"

He beamed with pride, and reached across to clasp my hand. "I'm glad you like it."

"Like it? It is fabulous!"

He laughed, his blue eyes sparkling in the sunshine. "I thought you saw it before?"

I nodded. "Yes, but it didn't look this pretty." I didn't explain that it was in ruins when I saw it more than 200 years into the future.

As we pulled up in front of the house, the servants began coming outside to greet us. They lined up in a row, with Fancy and Tobias in front. Tobias helped young Gabriel and me down from the saddle, and Fancy and I embraced as Will climbed off Zeus to come around and clasp Tobias's hand. Gabe's eyes looked like they were about to bug out of his head.

What's the matter, son?" Will asked, as he passed Gabriel.

The boy blinked. "Uh...uh..."

"It's okay, Gabe. You can answer Mr. Will. It's no trick. You won't get in trouble," I coaxed.

He swallowed hard, and then stood up as tall and straight as a 7 year old boy can muster.

"I jus' ain't never seen no white man that friendly wif' no n..."

"We don't use that word here, Gabe. That word is an insult to the hardworking people here and everywhere else who have darker skin than mine," I said. "If you feel a need to identify someone by their color, I would prefer you to say black. Okay?"

His eyes round, he nodded.

Tobias laughed, as all the servants looked stunned by my words. "Young fella, looks like we need to get you cleaned up. How 'bout you come with me, and we get you a bath? I reckon that's what you want, Miss Sassy?"

I smiled and nodded. "Yes, thank you, Tobias."

Arm in arm with Fancy, I walked over to the other house servants. Will held my hand, and said, "This is Miss Sassy. You all know that we're going to be married here on the 4th of July. We were hand fast in March, and were married by Shadow Wolf in a Cherokee ceremony, also. Sassy is my wife right now. My will states she is my wife, if anything happens before the wedding next week. Please treat her with the respect my wife deserves."

I blushed. Just then, out trotted Hawk and Mia, followed by their puppies. I squealed with delight and bent down to hug the dogs. I grinned at Fancy.

Fancy spoke up next. "I told you I'd bring them! Miss Sassy is one of the finest ladies I ever met," she said, causing me to blush even more. "And you all know I thought mighty highly of Miss Belle. As I call out your name, please step forward, so she can meet you. Hattie Mae."

A heavy set, older woman with a dark complexion and curling, grey hair stepped out and curtseyed. "I am Hattie Mae, Miss Sassy. I be the cook."

I smiled at her. "William raves about your cooking. I'm delighted to meet you, Hattie Mae. Have you lived here long?"

She chuckled. "Yes'm, Miss, Sassy, all my life."

I figured that was about 50 years. She stepped back into line.

"Mina."

A trim, petite girl with a café latte complexion and neat, curling hair held back under a cap stepped out next and curtseyed. "I be Mina, Miss Sassy."

"Mina is the downstairs maid, Miss Sassy," said Fancy, ignoring the scowl I gave her as she called me Miss. "She is small but very efficient."

"I'm happy to meet you, Mina. I am sure that you are doing a fabulous job."

She blushed, curtseyed again, and stepped back into line.

"Dolly."

A light complexioned, plump girl with red hair and freckles stepped out next. "I'm Dolly, Miss Sassy. I'm mighty pleased to meet you! We all been so excited about Mr. Will bringing you home!"

I smiled back at her ready grin. "I am pleased to meet you, too, Dolly. Where do you work?"

Dolly blushed, and curtseyed again. "Oh, Miss Sassy, I'm so sorry! I am the upstairs maid."

Fancy frowned at her. "She'll be your maid, Miss Sassy, if she pleases you."

"I am sure she will, Fancy."

"Randall."

A tall, slender, elegant looking young man of mixed blood stepped out next, and bowed to me. His hair was cropped close to his head, and his soft brown eyes shone with intelligence. "I am Randall, Miss Sassy. We are all so pleased to meet you. I am the doorman."

Fancy smiled. "And he is very adept at his job. He is an asset to Belle Rose."

I could not miss the smile he gave her in return.

"Jeremiah."

Another, tall, handsome young man stepped forward and also bowed. "I am Jeremiah, ma'am, and I am Mr. Will's footman."

"I'm pleased to meet you as well, Jeremiah. And you must be very good at your job, if my Will has you working as his footman."

He blushed with pride. "Thank you, ma'am. That's most kind o' you to say."

"Moses."

A darker skinned man a bit older stepped forward next. He was also tall, but broader than the two younger men, well-muscled. His grey hair was close cropped, with a balding pate. He looked at me with intelligent, grey eyes. "I am pleased to meet you, Miss Sassy. I am in charge of the stables."

"Oh, you lucky man, you're in charge of Zeus!" Everyone laughed. "I'm happy to meet you, too, Moses."

"He's the best horseman in Virginia," said Will said with pride. "I don't care what George says about Billy."

"I figured he was pretty good if you let him touch Zeus." They all laughed again. "I am sure you will be talking to him about my Fiona."

Will nodded, as a hint of a grin played at his lips. My pretty mare, Fiona, was coming into season. The men were going to decide if Zeus was the appropriate mate for her, but I knew that was not a topic for 'polite society' to discuss.

"This is Raymond."

A slender, older gentleman also of obviously mixed heritage with his greying red hair and grey eyes stepped forward. I wonder if he's related to the Jefferson's, I thought.

"I be Raymond, Miss Sassy. I be in charge of the gardens."

I blinked and then smiled. "Oh, Raymond, your gardens are exquisite! I was in awe of them all the way up on the drive. My late husband loved roses, but we never managed to grow any as beautiful as these! I commend you, sir!"

He beamed in pride. "Why, thank you, Miss Sassy! Mr. Will said you do like flowers. I planted them roses for Miss Belle many years ago. Her name was Belle Rose, you know. The plantation was named after her. She sure enough loved roses, and I sure am mighty pleased someone new will appreciate them as well! I believe that would make Miss Belle mighty proud!"

"Oh, I do appreciate them," I assured him. "We will have to talk more about the gardens." He smiled as he stepped back into line.

"I really appreciate you all meeting me today. Please bear with me if I have to ask your names again a time or two." They all laughed. "We're all just human beings, and I can sure make mistakes or forget. I am delighted to be here, and I am delighted Fancy is here with me. I have tremendous love and respect for Fancy, and I am pleased to see that she has resumed her position here as housekeeper."

"It's high time Fancy's treated proper again," Hattie Mae said. Everyone murmured in agreement.

I smiled. "Now, let's get inside! I want to see this beautiful home my Will brought me to!"

As we approached the door, Will surprised me as he swung me up into his arms, and carried me across the threshold. "A man has to carry his bride across the threshold for good luck, Sass."

I smiled, as I wrapped my arms tight around his neck, and kissed his cheek. "I love you, William."

He beamed at me, and kissed me as he lowered me to the ground. "Let's have a round of applause for the new lady of Belle Rose!" he exclaimed.

The servants cheered, and my eyes misted over. I was home, and the old saying is true: home is where the heart is.

Chapter Seventeen

The next week flew by as if in no time at all. The staff and I went into overdrive to make sure the house looked perfect. We wanted it to shine for Will, and not in any way to embarrass or humiliate him at the wedding. Too many important people would be there for it to look anything less than perfect. And I was having so much fun exploring my new home!

It was tragic in a way that I was able to see and do all the things Owen would have loved to have done. Owen would be dying over this, I thought. If he weren't already dead.

I'm not dead, Sassy. I'm not born yet.

I started at the words in my head. Owen had been unusually silent of late. His words rather startled me. I smiled. *Well, I sure would be in one fine kettle of fish if you were here now, Owen.*

I could have sworn I heard him chuckle, *Pretty much. But in any event, you're ready to move on. I wish you well, my darling. Live long and prosper.*

I chuckled at the Star Trek reference. Owen was a historian, but he loved sci-fi and loved that phrase.

Fancy made last minute alterations to my dresses, and began working on others as well. I gasped at the transformation she had made from the elegant 1720's panniered mantua gown into the much smaller profiled gown that still maintained the tailored integrity of the gown that I wanted. "Will it fit me?"

She nodded. "I made the stays lace up the back, with extra-long lacings. I can extend the stomacher with matching material on the sides, if need be, to make sure it would reach from side to side with no problems, I think it'll be fine." She smiled as she patted my hand. "Now, look at these."

As usual, Fancy'd outdone herself. She had made a gorgeous Indian chintz petticoat, with a cream background and red and blue floral designs, hemmed to just the right length for me. With it was a chintz jacket again with a cream background, in a smaller coordinating print of primarily red flowers with blue accents. A solid, cream colored, lace fichu was pinned to the jacket, so I could see the entire outfit at once. "Oh, Fancy, I love it! It's gorgeous!"

"I thought the cotton chintz was a good choice for the summer," replied Fancy, who was beaming with pride. "I picked several up on the way home when we came through Williamsburg." She grinned at me, as I realized they made a special trip to Williamsburg to buy fabric. "This one, too." She pulled out another chintz petticoat, with a dark blue background and red flowers, which could also coordinate with the first jacket. "And you can also mix it with this," she said, as she pulled out a jacket in red chintz with blue flowers in a smaller print than the petticoat, that also coordinated. Her eyes grew wide. "Oh! And I almost forgot! I did these!"

My eyes grew enormous as she pulled out an exquisite marigold yellow ensemble in a blend of silk and cotton. The bottom of the petticoat was embroidered with flowers dancing around the hem. The stomacher was made bigger to cover more as a woman grew during pregnancy. The short robe volante would cover the ensemble, cloaking the advancing pregnancy. A row of covered buttons ran down the front to close the robe volante until the woman's pregnancy would be quite advanced.

I beamed at her. "Oh, Fancy! I love it!"

"I remade some of Miss Belle's things. These were some of her things Hattie Mae said Miss Belle wore while she was biggin'." Beaming with pride, Fancy pulled out yet another lovely gown she had remade from Will's mother's stash. Made of cream colored muslin, it was heavily embroidered down the front of the robe volante, around the sleeves, and around the hem of the skirt in rich reds, oranges, yellows, and greens. "You know, I called her Mama Belle when I was little, before she died. I loved her very much."

"Fancy, you have outdone yourself. She would be so proud of you."

"Thank you, but this was simple. I just cut down her old gowns. You are about the same height as her. I didn't have to do the embroidery. That was done years ago." Fancy grinned. "The rose silk and the one made with that pretty green painted fabric are done, too."

Now I had proper dresses for a lady to wear, I thought with a thrill. Fit for Will's Lady Ranscome to wear. Even if the title wouldn't last much longer.

Guests began arriving the day before the wedding. Fancy and I watched as the carriages pulled up in front of the house, with elegant couple after couple arriving. I felt ready to take on the crowd of well-dressed people in my new outfit, but I was still amazed at the richness and sophistication of the fabrics. I was wearing the dark blue chintz skirt with the red chintz jacket Fancy made me, with a pure white fichu at the neck, and matching lace apron, 'just for show', and lace sleeves. Lace mitts completed the outfit. I found red leather shoes in Miss Belle's closet that worked well with the outfit. I was thrilled to discover her feet were about the same size as mine, which meant that I had about a kajillion new dresses as well as matching shoes.

With a start, I realized General and Mrs. Washington were climbing up the steps from the Potomac into the house. Fancy repaired my hair, coiling my braid into a neat bun, and pinning a dainty lace covered wired cap into place over it. I hurried to the stairs, to meet the future Father of our Country. "Do I look okay?" I asked, uncertainty in my voice. "Everyone is dressed up so much more than I expected since they have been traveling."

"You look fine," Fancy assured me. "Very *au courant*, very modern. They will all be jealous of your new designs, not to mention the fact that you will be so much cooler than them in their silks."

I grinned at her, just as Will began shouting.

"Sass! Get down here, girl! These folk want to meet you!"

Lily, Fancy and I hustled down the stairs, Fancy a few steps behind me.

"Sassy, remember, George and Tom are both enlightened, but they are still 18th century men. They won't take advice well from a woman," Lily warned me before we got downstairs.

I nodded. "I know. I played the role of an 18th century woman many times at Williamsburg, not to mention in real life the past year. But, still! To be in the presence of such greatness! I am just amazed at the way my life has taken me!"

She stared at me, laughter on her face. "They still put their pants on one leg at a time. Just remember, brilliant or not, Washington and Jefferson are just humans. You and I both know they are imperfect men, and the future will not look with kindness on their slave holding. And, never forget that we are in the 18th century. Neither man will take advice from a woman well, and they won't appreciate your advice about slaves."

I was nervous as Will introduced me to his friends. I gulped as Thomas Jefferson held out his hand to me. "Mrs. Selk, it is a great pleasure to make your acquaintance. William has said very complimentary things about you."

I realized my hands were still chapped and rough and my skin was tanned golden with freckles obviously marring my nose and cheeks, from riding horseback for the past two months, not to mention from working the farm for most of the past year. I gulped, put on my best smile, threw back my shoulders, and said, "Governor Jefferson! I am delighted to meet you! William has said so many nice things about you!"

Will cut his eyes at me and tried not to laugh.

"Now, be honest, ma'am. Will thinks I am an eccentric child."

I refused to laugh. That was the exact words Will used about Jefferson. He did not have the same appreciation that I held for the drafter of some of our country's greatest documents.

Jefferson's big, freckled hand slid around my own, and he smiled as I hesitated just a moment before clasping it. His eyes sparkling with mischief, as he said, "What did you tell this girl about me, Will? Why, I do declare, she seems afraid of me!"

His Virginian accent was as charming as Will's.

Will laughed and clapped his friend on the back. "Nothing that isn't true, Tom! But to be honest, I don't think she's afraid of you. My Sassy ain't afraid of nothing! I suspect she is a little in awe of you. She says all the time that Tom Jefferson wrote the Declaration of Independence! You'd think she thought you wrote the Psalms or somethin' important! Now, don't let that go to your head!"

Jefferson laughed, and hugged me. I arched my eyebrows at Will as I tried not to burst into laughter.

"Oh, go ahead, Sass. Laugh at the man. He deserves it." Will grinned at his friend. With that, I burst out laughing, not because Mr. Jefferson deserved my laughter, but because Will cracked me up.

Jefferson was an impressive sight. Almost as tall as my Will, he was almost 10 years younger. Red haired, with a temper to match, they said, grey eyes, raw boned, he was down to earth, and often called the Man of the

People. He adored his wife and children. I knew his wife would die in childbirth in 1782. They would have had six children in all; only two would live to adulthood. He was a planter, educated at William and Mary, like my husband.

And both owned slaves. I was still coming to terms with that.

I knew Jefferson never served in the Continental Army. He would narrowly escape capture twice by Lt. Col. Banastre Tarleton in '81. Tarleton was the really bad guy moderns remember from The Patriot, a movie that starred Mel Gibson. Believe me, Tarleton was every bit as nasty as that movie depicted him to be, in fact, more so. But that story is for another day.

Jefferson became the Governor of Virginia in 1779, when he was just 36 years old. His original version of the Declaration was edited and revised by the Committee, into the version we all learned years later. I'd read the original, and knew some facts about him not many knew in the future. Just imagine. He was a mere 33 when he drafted it!

About then, Jefferson's wife walked up, and stuck her hand out to me. "I'm Martha Jefferson. My friends call me Patty. I hope you will, too. My Tom appears to have forgotten his manners. I'm delighted to meet you, Sassy."

I blinked. Martha Jefferson was even prettier than the paintings I'd seen of her. Rich, auburn hair and intelligent and thoughtful hazel eyes, a fair complexion with rosy cheeks and lips, slender, a tad shorter than me, and a sweet smile. Dressed demurely in a modest navy blue round gown of broadcloth trimmed with a white ruffle at the neck, and a white cap covering her dark curls, she looked petite next to her tall husband. Bless her heart. I'd bet my bottom dollar she dressed down for us, since we'd been traveling for two months, and I came from the wilderness. I smiled, and extended my hand to her. "Martha, I'm delighted to meet you. Will has spoken so highly of both your husband and you. I hear you have a house full of children?"

She reached out and patted me on the hand. "Oh, no, call me Patty. Everybody does, and I'm quite sure we're gonna be great friends. And it just confuses the tar out of some folks, with Patsy Washington and me! The house isn't full yet, but we're hoping for that passel of children." She grinned at Martha Washington, and they began laughing.

"And you really must call me Patsy, Sassy. No one ever calls me Martha!"

Mrs. Washington exclaimed. "And George is human, too. I swear my Old Man doesn't bite!"

George Washington was taller than I expected, taller than Will, if not quite as tall as Marcus. I knew they had known each other as boys. George and Tom had been the same age; Will and Marc were several years younger. Washington's skin had slight pitting from smallpox he suffered as a young man. I knew I shouldn't stare at his false teeth. I knew that he was sensitive about the poor fitting dentures. He wore his hair powdered, so the greying red was covered. Austere, elegant, quiet, refined, the Commander in Chief was indeed all that and a proverbial bag of chips. His petite, ebullient wife stood by his side. She went by Patsy because her father said she was too happy to be a Martha. A pretty woman, she appeared younger and more slender than pictures I had seen of her. Her hair was still dark but like her husband, she wore it powdered. Her eyes sparkled with what I was to learn was a bit of errant mischief that would show its head at times.

I knew Martha had four children, of whom just one reached adulthood, and I knew Jackie Custis would die of camp fever, or epidemic typhus, in 1781. George and she never had children. Lily and I suspected the smallpox he had at age 19 left him sterile. Lily had thought it might have been a Rhesus factor issue, since Patsy was O- and George was O+ when Lily tested blood types years before. Sometimes, it's just awful to know things about people before things happen. This was one of those times, since Jackie Custis was standing there with them.

Martha Washington was a formidable woman. She accompanied her husband to his winter camps every year. She was with him at Valley Forge the past two winters, including the winter of 1777-1778 when so many men died. It was said she was his strong sword, upon whom he depended. I knew they loved each other with their whole hearts. If I had not known it, I would have realized it then, seeing the great love and respect in the eyes of each for the other.

Lily came up and hugged Mrs. Washington. "Patsy, it's so good to see you!"

"Oh, my land, Lily! I didn't realize Marc and you were here! George will be thrilled!"

Will sidled over to Tom Jefferson. "Did you bring my papers?"

He nodded. "We'll talk later."

Will frowned. "But..."

Tom patted Will on the back. "Later, my friend."

I was quite impressed with the dinner that night. I remembered Owen said Jefferson appreciated fine cuisine. Apparently, so did my husband. Dinner began with a rich and hearty beef broth, followed by salmagundi, which is what they called chef's salad in the 1700's. The main course was a veal roast, cooked to perfection, with stewed okra and tomatoes. I smiled and forced myself to eat a bit of the hateful vegetable. I really can't stand okra unless it is fried crispy. I guessed I would have to teach them how to make it. There was also rice, which I knew would be a staple along the coast, sweet potatoes, and piping hot, fresh bread. Desserts were a choice of a rich pound cake, strawberries and clotted cream, or tipsy pudding. Knowing that the pound cake was so loaded with butter than a person could literally squeeze butter out of the slice of cake, I opted for the pudding with a few strawberries. While everyone else drank wine, I opted for hot tea. Since the Washington's and the Jefferson's were there, I wanted it to be really special. Oh hell, I wanted spectacular. I was relieved to see how easy it was for Hattie Mae to give me that. I was confident the wedding dinner the next day would be every bit as spectacular, not to mention fattening.

"So, what's happening in the War, General?" I asked over dessert.

Will frowned. "Sass, I told you no politics this weekend. We can all sit around and talk privately later, but not now."

I gulped. Damn, I wanted to see what these two men were thinking right now, but I knew Will was right. I nodded, tried to look meek, and said, "Of course, William."

The men looked surprised, and then they all started laughing.

"Dang it, Will, you said she would argue with you about that!" Jefferson guffawed.

I could feel my face reddening. "Well, then..."

Will reached over and placed his hand on mine. "Well, then, we will all talk politics another time, and Sassy can ask you all the questions she has then. Not... This... Weekend. Understand, Mrs. Selk?"

Silent, I nodded again, my cheeks still burning red with frustration as well as embarrassment, but also with an element of excitement. I would get to talk to the men, later. And Will said I could ask anything I wanted then. "Yes, sir, Mr. Selk."

The Historian could wait.

After dinner, Patsy Washington asked me to show her the house, and Patty Jefferson chimed in she would like to see it, too. I grinned, and started showing them through my beautiful new home. When we reached my rooms upstairs, they oohed and aahed over the extensive clothing I inherited from Belle Selk, in addition to the remakes Fancy and I were crafting from the beautiful gowns.

—

Will lead the men into the library, where he poured out glasses of the expensive French brandy that had been smuggled in earlier that week. Tom closed his eyes as the liquor slid down his throat. "Ah, Will, that is some fine brandy." He reached for a Cuban cigar.

"So, what about the papers?" Will pressed.

Jefferson frowned. "Will, you just can't do it."

"Well, why the hell not, Tom? They're my slaves. If I want to free them in honor of my wedding, I should damned well be able to free every one of them. I'll pay the taxes, you know that. Why the hell can't I?"

"Will, you know the answer to that as well as I do. Legislature says you can free slaves for meritorious service. You <u>cannot</u> free all of them at once. It would set a bad example for other slaves at other plantations in this area."

"Oh, bull hockey, Tom. You argued for freedom for slaves in your draft of the Declaration."

Jefferson shifted uncomfortably. "I knew I should never have told you that."

"Yes, but you did, damn it. These are human beings, Tom. Just like you and me. They have souls. They don't deserve to be sold any more than Marcus deserved to be sold years ago."

"Now, Will..." Jefferson began.

"No, don't start that nonsense with me. I never wanted to own slaves. They were my daddy's slaves. They were my brother's slaves. I never wanted slaves. I don't own a slave one at Bellas Flores in Puerto Rico,and that sugar plantation does just fine. How do I free them???"

—

Fancy came running up the stairs, and motioned for me. "Will's arguing with Mr. Jefferson. You have to go stop him right now, Sassy. This could be really bad. They're arguin' about slavery."

I jerked my head up in shock. "Are you serious?"

She nodded.

"Damned man won't let me talk to Jefferson about such things, but he does? Good lord," I muttered, hurrying down the stairs.

I heard them arguing before I entered the room. I stopped, smoothed my hair and my dress, and then threw the doors open. The men stopped shouting immediately, although it was clear that they had been exchanging angry words.

"William Selk, you told me I could not talk about this subject with Mr. Jefferson or with General Washington this weekend," I said.

He nodded. "Yep. I sure did."

"Well, then shut up, William. Right now. Do you understand?"

Jefferson started laughing. I stared at him, too. "You, too, Tom Jefferson. Shut up. Right now. I don't care if you did write the Declaration of Independence. This is my wedding. I will not have you gentlemen arguing like ... like... low class, backwoods, white trash, hillbillies at my wedding. Do you all understand me?"

"But... but..." Will sputtered.

I glared at him. "Not one word about this now, do you understand me, Mr. Selk?"

His lips thinned into an angry slash, but he nodded abruptly. "Fine."

"Jefferson?" I snapped. He nodded, also, with a look on his face that spelled astonishment. He was not accustomed to women talking to him like this.

"Washington?" I demanded.

George smiled. "I wasn't arguing. I was just standing there listening."

I stared at him, suspecting he wasn't being honest with me. I asked, "What about that cherry tree, General? Want to tell me the story?"

Thomas Jefferson started laughing, and leaned back on the sofa. "Yeah,

George, tell us that story."

George began to turn red and to sputter. "Uh... uh..."

"Oh, come on, General, is it true you cut down the cherry tree?" I cajoled, using my sexiest voice.

Tom was laughing outright now, as Will and Marcus looked increasingly nervous.

The General cleared his throat. "Um, well, you see, Miss Sassy..."

I leaned towards him, batting my eyelashes at him again as I placed my hand on his sleeve. With a conspiratorial tone, I asked again, "Oh, come on, George, you can tell me. We're all friends here."

He ran this finger around his neckerchief. "Well, you see, Miss Sassy, um, well, yes, I did chop down that tree."

Hmm. There was more to this story than I suspected. "And?"

Marcus cleared his throat. "Um, Sassy, perhaps William could tell you this."

George hung his head. "Oh, consarn it all, I'll tell ya. Yes, I chopped down that tree. Tom and I told my brother, Lawrence, that Will and Marcus did it."

My eyebrows shot up almost to the ceiling. "Uh... say what???"

He nodded, head still hanging in embarrassment. "Yes, well, they both got whupped, and sent back home. Later, a servant tattled on me. Lawrence confronted me and I admitted I chopped down the tree."

My jaw hit the floor. "And then?"

"I got switched pretty good, too."

"Tell her the rest, General," Marcus said.

The Commander in Chief turned even redder. "Well, it seems that Mr. Jo figured out Marcus and Will hadn't done it, and he switched them for admitting to doin' somethin' they didn't do."

My mouth fell open, shocked. "So, they got switched twice…"

"Yep," he answered woodenly.

"...for something you did?" I finished.

"Yep."

Every man in the room except Tom Jefferson was embarrassed. Jefferson just laughed. "Funny, ain't it?"

I looked at him with disdain. "Not so funny to Will or Marcus. Were you there?"

"Oh, no, ma'am! I was just a wee little tyke then! Remember, they're all older than me! I'm the innocent one!"

"Yeah, sure," I muttered while I exited the room, shaking my head.

But the argument stopped.

The next day came around in a rush of activity and emotions the likes of which I had never experienced before. At long last, it was dusk, and the wedding was about to take place. Fancy did the final touches to my elegant hair, replete with ribbons and hairpins beaded with pink tourmaline crystals through it, to accent the magical gown Fancy reworked for my wedding. The dress was a perfect fit, making me look trimmer than I ever dreamed possible with the utilization of a butt pillow, which made my waist look smaller and somehow miraculously managing to hide my pregnancy. I slipped into the rose pink silk slippers, fastened the diamond clips on them, and I blinked. Hot Damn! I have dressed up at Williamsburg for re-enactments before, but this was incredible! I really couldn't believe this was me.

"Sassy, come on! It's time!" Lily called out to me.

Fancy straightened my dress one more time, and smiled. "You look beautiful. Now, go on."

I squeezed her hand. "I feel beautiful. You did a wonderful job in altering the dress to fit me, and a great job with my hair. Everything. I can't remember a time in my life I ever felt prettier."

She beamed at me as I kissed her cheek.

I turned to Lily. "Okay, let's go."

Lily and Mark walked me down the stairs. About half way down, Will turned around, and smiled at me. I smiled back before it even hit me.

He shaved off his beard. Oh… My... Freaking… God! He kept the moustache, but shaved off his beard! I blinked and then blinked again as I stared in shocked amazement at the handsome man awaiting me at the base of the stairs. I whipped my head towards Lily, who stood there struggling not to laugh. "Oh, my freaking God," I whispered. "I'm marrying Matthew Quigley!"

She laughed out loud and nodded. "I wondered how long it would take you to figure out who he looks like. Or rather who looks like Will. Yes, that actor must be related. He looks just like Will."

I raised myself up a little straighter. My Gramma would be thrilled to know I was marrying the ancestor of her favorite 20th century actor!

Everything was gorgeous. Decorated in red, white and blue, for the fourth of July, there were small hurricane lamps all around the parlor, as well as on the porch and outside around the tables. The lamps each held blue candles surrounded with red roses and white babies' breath. The golden light from the glow of the candles gave a magical feel to the room. The dogs preceded me, Mimi with a basket of rose petals, Hawk with my ring tied on a pillow. At the base of the long, curving stairs, Will held out his hand. I reached out and took it. As he pulled me to him, our servants (I still refuse to call them slaves) began to softly sing.

Will looked startled. "When did they learn that?"

"Yesterday," I replied. "Do you like it?"

He nodded. "Very nice. I never heard it before."

"It's new. It's called 'Amazing Grace'. Will, how do you spell Selk?"

He smiled with a tilt of his head. "Well, it depends. In England, they spell it Selleck but Daddy spelled it Selk. Why?"

I grinned. "That is Selleck."

He grinned, those damned dimples gloriously flirting with me. "That's not the way my Daddy pronounced it."

I laughed. "Just curious, Mr. Selk. I love you."

And then the minister began. "Dearly beloved..."

I have been to hundreds of weddings in my life. I know the vows. I cannot remember saying my vows that evening. I just know as I looked into the eyes of my love, I was home. Not all who wander are lost, but you have to be lost before you can be found. I had been so lost last year, and now I was found. After the vows were said, we said that in unison. The minister looked a little confused, but we understood. This lost woman had been found. I was home. And home is where the heart is.

The servants sang a rendition of "Oh, Happy Day!" after the service that I taught them. It was different from the rendition written in the 1740's. The song began with a youthful, clear, true voice singing the words acapella before the other singers and musicians joined in. I was very proud of the job little Gabriel did in his solo.

After we were declared man and wife by the Anglican minister (the third time we had been married, by my tally, but who was counting?), we moved outside, where a sumptuous buffet dinner was set up for the guests. A half dozen Virginia hams glazed with brown sugar and cloves ready to be carved, and three enormous prime ribs of beef. Steamed crabs, raw oysters and fresh boiled shrimp had been brought from Chesapeake Bay that morning on ice. Men were laughing at Will, urging him to eat his fill of the raw oysters for extra 'stamina'. There was another salmagundi, along with fresh corn on the cob, green beans with bits of bacon and little new potatoes, fried cabbage, red beans, and bowls of piping hot rice. Fresh rolls as well as biscuits and cornbread were also available. There was iced tea for me, as well as cherry bounce and rum punch, two popular, alcoholic drinks that I avoided. Will also had a good supply of Jefferson's beer and Washington's whiskey in his office. Last, there was a beautiful wedding cake, at least 6 layers tall, piped with elegant pale pink roses up the sides and across the top. It was a feast fit for royalty. With a start, I realized this was American royalty, the tidewater planters of Virginia from whom so many important men would come in the early United States.

Fiddlers began to play for the diners. People ate and drank, and soon were laughing. As they pushed back their chairs, they started to dance. After an hour or so, some of us moved to the parlor, where Tom and Patty were sitting at the pianoforte and playing duets. I was really enjoying their music – they were justifiably well known for their prowess – when it became increasingly difficult to concentrate due to the racket in the front hall. Marjorie Cutter was caterwauling to everyone who would lend an ear of the injustice of it all, that I had stolen 'her' Will from her. It was rapidly becoming impossible to miss the little snot's whining and crying. After I had enough of her foolishness, I walked over, still in my beautiful wedding dress, and held out my hand to the sniveling little brat. "Hello, I don't think we have met before. I'm Mrs. Selk."

Marjorie sniffed. "I should be."

"Oh, believe me, if he wanted you instead of me, you'd be Mrs. Selk. But I remember Will said he wanted a real woman, not an immature child. I guess that cut you out of the running, sweetie."

Her eyes grew big, her mouth agape like a fish struggling for air out of water.

"You might want to shut that before flies get in, sugar pot," I purred. "Not the best look for a girl hunting for a wealthy husband."

Will chuckled behind me. "I reckon I didn't need to worry about you."

"Me? Hell, no. Worry about the sniveling brat who is telling all she should be your wife. Kiss me, Mr. Selk, and make it good. Let her see just what she is missing!"

And damned if the man didn't flat bend me over back asswards, for the most romantic, longest, sexiest kiss of my life. You know those clutch covers on romance novels, where the man is kissing the woman like that? This was ever so much better than those look. I was swooning when he raised his head from mine.

"That do?" he whispered.

I nodded. "Yes, but I won't object at all if you do that again. And again."

He dimpled before he resumed kissing me, the crowd cheering. As they cheered, little Marjorie Cutter was hustled right out into her carriage by her father, with her still crying that it should have been her wedding. We waved goodbye and good riddance to them both.

—

Sassy had gone upstairs when Tom pulled Will aside. "Legislature won't approve freein' all of them right now, Will. But I have papers for four. You choose who."

Will frowned. "Wonderful. I decide who gets freedom and who doesn't?"

Tom nodded. "That's how it works. You decide who merits freedom the most." He pointed on the documents to the line for a name and the line for Will to sign. "Just fill in the names, and then you sign. You can free some more next year, and every year after."

"Fine." Will wrote in the names of four and signed the Articles of Manumission.

Jefferson let out a low whistle. "You're freein' your cook? Are you crazy? I'll hire her right away from you!"

Will gave him a tight smile. "You can try. Hattie won't leave."

Tom laughed. "Yeah, sure. I'll remind you of that when she's cooking your dinner at Monticello."

"That's part of freedom. If they want to leave, they have the right. If they stay, they get paid a salary. But I still would bet she won't go." Lips tight,

Will handed the four documents to Tom. "Just see to it Legislature signs them. No bull. Get them signed."

He could free four. Hattie, Raymond, Moses, and Randall. Tobias and Fancy were already free, Fancy since even before birth, her mama free before her. Over a hundred servants worked at Belle Rose. Over half were freed by his father years ago. Now, there were thirty-six left to free. Damn it, he wanted these people free. They all deserved that. Sassy swore Legislature would allow him free them all in 1782. He sighed. He could free as many as possible every year until then. By damn, every one of the Belle Rose slaves would be free in 1782 if not sooner. But sakes alive, it hurt like hell that he could not even free his own enslaved people because of a damned law. Laws should not be set up to keep people enslaved. Laws should give freedom to all Americans, regardless of color. It astonished Will to know the first slave in the Colonies was made so permanently rather than by indenture by a free black man. How could anyone want to do that to their own? Hell, how could anyone do that to another human being?

He sighed. He realized he couldn't change the world by himself, and he damned sure couldn't change the world today. He'd do his part, and these four were a start in the right direction again at Belle Rose.

His father pulled some kind of legal shenanigan years back so all babies born to slave and indentured parents were born freed, contrary to common practice. Each freed person at Belle Rose received a salary. They always had when freed at Belle Rose. Hopefully, he put the idea into the heads of George and Tom that everyone in this country deserved to be free. He planned to keep pushing that on them. They had tremendous influence in this country. They fought in earnest for freedom and liberty for all people. That must include everyone, not just white men. Freedom didn't really even apply to white women, if you got right down to it. They couldn't vote or run for political office. Sassy would be a fine person to have in office. She knew more about where this country was headed, good and bad, than anyone else he would ever know. If anyone should be making policy, it was her!

Oh well, at least two of the puppies were leaving with George, and another was leaving with Tom.

He sighed, and headed up the stairs. It was his wedding night, and his bride was waiting for him. He'd deal with this mess later. Tonight, was for his Sassy.

Chapter Eighteen

The weeks flew by rapidly. Summer changed to fall, and I grew bigger and bigger. We began to count the days until the babies were born. But something happened in my 30th week that made Will restrict me to the house.

In mid-September, I went out to saddle my mare to take Will his lunch. I was accosted by two Redcoats in the barn. Hawk and I put short shrift to their idea of kidnaping me. Hawk started barking, Tobias speared one in the ass with a pitch fork while I shot the other one when he tried to drag me off my horse. I was still trembling, when Moses and Randall came running at the sound of the shots. My knees buckled and I fainted just as Randall hollered. I woke up on my couch with Fancy fanning burnt feathers under my nose and Will ranting and raving I would never leave the house again without accompaniment. I knew I was in big trouble when Lily stood silent, lips pressed into a tight slash across her worried face.

The Braxton Hicks contractions started after that. They all kept me under close watch and on a short leash once those started. Lily would not let me out of the house much at all, worried I might go into premature labor at any time. We all worried I could be kidnaped. As such, I was pretty well confined to the house, and Lily and Will tried their best to keep me upstairs.

I was going stir crazy, even with lots of sewing to do, both with baby items and my quilting. I knitted and crocheted when I got too bored with quilting and embroidering. After all, I needed multiples of everything. When I got tired of making baby things, I worked on things for our soldiers during the Hard Winter to come. The dogs stayed close by. I wasn't sure if they were protecting me or I were protecting them.

We figured the babies were due December 17th. I sighed with relief when Halloween came and went, with no babies on the ground yet. It was looking really good for them. Fortunately, Lily agreed to stay until they were born, to ensure the babies and I were okay. She'll never know how much that meant to me. I knew they had to go home at some point, but I felt so much better knowing I had a competent physician to deliver the babies. She wished she had shots to give for hyaline membrane disease, in case they came early, but we figured we'd do the best we could. With Lily, I knew my babies and I had a better than average chance. Let's face it: I sure did not want to be the one out of three women who would die in childbirth.

Come mid-November, Will got a pigeon from Mount Vernon with a message the General wanted to meet him to talk strategy before heading back north. Will knew Washington was hunting for supplies as well as advice. Will already told him we'd give him all the supplies we could spare, and the women and I had been quilting and knitting for the troops for months. You can make a lot of quilts when you are laid up for a couple of months. They weren't fancy, but they would definitely help keep the men warmer this year. We also knitted about 100 pairs of woolen socks and mittens so far, and hoped to finish more before Washington left. Patsy's servants as well as Patty's were working on similar projects, along with scarves and caps. Patty was also sending food and kegs of the Governor's home brewed beer, and Patsy would send food and kegs of the General's whiskey. (See why they have fun with the similar names??)

On November 17th, Will rode out to 'go fishing'. I didn't know the location of the alleged fishing expedition, for my own safety, although I knew little Gabriel knew where Will they liked to fish on the Potomac. The site was towards Pope's Creek, where the General lived when he was a boy, about 10 miles from Belle Rose.

I sewed all morning. I was having contractions enough that they were annoying, but I was pretty sure they were just more of the same old Braxton Hicks contractions I had been having for weeks. Lily went to Monticello the day before, when a man crushed a leg and she had to amputate it. She stayed overnight to make sure he was going to be okay, and was returning today, unless the man got a really bad infection. My back had ached for hours. It never did that before, but I was convinced that these were just Braxton Hicks. Surely, I could not go into full blown premature labor with both Lily gone and Will gone.

Yeah. Sure. Remind me to stifle such thoughts in the future.

Around noon, there was a lot of noise downstairs. I heard people shouting, cursing, doors slamming and people running. Hawk sat up, and began growling. I could hear Fancy telling people to calm down and to lower their voices, but no one listened to her. The shouting got louder and louder. I even heard English accents. I wasn't at all sure what the ruckus was about, or why there were Redcoats downstairs, but I was damned sure going to find out. This nonsense was going to stop, right here, right now.

I pulled myself out of bed, my big belly again in a contraction. I struggled to slip into a robin's egg blue quilted petticoat and slip on my gold colored robe volante, without stays, so it looked like appropriate afternoon attire. I was not putting on stays today. I winced as I slipped my swollen feet out of house slippers and into my most comfortable oversized shoes, and started for the stairs.

Okay, I'll admit it. I'd been having contractions every four minutes now about an hour. I still hoped they were Braxton Hicks contractions, but I was 36 weeks along, and knew I could domino any minute. My back was beyond aching. It hurt, dammit, and that worried the hell out of me. But something bad was going on downstairs, and I had to see what it was. As I reached the bedroom door, I called out, "Michael, can you help me?"

Michael came running to my aid. "Of course, Sassy, but you got no business goin' downstairs now. My Mum will have a fit."

"I don't care. I want to know what those damned Redcoats are doing here."

I looked around, and spotted Gabriel cowering in the background. "Gabe, come here, dear." He ran to my side as I wrote notes to go to Will and to Monticello. I marked both so he could tell which they were. In the note to Monticello, I added a note to Lily, to tell her that I was having contractions 4 minutes apart for the past hour. I handed the notes to the boy. "Tell Moses to get some men to find weapons and to come in when I sound the alarm."

Gabriel nodded. "Yes, ma'am, Miss Sassy."

"After you let the pigeons loose, saddle your pony, grab a fishing pole, and head down to where the General and Will are fishing. If anyone tries to stop you, say you're going fishing to catch me some fresh trout for supper."

He grinned, realizing I was getting him out of the house and off to safety while he would be helping us. "Yes, ma'am, Miss Sassy!" He took off without a sound as he slipped down the back stairs.

"Do the men know what is going on?" I asked Michael, as he slipped an arm around me.

He nodded. "I think so. Fancy slipped down a bit ago, and I think she passed the word."

"I heard Fancy. Good, then come on, Michael, let's get this show on the road."

I leaned on Michael as we traversed down the curved stairway, Hawk following right behind us. We stopped half way down, as I had another contraction, the strongest yet, so I could catch my breath. As entered the parlor, the men jumped up.

"Mrs. Selk! I did not realize you were here!" a flustered young English soldier stood at attention as I entered the room.

"Really, Lieutenant Gresham? I'd have sworn you were quite aware I was here. However, I must admit that I am a bit surprised to see you here. You were headed back to England the last time I saw you. In any event, I swear people could hear you all the way to Richmond. What can I do for you gentlemen today?"

The young Lieutenant stood twisting his hat in his nervous hands. He began to stammer, until I interrupted him.

"Let me try to help you out here, soldier. My husband isn't here. What do you need?"

The Sargent with him, a hard-looking man with small, beady eyes, turned to Lieutenant Gresham and said, "We should take her. Ranscome will come to get his wife back."

I eased the small pistol from my pocket, where it was hidden by the fabric of my voluminous robe volante. "Now, why would you nice young men want to do that?"

The Sargent turned with a swagger, to begin to saunter towards me. "Because the General done told us to come back with either your husband or you."

I smiled, raising the gun. The Lieutenant paled, and stepped away from the Sargent, as did the Corporal who had remained silent. "That might not be such a good idea, but you can try. As we say in the United States of America, come and take it. By the way, just who is the General?"

Sgt. Smarty Farty apparently did not see the shine of the metal on my pistol. Instead, the fool began to saunter towards me again. "Ain't no one you know."

My dog began growling. I smiled. "You need to stop walking, sir. In fact, drop your weapon."

He laughed. "We know you ain't about to shoot me with that little pea shooter. Now, you drop your weapon and be a nice little girly."

I smiled, and took aim. Hawk was barking like crazy. He really wanted to bite the little weasel. His eyes grew large in alarm (for small beady eyes, anyway). "Now, wait just a moment, lady!"

I did not even bother to correct his mistaken assumption that I were a lady. "Who sent you?"

He swallowed hard, and then raised his head to stare me in the eye. "Go ahead, do it then. Shoot me, bitch. I ain't gonna tell you nothing."

"Stupid Redcoat," I muttered, as I shot the sorry bastard. Nice center of mass shot. And then all hell broke loose.

Hawk barked, angry and frantic, as Moses, Joseph and Ezra rushed in from the front, armed with scythes and hay knives. Raymond, Jeremiah, and Tobias came in from the back, with a shotgun, a butcher knife, and a pitchfork. I still had 10 rounds in my little Sig, and another magazine in my pocket with 12 more.

"Gentlemen, I recommend you slowly drop your weapons, and raise your hands. Kick those guns away from yourselves. Moses, pick up their guns. Ezra, check if they have other weapons. Take those, too. Check their boots. I want you gentlemen to lay face down, hands outstretched, where my men show you to lay down. Moses, get someone to drag that worthless carcass outside. That damned fool man is bleeding all over my favorite rug."

It's refreshing to see how fast men respond to a lady's polite request when they take her seriously. "Now, let me ask again, gentlemen, who sent you? Or shall I guess? General Campbell? Or perhaps Lt. Col. Banastre Tarleton?" Both men looked uncomfortable. They realized I would shoot but they were not supposed to give this information away. That led me to believe that it could but be one man.

It was the fall of 1779, when it was first suspected that Benedict Arnold was a traitor. I knew his treachery was discovered by Madame X of the Culper ring, whoever she was. Her identity had never been learned. Arnold would not start ravaging towns and plantations in this area for another year. This was apparently an isolated expedition, which lead me to think it was related to the earlier hunt for Will in Georgia. I took the gamble. I smiled and raised my hands up to cover my eyes. "Oh, I can see it now. It is emblazoned before me plain as day. It's General Arnold, isn't it, gentlemen? General ... Benedict Arnold?"

Both men looked at me with horror written across their faces. I have rarely seen looks as shocked as those two when I said that name. As the Corporal began stammering, Lieutenant Gresham stared at me as if afraid. "It's true you have the Sight then, madam?"

I nodded. "Yes. I see the name Benedict Arnold will be equated with traitor as long as the United States shall endure. That will be a lot longer than you or I, or our children, shall live, Lieutenant."

"Yes, ma'am. General Arnold sent word to Col. Tarleton and General Campbell. Your vision was very accurate. It is frightening that it is so accurate."

It was all the more frightening because Arnold was still Governor of Philadelphia, wearing a United States uniform. Already under suspicion for treason, and I now had proof of more.

My men tied up the Redcoats. They rolled the dead man off my lovely, now ruined Aubusson rug, and stripped him before taking his corpse out to throw it in the pig pen, per my request.

"Is that necessary, ma'am?" asked the young Lieutenant.

"Yes, sir, I'm afraid it is. First of all, we don't waste clothing. We recycle it. Secondly, the pigs are hungry, and they like to eat garbage."

The Corporal paled, as the young Lieutenant spoke up. "Col. Tarleton on said you were a pistol, Mrs. Selk. I suspect he didn't realize you handle a pistol quite well, or that you are quite so ruthless."

"When you are paroled, you need to let General Campbell and Col. Tarleton know that."

I struggled to hide my increased pain at the ever strengthening contractions. I glanced at my watch. Three minutes since the last one. Lily needed to get back pretty quick, or these twins were going to be born right here in the parlor with the Redcoats watching! I walked across the floor to the large armchair I knew was comfortable for my sizeable girth, and rather ungracefully grunted as I lowered myself into it. "Fancy, could you send someone down to keep watch? And Hattie, could you please put the tea kettle on to boil some water?"

Fancy eyed me before she nodded, and then sent Jeremiah to watch out for Redcoats, my husband and our General, who I expected to return quickly once Gabe reached them. Gabe had been fishing with Will more than once, and knew the spot where the men were enjoying their morning. Hattie rushed to the kitchen, suspecting I needed water for more than a cup of java.

I winced and glanced at my watch. Three minutes again. The contractions were more frequent, and stronger. I struggled to stand during a contraction as my waters broke. Dammit, I hoped I hadn't to ruin my favorite chair! "Fancy!" I gasped. "Come back!"

She stopped dead in her tracks, stunned by my voice, and turned back to me. "You alright?"

"No. But these men need to be secured before we go upstairs."

The Lieutenant raised his head, and paled when he looked at my soaked skirts. "Oh, my word."

"Tobias and Raymond, would you gentlemen keep watch over our guests? Randall, could you help Michael get me back upstairs?"

Fancy took control. "Are there any more of you Redcoats on Belle Rose property?" she snapped at the two men, a marble rolling pin leveraged over their heads.

"No, ma'am," the Lieutenant said. "General Campbell definitely underestimated the Selks."

I chuckled, then grimaced as another contraction began. *Damn, just 2 ½ minutes since the last one.* I struggled to control my breathing like Lily taught me. When the contraction ended, and I spoke. "Good. Then, if you gentlemen don't mind, I'm retiring to my boudoir to deliver this baby. Hawk, stay. Guard."

Hawk positioned himself in front of the men, hackles raised, teeth bared.

Randall swung me up, and headed to the stairs. "Come on, Miss Sassy, we'll get you all situated and comfortable for this birthin'."

Fancy ran along behind him up the stairs, shouting out commands to him. Randall grinned, as he ignored her and carried me straight to my bed, where he sat me on the edge with care.

"Thank you, Randall."

"My pleasure, Miss Sassy." He bowed, turned, and started to leave my room. "We'll take care of them Redcoats."

Dolly's eyes were huge as saucers that Randall carried me upstairs. "Oh, my land, Miss Sassy! You don' mean to say your in labor, do you?"

I laughed. "Well, Dolly, it sure looks that way." I grimaced as the newest contraction hit, 2 ½ minutes after the last one.

"But Miss Sassy, I don' know nothin' 'bout birthin' no babies!" she protested, and I laughed at the comment that would someday be famous in Gone With The Wind.

"It's okay, Dolly. We do," Fancy said in a low, calm voice. The women eased my petticoat, and robe volante off, leaving me in my short shift. Fancy fluffed up the pillows and spread extra, clean sheets across the mattress. She then helped me back onto the bed, and sat beside me. "Betsy, fetch some extra clean sheets and some old quilts. Uncle Tobias, please send this note to Lily at Monticello?" Fancy scribbled a note to Lily to advise I was in full blown, active labor and my waters broken. She let me hold her hand as wave after contracting wave rushed over me, again and again.

I almost wept with tears as I heard Lily's strident voice, and I realized she was running up the stairs.

"Leave it to you go into labor when I'm gone," she snapped. "Let's see how you are doing." She turned to the wash basin to scrub her hands.

I sighed with relief. I'd been about at the end of my rope. I knew everything would be all right now that Lily was there. "This is hard, Lily. I had no concept how hard."

"Yes, you little ninny, that's why they call it labor. It *is* hard work. The hardest work any woman will ever do in a life time." She peered at my nether regions. "Very good. You're almost there, kiddo. A few good, hard pushes, and this baby will be out."

Just then, another contraction started, and I could tell something was different. "What is it??"

"You're crowning. Okay, here we go, push, girl, push!"

Pushing felt so good. I pushed hard, and soon, I heard the squalling of a new baby, even before he was out of my body. "Let me see my baby."

Lily finished wiping off the screaming child. "It's a boy, Sassy. Will has his heir."

I blinked. Dark, curling hair like his daddy. And eyes that beautiful, azure blue. Of course, that could change, but somehow, I knew Thomas William Selk would keep those eyes.

I gasped as another contraction started. Fancy took Baby Tom and handed him to Dolly. "Clean and swaddle this baby and put him in that cradle."

Silent, Dolly nodded, doing as Fancy ordered.

Soon, I crowned again, and was ready to push. But this was different. The caul around him was still intact. These were fraternal twins.

"Don't push," Lily snapped. "Pant. Like a dog." She showed me how. I nodded, and began panting as she broke the caul and lifted the umbilical cord from around my baby's neck. After what seemed like an eternity, she said, "Now push!"

And once again, that glorious, heaven-sent release as I pushed my second baby out. His face was a little blue at first, but he soon became oxygenated and began screaming like his four-minutes-older brother. And merciful heaven, he looked like Jim! Ginger red hair, ruddy cheeks, and the very fair complexion Jim got from our Irish American dad. "Oh, Fancy, he looks like my brother!" I cried and laughed. Fancy and Dolly took the baby, and cleaned him up, too, before swaddling him and placing him in the cradle next to his brother.

I was 36 years old. I never dreamed I would have a child born of my own body after I learned Owen had that vasectomy. Now, I had a whole new life, in a whole new world, a second chance at love and not just one, but two beautiful babies.

God is good.

Chapter Nineteen

I heard him before I saw him. Footsteps pounding up the stairs, as Will yelled, "Sassy! Are you all right?"

I smiled. I was nursing the boys as he entered the room. "Yes, love, I'm fine. Come see your sons."

Will stopped dead in his tracks, turned white, mouth agape, as he realized just how busy a day I had while he was 'fishing' with Washington. "Damn, Sass, here I was worried about Redcoats."

I waved my hand dismissively. "Oh, that was the easy part. Shot one, the other two are in your library waiting to be questioned. They verified Benedict Arnold sent info to Campbell and to Tarleton, to send them here, as I suspected."

Will blinked, stunned by my words. "One shot?"

I nodded. "Dead."

He whistled. "Well, you are one fine shot, little lady." I laughed. "Two more captured?"

I nodded again. "The men are guarding them downstairs. The Lieutenant is a decent guy. Same guy from the Corner. Seems they sent him to complete his mission and find you. The Corporal is scared shitless. The Sargent, now fodder for the pigs, was an A-hole Deluxe. I would go so far as to say the man was... deplorable." I chortled at the significance of the term, unknown to Will. It would be over 200 years before the "Basket of Deplorables" comment would be made.

Will stammered in disbelief. "In... in the pig pen?"

I nodded again. "That's where we throw the scraps, right? And can't a hungry pig eat a human carcass in 8 minutes? I figured it would be good to dispose of the evidence as fast as possible."

Will started laughing. "Damn it, woman, I was scared witless you were hurt and here you were running the day, as usual. And then I come up here, and you are all calm, serenely nursing our babies. Let me see those little scamps!"

"Wash your hands," said Lily. Will immediately complied, and threw a clean sheet over his shirt before he came over to take the baby.

I handed him the dark haired boy I knew would look so much like my husband. "Here's your first born son, Mr. Selk."

He took Tom like he was the most precious gem in the world. I was pleased to see he knew how to hold a baby. He stood up, and walked around the room, talking softly to his son. He walked to the window, and pointed out over the land as he talked to the baby, staring up at his father, taking in every word.

Will stopped talking.

"What is it?" I asked.

He turned back towards me so I could see. The baby had taken his father's thumb, and was sucking it. He tried to grin, as a tear slid down his cheek.

"Why are you crying, you big goof? Here, if he is upsetting you, come get your other boy." I held out our red haired son.

Will shook his head. "I'm not upset. I just never had a brand-new baby grab me like that, before. It's almost as if... as if..."

"He knows you're his daddy?" I whispered.

He nodded. "Yeah." After a moment, he walked back to me, and handed Tom back to me, before taking our other son. "Now, boy, what are we gonna call you? And where did that thatch of red hair come from?"

I laughed. "Jim has red hair. He's the spitting image of Jim, from our baby photos. Oh, Will, I can't believe they are here!"

"I can't believe I missed it," he muttered. "He's supposed to be George Marcus."

"Well, the General has red hair. Marc almost does, with his strawberry blonde. Ask if they mind if your red-haired son is named after them."

His head whipped up. "The General! Oh, hell! He's downstairs!" Will handed Boy 2, name yet to be determined, back to me, bent over, kissed me, and then ran down the stairs. "George! You're never gonna believe what happened while we were gone!"

"I have a pretty good idea, Will. How is she?"

"Seems pretty good. Lily's with her. Both babies seem fit as a fiddle. First one will be named Thomas William, after my brother and me."

The General grinned. "Not after Jefferson?"

Will laughed. "We'll let him think he was named after him."

The General said, "And the second one? Is it a boy, too?"

Will nodded. "Yes. George, he has red hair. We planned to name him George Marcus, after you and Marc, but are you okay with that? Especially since the little rascal has red hair? Sassy's brother has red hair. She's really excited, and says he looks just like Jim."

George cast a fond look at Will. "Will, he can be George or whatever you want to name him. Anyone thinks he is mine because he has red hair, well, let them. If she wants to name him after her brother, I understand."

Will blushed. That was what he wondered, if Sass wanted to name the baby after Jim. "I'll ask her."

"When she feels up to it, I want to talk to her."

Will's head jerked up. "What about?"

"How she knew Arnold gave the order that sent these men."

Will thought for a minute before answering. "That's a question you need to ask Sassy."

—

"George wants to talk with you."

Will sounded funny. I looked up, and saw worry on his face. "Why?"

"He wants to know how come you think Arnold was behind this. I didn't attempt to explain."

I glanced over at Lily. Worry was etched all over her face. "Oh, dear," she murmured.

I sighed. "I take it he's not buying that I have the Sight?"

"He already knows we say that. I told him it's a question you need to answer. Are you up to this today?"

I looked at Lily. She nodded. "If you feel up to it, it's okay. Will can carry you down, or the General can come up here."

"No, I'd rather go down. I don't want the babies around any more people and germs than is necessary right now."

Lily looked relieved as she nodded. "Good."

I got out of bed, and slipped on my dressing gown. Will carried me downstairs. It would have been quite romantic if I hadn't known a difficult scene was about to unfold.

Washington stood facing the fireplace as Will carried me into the parlor. As Will sat me down on the settee, I noticed my favorite chair had been removed, hopefully to be cleaned. Otherwise, I would re-upholster it. Will sat next to me and put his arm around me. I leaned my head against Will as Lily and Marc entered the room.

Washington turned around, and took in the four of us. "It might be best if I had this talk with Sarah alone," he suggested, with his intent clear in his quiet words.

Lily shook her head. "No, sir, we're all here. We might have answers you need."

He stared at her for a minute, before he spoke. "You know I have to ask it."

I nodded. "I know."

"How could you have known the order was from Arnold?"

I heard the anguish in his voice. "You know I have the Sight, General," I began.

"Oh, hogwash, Sassy! You've said that for months. That is just so much blather. I would just as soon believe that dog of yours has the Sight! Come to think of it, I might just believe it of Hawk. Now, I want the truth and I want it now. How would you know anything at all about Benedict Arnold, much less that he might be aligned with the British?"

When that man was serious, there was steel in his voice. Add upset, and it was honed Damascus steel. I flinched, and glanced at Lily, who nodded at me.

"What's that all about?" he snapped. His eyebrows arched, as he looked from me, to Lily and Marc, to Will. "Well, this should be interesting."

"Oh, believe me, sir, it is," Will said, his voice gravely serious.

"General, I know Arnold is your friend."

Washington nodded.

"I know he resents he wasn't promoted and that Gates took credit for the win at Saratoga, which was, to be blunt, Arnold's win."

His eyebrows popped up. "How the blazes do you know that?"

"Sir, if you will humor me, I will tell you. You see, my late husband was a history professor."

"What does that have to do with this, Mrs. Selk?" he snapped with a frown.

I sighed, frustrated. "Really, George, I gave birth less than 2 hours ago. I did not have to agree to see you today. I am seeing you as a favor. Take it down a notch, or we are done today. D.O.N.E. Done. Do you understand?" I snapped.

I thought his false teeth were going to fall right out of his mouth. He slapped his jaws shut again, nodding abruptly as his cheeks turned bright pink. "Please proceed. I will try to contain my curiosity."

"Fine. As I was saying, my late husband was a history professor. So was I." His eyebrows shot up again. "When Owen died, we'd just bought a house in Georgia, outside a town called Acworth. I went hiking up into the Cohutta Wilderness to go find this property I heard was for sale. I thought I might buy it and build a 'bug out cabin'...you know, an off grid cabin."

"A what?" he inquired.

"A place to go hide out if needed. Things are... different... where I came from. Anyway, the land I was going to see was Marc's land. Along the way, I fell. When I came to, I couldn't find the path I'd been on. After hours, a Native American man ..."

"A what?" he asked.

"An Indian, sir. Shadow Wolf found me. He asked if I was from Beyond. At that time, I did not know what he meant."

I couldn't believe the change in his face. "Wolf asked if you were from Beyond?"

I nodded. "Yes, sir. He said I was a Lost Woman. He led me on to McCarron's Corner. That was when I found Lily and Marc."

He studied my face for a long pause before he spoke again. "Proceed."

"Well, sir, you see, it was July 4, 2018 when I started up there, and it was July 4, 1778 when I arrived at McCarron's Corner."

He again studied my face. Long and hard. He looked at Will. "Do you believe her?"

"Yes, sir, I do. We all do," Will strongly asserted.

"Why?" the General pressed.

"Because I came the same way in 1763," said Lily. "Except it was 2001 when I left to go hiking and fell through the same hole in time."

Silent, Washington stared at both of us. "Amazing. Wolf used to tell us stories of people who came from Beyond. I thought they were fables."

My heart leapt with excitement. "No, sir, it can really happen. You can pass when God sends you to meet your heart's true love. Otherwise, you cannot."

His face softened. George Washington adored Martha. "So, if my memory is correct, Marc was supposed to be Lily's love, and Will yours?"

We all nodded.

"Tell me what you know about Arnold."

I told it all. "I taught history, General, and the Revolutionary War was a special favorite. I guess that's why the Good Lord sent me to this time. I could be of use here in some way. I knew Benedict Arnold was a great hero of the Revolution. I won't go into all of his military achievements, but we know that despite his years of heroic service, he felt he didn't receive deserved recognition from the Continental Army. He resigned in 1777 after Congress promoted five other junior officers over him."

Washington's eyebrows popped up again. "That's not common knowledge."

I chuckled. "Not common knowledge information today, sir, but it is known in the future."

He nodded curtly again. "Proceed. I will try not to interrupt you again, my dear."

"I know you urged him to reconsider, and as a result, Arnold rejoined the Army in time to participate in the defense of central New York from British forces invading under General Burgoyne in the fall of 1777. In the battles against Gentleman Johnny, Arnold served under General Horatio Gates. Arnold held Gates in blatant contempt, and Gates was no fan of Arnold either."

"That's putting it mildly, m'dear. They hate each other," Washington said.

I nodded. "At one point, Gates relieved Arnold of his command.

However, at the pivotal Battle of Bemis Heights on October 7, 1777, Arnold defied Gates and led his troops in an important assault against the British. This attack threw the enemy into disarray and will contribute to the American victory. Ten days later, Burgoyne surrendered his entire army at Saratoga. That win was attributable to Arnold, but Gates downplayed Arnold's contributions in his official reports and claimed the credit for himself."

General Washington sat down. "Please continue. And may I say you have a better grasp of Arnold than most of my generals do, and better than Gates ever did. Or Congress, for that matter. Although they are getting there."

I smiled. "Hindsight is 20-20, General. And Gates was threatened by Arnold, who is frankly, a superior military man. At Saratoga, Arnold was gravely wounded again in the same leg he injured at the siege of Quebec. Temporarily incapable of a field command, he accepted the position of military governor of Philadelphia in 1778, but that will be the worst thing that ever happens to him."

Washington frowned. "I appointed him to Philadelphia. Why will it be the worst thing that happens to him?"

"While there, he met and married Peggy Shippen, the daughter of a Loyalist. Since their marriage, Arnold's loyalties increasingly come into question. His loyalties are changing. I am convinced Peggy has a lot to do with that. He's also accruing enormous debt hosting fancy balls and buying little Peggy everything her heart desires. You know he'll be brought up on charges in January. He'll be brought up again in May next year. He will be found guilty of abusing his position as Governor. Most of the charges will be dismissed, but he will be court martialed, and you will reprimand him. Even if mild, I don't think he will ever recover from that, sir."

Washington looked stricken.

I paused before I continued. "Peggy has already established correspondence with a number of British soldiers, including British Major John André during the British occupation. I suspect that they were lovers at some point, might still be even though she is married to Arnold. After the Brits leave Philadelphia, she develops ways to communicate with André across the lines."

Washington's head snapped up at me. "You mean...?"

I nodded. "Yes, sir, I do. Peggy spies for the British, and wants to bring Ben over to them. She's already begun passing letters back and forth between Ben and John André. Right now, Arnold is negotiating with the British regarding troop locations and munitions locations. You send him to West Point next August, where he will begin draining supplies, failing to make necessary repairs, just generally weakening the fort's defenses. He also starts transferring his personal funds to England, because Peggy and he plan to move. He meets with André on September 20, 1780. Several days later, André is captured, dressed as a civilian, carrying vital information about Arnold's treacherous betrayal of your trust with arrangements to surrender West Point to the British in return for a lot of money and command as a General in the British army."

Washington pondered all I had dumped on him. He leaned back against the back of the chair, with his eyes closed. "Dear Lord. West Point is essential. If he gives it to the British, we're finished. From there, they have the whole Hudson, then all of New York in addition to a goodly part of the South." Washington sighed. "You haven't told other people about this, have you, Sassy?"

"No, sir. You will be able to intercept the delineated arrangements before the transfer occurs, thus thwarting the plot. I told Will to be wary of Arnold. When the men showed up, for the second attempt to kidnap me, I just guessed and asked if Arnold was behind the attempts. I was surprised they admitted he was. I didn't think he would be working with the British for almost a year."

Washington arose and walked to stare outside, where he stood looking out across the Potomac. The sun was about to set, and the water shone red and gold with the fires of the setting brilliance. It almost seemed he had become lost to it, when he began speaking again.

"I'm relieved to hear that. I hoped we had not leaked news of his ill intent to the community. Who is his chief intermediary with the British?" Washington asked.

"Major John André, who will be captured on September 20, 1780 disguised in civilian clothing. Of course, a British officer found in civilian clothing is immediately considered to be a spy."

Washington nodded, impressed with my understanding of the workings of the politics of war.

"Papers found on André in his boot will incriminate Arnold of treason. Arnold will flee to the Brits before you can arrest him. West Point remains in U.S. hands. Ironically, Arnold will receive a fraction of the money promised to him. Peggy plays crazy for you in an attempt to avoid any prosecution. You let her go to her father in Connecticut. You offer to trade André for Arnold, but the British won't trade. André will be hanged as a spy in October 1780. After that, it becomes publicly known General Arnold turned coat, and is working for the British. He leads numerous attacks on towns and plantations in Virginia. Yorktown falls."

The General let out a long sigh. "So now what do I do? I can't just go arrest him. We are, indeed, watching him, but I have bigger fish to fry than just Ben."

It hit me like a sledge hammer. "Madame X," I whispered, as I glanced at Will.

"No, Sass..." Will began with a shake of his head as well as his hands.

The General looked puzzled. "Who's Madame X?"

"No one knows for sure, General. It's just known she was the sole woman in the ..." It hit me I was saying something I wasn't supposed to mention. "Uh..."

Will put his head in his hands. "Go ahead. Finish it."

I swallowed hard. I sure hoped he believed me, or I would be the one hung for treason. "Well, uh, sir, she's the sole woman in the Culper ring."

The General looked startled, and then shock was replaced with fury. "By, damn, William, have you told this woman national secrets?"

"No, sir," I interrupted. "I researched the Culpers for the past 14 years with my husband before I came here. We wrote two books about them. By 2018, every member of the group is known, except Madame X. By the way, how is Mr. Talmadge?"

"Talmadge is fine," he said automatically before his eyes narrowed.

"She tells you about André and Arnold. But, General, let me assure you of one thing. News of Arnold's treachery re-energizes the Patriots, and keeps us fighting this war. And never forget that if the musket ball that shattered his thigh bone had hit his heart, he'd be remembered as a great hero. Instead, his name will be synonymous with treason."

Washington smiled again. "Sassy, it's clear you know what you're talking about. History, which is our current events, is obviously your passion. But something else is obvious to me as well. I am a blessed man. The Good Lord sent you to me as my ace in the hole. You are my, what is it you say? My dunk slam."

"Slam dunk," I corrected absent mindedly. "Oh, I am sorry, sir, please continue."

He chuckled. "Don't you see, girl? You can tell me what is going to happen before it happens, and guarantee we win. You, Sassy Selk, you are the woman who shall be known to all posterity as Madame X."

Well, shit. I really had not seen that one coming.

Chapter Twenty

"Well, now, George." I began.

"No but's, girl. It is plain as the nose on Will's face to me." We all laughed. "You have the ability to give me information which will be a great aid in the war effort." He leaned back again, and grinned. "Think about it, girl. Who else could it be? No one knows her name in the future? But you're the historian who came from the future, who wrote books about this war, even about Madame X and her contribution to the war effort."

I nodded. "Okay." It made sense.

He smiled. "You send me missives as Madame X, in my code, delineating what I need to know about upcoming events and battles. I assume you know my code." He smiled as I nodded. "You tell me who to trust and not to trust, like Ben Arnold. Damn, I like that young man. Makes me sick to think he's going to turn coat." He stood up abruptly. "Your assignment is this: Before I leave next week, outline the information I need for the next six months. About the weather, as well as upcoming battles of importance in the North and in the South. Who to trust, who not to trust. I may attend parties in Philadelphia, but now I know to be very careful what I say around Ben, Peggy and this John André fellow. Going to be damned hard not to just hang them all, but I can be a wily old fox. I can bide my time."

I laughed. "You're not old."

"I feel mighty old some days, girl. Earning every one of these grey hairs, fair and square." With that, he arose, bowed, and exited my parlor with Will and Marc to go interrogate the prisoners.

I worked on key events and battles on land and at sea for the next few days. The following Friday, George and Patsy sailed down from Mount Vernon to Belle Rose. He looked over the list, somber at times, pleased at others. He slowly raised his head. "You're sure we are going to win this war, aren't you?"

I nodded. "Yes, sir. Like I said before, morale will be pretty bad when Arnold turns traitor. We will have been losing a lot. That's part of the reason he turns. But the nation rallies behind you with his rejection and we go on to win the war in '82. But an important event is happening right now."

His eyebrows shot up. "What is it, Sassy?"

I smiled. "The French will throw in with us. A new ambassador should be arriving from France any day. They decide to back us and send troops, weapons and munitions."

He sat down heavily. "Thank God. I didn't know what to expect when I learned they were sending a new Ambassador."

"Next year, the Spanish also support us and send aid. They already have munitions for us in New Orleans and Havana. Where do you think Will gets those cigars you like so much? Havana. The aid from the French and the Spanish will be important. And, you're going to winter in Morristown this year."

His head snapped up. "I haven't discussed a possible change for winter lodging from Valley Forge to Morristown, little missy."

I chuckled. "George, like I said before, hind sight is 20-20. You thought last year was hard, and the winter of '78 at Valley Forge will be remembered for the huge loss of life, but this winter will be the worst of the century, known as the Hard Winter. And yes, I know you are wintering at Morristown, New Jersey. You take pigeons and let us know when to send more food and supplies. We'll keep working for you, sir."

Will and the General both looked shocked. "Worse than last year? Or the year before? That was by far the hardest winter anyone can remember in this century."

"Like I said, this will be remembered as 'the Hard Winter'. New York Harbor will freeze so thick the Redcoats march from Manhattan to Staten Island. When you arrive at the encampment site at Morristown, there will already be a foot of snow on the ground."

"Good lord, if I didn't know better, I would think you had the Sight," he muttered.

"In a manner of speaking, I do. You'll take your troops there next month.

It's going to be the most tremendous snowstorm ever remembered. Your men won't be able to endure its violence for many minutes without danger to life and limb. When it subsides, the snow will be over six feet deep and will obscure the roads and fences from view."

Washington looked worried. After all, I knew my facts. This was my area of expertise.

"General Clinton sails from New York against Charleston right after Christmas. To be honest, I never understood how he would manage that with the harbor frozen solid. Charleston falls. You reprimand Arnold in January 1780, by order of Congress, for misconduct. But, George, over 2000 men died at Valley Forge. Less than 100 Patriots will die at Morristown. You're right to move your winter camp."

He sighed as he sagged with relief.

"In March, you send Gates to replace Baron de Kalb, and in April, he lays siege to Charleston. I have more details delineated in code for you, but those are the big issues for you for now. Don't tip your hat too soon about Arnold."

He stood up. "It still just about kills me to know Ben will turn coat, but I sure am glad I have you on our side instead of their side, Madame X."

"You also need to be aware of the danger of Lt. Col. Banastre Tarleton, whom the troops call the Butcher. He's relentless. Under Clinton's orders, he takes Tarleton's Raiders to North Carolina early in 1780. After he takes Moncks' Corner, he captures Savannah, but not before one of his soldiers rapes a local woman. Very nasty business. From there, he raids into Virginia with Arnold a number of times. Jefferson narrowly escapes capture from him. In May of 1780, he massacres 113 soldiers. Another 203 will be captured, with 150 sustaining serious injuries. That's why he is called the Butcher and why the phrase 'Tarleton's quarter' will mean 'no quarter offered.' I will send you more in my next missive."

"Again, my dear, your assistance will be invaluable. You're a jewel I never expected to discover in this bitter rebellion against tyranny."

I felt my cheeks blush. "Thank you, sir. I am more than happy to assist the cause."

"Excellent. I need you to come to Philadelphia in January for the Military Governor's Winter Ball."

My heart sank. "Oh, now, George..." I began.

He was adamant. "I'm not going to hear any arguments, Sassy. I need you there when we have that damned Ball, to help me read the people."

"But my babies..." I tried to interject.

"I realize your babies won't even be two months old then. But I need you there. You just promised you would be available to help me. I believe you said you'd be more than happy to assist the cause. Well, I need you then. We all have to make sacrifices in this war. This is yours." He sounded sympathetic, but firm.

I realized there would be no winning this argument. His Excellency had issued a command to Madame X. I struggled not to cry as I nodded wordlessly.

"Bring a real pretty gown. Somethin' very elegant and warm. And somethin' elegant for the next day, at the Congressional Hearing. Will, if your mama had a fur, this is the perfect time to get it out to be altered for your pretty wife."

I tried to control my frustration as Will and the General laughed.

Will and I stood together and watched as the servants helped the General and his Missus load the winter supplies we were sending with them. I checked on the boys, and then came back to lean against my husband as we watched them sail out to head north to Morristown.

The weeks flew by before I knew it. Fancy and I discovered a beautiful midnight blue silk velvet mantua, with heavy silver embroidery and silver lace trimming the neck, sleeves, covering the stomacher, down the front, and around the hem. We figured out how to restyle the outdated gown, into a lovely gown in the English style, with a slight train. We made a cloak to wear over it from the outdated, long train. We found an ermine muff, and Will bought me an exquisite ermine cloak with an attached hood. I would be dressed fit for royalty.

A month after the babies were born, Will and I drove over to Monticello for an intimate dinner party with Tom and Patty Jefferson. Bitter cold but snow-less, we bundled up and made the carriage drive in record time. I wore a gown in a red and green plaid wool, with a white blouse with a big bow at the neck underneath the plaid wool. I wore a jaunty red tam on my head, a swirling red wool cloak trimmed with black velvet, red wool gloves trimmed with black velvet bows, and jaunty, fur lined, black leather boots. The ensemble was pretty and warm, what I really wanted. Will looked handsome as ever in a dark blue wool jacket, crisp white shirt, a pair of his much-loved buckskin pants, and highly polished black Hessians. As we pulled up to the gorgeous Georgian mansion, I stared in awe at the almost-new building Jefferson built just a few years earlier for his beloved wife.

We sauntered through the portico, where I could see the clock Tom made with just one hand, for the hours. I would ask about it, even though I knew the story well. I would also have to be sure to ask about the grass green floor cloth covered the floor, Jefferson's intriguing 'essay in architecture' that invited the spirit of the outdoors inside.

Patty and I went into the parlor, arm in arm, as she began telling me about the children. She was excited because Patsy, the oldest, was both learning to read, write, and speak French, and to dance, along with her ongoing developing equestrienne skills. "She went over her first jump just this morning!"

I smiled and bit my tongue to keep from telling her that the French would be well used when Tom and Patsy went to France in a few years. TMI. My hands went almost instinctively to a needlepoint pillow on the camelback couch. "Beautiful work. Yours?"

She smiled. "I love to do needlework. My one regret in this room," she said, as she glided across the floor to the windows, "is that I can find no more fabric like this. I wish I could find more to make more drapes and to upholster some of the pieces in here."

I joined her at the window, where I blinked. The fabric was a dove grey and cream pattern I often made at Williamsburg, a pattern known in the future as Jefferson chintz. I chuckled. "You can't obtain this at Williamsburg?"

"No, they don't make it any more. If I'd realized that, I would have ordered more when they made this for me. I've begged and pleaded, but the person who used to make this passed on."

I fingered the fabric I had seen so many times in the future at Monticello and would never have dared to touch, even though I made the replica fabric at Williamsburg. "How much more would you want?"

"At least 20 yards, more if they had it. But, alas, it's not to be..."

"I could make this."

Her head whipped around to me. "Are you serious?"

I nodded. "Oh, yes. I just need the cream linen, and you need a lot of patience. It's a simple design. I can replicate it. I just need to take a pencil and paper and trace a bit of the pattern to get it on the fabric sized right before I apply the wax to keep the fabric from dying all over the same color."

Stunned, she gaped at me.

"Uh... well, if you want me to..." I stammered.

"Oh, I would be delighted! But this is a big project. I never knew a white woman who could dye fabric, much less make designs like this! Oh, yes! I would be so grateful!"

I was delighted as I realized that the lovely, classic curtains I always admired were something I would help make. I smiled and reached around to hug her. "I know lots of women who can dye fabric. This would be my privilege. Just let me wait until after Christmas!"

She beamed. "Yes, it's in just two weeks now, isn't it? And Patsy Washington is very excited about hosting the Winter Ball for the Governor in Philadelphia. You're going, aren't you?" She pouted at Tom. "Tom won't go. He says he has too many responsibilities here, and fears it will be too cold. Oh, Fancy, please come in. Sassy, I see you brought your girl over to help you. I thought you might choose to rest here a few days before going home. I imagine you could use the rest. Fancy, did you bring the ball gown to work on? I really want to see it."

Fancy bobbed a quick curtsey. Clad in dark blue serge with a white fichu and apron, she looked the epitome of an upper-class servant. I noticed Fancy's eyes stayed averted from Patty Jefferson's face. "Yes, ma'am, Mrs. Jefferson. I done brought that dress and a day outfit to work on fo' Miss Sassy. I figured I could work on those, so she would have that pretty ball gown and somethin' else to wear in Philadelphia."

I bit my lip as I tried not to laugh. Fancy was back in servant mode, not about to look 'uppity' to Mrs. Jefferson. "Well, let's go look at the dresses we brought!"

Patty Jefferson's eyes flew open at the sight of Fancy's exquisite needlework. "Fancy, you do such lovely work. I'd have tried to buy you from William long ago if I realized you sew like this!"

I frowned. "Fancy's not a slave,Patty. She's a free woman." I did not add that she was also Will's sister – just like Sally Hemmings was hers.

She looked surprised, and then smiled again. "Well, my land, I should just hire you away from them!" She tittered.

Fancy's face remained impassive and she made no response.

"Fancy's a dear friend, and my business partner. I would hate to lose her." I didn't add that I knew she would never leave to go work for another planter, especially after what happened with Le Grand.

Martha looked shocked and surprised. She blinked rapidly, and then got her 'game face' on, and said, "I understand! I feel the same way about my girl. I don't know what I'd do without her, too."

Patty did not see Fancy wink at me.

Dinner was a sumptuous, gourmet feast prepared by the Jefferson's French chef, filled with fancy dishes of which I could not pronounce half the names. Tom and Will both laughed at my attempts to pronounce the names of the fancy foods. The lamb was cooked to perfection, the vegetables were hot, still crisp, and tasty, with exquisite sauces, and the desserts were 'to die for'. Patty made her famous Monticello pound cake, and I ate two pieces. Exquisite French wines and piping hot coffee and tea further enhanced our dinners. It was fabulous.

At the close of the evening, we all went into Tom's library, where he presented Will with the signed Articles of Manumission for the now freed men who assisted in repelling the British when they attempted to kidnap me in November. My eyes filled with tears as I realized they even freed Gabriel, 'for service above and beyond the call of duty, which lead to the rescue of Mrs. Selk, who was in labor when the Redcoats tried to capture her.'

He patted me on the back. "We can't have them thinking they can kidnap our womenfolk, can we? I know this is important to you, Sassy. Merry Christmas."

Two mornings later on the way back to Belle Rose, I leaned over in the carriage and kissed Will. "Thank you."

He looked puzzled. "For what?"

"You persuaded Tom to obtain those papers. Thank you, darling. You really are the very best husband in the whole, wide world." I snuggled up against his shoulder, where I fell asleep, safe and secure in the warm and loving embrace of Will. Fancy sat across from us, humming as she hemmed the sweeping skirt of wool ensemble I would wear in Philadelphia to appear before Congress.

I was disappointed Lily and Marc went home before Christmas. Will said Marc gets moody when he's away from McCarron's Corner very long. I knew Fancy and Marc quarreled. No one knew what it was about. Fancy sure wasn't talking, although I caught her crying several times. I told Will, but we agreed it was wasn't really our business. Will looked stressed by the whole situation. I figured he knew more than he was telling. I just knew I sorely missed my friends.

Soon, it was our babies' first Christmas. Despite the snow and cold, we had a wonderful time. We gave a Christmas party and everyone at the plantation received presents, new clothing, and extra food. Will gave me a beautiful coral necklace and earrings set. I gave him a new pocket watch I found in Charlottesville on the trip to Monticello, and a pair of felted wool slippers I made for him. I gave Fancy a new quilt in her favorite colors of roses and greens for her room. She gave me panniers and new stays to wear with my ball gown. The boys received new blankets, caps and gowns, and hand carved toys from their daddy and several of the servants. Bella played with her new dolly, changing her doll's attire from gown to gown in the collection her mother and I crafted from remnants of remade dresses. Bella hummed, showing the twins and the dogs each outfit as she tried it on her doll.

We all agreed the best presents were the manumission papers Tom Jefferson gave us for Moses, Joseph, Jeremiah, and Gabe, for their heroic and valiant efforts in capturing the two Redcoats and saving the plantation and me when I was in labor. The Virginia legislature fussed at freeing more of our slaves, but eventually they caved in. After all, it was Christmas, and they saved the Selk boys and their mother.

Gabe stared at the manumission papers for a good hour before he came to us, tears in his eyes. "Thank you, Miss Sassy, Mr. Will. It's the best present I could ever have dreamed of getting. In fact, I never, ever dreamed I would get ... get..." The boy choked up.

Will patted Gabe on his back, awkward in his embarrassment. "You earned it, Gabe. You helped save Miss Sassy and the boys, and I will always be in your debt, young man."

Gabriel raised his tear-filled eyes, and beamed at my Will. "Oh, no, Mr. Will. I will forever be in your debt. You saved me from Mr. Cutter. You taught me I have value as more than just a work animal. You treat me like I'm a human bein'. Miss Sassy and Fancy been teachin' me to read and write. And now this. I ... I..." The young boy threw his arms around Will. "I will never forget, sir. Never. You are the finest man in all the world." Gabe looked embarrassed by his emotions as he hurried towards the servants' quarters.

Will wiped at the corner of his eye. "Must be dust," he muttered, his voice husky with emotion.

I hugged him. "Undoubtedly."

We had roast turkey, oyster dressing, ham (of course, it is Virginia, after all!), winter squash, green beans, and pecan pies with fine French wine for all the adults. The children had to make do with milk or non-alcoholic fruit punch. Everyone said it was the finest Christmas since Miss Belle died. Their words thrilled both Will and me. As the day ended, everyone headed to their own quarters for the evening.

Will kissed my forehead, and then frowned. "Why are you crying, Sassy? We have two beautiful, healthy babies. Life is great, darlin'! Be happy!" He kissed me again, soundly on my mouth.

I looked up from my babies to my handsome husband. "It's just..." I started crying again.

"Women feel a bit emotional sometimes after they have a baby. Mayhap more so with twins."

"No, I'm grateful for you and our babies. Life is good. But I promised Rick I'd always be there for him. There's no telling what he's going through." I sniffed again, voice trembling. "He was … very sick when he was 15. He was in the hospital for ... well, for a while. I told him I would always love him and I would always be there for him."

My voice cracked. For a moment, I was lost in the memory of that desolate time, after I tripped and fell down the stairs. Like Will and Lily, Rick was convinced his dad pushed me down the stairs. He attacked his father, and even drew blood. As a result, Owen had Rick committed to a local mental hospital. When I got out of the hospital, I realized what Owen had done. I filed for divorce, and asked the Court to give me custody of Rick. The Court did, and released Rick to my care after almost two months in the mental hospital where he didn't need to be. The Court even allowed Rick and me to move to Williamsburg, Virginia where I began teaching as a History Professor at William and Mary.

Owen followed a few months later, after he accepted a position as Dean at the same college. I was furious when he showed up on our doorstep, smug as that proverbial bug in an Aubusson rug. I will always remember his startled look when I slammed the door in his face that afternoon. I flooded with emotions ranging from fury to my own love for the man I desperately wanted to hate.

We went to months of therapy. I gave in and I took Owen back the next summer. I always loved Owen, even if I never trusted him the same after that fateful day when I found him in the office with that damned girl. Our wounds healed with time, and I grieved when he died. But a piece of my heart died that day in Boston. No matter how hard I tried, no therapy could ever erase that picture from my mind of my husband leaning back, in the throes of passion, as that girl blew his pipes.

Will sank down in front of me. "Sassy, darlin', you couldn't prevent the Good Lord from bringing you to me. No more than you can go back now."

I nodded. "I don't want to go back. I'm quite deliriously happy here. I just wish Rick knew what happened to me. To have some peace, not to worry about me. Because I sure got my wonderful happy-ever-after."

Will leaned his head against mine. "It'll all work out just fine, Sassy. Some way, somehow, you'll manage to get word to them that you're safe. I'm sure of it. You'll see."

A few days later, Will came into our bedroom grinning as I was playing with the babies.

"Yes?" I asked, without taking my eyes off my smiling and cooing babes.

"I think I figured it out."

I turned to look at him. He was grinning with excitement. "Okay, I'm game. Figured what out?"

He dipped his head down to catch a kiss from me. "How you can write to Rick."

I frowned. "Uh, Will darling, I don't think they have time travel mailmen yet."

He laughed. "Nope, but didn't you have relatives in San Antonio? Who moved here from the Canary Islands?"

My mouth fell open. I was very glad I was not wearing George's wooden dentures. "Yes, I sure do! My great-great-great-whatever grandparents came over in 1738." I got up, excitement mounting as I rushed to my cell phone.

"Sweetheart, I don't think you can call those folks on that contraption," he laughed.

I shrugged. "Smart ass. I understand that. But, I have our family genealogy downloaded in my eBooks, and I know some of them live in the house where I grew up. Here it is! Genovio and Marcellina Consalvo were Gramma's ancestors who came in 1738. Ah! And here are Papi's ancestors, who came in 1743. Martin and Antonetta Suarez. I can write them both, Will! And hopefully, they'll keep the letters and someday, the letters will get to Richard!" I pulled him laughing down to my arms. "Oh, you're the smartest, handsomest, cleverest man in all the world!"

Two weeks later, we bundled up our belongings onto the Ranscome's Revenge, to head to Philadelphia. Even though the Revenge was the most modern of the ships in the Ranscome line at that time, and reputed to be the most comfortable for sea travel, I was nervous about the winter sea journey. I'd never been a really good sailor, even in a decent sized sail boat, in calm water, and I'd never been out in rough waters on open seas in the winter. I bundled up in a woolen round gown, with two quilted petticoats, and warm, corduroy leggings underneath. I covered up against the roaring, frigid wind with a double layer wool cloak. We put two layers of batting between the layers of wool, and quilted the cloak as well. With two pairs of woolen socks beneath my new fur-lined boots, I hoped I would be warm enough for the trip to Phillie.

Snow swirled almost as fast as my stomach flipped. I felt unsure if I were more unsettled at leaving my babies or by my inordinate trepidation over traveling by ship. Then again, maybe it was the fact that we were going to a ball being given by General Arnold, at which I would be spying for Washington.

Between the pitching of the ship and the sea sickness I would have had any way, I was quite ill within an hour of leaving shore. Because of the weather, it took about 30 hours to get there, twice as long as expected. Will estimated it would have taken at least 4 days if not 6 by carriage, maybe more, assuming we could have traveled the roads with all the snow and ice.

I was exhausted and dehydrated when we arrived in Philadelphia. Will carried me to the waiting carriage, and into the house where we would stay during our sojourn in the Friendly City.

Then things went from bad to worse.

We were greeted at the door by a dour, frowning woman who identified herself as Lydia. Her accent identified her as Irish by birth. Dressed an ill-fitting gown and a homespun apron, with a cap covering her lusterless dirt brown hair, she did not speak another word as she curtly motioned for us to follow her. She led us to our rooms, and watched sullenly as Will fretted with me.

Will spoke, frowning. "I thought you expected us. This room looks like it has been abandoned by a gang of drunken gypsies after a wild night of revelry." He bent over, and flipped back the sheets. "These are filthy. The room stinks of body odor, cabbage and turnips. My wife will not be sleeping here, nor will I for that matter."

The woman shrugged. "That's your decision."

Will's eyes narrowed, and I saw silver sparks in the azure of anger in his eyes. Her eyes widened as he snapped something at her in Irish Gaelic. "Madam, rest assured, it is your decision. You can clean this room, or we will go to His Excellency. His staff made the arrangements for us to stay here. He will be most upset that you have tried to foist off these shabby, filthy rooms to his friends."

Her light brown eyes widened in shock. "His... Excellency?" she gasped.

Will nodded. "You have thirty minutes to remedy the room. If it is not ready then, I will summon a hansom cab to take us to the Washington Manse."

"Will, can we just go back to the ship? I feel horrible," I murmured.

Will looked back at Lydia. "Is there a doctor who could come see her? She's been throwing up for three days."

The woman looked disconcerted. "I didn't agree to keep no sick folk. Iffen she be sick, you cain't stay." She squared her shoulders and glared at Will, animus all over her face. "Mister Brighton don't allow no sick folk to stay here."

"Mr. Brighton can explain that to General Washington. Brighton's been paid in advance. I expect quality for payment rendered." Will frowned, standing up to tower over her. She stepped back a few feet, and raised her arm in a protective stance. "Oh, for God's sake, woman, I don't hit women. She's seasick. The General wanted us here, or we wouldn't have come in this freaking storm. She needs to feel fit by tomorrow night for Governor Arnold's damned ball. Now, where can I find a doctor for my wife?"

She blinked, and began to stammer until she gasped, "Doc Koursandi is a few blocks over. You could send yer boy to fetch him back."

Will looked disgusted. "Oh, for heaven's sakes… what's the doctor's address, woman? There's a blizzard out there, and this child doesn't have any idea where to go in this town. I reckon I can find it. At least I've been here before."

She blinked again as she realized the master would leave the servant to fetch the doctor rather than risk the child's life. She stammered, "no, sir, I'll send m' boy to fetch him. It ain't right for you to have to go."

"Then, I'll go with the boy in case we have to send for the doctor again." Will sighed as he pulled his heavy seaman's pea jacket and wool cap back on. Lydia nodded abruptly turned and hurried out.

I was so proud of my Will, and reached up to squeeze his hand. "Really, darling, I feel better now. Just let me rest, and I'll be fine."

"Oh, bollocks, Sass. No one could be fine after puking for this long." He eased me out of my cloak and my gown before he settled me into the big oversized armchair, clad in my shift and a warm bed jacket. He wrapped my cloak around my legs, and bent down to kiss my forehead. "I'll be back as soon as I can find the damned doctor. You stay right here until she cleans this room and changes the linen on that bed, you hear?"

I nodded. I wasn't up to arguing with him. Will left with a slender boy about Gabe's age.

I dozed for a while in the big armchair before I awoke to loud voices and heavy footsteps coming up the stairs. I was pleased to see dour Lydia had cleaned the room from top to bottom and put fresh linens on the bed. Gabriel rushed over with my bed robe, and helped me pull it on just as Will came in with a man about Will's age in tow.

Dr. Koursandi removed his hat and coat. He was just a tad under 6 feet tall. He had curling dark hair, with a greying widow's peak, and greying temples. I was impressed with his intelligent dark brown eyes, and serious demeanor. I was even more impressed he did not immediately say I needed to be bled. After a quick, efficient examination, he surmised I was dehydrated from my sea sickness. He prescribed I sip boiled water, drinking no less than 8 ounces every hour. Wordless, Lydia slipped away as she realized I wasn't dying of some dire illness. Will sighed, and slipped out to go smoke his pipe.

Lydia fussed, but boiled the water, and brought me a glass every hour on the hour.

By the next day when Dr. Koursandi came back, I looked and felt much better. He grunted in pleased satisfaction as he checked me. "Much improved, Mrs. Selk. I must ask: why did you come through a blizzard to be in Philadelphia this fine wintery day?"

I laughed, uncomfortably aware that I could say too much. "When His Excellency summons, you come."

He frowned. "Yes, I have heard that. Well, you rest today, take it easy tomorrow, and enjoy the ball tomorrow night. I still think your husband is a fool to have brought you, but that is between the two of you. I'll come back again tomorrow to check on you."

I reached out to shake his hand. "Thank you, doctor. But my Will is no fool. There are exigent circumstances."

He nodded. "We won't discuss those. I am fully aware who the Military Governor is. Just... be careful. This town is rife with British spies."

"So I understand." I gulped, slapped what I hoped was a pretty smile on my face, and nodded. "We plan to enjoy the ball, and go back home before week's end."

"Easy on the alcohol, no heavy foods, try to keep it bland. And remember: loose lips..."

"Sink ships," I replied with a grin. "I understand."

The next afternoon, Patsy Washington bustled into the boarding house with her maid in tow. "Sassy, darling, I brought Eva to do your hair! I know you want to look spectacular tonight! Tell me how the boys are doing, and how Christmas was. Will told George you went to see Thomas and Patty right before Christmas. Tell me all about that, too!"

I smiled. I loved Patsy Washington, and no one could be a better wife to George than her. She adored her man, and traipsed north with him every winter to make sure His Excellency was safe, sound, well fed, warm, and stayed healthy. She knew he was important to our country; she did not yet realize just how important he was. I hugged her, and then showed them my gown for the party.

"Magnificent! How did you ever manage such an elegant gown so fast?" Martha asked, impressed.

I chuckled. "Miss Belle's closet came to the rescue yet again. We found the old mantua, altered it and voila! Here I am with this gorgeous gown!"

We talked about hairstyles before Patsy instructed Eva how to fix my hair. I sat down as Eva began to brush pomade and powder through my long tresses. We chatted while Eva worked her magic. I trembled with excitement as Eva slipped diamond pins into my hair, to catch the glitter of the silvery powder in my hair. The front was relatively high by American standards, with lots of curls, and more curls trailing down over my shoulder provocatively. Next, we did my makeup, with powdered skin, and rouged cheeks and lips. Once makeup and hair were completed, Martha's lady and Lydia helped me into my ball gown.

I stood stunned as Will came in with a jewelry box, and lifted a beautiful diamond parure set out of the velvet case to slip the necklace around my neck. He next fastened a bracelet around my wrist before he slipped the earrings into my earlobes, and then bent over to rakishly kiss my daring décolletage neckline.

"You look fabulous," he murmured.

"So do you." I eyed him, clad in blue velvet with silver embroidery, with his hair clubbed back and powdered before. He looked spectacular, every bit the urbane charmer I'd heard about. Daddy Jo had some pretty nice clothing that we could renovate for Will, too, as we found out getting ready for this ball.

Will helped me into the velvet cloak, and then extravagant ermine wrap and hood. The ermine muff finished the ensemble.

The carriage carried us to the Governor's Mansion, where the ball was held. Elegantly clad footmen helped us down from the carriage and ushered us into the great hall, where Will took my fur wrap and ermine muff. As I turned around, George slapped a man dressed in exquisite party wear on the back.

"Ben, I want to introduce you to my friends, Will and Sassy Selk," the General said.

Tall, elegant, his tawny colored hair powdered and queued back, wearing ice blue silk evening attire, he turned around and extended his hand to me.

My eyes grew wide with shock as the room began to swirl. "Owen," I whispered, as the ground swam up to swallow me.

Chapter Twenty-One

I waited for Owen beneath a chestnut tree outside the Episcopal Church in Williamsburg. I wore a lovely pink and white striped silk redingote, a turquoise sash at the waist. The skirt was cut right at my ankles, as the fashion in the 1780's, and my white clocked stockings showed beneath the skirt, along with the turquoise silk slippers on my feet. The outfit was completed with a bergere hat, with a turquoise silk ribbon tied jauntily at the side of my head, and my hair curled down my back. It was one of the prettiest dresses I ever wore at Williamsburg, and I felt quite fetching.

I heard the chuckle, and turned to see my handsome husband leaning against the gate to the church, as he puffed on his ever-present pipe. His tawny blonde hair was covered with a powdered wig and he wore an elegant cream linen suit. He took a long draw on his pipe, before he exhaled the smoke, and then smiled at me. "Exquisite, my dear. You are ... simply exquisite."

I blushed, charmed by his compliment. We'd been back together a few months, and he'd been trying hard to be very attentive. Compliments were not his forte, and each was precious to me.

Just then, a friend came up and clasped Owen on the back. "Damn, Owen, if you looked any more like Benedict Arnold, we'd have to give you that role to play here all the time!"

Owen frowned. "I am not goin' to play a Redcoat at this point in my life, Brian. You know me well enough to know that about me."

And then Owen totally surprised me as he dropped to one knee while he clasped my hand in his. "My darling, will you do the honor of marrying me?"

I laughed and I reached over to caress his smooth shaven face as I stared into his hazel eyes. "You goose, we are married."

He smiled. "Let's do it again, darling. Let's renew our vows. I promise I'll do better this time. Really, Sassy. I love you so very much." He kissed my hands.

My heart overflowed with emotion at his words. "Yes, Owen. Of course. I love you, too."

—

I regained consciousness in Will's arms. General Washington and Governor Arnold fluttered about me, terrified and fascinated by whatever made me faint. My heart in my throat, I was afraid to look at Arnold again, and yet knew must.

It was true. My Owen was a dead ringer for Benedict Arnold.

I knew Owen was somehow related to Arnold. He was always a bit vague about the connection. I heard people at Williamsburg comment he had a striking resemblance to the renowned traitor. Owen always huffed up at the comparison. But Arnold looked enough like Owen standing there dressed in fancy dress clothing with his hair powdered that for a moment I thought my Owen was standing there before me. Coming face to face with Arnold was one hell of a shock.

"Are you alright, darlin'?" Will fretted over me like a mother hen.

I nodded. "Yes. It's just a shock. I can't believe how much they look alike. For just a minute, I thought Owen was standing there..." I choked up again.

Will kissed my forehead. "Poor darling. Do you feel like getting up yet?"

"Heck, yes. We have a party to attend, and after coming all this way, I don't intend to miss it!!" I repaired my makeup and hair, and we proceeded into the ballroom. General Arnold as well as General Washington still looked rattled by my unexpected fainting spell.

I enjoyed listening to the music and observing the beautiful gowns. I saw one man in an incredibly elegant suit of pale aqua silk, the jacket embroidered with pink roses and gold leaves. Heavy pink lace dripped from the cuffs of the jacket. The tall, slender man sported a pale pink powdered wig, white face powder, cheeks, white clocked stockings, and elegant aqua pumps completed his ensemble. I could almost hear Owen making catty comments about the outfit. Will saw me staring at the man, and winked.

Apparently, Will had the same opinion of the outlandish outfit that Owen would have had. That outfit might work in Paris, the fashion center of the world, but not in the Colonies!

Arnold came over, extending a flute of champagne to me. "Perhaps we could attempt this again, madam. I am Governor Arnold."

I took the wine with a smile. "Governor, it's a pleasure to meet you. I've heard so many things about you."

His tawny hazel eyes blinked at that, as if he were unsure how to respond. "I hope at least some of those have been complimentary."

I felt my cheeks dimple as I smiled engagingly at him. I sipped of the bubbly wine. "Oh, yes. This is wonderful."

He blinked again, and then nodded. I could tell I disconcerted him, perhaps on many levels. At last, he responded. "I believe the new Ambassador from France brought it. Champagne, I believe he called it. He brought it on one of your husband's ships."

"The Ranscome's Revenge," I said as I took another sip. "The ship we sailed on from Virginia. Mmm. Excellent vintage. Elegant, fruity, light on the tongue, with a delightful effervescence. The Ambassador is to be commended." I turned to watch the dancing which was already in progress. "Do you dance, sir?"

He looked dismayed. "Not really, madam."

I turned back, to see his face ashen. "Oh, I am sorry, I forgot. Your injury at Saratoga, as I recall."

He looked stunned that I would know that, and began to stammer.

I held a finger up to his lips. "No need to apologize, sir. You're a hero. It's an honor to be in your presence tonight, General Arnold."

"I am sure you will excuse us both if I take my beautiful, beloved bride to dance, General," Will said.

Arnold appeared speechless as my husband took me by the arm, sat my glass down, and moved me to the dance floor. As the set ended, we went back to the tables where Arnold and Washington stood chatting. As Will left to go fetch me another glass of champagne, Governor Arnold said, "I must talk to you, Lady Ranscome."

I looked at him through my lowered eyelashes (a practiced maneuver both Owen and Will said was very effective). "Why do we need to talk, sir?"

He swallowed hard, and glanced around us before answering. "Madam, I need advice."

I stared into those tawny hazel eyes, so much like others I knew and loved for all those years, wondering what was up. I nodded, and he led me out of the ball room to his offices. Will noticed Arnold lead me away, and nodded to let me know he was aware. I knew Will would stand guard outside Arnold's door for me. Still, I was wary. This man sent people to kidnap me once, if not twice. He had to know I was aware of that fact. I eased onto the edge of a chair (about all you can do in a panniered skirt) as I awaited him to begin the awkward conversation.

"Lady Ranscome," he began, "I believe that you are under the impression that I had something to do with an attempt to kidnap you in November."

I thought for a moment before even attempting to reply. Should I be coy? Should I be direct? After pondering my options for a couple of minutes, I smiled. "Yes, Governor, that is correct."

His color heightened his already reddened cheeks, and he ran a nervous finger around his collar. "Madame, I can assure you I had nothing to do with that."

Damn, even his New England accent sounded like Owen. Focus, girl, I warned myself. This is <u>not</u> Owen. This is Benedict Arnold. *The* Benedict Arnold.

"Balderdash. Or put another way, bull hockey, Governor Arnold. You are aware I have the Sight?"

He nodded, discomfited by the entire conversation. "So I have heard, Madame."

I smiled. "Well, I do. I have visions which show me what is going to happen in the future. When the men came to try to kidnap me, your name was emblazoned in my mind, plain as day."

He swallowed audibly. He looked like he might vomit, and believe me, I knew the look.

"You're aware what is happening tomorrow then?" he asked.

I nodded. "I am aware Washington is addressing certain, shall we say, discrepancies with Congress."

His lips thinned. "He has asked Congress to sanction me for abuses of power, one of which involves the alleged attempt to kidnap you, Lady

Ranscome."

"Really?" I acted as if this surprised me. I knew Arnold was brought up on charges in January 1780, and that there was suspicion he'd been working with the British that fall. I wasn't supposed to know Washington wrote him up for the kidnaping attempt. I acted like I didn't want my surprise to show, so I just nodded my head. "And...?"

He began to pace back and forth. "Madame, I swear on my mother's grave, I was not involved in that travesty. Someone used my name falsely. I swear!"

I swore at him under my breath, both aggravated by his lie and impressed with the slick way in which he managed to carry it out. Damn, he channeled Owen well.

"Washington has lost faith in me. He will never trust me again if this goes forward! Please, Madam, I implore you!"

I was stunned both by his vehement denial of any guilt as well as my own unbidden desire to believe the man who looked so much like Owen. At least now I understand where Owen's innate ability to lie without effort came from. I stood up abruptly. "Fine. I will so advise the General."

"But..." he began.

"No, sir, you're a hero. If you swear to me that you were not involved, I must believe you. I will so advise General Washington, and ask him not to pursue that charge. As for any other charges, well, that is between Congress and you. Are we done?"

He sagged with relief. "Thank you, Madame."

I started for the door, and then turned back. "Just remember, do not make permanent decisions based on temporary feelings."

He blinked, confused by my words. "What do you mean, Lady Ranscome? I do not understand."

"Do not make a decision about something that angers you or upsets you that will have permanent, long-lasting effects, not merely on your own life and your descendants, but upon this nation as well, Governor Arnold. You are a brilliant soldier, a true hero of the Revolution. Do not throw all that away based on anger, on a desire to better your finances, or perhaps an effort to injure someone you feel has injured you. Please think long and hard before you make any decisions that you may later regret."

He pulled himself up to his full height. "Madame, I assure you I am not prone to impulsive decisions. Any decision I make shall be made with utmost careful determination of all the facts."

I was fascinated by the righteous indignation in his voice. Owen, you had your great-great whatever grand pappy's temper as well as his looks. "Good. I would hate to see one of the finest heroes of our Revolution become the most hated, most reviled traitor ever to live on this Continent."

He paled at my words, and nodded his head. "I ... see. Thank you."

Will awaited me outside the Governor's offices, patient as he puffed on his pipe. I laughed to myself that the pipe went everywhere Will went. As I came out, he tamped the embers out, and tucked the pipe into his pocket, before striding across the hall to gather me into his arms. "Everything okay?"

I nodded. "Yes, just very strange."

As Will and I started back towards the ball room, a lovely young dark haired woman clad in an elegant gold silk frock slipped into the office. "Ben! What did she say? Did she believe you?"

"Shush, Peggy," I heard him respond as he got up to shut the door behind her.

Will gave me a knowing look as he nodded back towards the closed door.

"I must talk to the General. Now."

We strolled back into the ball, where Will picked up flutes of champagne for us both. I flirted coquettishly with my handsome husband, as we meandered through the crowds until we found the Washington's, gaily chatting with members of his staff. I sidled up to the Commander in Chief, sipping my champagne until he noticed me. Without looking at me, he patted my hand. "Oh, Sassy, there you are. I want you to meet my chief aid-de-camp, Lt. Col. Alexander Hamilton. As you know, aides de camp are persons who demonstrate abilities to execute their duties with propriety and dispatch. Alexander is just such a man."

I smiled at the brilliant young man destined to be influential in the writing of the Constitution and as the founder of the nation's financial system. He handled letters to Congress and to generals and drafted many of Washington's orders and letters. He was also the main author of the economic policies of Washington's administration. I also knew Aaron Burr would kill him in a duel in 1804. "I'm honored to make your acquaintance,

Col. Hamilton. His Excellency holds you in very high esteem."

Hamilton beamed with justified pride at the words of both the President and me. He responded, "I am a fortunate man indeed to have this opportunity to work with His Excellency. Now, if you do not mind, I will excuse myself. I believe you may wish to talk more privately."

I was pretty sure he knew what we would be talking about. Washington and I ambled over to look out at the snow-covered garden. "Lovely evening, George."

He smiled. "Yes, indeed it is. And may I say you look quite fetching, my dear."

"You just like the powdered hair." We both laughed. I glanced around the room before speaking, and just to be sure, I raised my fan in front of my mouth. "He claims he wasn't involved in the attempt."

George's eyebrows rose just a little. I knew he was an excellent poker player, and was surprised to even see this tell. "Well, we expected that, Sassy."

I nodded, dropped my fan, and laughed, as if he said something amusing. I nodded at several people as I did. I then raised the fan back. "I'm not sure he isn't telling the truth."

His eyebrows rose in obvious surprise. "What?!!"

"Really, sir. I'm not convinced he's lying. Perhaps it is because he looks so much like my late husband, but I could generally tell when Owen was lying. I can't tell if Arnold is."

He frowned. "So, what do I do?"

"Tell Congress I won't pursue that charge. Go on the others. I didn't think you would charge him with that. I should have, since you insisted I come and be there tomorrow. He's legitimately concerned that you will lose faith in him. That can't happen, George. He has to think you still believe in him. As horrible as it sounds, as hard as it will be to do, you have to let him proceed in order to get the people to be outraged when it is learned he turns. Otherwise, let me be blunt, we will lose this war. He has to turn tail. You just have to give him enough rope to hang himself."

"Damnation," he growled, as he paced back and forth in front of the windows. "But they could have killed you, Sassy. And the babies. Not to mention your people..."

"But they didn't, George. I killed one of them, the others gave us names. Drop the issue, George. Sanction him on the money issues. Warn him to stay away from Brits, like André, who is here tonight. Give him enough rope to hang himself."

He sighed. "Fine. If you're right, we need to watch to see who all he is consorting with, in addition to André. Have you met him?"

"André? No. He's supposed to be handsome, young, and charming, but so are about half the men here. I don't know who he is." I glanced around the room, and saw a handsome young man flirting with Peggy. I looked at them. "Is that him?"

George smiled – almost – and gave me an almost imperceptible nod. "You have a good eye. Yes, that's him. Can you try to get a fix on him?"

I smiled and laughed as if he said something amusing, and tapped his arm with my fan. "Oh, George, you read my mind!"

I slipped my arm through his, and we began strolling through the crowd. George stopped now and then to introduce me to people. John and Abigail Adams. Several other aides de-camp and their wives as well as several members of Congress. We gradually made our way to Peggy Shippen Arnold and Major John André.

"Oh, Mrs. Arnold, would you introduce me to your handsome companion?" I asked.

She looked up, obviously shaken to see George Washington and me standing before her, smiling amiably at her and her companion. About that time, Arnold came up, and clasped George on the back. "George! Sassy! Let me introduce my beautiful wife, Peggy, and our dear friend, Major John André. Major André is here in Philadelphia until he is paroled. He's hoping that will occur any day. We hope it takes a while longer." He laughed amiably.

George Washington extended his hand to André. "Pleased to meet you, young man. Even if you are wearing the red."

Major André looked discernibly shaken. Nonetheless, he took Washington's hand, and then turned to bow with a flourish. "*Enchanteé*, Lady Ranscome." He flashed me a dazzling smile. "I have heard many interesting things about you."

I laughed coyly. "I imagine you have, sir." I felt my cheeks flush pink as I coyly lowered my lashes.

We spoke a few minutes, before he bowed over my hands to kiss me goodbye, and then did the same to Mrs. Arnold. Her cheeks reddened at the attention, and she fanned her face feverishly as he left.

André was an attractive young man with an animated and pleasant manner. He was quite intelligent. I heard him speaking several languages during the evening. I was impressed with the silhouettes he cut of people attending the party. I have a set he did of Will and me later that evening. He had many friends among the Patriots. I knew he would be mourned by both sides in less than a year. I felt sorry for him, but he would make his own bed and thus his own destiny.

As we started to leave late that night, we thanked our hosts, the Arnolds. I whispered to the Governor again, "Remember, do not make permanent decisions based on temporary emotions."

He smiled and bowed. "Believe me, Lady Ranscome, anything I shall do will be done with the utmost careful and prayerful contemplation." He bowed again, kissed my hand, and we wished each other adieu.

The next morning came far too early. It had been a very late night, and I was still exhausted when it was time to arise. Will even let me sleep late, but we had to be at the Congressional Hearing at 10 a.m. Eight just seemed too early for humans to arise after getting to bed four hours earlier. An hour later, we were dressed and ready to go. Will wore a somber, dove grey outfit with cream colored hose and black shoes. He doffed a tricorn hat and swung a heavy, wool cape over his shoulders as we exited the house. I wore a gorgeous outfit styled after the Duchess of Devonshire's riding outfits, with a royal blue wool skirt and jacket, with white cuffs and collar sporting red trim, with gold decorative buttons. The white blouse beneath had a frothy lacy jabot at the neck. The red waistcoat had gold buttons down the front, and laced up the back like a corset, hidden from view by the jaunty jacket. The ensemble was topped off with a large blue silk hat with red and white feathers sitting atop my hair, styled high and curled for the day. My coral earrings and necklace were in place as finishing touches. I swung my warm fur cloak around me, and we left for our meeting with Congress at Independence Hall.

George smiled as we entered and nodded towards our seats. After a moment's hesitation, we sat down to await my call to testify. Minutes later, I was called to testify. I recognized some people I'd met before, others from paintings I'd seen in the future. It was an impressive and intimidating assembly.

At last, Washington arose to address the Continental Congress. "Gentlemen, we are here today to address charges which have been levied against Governor Arnold. One of those charges involves the attempted kidnaping of Mrs. Sarah Selk, wife of William Selk of the Belle Rose Plantation in Virginia. Mrs. Selk was unaware until yesterday that charges were levied against Governor Arnold. She would like to make some comments. I believe several of you have questions for her. I call Sarah Selk to testify at this time."

Words I never expected to hear in my lifetime! I wished I could leave a copy of this transcript somewhere for Owen to find in the future. I arose and walked to the witness's podium. I was to stand while I testified, but my knees were shaking so badly I hoped I could manage. I was in the presence of at least three future Presidents, John Adams, James Madison, and George Washington. I gulped, squared my shoulders, and put on a serious but hopefully pleasant face.

Next, John Adams spoke. "Madam, we understand on the 17th day of November in the year of our Lord 1789, at around noon that day, there was a rather significant disturbance at your home. Is that correct?"

I nodded. "Yes, Congressman Adams, that is correct."

"Would you please tell us about that incident?"

"Of course. As you may know, I was at that time *enceinte*, awaiting the imminent birth of my twin sons. My husband was away from the home, with His Excellency. They had gone fishing."

The men chuckled at the idea of Will and George out fishing.

I bristled. "I know they went fishing because they came home with a passel of fish. My cook prepared trout for dinner. Those men love to fish. In any event, around noon, there was a significant ruckus downstairs, and with the assistance of several servants, I made my way downstairs."

Adams looked perplexed. "Why did you need assistance, madam?"

I blushed. "To be blunt, I was in active labor."

The men murmured in surprise. They knew I gave birth shortly after that, but hadn't realized that meant I was in labor when it happened.

"I came downstairs to discover three Redcoats in my living room, demanding my husband. I advised them he was not home."

"Did you tell them where he was?" asked a nervous Adams.

"Oh, heavens, no! I said he was fishing, which was true, and he had promised me some fresh fish for dinner. Then, one told the others to just take me, that the General told them to take me if they could not find Will, because Will would come after me."

The men shuffled uncomfortably again, with much murmurs. I took a sip of water and then continued. "I inquired who sent them after us. The Sargent refused to say. When he made aggressive steps towards me, I was compelled to shoot him, in a purely self-defensive stance."

The men began arguing with that, with more than one comment it was preposterous to think that a woman in labor would have managed to shoot a man. I waited for the noise to quell before continuing.

"I assure you that I am a very good marksman. I killed the man with one shot to the chest."

Suddenly, it was deathly quiet.

"Pray continue, Mrs. Selk," urged Congressman Adams, eyes sparkling.

"Well, sir, after I shot the one, the other two were much more willing to talk. I questioned them about several British officers I knew to be in the South. They feigned ignorance of their involvement. You now I have the Sight, sir?"

Adams nodded. "General Washington has so advised, Madam. Although several of us question it."

I blushed as I lowered my eyes. "Perhaps you are correct to question it. Sometimes, my intuitions are correct. Other times, not quite. It was like I saw the name 'Benedict Arnold' emblazoned across the wall before me. I inquired if he were who sent them for Will, and if not Will, for me. The Lieutenant admitted it was Arnold."

Pandemonium broke out. Adams lowered his gavel several times before regaining quiet again in the assembly hall.

I took another sip of water. "Not long after that, it became imperative for me to retire to my quarters, due to the impending birth of my sons. Servants assisted me traverse the stairs, while others watched over the two surviving

Redcoats, who were taken prisoners by my staff. My servants acted admirably. In fact, several received their freedom as a result of the heroic behavior they demonstrated that day."

Adams' eyes narrowed. I realized he knew what I was supposed to say next. "You say your intuitions are not always correct, Madam?"

I blushed one more time, again lowering my eyelashes. "Unfortunately, not always. I fear General Arnold was not involved, and I have sullied his good name most scurrilously."

I peeked a look at Will and George. Will's face was impassive, but George looked like he might laugh. I narrowed my own eyes, and continued. "I had the opportunity to speak with Governor Arnold last night. He most vociferously denied any involvement in the attempt to kidnap me. I know he is a hero of the highest order. I believe he is being honest with me."

Adams feigned a look of surprise. "Why do you believe you his saw name that night?"

"Sir, I believe the men were supposed to tell me his name, to throw me off track of the real villains. I'm sure Campbell, Clayton, and Tarleton were behind it. Perhaps Major André mentioned his easy relationship with Governor Arnold and his lovely wife, and the brutes thought to abuse it. Mayhap it occurred because I was in labor. In any event, it was apparent to me last night that Benedict Arnold was not involved."

"How could you tell?" interrupted John Henry, a Congressman from Virginia who attended our wedding.

I smiled. "His aura indicated he was telling me the truth."

The men looked stunned. Adams spoke. "His ... aura? What is that, Madam?"

"Everyone has an aura, a light encircling their bodies which is unique to that person. For instance, Mr. Adams, yours is white, indicating a man of utmost integrity. Mr. Henry had spikes of red when he questioned me, indicating anger. His Excellency always has an aura of purple, indicating higher purpose."

Adams frowned. "How did Governor Arnold's aura appear last night when you spoke?"

"Clear white, with purple streaks. It couldn't be such if he were lying."

Pandemonium broke out again.

General Washington stepped to the podium. "Please explain, Sarah."

I smiled. "Your Excellency, if Governor Arnold lied to me, he'd have flashes of black, spiking as he lied. By the same token, had the Redcoats been lying, they'd have spiked black. Neither did."

Washington frowned. "How do you explain the disparity?"

I took sipped my water before answering. "I believe the soldiers were given the wrong name in case I inquired with too much rigor. When I asked about Governor Arnold, they admitted it. There was no indicia of lying. By the same token, when I spoke with Governor Arnold, there was no indicia of lying."

The men shifted in their seats uncomfortably murmuring amongst each other before James Madison spoke. "Well, then, Madam, what would you have this Congress do?"

I smiled. "Congressman Madison, I cannot speak to the other charges. Those are between you good men and Governor Arnold. But as for the charges brought on my behalf? I ask this honorable assembly to dismiss them for insufficiency of evidence."

His eyes narrowed. "Is it not true, Madam, that Governor Arnold looks much like your late husband? In fact, so much so that you fainted last night upon introduction to Governor Arnold?"

I looked at him in surprise. "Yes, sir, that is correct."

"Is it not possible, how shall I say this, that you might be influenced by that appearance to alter your testimony here today?"

My own eyes narrowed as did my lips. "Sir, are you accusing me of perjuring my testimony? I am offended by your very suggestion, Congressman Madison. Shame, sir, shame! Impugning my name in such a scurrilous manner! I didn't ask to come today, but when asked, I came hundreds of miles in a blasted snow storm 6 weeks after the birth of my precious babies in order that justice be served. Do you believe I would perjure myself here before God and Mankind because Governor Arnold resembles my deceased husband? For shame, sir! For shame!"

I shook with emotion as I ended my tirade. The hall was silent. Madison looked mollified. Will and George both struggled not to burst into laughter, which would have caused them both to get hit upside the head by one angry little woman reputed to have hair the color of firelight shining through good corn whiskey (I must admit that I had grown rather fond of Will's description of my hair).

I picked up my gloves. "Sir, I believe we are finished." With a flourish, I wheeled away from the podium despite the fact that I had not yet been released to leave, and stomped out of the hall, where I awaited Will and George.

Peggy Shippen Arnold slipped up beside me. "Thank you from the bottom of my heart."

George came out, clapping his hands together several times. "Well done, Sassy. You should be an actress."

"What makes you think I'm *not* one?" I retorted as I put my cloak on to depart. "Don't ever put me in a situation like this again, George. This was a bit much." I heard a low chuckle behind me, and I wheeled back around. "This man's life is at stake. I could be wrong, as you well know. Don't laugh."

George wiped the grin off his face almost as fast as he did the night I asked about the cherry tree.

"I just hope I did the right thing, Will," I fretted.

"You did not impede the future from what it is supposed to be, Sassy. Otherwise, the British might manage to take West Point, which cannot happen," Will murmured.

I nodded. We knew what would happen with Arnold. We didn't know what would happen if someone else instead turned. The country might not rally upon the turning of a man of lesser value than Arnold. It ached to know that Owen's ancestor who looked so much like him would so heinously betray our beloved country.

It would have killed Owen.

Chapter Twenty-Two

We returned to the inn to prepare to leave. Lydia surprised me when she came to our rooms, and asked to speak to me.

"Mrs. Selk, I ain't been very nice to you. I apologize. I have a tremendous favor to ask." Her voice was soft as she stood wringing her hands, glancing at the door as if worried we'd be overheard.

I frowned. "What's the problem?"

She stifled a sob. "Mr. Brighton says he's goin' to sell my boy. He's angry at me, you see, and whenever he gets angry he threatens to sell Jed." She glanced back towards the hall.

I walked over and shut the bedroom door, and then pulled her over to the settee. "Now we have more privacy. Tell me what's going on."

Lydia told me she came to Pennsylvania 15 years before as an indentured servant. She should have been free after she worked her 7 years. However, typical of many indentured servants, her master abused her during her indenture, both physically and sexually. By the time her indenture was completed, she'd birthed two children he sired. He threatened to sell the children unless she stayed and continued to submit to his sexual demands. Unwilling to abandon her children, she stayed and submitted. However, five years earlier, he became angry at her again, and sold her daughter, then 7. She had no idea where her daughter was. Lydia had been terrified to cross him since, knowing he would make good on his threat to sell Jed, also, unless she complied.

"I just can't take it anymore, Mrs. Selk, I can't," she whispered. "But if I leave, he'll sell my Jed, just like he sold my Liza. His own flesh and blood, and he sold her like a sack of praties. I knowed you was a good woman by the way you treat your servant boy. You treat him like he is family. I thought... well, I thought mayhap you could buy Jed."

I was flabbergasted. "You want us to buy your son?"

She nodded. "I know he'd be cared for well and you would not abuse him. I'd know where he is. Please, Mrs. Selk? Will you talk to your husband??"

"We'll take care of this, I promise. Don't do or say anything until I talk to Will."

A spark of hope sprang into her eyes as she clasped my hand. "Thank you, Mrs. Selk. I'll never forget."

"What will you do then?"

She held her head up for the first time since I had met her. "I'll leave."

Will came in a little later, saying the Washington's had invited us to dinner. I told him to send word we would be delighted to stay if it wasn't an inconvenience for us to stay another night at the inn. He'd already checked and they said it would be fine. Without further ado, we changed our clothes for the small dinner party the Washington's that night. I hoped Madison wouldn't be there, but I suspected he would.

The Philadelphia house was much more modest than Mount Vernon, but was warm, inviting, and cheery upon entering from the blustery cold. Servants rushed to take our wraps, as Patsy and George greeted us with hugs and kisses.

"Oh, Patsy!" I exclaimed upon entering the dining room. "This is quite lovely! What are we having tonight? It smelled heavenly!"

She beamed with pride. "Roast of beef, mashed potatoes with gravy, and green beans almandine. We have fresh bread baked this morning, and a lovely cherry pie for dessert. George does love a good cherry pie. I believe we have a nice bottle of wine from the French Ambassador. You look quite lovely tonight, dear girl. Rose is definitely your color."

I laughed. "Oh, thank you, love! Yes, this is one of my favorites of Mama Belle's pretty dresses. Will picked it out himself for me to remake." I did a little pirouette. "I'm pretty pleased with the result. You look wonderful, too. I guess great minds think alike. We both wore pink!"

I moved to the fireplace, where I was warming my hands and bum when I heard the voice I didn't want to hear. Great. James Madison was there to ruin my roast beef dinner. I expected some sort of verbal attack from Madison about poor dead Owen's resemblance to Arnold. I so did not need that. I took sighed and then turned around to face him.

Madison inherited his plantation, Montpelier, from his father. He owned literally hundreds of slaves. He attended the University of New Jersey, known in the future as Princeton. He was a member of the Constitutional Congress, where I had just appeared, and later became one of the leaders in the movement to ratify the Constitution. His collaboration with Alexander Hamilton and John Jay would produce The Federalist Papers, among the most important treatises in support of the Constitution. Madison would change his political views during his life. Maturing does that to a person. During deliberations on the Constitution, he favored a strong national government, but later preferred stronger state governments, before settling between the two extremes late in his life. He would be known as the Father of the Constitution and of the Bill of Rights. Still, he pissed me off that afternoon, and I was not as excited to be in his presence as I usually would be upon meeting significant historical figures. I just thought he was a smart assed punk with a chip on his shoulder. Silly me!

The men laughed with one another, as I stood haughtily aside, determined not to give Madison the courtesy of my smile. George came over, clapped me on the back. "Well, Sassy, I have to hand it to you. You pulled it off with panache. You couldn't have done better if we rehearsed you!"

I looked at him, confused. "What on earth are you talking about?"

Will laughed. "Sass, Jim baited you..."

"Really?" I snapped. "Gee, William, I would never have guessed."

The men all burst into another round of guffaws.

I frowned. "I don't see how this is amusing. Madison attacked me this afternoon, and had the nerve to state I perjured myself to clear Arnold. I... Am... Offended. And you're point was???"

George and Jim Madison laughed while Will turned beet red. Madison spoke. "Mrs. Selk, I apologize. We knew if you simply changed your story, some would question why, in light of your fainting spell last night. Will suggested ..."

My eyebrows must have flown up to the roof. "Will suggested??? My Will???"

He grinned, nodding as he responded. "Will suggested if we accused you of unconsciously covering for Arnold due to the resemblance, that you would get angry, tell me off, and it would convince Congress better than anything scripted could work."

I blinked. I felt my cheeks burning red, but now from embarrassment rather than from anger. "Uh... did it work?"

"Oh, yes, ma'am! The vote was unanimous to dismiss that charge against Arnold. He was found guilty on a number of others. There was no word whatsoever of you being biased in favor of him due to his appearance. Instead, men were fussin' at me for attacking you like that!"

George clasped me on the back. "Great job, Sassy! Great job!"

The taste of misjudgment is so vile. Crow really is better served with 12 year old Scotch whiskey instead of roast beef.

The next morning, we finished packing our things. I talked to Will, who was willing to buy Jed from Brighton. As we started downstairs, we heard arguing. Brighton screamed, "I'll sell him! I swear woman, you try to leave, and I will sell that boy!!"

Lydia was white with fear, but held her ground. "Ye've kept me enslaved too long, Weldon Brighton! I'll not stay and slave for you another day! Ye threaten to sell m'boy? Yer a damned fool. He's yer boy, ye'd be sellin', yer own kith and kin! Shame on ye, Weldon! Shame!"

Will's eyebrows popped almost off the top of his head. He glanced at me, and I nodded. He pulled out his wallet. "I tell you what, Brighton. If you want to sell the boy, I'll buy him right now. How much?"

Brighton obviously was not thinking that if he sold Jed, Lydia would have no reason to stay. "50£."

Will laughed. "That boy's not worth 50£, as you well know! I'll give you twenty, and that's more than he's worth." Will pulled the money out of his wallet.

Brighton turned his beady little eyes towards the money in Will's hand. "Sold. Take the damned boy. Get him out of here today. I never want to see him again. Hell, I never want to see either of them again. Are you happy now, Lydia? Go. Get out. But ye'll not take the boy with you." He snatched the money from Will, who wrote out a receipt for the boy, which Brighton signed.

Shaken and pale, Lydia turned abruptly and exited the parlor to fetch her own few belongings.

"We need the boy's belongings, Mr. Brighton, if we are to take him now."

Brighton's eyes followed Lydia as she left. As I spoke, his head snapped back around to me. "He has naught beyond the clothes on his back."

We took young Jed upstairs with us as we finished packing. Since Brighton would not allow the boy to take his shoes or coat, Will put two pair of his own socks onto the lad, and then we wrapped Jed in my wool cloak. Sailors carried our luggage downstairs to the carriage, and Will carried Jed down. The lad settled into the seat across from us next to Gabriel. He looked like he couldn't comprehend what happened. We went around the corner, and two blocks down, to the spot we had arranged to meet his mother. When the carriage stopped, Lydia rushed over to climb into the carriage with us. As young Jed threw his arms around his mother's neck, she hugged him close and said, "Oh, Mr. Selk! I'll never forget this, sir! God bless ye!"

Will chuckled. "Just keep the bed linens clean and we'll be fine, Lydia."

The return trip to Belle Rose was far less eventful than the trip to Philadelphia had been. The storm abated, the sea was much smoother. We made it back in 24 hours. Home rarely ever looked as good as it did that cold January morning.

Will had letters for Mount Vernon from Washington. He intended to drop us off at the plantation while he went on, and he would return by morning. I kissed him adieu, and watched the Revenge sailed towards Mount Vernon. I turned to trudge up the hill to the house.

About halfway up, Franklin met us, and whispered, "Miss Sassy, you cain't go in there."

I frowned. "Why not? What's going on?"

Franklin glanced around, fear etched across his face. "Mr. Le Grand showed up this morning."

My heart did back flips. "Simon Le Grand? Oh, my God! Where are the children?"

He patted my hand. "It's all right, Miss Sassy, we got little Bella and the boys hidden away in the cabins. The dogs are there, too. We was afraid he might kill them. But..."

I grabbed his hands. "But what? What's going on? Why can't we go in?"

He looked back towards the house. "He's got Miss Fancy."

I would have sworn the temperature dropped 20 degrees, if not more. I shivered as I hurried back down to the dock. The Revenge had already passed the bend in the river. I pulled out my handgun, and shot three times, paused and shot three more. I dropped the magazine out, stuck the half-filled mag in my pocket, and reloaded a fresh one with 12 shots, before I turned back to walk into my home.

"Take Lydia, Jed, and Gabriel to the other children. No one comes out until Will or I say it's safe."

Franklin gulped. "You ain't plannin' to gwine back in there, is you, Miss Sassy? Cause iffen you is, and iffen somethin' happens to you, Mr. Will gonna skin my hide!"

"Nothing is going to happen to me. But Simon Le Grand better watch out," I muttered through clinched teeth. "Or he just might wake up dead."

Upon entering the house, I heard muffled sounds coming from upstairs. Fancy crying as if in pain. A sharp smacking sound which seemed to stop her sobs. I dropped my wrap, removed my hat and jacket, and crept up the stairs, silent in my stealth. I didn't bother to knock before I entered. Even expecting the worst, I was ill prepared to discover Simon Le Grand on top of Fancy, as she sobbed, silent as a church mouse. I raised my gun, aiming it at Le Grand.

"Fancy, get away from that animal," I ordered, with steel in my voice.

Le Grand's head jerked up, and he looked towards the door. "Well, ain't this cozy? Who's your little friend, Fancy? Wanna come play, darlin'?"

As he lost interest in Fancy, she pushed hard and managed to scoot out from underneath her nightmare. She slid off the bed, and crab crawled backwards to a corner, where she huddled into a ball, still crying.

Le Grand, apparently not the sharpest tack in the box, stood up and started sauntering towards me. "So, who are you, darlin'? You come to play with ol' Simon?"

He wasn't a bad looking man, even naked. Blonde and blue eyed, slender, and well-muscled, the classic looks sought in this day and age. But I knew his soul was blacker than the depths of the seas. I aimed at the middle of his body, just like Owen taught me years before.

"Stop. Now. Or I'll shoot."

Fancy's eyes were wide with fear as she raised a hand to her mouth, to stifle another sob.

Simon just laughed. "Darlin', you know ain't' a 'fixin to shoot me."

I smiled thinly. "You reckon? Why don't men ever take a woman serious when she is holding a firearm? Come on, Simon, try me. Make my day." I was shaking as I said it, mouth dry, terrified, as I remembered another evening long ago when another fool tried to rape me.

Neither Owen nor Will was around to rescue me this time.

Simon blinked, unsure what to do. He laughed and started towards me again. "Never let it be said that ol' Simon didn't give a woman what she asked for." I startled as he ripped my blouse down the front. Buttons popped, careening across the room. My breast stung where his nails gouged delicate skin.

I didn't even blink before I emptied the gun into the sorry son of a bitch. His eyes grew round in shock and then glazed. He slid to the floor as death dragged his blackened soul to hell.

Fancy ran to my side. "I want my… my Daddy," she sobbed. "I need my Daddy."

I hugged her close. "It's okay, sweetie. Simon will never hurt anyone again."

Fancy and I were still standing there shaking when Will came running back up the stairs. He took one look at his sister, at my ripped blouse, the blood beading up on my scratched breast, and at Le Grand lying in a pool of blood at my feet. Face white with anger, hands shaking with rage, he finally spoke. "You girls okay?"

We both nodded. He grabbed the quilt off Fancy's bed to wrap her before he spoke again. "Feed him to the pigs, Tobias. Now."

Chapter Twenty-Three

Rick and Melanie were having a wonderful vacation in Washington, D.C. They attended the seminar for new emergency room physicians, and took an afternoon off to tour the Smithsonian before they would fly back to Atlanta.

"That's the dress my mom loved so much when we came before. Dad teased her that she must have lived another life and was married to another man in the 1700's. She stood and stared at that dress for over an hour that day."

Melanie laughed, as she snuggled closer to Rick. "Your mom sounds like she was a hoot. I wish I could have known her."

Rick nodded, lost in his own thoughts. He bent down, and studied the writing on an old letter sitting next to the exquisite dress Sassy loved so much. "Hmm... that looks an awful lot like my mom's handwriting." He looked up abruptly and spoke to the Docent. "Sir, I'm Dr. Richard Winslow. I believe Mrs. Selk may have been an ancestress of mine. Is there any chance I could see the letter up close? My parents were Sarah and Owen Winslow. I was trained very young how to handle archival treasures." He gave the man his best smile.

The gentleman nodded. "Of course, Dr. Winslow. In fact, It's a letter to her son. We have another one to her brother. You know the drill. Come with me. We'll arrange for you to see the letters."

Rick's heart beat fast with excitement as they led him into the archival research room. He spent long hours in rooms such as this one over the years and he indeed knew the drill. He donned a mask, to keep from breathing anything on the old documents which might damage them, and special gloves to handle the letters. He knew to touch as little as possible.

Rick began to shake as he looked through the letters.

"My darling Rick,

I never dreamed when I went up the Jacks River that those silly stories were based in fact, or that you cannot come unless if you are meant to find your One True Love.

Rick, I loved your dad. I really did. And I love you. Please never doubt that.

But, God has blessed me more than I ever dared to hope. He gave me a new husband, and a family. You have two little brothers, and another baby is on the way. I'm happy and I am safe. Always remember, I love you to the moon and back.

Don't make permanent decisions because of temporary feelings.

Love, Your Mother Always,

Sarah Selk, June 1780"

The Docent handed another piece of parchment to Rick, who unfolded it with care.

"Dearest Twin,

I'm fine. Give my love to Sue and the kids. Will and I have twin boys, Thomas William Selk and George Marcus Selk, born November 15, 1779, at the Belle Rose Plantation. We also have a daughter, Rosa Linda, born on December 30, 1780. I am again *enceinte.* I think I'm having twins; we will see. Maybe this time it will be a boy and a girl, like us! Our life is as full as our house is.

The war will be over here soon. We are safe. But we sure won't travel to France anytime soon, that's for sure!

George Washington is a nice man. I know the real story about that cherry tree. Patsy is a dear friend. Patty Jefferson was another very dear friend. She was such a sweet woman, with the most incredible singing voice, not at all like mine! I miss her very much. Tom was devastated by her death last year.

Benedict Arnold looks enough like Owen to be his twin. I met James Madison, Sam Adams, and John and Abigail Adams, John Henry, and Alexander Hamilton. The list just goes on and on!

Will is the best man. God graced me when he brought me here to find my Will. I have been blessed with two fine men who loved me, heart and soul.

Oh, Will's last name is spelled Selk, but it can also be spelled Selleck.

His great-great-whatever grandson looks so very much like him. I think Gramma would love him even more than she loved Owen, and that was a lot. He is rock solid, total patriot through and through.

I love you forever,

Sass, November 1782"

A third letter fluttered to the floor. Rick picked it up and unfolded it with shaking hands, and read:

"Gentlemen:

My name is William Ranscome Selk. I am the lucky man who found love with Sassy. She is a Godsend, not just to me but to the Cause of Liberty. I will love her, treasure her, and protect her all the days of my life, so help me God.

"William Ranscome Selk, January 1780"

Rick pulled out his cell phone and called his Uncle Jim, telling him about the letters at the Smithsonian.

"Hang on a minute. Let me go see if I can find something," said Jim.

Rick tapped his foot until Jim returned.

"Rick, you aren't going to believe what I have here. I have an old box filled with letters Gramma said we were supposed to open in 2024. I just did and it is cram packed with letters from Sassy. They were written in the 1780's. And, hey! Hang on! My God! It's got your mom's cell phone! I swear!!! There's photos here of Sassy at a wedding at some mansion, with what look like a lot of impressive people. If I didn't know better, I would swear that's George Washington and Tom Jefferson! There's some guy at another party who looks enough like your dad to be your dad. That's just weird. Your mom looks great. And there are lots of pictures of little kids, and even of her dogs. Pictures of letters she wrote us. Jesus, Rick! We hit the mother lode! We found her!"

Rick hung up the phone grinning ear to ear. "We found my mom! Come on! Let's go!"

It sunk in to Melanie. "Rick, you can't go after her."

Rick's head swung up. "Why not? She could go. Why couldn't I? Why would she send these, if it wasn't to tell me where she is and how to find her?"

Melanie reached out and gingerly touched Rick's hand. They weren't married. Rick had never been able to make that commitment. Melanie always thought he still mourned the loss of his mother and father, both gone so close together. "You know what she wrote you. Don't make permanent decisions because of temporary feelings. You have to be rational, Rick. You're a doctor. You can't just take off and go gallivanting through time."

Well, why the hell not? thought Rick. *Mom did. Why can't I?* He tried to calm his breathing, and smiled at his girlfriend. "I won't do anything foolish, sweetheart. Don't worry. I won't make a permanent decision based on temporary feelings. I'm just glad I know where she is and that she's okay."

But once I'm ready, I'm going to find her, he thought with determination. *I will be fully prepared and take with me a medical bag full of 21st century remedies. And whoever this William Selk guy is, he damned sure better treat my Mom right, or there will be hell to pay in Virginia, or wherever I find him.*

To Be Continued…

CPSIA information can be obtained
at www.ICGtesting.com
Printed in the USA
FSHW020123251118
53975FS